THE WEAVER

Old Blood Series Book One

B. Scott Hoadley

First published 2020 by Marco & Bee Books
London, UK

Copyright © B. Scott Hoadley

ISBN: 9798575067535 (paperback)

The right of B. Scott Hoadley to be identified as the author of this work has been asserted by them in accordance with the Copyright, Designs and Patents Act 1988.

This is a work of fiction. Names, characters, places, and incidents either are the product of the authors' imagination or are used fictitiously. Any resemblance to actual persons, living or dead, events, or locales is entirely coincidental.

All rights reserved. No part of this publication may be reproduced, stored in or introduced into a retrieval system, or transmitted, in any form, or by any other means (electronic, mechanical, photocopying, recording or otherwise) without the prior written permission of the author. Any person who does any unauthorized act in relation to this publication may be liable to criminal prosecution and civil claims for damages.

About the Author

B. SCOTT HOADLEY is the author of *The Weaver*, Book One of the OLD BLOOD Series. His second book, *Old Blood*, is due out in Spring 2021. He is also author of the upcoming ALEX WEBB Series, whose first book, *Alpha Six*, is due out in 2021. He graduated from Emerson College with a Master of Fine Arts in Creative Writing in 1997 and has worked in the product design and technology fields since. He is from New York but lives in London. He can be found at www.bscotthoadley.com where you can sign up for email updates and view his blogs. You can also follow him on Facebook (https://www.facebook.com/bscotthoadley), Twitter (@bscotthoadley) and Instagram (@bscotthoadley).

For my partner (best friend and personal reader and editor) and everyone who believed this was possible.

Homecoming

Chapter 1

He circled high up in the sky over a lone island. Far below, spread around a large crescent harbor, lay a glistening city and a network of roads radiating from its center like the fine silken threads of spiderweb. There were many ships anchored along the docks and in the water, and he could see many others entering and leaving through the narrow mouth of the harbor. At each point of the crescent at the narrowest part of the harbor stood two tall defensive towers. Thin tendrils led to smaller towns dotted around the island. It looked as if a master architect had designed the island before any construction had taken place.

Hills gave way to a small mountain ridge that ran along one side of the island, on the other side of which lay another smaller harbor, a small town and a narrow channel that led out into the bluish-green sea. A single road led from the main city to the opposite harbor, up through the hills, and through a canyon that cut through the mountain range. The island was alive with activity. Farms, animals, people, all living in harmony together. In the distance, cutting across the boundless blue sky, advanced a ridge of solid black clouds, occasional streaks of lightning arcing sideways, from one section of clouds to another. A tendril of ice-cold air reached out across the vast expanse, chilling him. The islanders seemed unconcerned, oblivious to what was coming.

Nathan Briggs woke with a start, blinked away the feeling of disorientation as he looked around him, and turned his head to peer through the port hole into the dark expanse below. The video screen in his pod indicated the plane was flying parallel to the Canadian coast. He couldn't see anything in the murky blackness apart from the regular flash of lights from the wing. He could feel the plane dropping altitude, making its gradual descent towards Boston. He had been lucky to get this flight, another passenger having cancelled at the last minute.

Twenty-four hours before, he'd received a call from his mother informing him that his grandfather's private jet had gone missing somewhere off the Pacific coast of the state of Washington. Hedlund Briggs was returning from a business trip, having handed most of the reins of running the family business over to his son, Nathan's father. The aviation authorities and Coast Guard had begun a search but had not yet located any debris by the time Nathan managed to book his flight from London, where he'd spent the last few weeks of a nine-month holiday traveling around the world.

As the pilot made several announcements, his thoughts turned to his departure the previous June from Boston's Logan Airport. His mother had cried. His brother and sister had hugged him. His grandmother held his grandfather's hand and they both smiled with pride at the determination and adventurous spirit of their grandson. He was a bit nervous, at twenty-one, heading off on his own. But he'd felt it was something he really wanted to do before he committed to joining his siblings, father and grandfather in the family business.

His father, on the other hand, was angry that his son was leaving, having just graduated from university, and having deferred his entry into the company by a year. He had stayed at home instead of accompanying the rest of the family to the airport. He didn't want to give anyone the impression that he supported what he saw as Nathan's irresponsible decision to travel and avoid his obligations.

In many respects, Jonathan Briggs' behavior was to be expected. He'd always been hardest on his youngest son. Where Nathan's older siblings were given a higher degree of autonomy, their father had been more disciplined with him, at times seeming to express unmistakable disappointment. He never understood what it was he'd done to deserve being treated so disrespectfully by his father. He was a bright, independently motivated student, had excelled at sports in school, and helped out around the house and company during his holiday breaks.

His desire to travel wasn't to avoid his responsibility to his family, or to rebel against his father. It had grown out of a genuine desire to see the world before he had to take his place in it. He wanted the chance to be his own person before he had to be everyone else's. Of course, it hadn't helped that his grandfather had always treated him as a favorite grandson—perhaps that had added to the tension between Nathan and his father, especially as his father and grandfather didn't always see eye to eye when it came to raising family or running the business.

As Nathan's thoughts returned to the moment, his eyes teared up at the thought of his grandfather, missing, and presumed dead. When his trans-Atlantic flight departed London there still hadn't been any news. All that he knew was that his grandfather's plane had taken off from Tokyo, had regular check-ins along the way and then, as it approached the West Coast, had suddenly disappeared from radar. There'd been no further communications and no signs of wreckage. Despite the emotion he felt, he held out hope that he might get good news by the time his plane landed—that it had all somehow been a misunderstanding.

He rearranged the belongings he'd carried onto the plane in his upper-class pod and settled back for the remainder of the flight. He closed his eyes and let his thoughts wander to the last nine months. He searched for a good memory, something to take his mind off the moment, and recalled something that had happened relatively early on, and that he'd been unable to put out of his mind for the rest of his journey.

When traveling through Croatia, one evening he had met a pretty girl in Dubrovnik. Her name was Serena. Though she said that she was originally from Croatia, Nathan couldn't detect an accent like those of the many other people he'd met as he traveled down the coast of the country from Slovenia via Austria. In fact, if she hadn't told him that he would have thought he was speaking with another American who, like him, was traveling around the world. She explained that she had traveled a lot with her family since she was quite young, and that speaking English had changed her accent over the years. She told him that she hadn't been back to Croatia in some time and was in Dubrovnik visiting old friends.

They spent evenings together, wandering throughout the town, along the wall and down by the water's edge, Serena providing a rambling history lesson as they walked. She had a long and deep knowledge that spoke of her love of country and ancestry, something that struck him as unusual coming from one who must be nearly as young as he was.

It turned out that her family—like his own—had global business interests and spent a lot of time traveling when they weren't visiting their homes in London and New York. They even had business interests in Boston, a place where Nathan had spent a great deal of time growing up, and the center of his own family's businesses. They appeared to come from similar backgrounds: siblings and fathers always busy, high expectations, and everyone involved in making the family businesses a success in one way or another. To Nathan, Serena seemed like a kindred spirit, and as a result he grew close to her very quickly.

Because of prior commitments, it turned out, she wasn't able to spend days with him, but every evening for nearly a week, like clockwork, she appeared at the entrance of his hotel ready to act as a tour guide and traveling companion. It seemed she enjoyed spending time with him too. But after a week of evenings together, and just as he thought everything was going really well, Serena disappeared. He came downstairs to the lobby one evening and was called over by the receptionist. There was a message for him.

Nathan,

I'm so sorry. I've been called back to London by my father. I didn't mean to leave in such a rush, but I'm sure you can understand the needs of family. I will find you. Enjoy the rest of your journey.

Serena

He was disappointed that she'd had to leave so quickly, with saying goodbye. In the event that she was able to return, Nathan hung around Dubrovnik for a further week, longer than he'd intended, in case she showed up—but she never returned. A week later he departed across the Adriatic for Italy, sad and disappointed, leaving Serena, her history lessons and companionship behind him.

He was already a couple of months into his journey and as he traveled around Europe, he occasionally thought he caught glimpses of her—or someone that looked very much like her—out of the corner of his eye. When he'd turn to look, there was never anything but darkness and shadows. After a time, he concluded that his mind was playing tricks on him.

Eventually the visions passed, and he settled into the routine of his daily travels. He met new people and had new experiences. He learned about different cultures by doing his best to experience them. He absorbed everything he encountered along the way, realizing that the world was an incredibly diverse place. As his view of the world grew, the thought of returning home to New Comfort on the north coast of Massachusetts grew distant. And still, one day, he knew this would all come to an end.

When the plane finally landed and taxied to its terminal, he was ready and one of the first people to make his way off. He rushed down the long corridor to Customs, where he dug out his passport and took his place in line. He thought about taking his cell phone out and phoning his sister, but there were security guards within sight and large posters on the walls declaring cell phone use a crime, and the last thing he wanted was trouble and delays when he was in such a hurry.

As the line of tired passengers wound its way through the large lobby, he stepped up to the biometric machine, placed his passport face down on the scanner and stood on top of the footprints painted on the floor. The machine made a whirring sound as it scanned his passport; then the light turned green and he quickly made his way out of Customs. He followed signs to the baggage area, located the conveyor belt for his flight and, after a short wait, watched as his bag appeared and slid down onto the long stainless-steel conveyor. He elbowed his way through the throng of people waiting for their bags, threw the well-traveled backpack over his shoulder and, with nothing to declare, made his way through the rest of the Customs area and out into the arrivals area of the terminal.

It took him a bit to acclimate to his surroundings. There were dozens of people waiting for recent arrivals. He scanned the crowds for familiar faces and, after a moment, saw his sister standing at the farthest edge of the crowd. The first thing he noticed about Sam was her pale, drawn face. She looked as if she hadn't slept in a while. At that moment, as he looked into her tired, emotionally drained eyes, he knew that any hope he'd held out that his grandfather was still alive was dashed.

They hugged and exchanged a few words as they made their way out into the parking area, where there was a chauffeur-driven Range Rover waiting. He threw his gear into the open back of the black SUV and then joined his sister in the rear seats. Their driver took up his position behind the wheel and slowly pulled away into traffic. As they made their way home, he turned toward her.

"So… anything?" he asked.

She retrieved a tissue from her bag and blew her nose. He could see now that her eyes were red-rimmed from crying.

"They haven't found anything yet. The Coast Guard is out searching the area where the plane was last reported. And so far, they've found nothing. No debris, no plane, nothing."

He sat quietly, taking it all in.

"Dad?" he asked tentatively, already anticipating the answer.

"He's flown out to the West Coast to be on hand in case there's any news. Grandmother is home with Mother. She hasn't been feeling well lately and this is all too much for her."

They settled back in their seats for the drive up to their parents' home. There wasn't much more to say at the moment. No news wasn't necessarily bad news, but it wasn't what he'd hoped to hear after his long flight. As they passed through traffic on the expressway heading north away from Boston, he recalled the last time he'd been there—when he left nearly nine months previously to begin his journey. Unlike his sudden return home, everything had seemed so exciting back then.

Everyone apart from his father had been supportive, if a bit worried, at his decision to go alone. Originally his best friend, Ben, was going to travel with him but at the last moment, he'd backed out to attend graduate school. Nathan believed it was really because his friend couldn't afford it, even though his own family had offered to pay Ben's way so that he wouldn't be traveling alone. Ben was too proud to accept their offer and decided only a week before they were meant to fly out together to walk his own path.

Despite having to go it alone, it was his grandfather who had strongly encouraged Nathan to attempt the journey. Hedlund Briggs had told him that there was no shame in going and then cutting his travels short if he decided that it wasn't for him. He told him that if he decided not to go he would always regret not having made the effort. In the end he went, knowing that his family would be there when he returned—though he would have to deal with repairing his relationship with his father when the time came.

His sister placed a hand on his shoulder.

"You're looking good. Nice and tanned. Maybe a bit thin?"

Nathan smiled.

"Well, before arriving in the U.K., I was in Australia for two months. I got a lot of sun there, which was just as well, because England in March can be pretty grim."

"How long were you in the U.K.?" asked Sam.

"I was there for a few weeks. I spent most of it taking trains to different places, like Scotland and Cornwall.

It's really beautiful. Cornwall reminded me a bit of the Cape. Scotland was pretty dreary. I had lots of time to think on the train. I loved it, even if the weather was a bit crap."

"At least it sounds like you had a great time."

His sister looked out of the window and into the distance.

"Sam, do you think there's any chance? I mean, do you believe that he's really gone?"

"I don't know what to believe, Nathan. It seems odd they haven't found anything, but then again, they haven't really been looking for that long. I don't understand it. I mean, there was a bit of rough weather out that way, but you know Granddad. He kept that jet in immaculate shape."

He nodded. His grandfather was meticulous about things. He would never have taken off if he'd thought there were the slightest danger. It was difficult to know what to think. After a time, the driver exited the motorway onto a road that took them through several small towns, until eventually, at the edge of New Comfort, a town that had grown from a small New England settlement that the Briggs family had emigrated to from England, he turned off and drove up a narrow country road to their family home, built on a hilltop overlooking the town and the sea.

The large, imposing house was the kind of home that looked more as though it belonged in the Westchester County countryside outside of New York. Their home was a three-story brick edifice with black shutters and a large black front door and white portico. It stood in stark contrast to the pastel-colored wooden New England coastal community homes that made up the town below. The house had been built on the same site as their original family home, built in the mid-seventeenth century, which had burned down in a fire in the mid-eighteenth century. The family had originally moved from England to the colonies to escape taxation and laws inhibiting weavers in practicing their trade. The Briggs family came from many generations of weavers, his grandfather had always said, going back centuries even before their migration from other parts of Europe to England.

When he was growing up in this large home, his friends had always been in awe and fear of it when they came to birthdays or sleepovers. It wasn't what they were used to, and the place had an eeriness about it that made many visitors feel uncomfortable. His grandfather had always said that their ancestors had built the imposing brick building like a fortress, to protect their family. Nathan never understood what it was they were supposed to be protected from—he wasn't even sure whether or not his grandfather was being serious or just taking the opportunity to tease him. Returning now, after his long absence, the house felt warm and inviting. Perhaps it was the nine months he'd spent on his own away from home and family. It felt as though the house welcomed him, and he suddenly felt very glad to be back home.

They drove around the circular driveway, stopping in front of the impressive front entrance to the house.

Hedges and rose bushes ran along the front, reaching out from either side of the steps that led up to the front door. He could see movement through one of the curtained windows. A moment later, the front door opened, and a woman with gray-streaked blond hair, resplendent in a dark blue cashmere wrap, stepped outside.

He stepped out of the SUV and straightened his rumpled clothes before walking up the steps to greet his mother, giving her a long hug. Sam followed. The driver retrieved his bag from the car and carried it up to the steps, where he set it down and said his goodbyes.

"It's really good to have you home Nathan. I'm just so sorry about the circumstances."

He looked into her green eyes.

"Has there been any word? Anything at all?" he asked.

She shrugged her shoulders.

"There's been no word yet. The Coast Guard is still searching, of course, but they haven't found anything. Your father's out there in the event they do find something."

He felt deflated, having hoped for some good news. His personal journey over the last nine months had been challenging and exciting. He'd felt like he'd grown up, having experienced so many things on his own. He'd never expected it to end like this. Not like this. His mother led them all inside the house and closed the large imposing black-lacquered door behind them. It would be a bittersweet reunion for everyone.

Chapter 2

As the next two weeks passed, the family received daily updates from Nathan's father. The Coast Guard had searched extensively but had turned up no sign of the jet's wreckage. To all intents and purposes, it had simply disappeared. The aviation authority said that depending on the nature of the accident something might turn up over time, but that there wasn't anything more that could be done. The search was being called off for the moment. No wreckage, and no closure for the grieving family.

His father had phoned the house late one evening to say that he would stay for a few days longer and then would return home early the following week. Sam and his other sibling, Christopher, would continue to look after the business from the company's Boston headquarters until their father eventually returned—or until he was ready to re-engage with things.

Like his mother and grandmother, Nathan felt shaken by the call. They'd expected to have something tangible to hold onto by now and knowing the search was being called off was like a kick in the gut for all of them. His grandmother took the news with a certain amount of resolve and said she would start thinking about making arrangements for some type of service. Over the last couple of weeks her strength had returned, and her health had improved, even if her spirit seemed broken. Still, of all of them, she seemed the most focused on carrying out what needed doing. She disappeared upstairs to have some privacy and think about what to do next.

His mother brushed aside a lock of hair and momentarily looked away with a deep sadness in her eyes. She was a tall, slender woman in her fifties who had always walked with a certain poise. Since his return, she looked older, creases appearing at the corners of her eyes, and slightly stooped from the weight of carrying the emotions of the family while holding them all together. This was a difficult time for everyone, and Elizabeth Briggs had done her best to take their minds off things. But her husband, her own personal support, was away and she was carrying all this responsibility with little support for her own feelings.

"I'll call your brother and sister and let them know."

Like his grandmother, she turned and disappeared upstairs, leaving him to ponder the situation alone. He sat on one of the large sofas in the sitting room listening to the sound of a fire crackling in the fireplace as various thoughts circled around inside his head. The house felt warm and still. It creaked and groaned in the way that old houses do, something he'd gotten used to when growing up there. It was dark outside. He felt a sudden emptiness in the pit of his stomach as the eccentric old house comforted him.

He had looked forward to seeing his grandfather when he eventually returned from his journey. Hedlund Briggs was a kind man who'd inherited the family textile mill business from his father and had diversified the business into global real estate, imports and exports and other investments, and who had significantly grown the family fortune during his lifetime. He'd certainly done his best to secure the legacy that would pass on to Nathan and his siblings one day. And yet, through all of it, Hedlund never acted like a man possessed of great wealth. He was down to earth, kind and cared a great deal about his wife, family and their community.

As he sat quietly in the sitting room, Nathan realized that while he had learned many things over time, he still had no idea how big the family business was or what they were worth. No idea of the legacy his grandfather had left behind. He knew that it was substantial but growing up he'd never paid much attention to the business. Although he had known that one day he'd have to step up and take his place in the family, he'd always treated that day as though it was a long way off. In recent years, his father had taken over much of the operation with Nathan's siblings, while their grandfather stepped back to focus on his own special projects. Nathan wondered now what those projects might have been, and what would happen to them now that he was missing.

His grandfather had supported his desire to travel, feeling that having graduated from university the previous year, and before committing to the family business, he should see something of the world that he was about to take on. Their businesses had a strong presence and trade across Europe and given their European heritage, his grandfather had thought travel might give Nathan a deeper appreciation for their history and a view beyond the small New England town in which he'd grown up.

Unfortunately, his father hadn't been as happy or supportive about him taking the time off and didn't appreciate his own father's meddling in the life of his youngest son. There had been rows between all of them prior to Nathan's departure. He only hoped that his father had calmed down and made peace with his son's decisions in the time since he'd been away. Though under the circumstances, he didn't hold out much hope. His father was a stubborn man who was more likely to return from the West Coast holding onto his previous feelings, now exacerbated by the loss of his own father. Seeing Nathan wasn't likely to improve his mood.

On Monday, his father returned as expected. Nathan could hear the commotion as he entered the house with the driver following him in with his bags. He heard the sound of his mother and grandmother's voices greeting him. He waited in the kitchen as long as he could but realized that if he didn't go out into the hallway to greet his father, Jonathan Briggs would likely find some fault in his lateness.

As he made his way down the main hallway, he could see his father consoling his grandmother. Or perhaps it was the other way around. His grandmother was a very slight woman, standing only a little over five feet tall at the best of times. He could see tears in her eyes as she hugged her son, his six-foot-three-inch-tall frame hunched over to hug her. His mother stood to one side, a hand covering her mouth and her eyes wet with tears. He quietly entered the main reception area and stood waiting, not wanting to interfere. Eventually his father and grandmother parted. His father stood to full height and turned to face his son.

"Well, it's good of you to make time to come home for your grandfather's funeral."

He pursed his lips as if he were about to say something further, and then shook his head, turned and walked towards the rear of the house, leaving Nathan standing in silence with his mother and grandmother. They all looked about, lost for words, and after a brief moment his grandmother broke the silence.

"He's upset dear. You know that your father isn't very good with his emotions. I'm quite sure that he didn't mean anything by it. You just need to give him some time."

He nodded. As he turned over his father's reaction in his mind, he thought that coming home, though it was the right thing to do under the circumstances, wasn't going to be easy. He wasn't sure how they were going to get through this.

"Come Nathan. Let me get you some tea."

His mother took him by the hand and led him back into the kitchen. His grandmother, a firm look of resolve on her face, turned and walked off to look for her son. She found him in the study in the back of the house, staring out of a large window that overlooked the lawn.

"Jonathan," she said.

He stood still, back stiff, and continued facing out of the window, across the lawn and gardens to the forested hills beyond.

"Jonathan." She spoke more forcefully. "You need to put this foolish issue between you and Nathan aside. He's your son. Family is important, especially now. I'm not going to have you tear this family apart. It's not what your father would have wanted."

Jonathan stood resolute by the window. After a moment, he turned towards her.

"Did you know?" he asked.

"Know what, Jonathan?" she replied.

"I had a call from Father's lawyer yesterday about his will. Did you know he left a major portion of his shares in a trust for Nathan, to be inherited by him when he turns twenty-five?"

They stood for a moment staring intently at one another.

"I'm not surprised by it. You know that he and Nathan were very close."

"He leaves a large percentage of the company to a child who shows no responsibility or desire to be a part of the family business? It's inexcusable. Irresponsible. I'm going to contest it."

The momentary silence that followed was deafening. Alexandra Briggs shook her head, took a deep breath and spoke.

"I have never been so disappointed in you. Hearing you talk this way about your own son and your father at a time like this. You need to think long and hard about what you are saying. It was your father's wish that Nathan take his place in the family business… and fulfil the legacy that he was born into."

The words hung in the air for a moment as neither of them spoke.

"Legacy?" Jonathan stuttered.

"You can't mean?" he started.

"Your father thought so. If you ever trusted your father, Jonathan, don't let him down now. This was extremely important to him. And you know that it's important to honor the legacy of this family. Blood runs deeper than the family business, this house, or all the money in the world."

Jonathan Briggs turned and quietly stared back out through the window.

"I'll think about it," he muttered.

"That's all I'm asking. Now I'll leave you alone to consider things," she said.

Alexandra turned and walked quietly out of the room, leaving her son in the solitude of his study. She knew that he carried a lot on his shoulders at the moment. She had hoped that his issue with her grandson would have gone away by now and only hoped she hadn't just made things worse between the two of them.

She knew that they would all choose to grieve in their own way. She knew that her own son was dealing with the loss of his father, and the return of the son who he felt had abandoned him. But she was also convinced that things would settle down with time. For the moment, she had her own feelings and thoughts to consider. Her son would have to come to his senses in his own way, in his own time. On her way back through the house she came upon Nathan, alone in the sitting room, seated quietly by the window with a cup of tea. He was clearly lost in his own thoughts.

One Briggs staring out of the front window pondering his future, while another one stared out towards the rear gardens sunk in his own terrible thoughts and emotions about the past. Both standing with their backs to the other. If they didn't find a path back towards one another soon, these two would need sorting out. Alexandra sighed, shook her head quietly and went upstairs to her own rooms.

Later that week they organized and held a funeral in the local church. There was no body to bury so the formalities had been easy to arrange. They had decided to keep it a close family affair. There would be time to reach out to friends and business associates later. Their father spoke at the service and afterwards, Nathan's brother Christopher read out a poem that was a favorite of their grandfather's. He looked good standing at the podium. He'd obviously been spending time at the gym in Nathan's absence and had begun to turn his once scrawny frame into something more athletic. He was unusually tanned for April—Nathan thought he must be hitting the tanning beds as well. His light-brown curly hair flopped over his forehead and brown eyes reflected the glistening lights in the chapel. He'd always hoped his curly hair would straighten out as he grew older, but it never had. His wife, Emma, sat in the second row with their sister.

Sam looked better than she had when they'd met Nathan at the airport. She looked more composed now. She was tall for a Briggs woman, standing at nearly five feet eleven inches. Her blond hair fell to her shoulders and her black dress was enlivened by her bright blue eyes. She was beautiful by any standard, though he still remembered her as a bit of a tomboy growing up, always competing with her brothers and showing them she could do anything they could do. He was glad to see she'd mostly grown out of that. He liked his big sister. She'd grown into a smart, talented, beautiful woman.

He and his father kept a civil distance from one another after the funeral. He'd been left on his own to ponder what the future held now that his father was back. He wasn't even sure if Jonathan wanted him to work in the company anymore. He didn't seem to want him around at all. His mother and siblings had welcomed him back warmly and his grandmother had taken tea with him a couple of times since his return. He was far more concerned about her at the moment than he was about his own future, and he found spending time with her a welcome distraction from the lack of reconciliation with his father.

No one had spoken of his grandfather's will, so he was none the wiser when his father approached him at breakfast one morning and asked to see him in his study at eleven that morning to discuss it. Time passed slowly as he anticipated the meeting. When the family lawyer arrived around fifteen minutes before he was due to meet with his father, he knew that something was up. He felt sick to his stomach and wished that he was anywhere other than here.

At the appointed time, he approached the door to his father's study. From inside he could hear the murmur of voices. He stood for a moment in the hallway, composing himself, before he reached out and knocked on the dark-stained oak door.

"Come in," called his father's voice from inside.

Nathan gently pushed the door open and walked into the study, the wide floorboards creaking under his feet as he entered. He'd always loved this room. Dark wood paneling covered the walls, and the shelves of the bookcases were stuffed with a mixture of old and new books. A large mahogany desk sat between two large rectangular windows with two leather chairs facing towards it. The large room also contained a couple of leather wing-back chairs, two sofas and several tall antique chests of drawers. Along one wall was a large fireplace that, for the moment, lay dormant.

He didn't know how old the furniture was or how long it had been in the study, but he suspected that some of it dated back to the construction of the house. The floor was lined with polished oak boards with the patina of centuries of use, and a large rectangular oriental rug framed the area in the middle, softening the dominance of the wood. His father sat behind the desk and the family lawyer, Arthur Johnstone, sat in one of the leather chairs facing his father. A briefcase was perched on the edge of the desk. Both men appeared to be reading sets of papers held together with clips.

"Please, sit down," his father said.

He walked over and sat in the chair next to the lawyer. The desk had always appeared vast and slightly intimidating from that perspective. He suspected it was meant to have that effect. Though he had sat in these same chairs many times growing up, as his grandfather had previously used this study, he had never thought of it then as imposing. Sitting quietly by while Hedlund Briggs worked had always made him feel connected to both his grandfather and the important work that he did on behalf of the family. Now, with his father sitting across from him, scowling, the large desk seemed to exacerbate the gulf between the two of them.

"You know Mr. Johnstone," his father said.

It was more a statement than a question.

"Yes, of course," Nathan said.

They nodded at one another, the lawyer affording him a sly smile.

"Shall we get on with this, Arthur?" Jonathan said.

"Yes, of course," the lawyer said as he handed Nathan a bunch of papers. "Because of the unfortunate circumstances, your father has asked me to review your grandfather's will. Now of course nothing is immediately binding, as your grandfather will have to be declared legally dead, which will take some number of months, but we thought it best to review parts of the will with you as they also pertain to your interests."

He paused for a moment before continuing. Nathan nodded, looking between the two men and thinking to himself how cold and calculated the conversation felt. He wished now more than ever that he could be anyplace but sitting in that chair.

"As you know, the family business is one hundred percent owned by the family. There are no external investors involved. Over the years, shares have gone through a fair number of redistributions, resulting in what is owned by your father, grandfather, grandmother, brother and sister. Of course, as you were in university, and then traveling, you hadn't yet been allocated any shares in the business."

The lawyer flipped through the pages of the document he held. Nathan's father sat quietly, staring off into the distance.

"Your grandfather still held sixty-two percent of the company shares, which means he held a controlling interest in the company. Of course, your father has held joint control of the company for a number of years in the event that anything happened to either of them, ensuring it would continue to function. Do you understand so far?"

Nathan nodded.

"Please Arthur, get to the point." Jonathan spoke impatiently.

Arthur re-shuffled the papers, unclipped them and pulled one sheet out of the bunch.

"It would appear, Nathan, that your grandfather has left some of his shares to your father and siblings, and a large proportion of shares to you. In point of fact, in the event of his untimely death, he has left fifty-one percent of the company shares to you."

The lawyer's words hung heavy in the air between all of them. Nathan slowly processed the information, feeling the weight of each and every word. Was this the reason that his father had such an issue with him? Had he known about this a year ago when he accused him of shirking his responsibilities and instead leaving home to travel?

"So I'll inherit a controlling interest in the company, is what you are saying," he said slowly and very quietly, not daring to look at his father. He could feel the heat of anger emanating from across the large desk and he felt a strange tingling sensation at the back of his neck.

"Yes, that's about the size of it. Now of course there are formal processes to go through before this can happen. And in any case, your grandfather stipulated that it will be held in a trust managed by your father for you until you turn twenty-five. But at that point you, like your grandfather before you, will have the ability to control the direction of the company. Your father will retain the ability, as he has had with your grandfather, to make joint decisions, unless of course you decide to do differently. However, I would always advise that the company is safer if it is managed between the two of you than if only one person has control."

The lawyer looked uncomfortable as he sat back in his chair, allowing Nathan time to process what he had just been told. Was the issue between him and his father as simple as control over the family business? Was his father that petty? As if sensing what Nathan was thinking, his father broke the silence.

"Before you ask, I didn't know about this. I only found out after I returned home from Washington the other week. If I'd known about this a year ago you can be sure that I would have done my damnedest to talk your grandfather out of this irresponsible decision."

His father's words hung in the air between all of them. It was clear that he wasn't going to let go of his issues with his son so easily; if anything, his anger had strengthened with his son's absence and the death of his own father. Clearly, the issue with the will would only further cement their poor relationship.

"I have a lot of work to do before we can invoke this will," the lawyer said. "But absent your father or another family member contesting it, this will likely be the final outcome."

He looked at the angry face of Jonathan Briggs and the pale stunned look on Nathan's face and reached over, placed his papers in his briefcase and closed the lid.

"I think that I should leave as I believe you both have a great deal to discuss and think about. I'll be in touch in due course to let you know the next steps that we need to follow."

He locked the clasps on his briefcase, stood, nodded at both of them and took his leave, closing the study door behind him. Nathan and his father sat quietly for a few moments, neither seeming to want to break the silence first. When his father finally spoke, his words were bitter and clearly angry.

"This isn't over Nathan, not by a long shot. You chose to leave this family and left behind your place in the business for selfish reasons. I am going to speak with your brother and sister about our options, and we'll discuss this with you in due course. But I can assure you, you are going to have no part in this, and those shares won't be going to you. The rest of us have worked too hard for this company and I'll be damned if I'm going to let you waltz in and ruin everything."

His father spoke like he was serving legal notice to a business associate, or a stranger—cold and dismissive. He swiveled his chair around and faced back out of the window. In every respect, Nathan was being dismissed. For the moment, this conversation was over. Feeling as though he'd been slapped in the face, he pushed himself up from his chair, stood uncertainly for a moment, then turned and walked out of the study, closing the door behind him.

The house suddenly felt claustrophobic and hostile. For all that it was such a large house, with plenty of room for all of them, he suddenly felt as though he were trapped in a small box. He felt the need to get out. Not just to go outside, but to leave. The last couple of weeks had been very difficult and the tension between him and his father felt insurmountable. He needed time and space to think about things and understand the implications of what he'd just been told. As his father was angry with him anyways, he decided getting away from the house for a while might just be a good option. Both of them under the same roof would only lead to further difficulty for the family, and he just couldn't take that at the moment.

He walked purposely upstairs to his bedroom and

hastily packed his backpack—something he was very familiar with doing. He had an idea of where he might go—someplace secluded and quiet. Someplace where there were wide open spaces, room for him to think, no intruding emotions, and no hostility. He would head to the Cape, where the family owned a summer home in Truro. Nobody would be using it at the moment, and it would give him time to consider the death of his grandfather, everything that had happened since his return, his father's anger and this ludicrous inheritance that he'd never asked for. He decided his best bet was to walk into town and get a bus to Boston, from where he would grab another bus out to the Cape.

As he left the house and walked down the long driveway, he turned briefly to look back on the home he'd grown up in, often a place of great happiness, but more recently a house of great despair. He shook his head, bit back the tears that were forcing their way out, shouldered his backpack and walked silently down to the road that would take him to New Comfort and away from this house, the loss, and his father.

Chapter 3

It was nighttime in a city of stone and lights. He stood on a rocky promontory overlooking the perfectly symmetrical city that radiated out from a central square, in the middle of which sat a massive round building made of white marble—a church or a gathering hall of some sort. He was overcome by a tremendous sadness as he watched over the bustling city.

Along the coast, he could see beaches and a major seaport, where many hundreds of ships were berthed. Further inland he could see small clusters of lights, farms, villages and towns. They stretched into the far distance and ended at the distant shoreline. This entire expanse was an island. A large, beautiful island populated by a unique people. His mind reached out into the darkness and he could hear distinct voices, thoughts, reveries and secrets. He was privy to them all. He was a weaver—someone who was able to access the power and energy that resided in every living thing on the planet and bend it to his will. There were few like him, and they were revered amongst the people of this island.

In the distance he could hear a low rumble that slowly grew into a roar. It was happening again. He could see it in his mind, and he wasn't sure if it was happening now, had happened in the past, or would happen at some point in the future. He could vaguely make out a growing wall of water in the distance. Within moments the entire island would be engulfed by it, and before long the island itself, with all of its inhabitants, would disappear into the sea. An entire race of people… gone in an instant.

If only they'd listened.

⁕

He woke with a start, a sudden and frightening realization that he was running from home, his father, his grandfather's untimely death and everything that it entailed. He shook his head gently and blinked his eyes to clear away the sleep and the rapidly dissipating strange dream and, after a moment, he realized that he was still sitting in a bus station, awaiting the next leg of his journey. He'd made his way into Boston and bought a bus ticket to the Cape and had then promptly fallen asleep while waiting for the next bus.

For a brief moment, he considered heading back, feeling embarrassed and ashamed at having run away. It wasn't like him. He was much stronger than that. Even so, he wasn't quite ready—or in the mood—to head home and reconcile just yet. His father needed to understand that there were consequences for his poor behavior, and if that meant shunning him for a short time, then so be it. Nathan needed some time to think about what to do next. And he wasn't going to get that under his father's antagonistic gaze.

Their conversation had filled him with despair. His father never understood why he had decided to take time off to travel after finishing university. He was a company man through and through. Not creative. Not curious. A straightforward businessman who felt dedication and hard work were the only ingredients for success—and life. Happiness or balance never seemed to be a part of the equation for him. His grandfather had softened his father's rough edges. With him gone, all that stood between Nathan and his future was the raw, unbridled focus of a passionless man.

When he'd left home to travel, he was more interested in life and events outside of his small town. He'd left university a precocious twenty-something, perhaps a bit immature and schoolboyish. He felt like he'd returned home capable of understanding so much more than he had when he'd left. Having independence and exploring new things had helped him to better understand the family business, the meaning of heritage and, more importantly, the importance of family.

He traveled through many places where people still made things by hand and valued the quality of what they produced. Making something was important. Making things for others and leaving something behind was important. He had a better appreciation of his family's place in the world than when he'd set out to explore. This was something he hadn't been able to convey to his father, and it wasn't something that he thought his father would believe or understand even if he had said it to him. His father still saw the last nine months of Nathan's absence as rejection of family, of obligation, of him. He was too blind—or too closed-minded—to appreciate how his son had grown during his time away.

"Bus boarding for Cape Cod on platform three!"

Nathan stood, found the platform and shoved his backpack into the baggage compartment at the side of the bus. He got onto the bus and found a quiet solitary seat next to a window at the back. He wanted peace and quiet and to be left alone. As he settled into his seat, he could still smell the sickly-sweet scent of primrose through the open windows. The colorful flowers were planted in concrete planters all around the station.

He settled back into his seat and considered his time away from home. He'd often traveled on buses or trains and was well versed in getting around by whatever means took him to where he wanted to go. It wasn't like growing up and being shuttled to a private school nearby in a Mercedes, or traveling first class when they went on holiday. Over the last nine months Nathan had felt more connected to the people and places he visited than he had ever felt when he was growing up. He was just some non-descript young guy traveling on his own, as many European youth often did before going on to university. He wasn't a Briggs. He was just Nathan. And he'd enjoyed that anonymity.

One of the things he enjoyed most about his travels was that he met lots of different people and made many different acquaintances—though he was rarely in any one place long enough to develop deep friendships. Even now, his room back home held a stack of notebooks filled with journal entries, phone numbers and addresses of people he'd met. He wasn't sure when—or if—he'd find the time to get back in touch with all of them, but it was good to know that if he wanted to, there were people beyond his small town that he could reach out to and say hello. People who'd shared a piece of his journey with him.

As he sat there, he considered that he would eventually have to return and find a way to reconcile things with his father. The situation that caused him to leave was ridiculous on the face of it and he would have to bite the bullet and come to some kind of understanding with him. They would have to find a way to make peace of a sort. But first, he wanted time to clear his head. He wanted to feel that sense of independence he'd gained while away, to be in charge of his own life before going back to his old one.

His cell phone buzzed in his pocket. He took it out and saw that it was his mother calling. He badly wanted to answer it, as he didn't have any issue with her and didn't want her to worry, but as he wasn't quite ready to speak with anyone, he decided to let the call go to voicemail. After a few minutes he texted Sam to explain the situation, and asked her if she would let their mother know. He said he would call and explain everything to her later.

As the bus pulled away from the terminal, his thoughts traveled back to the conversation he'd had with his father when he first told him he was going to travel instead of joining the business straight away. They'd spoken—argued really—at length before he made the final decision to go. The worst part from his father's perspective was that it was being funded by Nathan's grandfather—Jonathan's own father was supporting this, setting up a generational battle of father against son. For Jonathan, it felt like a personal betrayal.

"Isn't it time you took your life seriously? The mills have supported our family for generations. Your grandfather and I have worked our backsides off to ensure the business is diversified so that you and your brother and sister can have a decent future. It paid for your university. It pays for our way of living, everything you've enjoyed in life. You might want to consider giving something back to it, back to this family, instead of pursuing this insanity."

It was clear from the start that he was against Nathan's decision.

"I'm not even sure if the family business is what I want," Nathan had responded. "I haven't had the chance to think about what's right for me yet. Shouldn't I have an opportunity to decide before I commit to anything?"

It was clear there wasn't any answer he could provide that would suit his father. The only right answer would be to give up his plans, stay at home and take his place in the business. He wasn't willing to do this. They simply weren't going to agree on this issue. In the end, his father had no choice but to give up in disgust and leave his son to sort himself out.

Of course, his grandfather hadn't been the only influencer in his life. His mother, Elizabeth, had also traveled the world before meeting his father. In many ways, it was her rich stories about interesting places and their history that she had told him when he was younger that had made him curious about the world. As he grew up, he'd realized that as beautiful as those stories were, they would always be somebody else's stories and he should go and experience things for himself.

After he'd left, his father poured more time and effort into working with his siblings. Much like their father, Chris and Sam enjoyed working in the family business and Nathan had hoped their enthusiasm would ease some of the disappointment his father felt towards him. Perhaps it had even worked to some extent. He'd never know now, as his grandfather's untimely passing had surely stirred everything back up. Maybe some time apart would help to settle things back down again.

The bus drove south out of Boston, making a number of stops until it reached Hyannis, where he retrieved his backpack and sat waiting for the bus that would take him to Truro. As he breathed in the fresh salt-tinged air of the Cape, and listened to the gulls flying overhead, he could already feel some of the strain from his morning encounter slip from his shoulders. A bit of distance and some fresh air would do him some good.

After a while the bus arrived, and he boarded for the final leg to Truro. Where the journey from Boston had taken around an hour and a half, this bus was only going to take about an hour to get him to his destination. He found a seat in the middle and sat down. As it pulled away from the station, and before he could get comfortable, he felt the hairs on the back of his neck stand up—the strange sensation of being watched. He looked around the bus and didn't notice anyone looking his way. Across the aisle, an old man sat quietly back in his seat, eyes closed, smiling to himself.

He settled in for the remainder of the journey. As the bus continued down the Cape, he considered that it wasn't the first time over the last nine months that he'd felt the sensation of being watched. The first time had been at a cafe in the Old Town in Stockholm one evening. He was sitting outside drinking coffee and writing in his notebook when he felt an itch on the back of his neck and the strong feeling of being watched, but when he looked up from the table, he couldn't see anyone who might be watching. He couldn't shake the feeling though, and eventually left the cafe and made his way back to the hotel where he was staying for the week, locking himself in for the evening. There were a few similar moments as he traveled, but he never actually saw anyone and, in the end, he decided it was probably just a bit of traveler's paranoia.

As the bus lurched away on its journey, he pushed himself up in his seat and peered around. There was a mix of people—elderly people on their own or together, younger couples and a couple of young groups of friends. There were a few who, like himself, appeared to be traveling alone, reading, listening to music, or just watching the scenic miles pass by outside the windows. And of course, there was the old man across the aisle. Everyone appeared preoccupied, sleeping or engaged in conversation. He didn't notice anyone unusual.

After a while he calmed himself, shook off the feeling and turned to gaze out of the window. Inland scenery gradually gave way to sand, scrub brush, Cape houses and tourist shops as they progressed mile after mile towards his destination. His family owned a beach house outside of Truro, near a long sandy stretch of beach. Though there were a few neighbors along the road their house occupied, their property was fairly secluded, surrounded by trees and a concrete and cast-iron wall.

"You visiting? Where you from?"

The sudden intrusion startled him. The old man across the aisle smiled and laughed.

"Sorry, boy. Didn't mean to scare you."

He shrugged it off.

"No, no, it's okay. I've been away for a while. So, I'm heading home really."

"Been away? Sounds interesting. Anyplace nice?"

The old man had the weathered face and hands of a fisherman, which was not all that unusual here. He looked to be in his seventies, with a thick shock of white hair and watery blue eyes. He had a warm, friendly smile that put Nathan at ease. Growing up in New England, he'd encountered similar people and knew the type—curious and social, but harmless.

"Yes, I spent time travelling around Europe and Australia. I came back a few weeks ago from London."

He stopped short of explaining why he'd come back.

"Quite an adventure for such a young man. Sounds like quite an adventure indeed."

The old man nodded to himself and returned to reading a wrinkled newspaper. Their conversation was over as quickly as it had begun. Nathan returned to staring out of the window and after a while, sat up in his seat, recognizing that they were getting close to his stop. As the bus pulled into Truro, the old man looked up from his newspaper, smiled and nodded.

"I hope you find what you're looking for."

He returned to his newspaper without another word, leaving Nathan to depart the bus and retrieve his backpack from the storage compartment. He laughed to himself as the bus lurched away from the stop to set out on its final leg towards Provincetown. He also hoped he found what he was looking for—a bit of peace and quiet. He shouldered his pack and walked to a nearby shop buy food and other supplies. He would get a taxi to the beach house, which was just west of town. Once he had stocked up, he walked down the street to a taxi rank and hopped in the first one available. The driver took him out of town, driving down country lanes towards the beach. It took about ten minutes.

The taxi arrived at a walled, gated property with a long driveway ending in front of the entrance to the old gray clapboard beach house. Large white-trimmed windows peered out across the yard. Though he couldn't see it from that vantage, he knew that just beyond the house lay the cold, glistening waters of Cape Cod Bay. He paid the driver, who turned around promptly and set off down the quiet country lane back to Truro. He fumbled around in his backpack for what seemed like an eternity before finding his key ring, hoping his parents hadn't changed the locks for any reason in his absence. He opened the door set into the wall next to the main gate and stepped through onto a white gravel path that led up to the house.

Standing at the front door, a light breeze blowing past carrying the scent of the saltwater, he unlocked the door and entered the quiet house. He looked around at the furniture covered with sheets, made his way to the kitchen and set his backpack down on the kitchen counter. He had the house to himself. No voices. Just silence and the distant sound of waves crashing on the beach. He was finally alone. He'd made it.

He quickly put away the food he'd bought and made his way up to his old bedroom. He spent a few minutes unpacking and sorting through the clothes he'd brought with him—he'd thrown the pack together so hastily he wasn't sure if he'd remembered to bring everything he needed. Afterwards, he rummaged through a chest of drawers and his closet and decided he'd left enough of an assortment of clothes there the previous spring that between the clothes he'd left and those that he'd stuffed into his bag, he'd be alright.

With food and clothes sorted, he spent the next hour removing, folding and putting away furniture covers and cleaning the house. He turned on the heat and hot water so that they would be ready when he needed them. As it was April, the New England days and evenings were still cold. He briefly thought that some Australian summer heat would feel good right about now. He walked around checking the downstairs radiators were working and was pleased to see that they were already beginning to warm up. He reckoned the house should be in good working order, as his family used someone local to periodically check on it throughout the winter. As he returned to the kitchen his cell phone buzzed.

It was a text from his sister. She was checking to see if he'd made it okay and said that if she could get away over the next few days, and he was still there, she'd drive down to see him. He messaged back that he was fine, and all settled in, and that she was more than welcome. He felt relieved that Sam wasn't texting him from the car on her way down. He needed some time to sort his head out first. She'd want to talk about what was going on between him and their father, and he wasn't ready to discuss it with anyone at the moment, which was also why he didn't ask if his father knew he'd gone. While he wasn't sure if solitude on the Cape would help the situation, he figured that under the circumstances it couldn't really make matters much worse. The time apart might do them both some good.

He decided it was time to go for a walk down by the beach. Leaving his phone on the counter, he found an old pair of sandals he'd left in the house on a previous visit, strapped them on, and walked outside. The back yard stretched from the house until it tapered off against an expanse of dunes that ran parallel to the beach. Through the peaks and valleys of dunes and waving sea grass he could see the cold blue-gray expanse of water. He loved everything about the ocean. He quickly walked through the dunes and sea grass and out onto the beach.

He made his way across the glistening sand and found a spot just above the tideline. He sat down, slipped off his sandals and sank his bare toes into the warm sand. The air was cool, but the sun had warmed the silicon grains. No matter what was happening in his life, the simple act of sitting on the beach and listening to the sound of the surf always soothed him. As he sat, clearing his mind and looking out over the water, he felt the sudden irritation of that itch on the back of his neck again. He glanced up and down the beach and back towards the dunes and the house. He didn't see any other people. In the distance, out on the water, there was a motorboat making its way past. Apart from that, he was alone.

He had no reason to think that anyone had an interest in watching him. But it was a strange feeling, and one that he couldn't easily shake once he'd felt it. It felt like a small alarm buzzing against his skin, annoying and determined, until he looked about, at which point it ebbed away. As usual, he shrugged it off. It was probably nothing more than lingering agitation caused by his encounter with his father that morning.

He looked at his watch and noted that it was already early evening. His journey had taken longer than he'd anticipated. The sun was low on the western horizon, setting out over the water. He gave himself a few more minutes, then pushed himself up from the sand, stood at the water's edge and then slowly, almost reluctantly, turned and made his way back to the house. As the shadows deepened, it felt more foreboding than when he'd arrived. For a fleeting moment, he wondered if staying alone at the beach house was such a great idea.

When he got back to the house, he turned on the outside and downstairs lights. That helped to cheer things up almost immediately. He considered making dinner. But more solitude wasn't the answer. What he really needed was to be around other people. He would head to Provincetown for dinner. He went into the garage and found the two motorbikes the family kept there. He checked their gas and oil, decided to top them both up from a gas can they kept for emergencies. He ran inside and grabbed a jacket. He locked up and walked the bike out into the lane and fired it up.

Chapter 4

Arriving in town, he found a space to park his bike, locked the helmet to it and set out to find a place to have dinner. Provincetown was a mixed community. Artists, old hippies, people from Boston who owned summer homes, tourists, and a large seasonal gay community. It was an eccentric town offering up an eclectic mix of activities. Having spent many summers on the Cape since he was quite young, Nathan was used to it. In fact, he knew many of the longer-serving business owners from the many visits he'd made with friends and family.

As he walked, he pulled the collar of his jacket in closer. The night was growing colder, and he was beginning to think he should have worn something a bit warmer. He thought about grabbing a quick slice of pizza at an old haunt that he and his friends used to go to. But tonight, what he really wanted was a place where he could sit down for a while, listen to people talking, eat, and let the events of the day wash away. In the end, he made his way to a restaurant that was a town favorite for its lobster. It was sure to be lively and provide him a comfortable amount of anonymity.

The noise was the first thing that struck him as he walked through the front door—people talking over one another, scattered around the tables and bar, and background music filling in the gaps. Without hesitation, he smiled and walked up to the host. This was just what he was looking for.

"Table for one, please?"

"Sure honey, wait one second."

He wandered off into the sea of people as Nathan watched plates of seafood, lobster and steak being delivered to various tables. The smell of the nearby sea air mingled with strong food smells coming from all around him. It was a familiar smell, the kind reminiscent of home. In a few short moments the host returned with a smile.

"Right this way, honey. You don't mind sitting in the bar area, do you?"

"No not at all."

Nathan followed him to the back of the restaurant near the bar and was seated at a table overlooking the water of the harbor. The windows were partially open, and he could smell saltwater and seaweed on the night air. He breathed in deeply as he considered what he wanted to order. He didn't need to look at the menu. He'd eaten here so many times over the years he'd memorized it.

After a few minutes a waitress walked up, and he ordered beer and a lobster plate. He hadn't eaten lobster in a year, and he couldn't wait for it to come steaming out of the kitchen. He was halfway through drinking his beer when he noticed another solitary figure at the opposite end of the bar seating area. At first glance he appeared to be in his mid-twenties. He had dark eyes, intent and serious, the kind of eyes that looked straight into you as if they knew something you didn't. Nathan quickly looked away, not wanting to give the wrong impression.

When his food came, he tucked into the side salad first. While traveling, his meals had varied widely. He'd tried to cook for himself a few times but there were very few opportunities to cook a proper meal. Fortunately, there was a lot of varied local fare to sample everywhere he went, and he'd made good use of it, taking notes in his notebooks of different things he'd eaten and ingredients he'd never seen before. Luckily, he had a good metabolism and was on the move a lot, or no one would have recognized him when he returned.

The easiest thing to make was salads, as they were simple to throw together and light to carry. In Italy he'd enjoyed all the fresh food he found, but really, he'd made out quite well in most European markets. In Australia he was amazed at the size of all the fruits and vegetables. The stores had mountains of beautifully colored tropical fruits and he did his best to try as many of them as he could eat.

As his attention turned to the lobster, he looked up at one point, butter dripping from his chin, and noticed the guy at the end of the bar looking straight at him. He briefly returned the stare and as the other guy looked away, he wiped his chin and returned to eating his dinner. Each buttery bite reminded him more and more of home. Despite the circumstances of his return to New Comfort, and now his unexpected stay on the Cape, for the moment he was really happy to be home.

As he continued to pick his way through the lobster, he noticed that the other guy didn't seem to be eating. He had a half-empty pint glass of beer sitting in front of him that he slowly slid back and forth between his fingers. Nathan, on the other hand, was on his second pint of beer thanks to an attentive waitress. As he continued to eat, a group of three people were ushered into the bar by the waitress and seated between him and the other diner. Soon the bar area was filled with the sound of laughter as the new arrivals livened up the space.

Between eating and the effects of the two beers, he was beginning to relax. Coming here was a good idea. Even though he'd questioned his decision on the way down, he now thought maybe having a bit of space from one another was what he and his father needed. His father could be really hurtful sometimes. In the past, Nathan would just suck it up and wait things out. But he felt different now. He didn't have to take that crap anymore. Maybe it would teach his father a lesson.

As he listened to the conversation and laughter from the next table, his thoughts turned to his grandfather. He couldn't fathom what he must have experienced knowing his jet was going down. He hadn't wanted to think about it at all, but the thoughts came now despite his best efforts to suppress them. He wondered if they would ever really know what had happened to him—if they would want to know. He turned and looked out at the harbor lights reflecting on the dark water as a distraction from his thoughts. Everything was quiet and still outside apart from the periodic sound of the rolling surf.

He considered having one more beer and then decided against it as he had to ride back to the house. It had been a while since he'd been on a bike, and he really didn't want to take any chances—particularly in the dark. He decided to give his body some time to process the alcohol and the meal and started thinking about what he might do the next day to keep himself occupied. As he had no idea how long he might be staying at the beach house, he wanted to make the most of it.

His first thought was that he should get a haircut. That was one difference on his return that his family hadn't gotten used to. He used to have neat, tidy hair—the kind of hair a prep schoolboy would have. Over the course of his journey, he'd experienced longer and longer periods between haircuts until finally he just let it grow to shoulder length—something completely new and different for him. His father hated it, and even if that might be a good reason to keep it, he decided that now might be a good time to do something about it.

He pushed his plate away, signaled the waitress and settled his bill, leaving her a generous tip. As he stepped outside, he decided to walk around town for a bit to clear his head before getting back on the motorbike. He strolled down Commercial Street stopping occasionally to look at window displays, until the shops began to turn into houses. He walked around a bend in the road and found himself at the start of the causeway that extended across a corner of the harbor to a landmass on the far side. He stood for a while at the edge of the stonework looking out into the darkness and could hear the sound of muted horns in the distance.

There was a misty fog winding its way in over the water—not uncommon for this time of the year. The air was beginning to grow heavy and damp. Nathan pulled his jacket in more tightly to keep warm. The cold, dark water slapped against the stone causeway, sea foam landing on the legs of his jeans. At the other end was a sandy jut of land that used to be the home of local fishermen—and going way back, the odd pirate. Some of the surviving houses had long since been floated across the water to the main town, and now it was a mass of sand and seagrass and wildlife.

When he was younger, he and his friends would often sail around to that spit of land, moor their boats just offshore and go swimming. When the tide made the causeway impassable, that sandy stretch was deserted and a perfect place to visit, always giving the feeling of being on some remote, deserted island—even if the town was completely visible across the harbor.

He recalled that as he passed through Greece, he'd

sailed on the Mediterranean with some people he'd met. The waters were a bluish green and made for beautiful sailing in the warm sea air. They'd spent a couple of weeks sailing around the islands, coming ashore only to stock up on food and drinks. Sailing was something that he hoped to get back into once he eventually settled down.

The night air continued to grow colder, and his clothes were beginning to feel damp. He decided it was time to turn back. He made his way back up the street until he found where he'd parked the bike. It was pitch black and the fog was starting to creep inland, so he took things slowly on the way back. It was a welcome sight when he finally got to the end of his lane and pulled up to the gate. That last mile had felt more like ten.

As he removed his helmet, he could feel the wind begin to pick up and by the time he pushed the bike into the garage, a light rain had begun to fall. He was both happy to be inside and exhausted from the long day. It was hard to believe that he'd only left home that afternoon. After locking everything up, he stumbled his way up to his room, shed his damp clothes on the floor and crawled into bed, where he slowly drifted off to the sound of the gusting wind and rain falling against the roof of the house.

※

Further down the lane, snug in a warm car, a pair of binoculars watched the house through the falling rain.

The fog had dispersed as the rain and wind settled in. The middle-aged man peering through the binoculars watched the downstairs lights go dark, and the upstairs lights switch on. He continued to watch as the house descended into complete darkness. Earlier he had observed Nathan as he entered and left the restaurant and had waited near the parked motorcycle for his return. He'd periodically kept tabs on him since he'd landed in Boston a few weeks previously and had followed him as he moved between buses earlier in the day. He was the kind of man who was used to hiding in shadows.

Under the eaves near the garage, undisturbed by the wind and the rain, a separate pair of steel-gray eyes peered out from the darkness. This shadow had followed Nathan from London—and was aware of the other man sitting in his car. He chose not to disturb either of them and, instead, quietly and stealthily observed their every move—all at his own mother's request. There was something altogether more sinister about this observer. He was the one that Nathan would fear—if only he'd known of his existence.

After a short time, the man in the car decided there was nothing further to see and drove off into the distance to get some rest. The area near the garage was also now free of its shadow. Nathan slept into the night, oblivious, seemingly safe and undisturbed.

In the morning he woke to heavy rain and wind lashing the house and the distant rumble of thunder. Through the windows he could see the dark, slate-colored waters of the Bay, with violent whitecaps churning across the water's surface. Waves crashed against the beach, throwing sea spray high into the air. He had hoped the storm would have passed by the time he woke in the morning, but not only had it not passed, it looked as though it had intensified overnight. He'd been so focused on leaving the house that he hadn't checked the weather forecast. He was glad that he'd at least done a bit of shopping the day before. He had enough food to last him for a couple of days in the event the storm didn't pass quickly.

He walked down to the kitchen to grab something to eat and then sat in the living room. He turned the television on and settled back into the sofa with a glass of orange juice and a bagel. There was no way he was going to take the motorcycle into town to get a haircut in this weather. He had no choice but to wait out the storm. The weather channel said it would last for a couple of days and then pass out into the Atlantic. There was something about low pressure holding the storm over the coastline. He could hang tight for a couple of days. Then he'd have to either return home or go into town and get more food.

The morning dragged on slowly. He had grown unaccustomed to watching television during his travels. He was more used to taking breaks on a beach or in a field or up on a hilltop. He had spent other times in cafes, restaurants or any place he could find to sit and watch people as they passed by. He'd done a lot of people-watching when he was away—and as a result, a fair amount of socializing. There wouldn't be any socializing today. As he soaked in the solitude, a part of him wished he could just stay in the beach house indefinitely. But he knew that wasn't really an option. He would have to return home eventually.

As the time passed, he drifted off to the sound of the storm, letting it lull him into a light sleep. Before too long he lay across the sofa, sound asleep, the television having shut itself off. He was just starting to dream when he suddenly woke to a large bang and someone shouting.

"Christ, Nathan, you'd better be here you little brat."

Chapter 5

"The drive down here was insane. I can't believe I did that in this crappy weather. That's love for you!"

She threw her wet coat over the back of a dining table chair and followed her brother into the kitchen. He made them both a cup of tea, hers an English breakfast with milk and two sugars, just the way she liked it. He also grabbed a towel from the downstairs bathroom for her wet hair. It was still dripping from her run into the house. He asked why she hadn't parked in the garage and walked in through the kitchen entrance.

"I couldn't find the damned remote control for the garage doors. It's been a while since I've been down here. I'm sure it's in there somewhere."

She swore when she was flustered—and even when she was not. All of her boarding school's attempts to teach charm and etiquette had been wasted on her. She smoked occasionally too but would never openly admit that to anyone. More than a few times over the last few years he had seen her stamping out a cigarette when she thought no one was looking. As he handed her the hot cup of tea, he could hear the wind and rain continuing to lash the side of the house. It was such a miserable day outside.

"How are Mom and Dad?"

She rolled her eyes.

"How do you think? Dad doesn't want to talk about it, and Mom is worried. I told her I'd check in on you. I hope you don't mind. You know how she is."

He knew exactly how his mother was. Him being the baby of the family, she could sometimes over-mother him—not that he really minded. He knew that at least one of his parents would be relieved and happy to know that he was okay.

"I trust Dad is either pissed off and wants to send me away, or has put together a plan to keep a close eye on me and bury me in the business?"

Sam laughed and shook her head.

"It's probably a bit of both to be honest. Look, I know you two are struggling with one another right now. But I know he loves you. I could see how worried he was about you while you were away. He always hung around the edge of the room when you called and spoke to Mom. He might not be able to admit it to your face, but he does care about you. He's just struggling right now with the loss of Granddad. We all are. It's not a great time right now."

He nodded thoughtfully, taking it all in. Sam probably understood their father better, because she'd spent more time with him and knew him both at home and at work. He was still trying to figure his father out. He knew that his father would feel the need to assert control when he returned. That's just the kind of thing he did when he felt under pressure. He'd just lost his own father. It was a difficult loss for all of them as their grandfather had been such a strong presence in their lives. Thinking about what his father must be feeling, he started to feel a bit guilty. Perhaps he shouldn't have reacted so quickly and instead have allowed a bit of time for things to settle down.

They watched television together until early afternoon. Eventually growing bored of all the channel-hopping and arguing over each other's choices, they decided to head into town and have lunch. As Sam had her car, it wouldn't be too bad a trip even with the awful weather. They locked up the house and made a mad dash through the wind and the rain. The drive into town was wet, and heavy winds against the side of the car caused it to weave about. Sand drifted across the road in spots, but his sister was a good driver and used to driving in all the different weather conditions that New England could throw at her.

When they arrived they parked in the same lot where he'd parked his motorcycle the night before. They hurriedly got out of the car and made their way into a small restaurant near the waterfront, shaking the drops of rain off as they entered. Sam asked for a quiet table in the corner overlooking the harbor. It was relatively empty, which was not surprising given the weather.

"Is this okay?"

The waitress pointed them to a table at the back of the restaurant with a view over the dark, frothy waters of the bay. They nodded and settled into their chairs, and took the menus offered to them by the waitress.

"I'll give you a few minutes to decide," she said.

He was happy to see his sister. It was comforting to have a friendly face, and some company. He hadn't seen much of her since flying home from London. She'd had a lot to take care of with work given the absence of their father and grandfather. Just thinking about everything she must have been going through, holding things together, made him feel emotional. Sam had always been more than an older sibling; she was a good friend. Even with so much on her shoulders, she still she made time to come down and see him.

Having looked through their menus, they placed their order with the waitress. Afterwards, Sam was the first to speak, skipping past the issue with their father and asking about his time away. It was a nice distraction from everything else that was going on. She had done a bit of traveling herself since graduating university and joining the company, though nothing as epic as Nathan. Much to their father's delight, she'd chosen to travel over a series of successive holidays instead of disappearing after university as her brother had done.

He settled back into his chair and began his story with landing in London a little over nine months previously. Over the next two hours he talked about experiences he'd had and places he'd visited. Their food arrived at points along the story and they ate slowly, making each course last for ages. Sam interrupted from time to time with questions, but it was mostly Nathan who spoke while they ate.

Outside the restaurant the storm continued at pace, punctuated with flashes of lightning and rumbles of thunder. Nathan occasionally glanced around the room as other customers came and went. At one point he was sure he saw the guy from the bar the night before. He shrugged it off though, as the town was the kind of place where you were likely to run into the same people in a short span of time—particularly as tourist season wasn't in full swing yet. As he considered the stranger it reminded him of his strange experience in Stockholm. He briefly recounted to his sister his feeling of being watched at various times during his journey.

"I was in the Old Town in Stockholm when I first felt it, Sam. I don't know how to describe the feeling. It's like when think someone is looking at you, the hairs stand up on the back of your neck, you get this itch, and you look around to find someone staring at you. Only whenever it happened on my trip I'd look around and there was no one there. It was such a strange feeling when it happened. There were times when I wished that Ben had come along with me so that I wasn't alone."

"It was probably just that. You were on your own—which was stupid by the way—and maybe it just got to you sometimes. Lesson learned. Next time don't go by yourself."

She tried to make a serious face as though she were their father, and they both laughed. She was probably right, he thought to himself. Sam was fairly grounded and pragmatic. She would never have thought to travel alone. He probably shouldn't have either. They sat quietly watching the white-tipped surf through the windows. After a few moments, his sister spoke.

"Not to put pressure on you, but when are you coming home, Nate?"

"Nate." He hadn't heard that for a while. When he was younger his friends and family had taken to calling him Nate, though when he was really young, and occasionally when he was being a brat, Sam called him "Gnat." He recalled not liking that very much. He'd known that she'd get around to asking him about home eventually. Even so, he hadn't really given it a lot of thought. It wasn't as if he'd planned on leaving home to begin with, and whether it was a day, a week or a few weeks, he wasn't ready to go home and face his father— not that he thought time or distance would help the situation. It was just that he simply wasn't ready to go back.

"Honestly Sam? I'm not sure. I feel like I need some space. Everything over the last month happened so quickly that I really haven't had time to process it all. I miss Granddad. Dad's being a dick, forcing how he feels onto everyone else. Onto me. It's like I'm not allowed to have my own feelings about things. Maybe I just need some time to figure things out for myself."

He wasn't entirely sure if that was the full truth. The

chaos of coming home was a big departure from the solitude and independence that he felt during his time away. It was possible that he wasn't entirely ready to be home yet. While some of the issue related to his father, there were parts of the situation that were his alone. It was on him to sort that out.

"I'm hoping it won't be more than a few days or a week. I don't know Sam. I just need some space where I'm not shouted at or made to feel worthless. Some space to decompress."

He took a sip of his coffee and looked up with a smile.

"I'm happy you're here though."

His sister brushed away a lock of her blond hair and looked at him intently through her deep green eyes—the same color eyes as their mother's. He loved his sister and didn't want her to feel as though she were intruding. He was happy that she'd made the trip down to see him and he wasn't going to let anything ruin that. He wanted her to go back and tell everyone that he was alright—he didn't want his father to have one of his moments and drive down himself to take charge of the situation. He felt that he could reasonably get away with Sam telling them that he would be away no more than a few days to a week. After all, his father might want some time to think through things as well.

"What about you Sam? How are things? How is it being a big cheese in the company?"

She laughed.

"Hardly a big cheese."

Their father believed that anyone from the family who got involved in the business should start at the bottom of the company and work their way up. This was one of the many reasons that Nathan wasn't looking forward to going back. He had a quick mind and too many ideas. He worried that he would get bored if he were in any one role too long. His traveling had only sharpened that desire to push against boundaries.

"I've learned the milling side of things. Dad has me working in head office in Boston now, learning the other sides of the business—property, investments. I never realized how complex the family business was. You'd be surprised how interesting it is once you get into it. When I was at the mill, they taught me how to make things. I could even make you a scarf now."

He raised an eyebrow and they both laughed.

"I'm spending a lot of time in communication, public relations and marketing. Dad's actually relaxed his strict bootcamp rules a bit. I spent three months each in a bunch of different departments across the businesses and at the end he asked me what I thought. We decided marketing and communications was a great place for me to work."

It didn't entirely surprise him. She had studied humanities and business at Yale. She was incredibly smart, and he knew that she'd excel at whatever she tried her hand at. He also knew how proud his father was of her—not least because she'd actually gone straight into the family business after graduating. Unlike him. Even though he felt he'd learned an awful lot by taking time off and traveling, his father would never see that as real experience. For him, his son had just gone off on a jolly, squandering money needlessly. But the past was the past, and now there were other things troubling him.

"How do you think Dad's going to react when I get back?"

He didn't really want to ask, but figured he might as well since they were on the subject. And it helped that he valued his sister's insight.

"Well, as you know, he wasn't all that happy when you made the decision after graduation to travel. But I actually think he'd come around on that before you returned. It didn't hurt that your friend Gareth from prep school got into some trouble—something about growing plants of a certain nature in his parents' back garden. You know how Dad always used him as an example of someone who was responsible and knew how to show respect."

He laughed. Gareth Hanson lived in a nearby town and his father was a wealthy property investor in Boston. The last time he saw Gareth was the summer before he graduated university, when they'd both gotten high from that same medicinal patch in his back yard. It was a shame he'd been caught out.

"What happened to him?"

"Well, the gardener found it actually. He was giving a tour of their gardens to the local Daughters of the

American Revolution when they came across the patch. You know the one I mean."

She winked conspiratorially and laughed. He turned red.

"Yeah well, and his dad?"

"Well, he obviously had the gardener rip it all out and dispose of it. He probably sold it all. Last time I heard Gareth was working on one of his father's construction crews learning the business. You know the story."

Well, he thought to himself, he didn't know that story personally just yet, but he suspected that once he returned home, he was going to find out what it meant to be one of the crew.

"Do you think Dad will have chilled by the time I get back?"

"I don't see why not. Look Nathan, the whole thing with Granddad was so sudden. You know Dad—he hates change, and he's not spontaneous. He likes to wake up in the morning and have things work the way he left them the day before. This whole thing has really shaken him up. Granddad dying is a lot for him to take in. He's shaken up is all. It's not about you. He's just angry and you're the nearest target for him to take it out on. I'm sure that he'll calm down. Especially if Mom and Grandmother have anything to say about it."

She looked at him over the top of her coffee cup.

"You are ready to join us, aren't you? We don't bite."

He shifted uneasily in his chair. He'd spent nearly the

last year pondering that very question—or more truthfully, avoiding pondering it too deeply. Because his trip was cut short, he'd not had the time he expected to have before returning home to fully think it through. Now he would have to make a decision over the next few days. It was a lot to take in.

"I can promise that I'll be back soon, Sam. I just want this one last bit of time to chill and clear my head before going home—and to give Dad some space. I'm sure I'll be ready to start work—what else am I going to do? It's not like I have a place to go if I don't."

His sister laughed. He looked back out of the window. That was about the best answer he could give at the moment. It would have to be enough for now.

※

They drove in silence back to the house. Sam was concentrating on the road and he was running through their conversation in his head and trying not to think about returning home. Still, a part of him knew that going home would be for the best. Having a job would allow him to begin earning a living of his own—and to get a place of his own to live.

Having his own place was important to him. He'd only grown more independent in his time away. He didn't want to feel like he was living off his parents, even if his employment was with the family business. His sister had moved out while he was traveling and purchased her own house. His brother Christopher had moved out a couple of years before when he got married. He didn't really want to be the only sibling living at home—the baby of the family in every respect.

When they got back to the house, Sam pulled into the garage. He had remembered to take a spare remote for the garage doors so they didn't have to get soaked this time. He grabbed an armload of dry firewood and kindling from a stack along the back wall on his way into the house, with the intention of getting a good fire going in the large fireplace in the living room. That would warm the damp air. His sister retrieved a small carry bag from the back seat before following him inside.

She went directly upstairs to her old room. She left her bag on the bed and looked quickly through the clothes that she'd left the previous season. By the time she came back downstairs, he had made a roaring fire and two mugs of hot chocolate. They sat in front of the fire and watched the storm outside through the large floor-to-ceiling living room glass wall that faced out into the bay. It showed no sign of abating anytime soon.

"I forgot to ask. How long are you staying?"

"Trying to get rid of me already?"

They both laughed.

"Only until first thing in the morning. I have to get up early and drive back for work tomorrow. And we don't really want Dad asking where I was, right?"

She smiled, and he agreed that wouldn't be the best idea. They sat quietly sipping their hot chocolate, listening to the fire crackling, the rain falling and the wind howling outside. By contrast, inside the house it was very calm—and warm and dry.

"You know, Nate. Working with Dad isn't really so terrible. He's got his quirks, but once you've spent some time with him, you get to see how smart he is. I'm really proud of how he's modernized the mills and our distribution. The competition keeps quite a close eye on him now. And he and Grandfather have been quite savvy about the investment and property side of the business."

Her words hung in the air for a few moments, both recognizing that their grandfather was no longer a part of that story. Though he felt more skeptical about their father, Nathan was sure that his sister was probably right. He was dedicated to his work. That was also one of the problems that he had with him. He wished that he'd been a bit more dedicated as a father when he was growing up.

He had never been one of those kids whose dad showed up at baseball games or soccer matches. He didn't show up at any school events. But he was always quick to make remarks about how Nathan could have used his time more productively, such as coming by work after school or helping out during the summer. To his father, the family business was an all-consuming life. Unlike his father, he didn't want to be consumed by it. He wanted time to establish his own likes and dislikes, make his own friends and indeed his own mistakes. He didn't like the idea of being plucked up and stuck into a machine—like a cog.

It was his defiance about the idea of living that kind of life that led him to hatch his plan to travel in the first place. If it hadn't been for that money from his grandfather, he'd never have been able to pull it off. But in the end, he managed to plan it all by himself and go. He sometimes wondered if his independence scared the father who liked everything to be part of a plan—his plan.

"Of course, he'll put you through your paces," Sam continued. "You'll have to experience different roles and all that for a period of time like Chris and I did. But you get used to it. The only thing you have to watch out for is the people you're working with. Most of them are great. But some of them don't like the idea of the owner's kids working with them and they can be a bit mischievous and make things difficult. It's just a small percentage of them though. Most are just really good, hardworking people."

He knew that he could be a bit of a brat sometimes. He was convinced that, between that attitude and his not completely wanting to be there, there would be trouble. He'd do his best, though, to do his time and stay out of it. Sam and Chris had done it, and he was a smart guy, and capable of hard work. He wasn't planning to do anything stupid and let them or the rest of his family down.

"I'm sure it'll be fine, Sam. Can we talk about something else?"

She obliged and dropped the shoptalk and they sat quietly for a bit. Outside it almost seemed as if the storm was beginning to let up. The wind had died down a bit and it wasn't raining nearly as hard as it was when they'd settled in front of the fire.

It was just turning dusk as the rain and the wind finally blew themselves out. Clouds dispersed and evening stars began to poke through until the sky was absolutely clear and filled with them. The air smelled fresh and clean, as it always did just after a storm passed. Sam decided to take a quick walk along the beach while he prepared dinner. The day before he'd picked up a couple of fillets of striped bass and some fresh vegetables, herbs and seasonings to make a marinade and a salad. He began to cook while she headed out.

※

Sam walked along the beach reflecting on her visit with her brother. She felt that from what she'd seen since he'd returned, he had grown up a lot in his time away. He seemed more thoughtful and introspective now—less impetuous. She thought that maybe the time away had actually done him some good. If their father would only give him a chance, he might see that for himself. She still wasn't sure if he was any more prepared to go to work for their father than when he'd left, but at least now he seemed willing to give it a go—and she believed that he would give it a proper try before making any decisions. That wouldn't have been as likely a year ago.

He'd matured physically as well, from the slight

scruff of his unshaven face to his long hair. She wasn't sure how well all of that was going down, but then he was more his own man now, and their father couldn't have his own way in everything. All in all, she liked the changes. Nathan had had the courage to do something that she and Chris would never have done. In some ways, the thing that made him the black sheep in their father's eyes made him a bit of a hero to Sam and Chris—not that they'd ever admit it to anyone.

As she walked along the beach, she couldn't see anyone in either direction. Even the surface of the water was clear of boats, which was not surprising given the storm had so recently passed. Still, she began to feel a strange itch at the back of her neck, as though someone was watching her. She scanned the beach and dunes but couldn't see anyone. It was incredibly peaceful. There was just the crash of the waves, and the waving sea grass on the dunes.

She shrugged it off. Her brother's stories of feeling watched on his journey had gotten into her head. She laughed at her own silliness. Who would have the time or inclination to follow someone across the great distance that her brother had covered? And why on earth would anyone be that interested in her little brother anyways? Shaking it off, she eventually turned and walked back to the house, where she hoped that he was getting along with his dinner prep.

From the dunes a pair of cold gray eyes watched Sam as she walked along the beach. At one point she turned and scanned across the beach and the dunes. She seemed to look straight at him, her gaze lingering for a few seconds before she shrugged it off and continued on her journey. He watched as she made her way back towards the house.

It wasn't intrigue or curiosity. He'd been sent by his mother to keep an eye on Nathan. He still wasn't sure why. His mother, Jelena, played things close to her chest, and Dragan knew better than to press the issue. He crept to the edge of the property and glanced up toward the road to see if the man in the car from the previous night had returned. He hadn't. The road was quiet and deserted. Through the large window he could see Nathan preparing dinner in the kitchen. Dragan settled in for a spell. Soon he would have to head off to find his own dinner.

Chapter 6

That evening, they sat at the dining table and ate together.

"I see you haven't lost your touch in the kitchen."

He smiled and blushed. He'd always enjoyed helping out in the kitchen. They had a cook who helped their mother and grandmother, and he had stolen as many of the cook's moments as he could over the years to learn as much as he could about cooking. It was a good thing to learn and he looked forward to doing more of it.

"Thanks Sam."

They ate in relative silence and enjoyed the respite afforded by the storm's passing. In the distance they could hear the crash of surf on the beach. Once they finished eating they retired to the living room, where he stoked the fire and gathered a few more logs from the garage. Those would see them through until bedtime. They spent the remainder of the evening catching up on everything else that happened while he was away. Though he had emailed and phoned Sam periodically, nothing beat just having some good old face-to-face time to sit back and chat.

She filled him in on activities with the family business. They had acquired more properties to add to their investment portfolio, and there were new trade agreements in place in different countries for materials and fabrics. Their father and grandfather had been exploring expanding the office they had in London into a European hub for the company. Sam and Chris had both managed to convince their father to set up a venture capital fund to invest in technology companies. The siblings were heavily involved in managing that fund. Though it was too early to tell, they thought there were already a few potential high-value opportunities.

Not much had transpired in their hometown while he was away. New Comfort was a sleepy little New England town with roots going back to the early settlers of the area. His family being founding members of the earlier settlement wouldn't mean very much in most places in the country, but in a town like New Comfort, your heritage had the benefit of giving you status—and with the success of the Briggs family, that status was amplified.

"There was a lot of talk after you left. Everyone was speculating about why you'd gone away. It was insane. It drove Dad crazy. Chris and I thought it was funny though. Anytime people would ask, we'd act all mysterious, like there was something we were hiding."

"Oh thanks Sam. I'll have a reputation when I finally head back."

She laughed at the idea. For all of his younger impetuousness, he was a smart, fairly steady kid. He'd gone to a good boarding school nearby and then on to Harvard. He'd worked hard and received all the right grades and done all the right things—apart from taking a year off after graduation and going traveling.

"I wouldn't worry about it. Mom told everyone that it was a very European thing to do to take time off and go traveling—a gap year I think she called it. I think once that story got around people were quite envious. You'll probably have a lot of people wanting to hear your stories. I hope you took lots of pictures."

He had definitely taken loads of pictures. In addition to his iPhone, he had a good digital camera that he carried with him. It was one of the few objects other than his laptop that he'd stuffed into his pack before leaving. And somehow, he'd managed to hold on to all of it throughout his travels, even though he'd encountered some incredibly questionable people and places along the way. He thought better of mentioning that to his sister or, in fact, anyone back home.

"I took thousands of pics, sis. It'll take me ages getting them all sorted once I'm back. I loaded a bunch onto social media while I was traveling, when I could be bothered. I'm going to have a hell of an Instagram when I'm finished!"

"That sounds great! I can't wait to see them all."

"I might tackle some of it this week while I'm here. It might help me to take my mind off things and give me something to do."

While they talked, they'd opened a bottle of wine

from the cellar their parents kept in the house. They didn't keep a lot of stock there, but there were a few bottles of the good stuff hanging around for them to enjoy. As he topped up their glasses, he decided to change the conversation. There were some things he wanted to know, especially about his best friend, Ben.

"So, on another note, how's Ben doing?"

Sam took a sip of wine and leaned back into the sofa, taking in the smooth, full taste of the Bordeaux and the warmth of the crackling fire.

"He's doing well now actually. He's back at grad school. He was keen to get started on his degree after you'd left. He'll be really happy to see you. He's had a lot to deal with while you were away."

Though Nathan and Ben came from different backgrounds, and while his best friend could be a little uptight about life at times, they'd found a happy medium and had become very close over the years. He was aware of some of the things that had happened after he left. Ben had decided it was time to come out as gay to his mother. Not surprisingly, being very religious, she took it quite badly. She was a devout Baptist, and the tight black religious community to which they belonged took a dim view of the gay community. Ben's mother had been strict with him and even though he had graduated from university, she still exercised a great deal of control over her son.

One night, after a particularly difficult week, she'd come home and found that Ben had taken an overdose.

Luckily she was a nurse, and she took care of him until the ambulance arrived. He ended up in hospital for a while and then began seeing a therapist. As far as Nathan was concerned, what he really needed was to move as far away from his mother as he could possibly manage. At least after the incident she had backed off and given him more space. She still didn't fully approve, but she also didn't want to lose her only son.

He'd always known that Ben was gay. Respecting his privacy, and also in the event that he might be wrong, he never pressured his friend into coming out. He'd come out when he was ready. They never talked about it before Nathan left, and he had only learned about what happened from his sister during one of their calls. His friend never mentioned anything when they messaged one another; maybe he assumed that Nathan didn't know—or maybe he felt too ashamed to tell him. It would never have made a difference to Nathan. They were best friends, and the world was a big place—big enough for all different types of people. It wasn't the sort of thing that would ever affect their friendship.

"It'll be good to see him. I probably should have tried to get over before now, but you know, with everything going on, it's all been a bit too busy and weird."

They talked and finished the bottle of wine as the fire began to slowly burn down. Unlike the night before, it was now peacefully quiet outside, and he knew that he would be able to get a good night's sleep. As they sat there, he thought to himself how glad he was that his sister had come to see him. He felt a lot of anxiety about the situation with his father, but spending the day with Sam had already gone a long way to making him feel more relaxed about things. He didn't want to be at odds with him, and despite the strangeness of their relationship, he still had the rest of his family, who loved him very much. He knew that he could count on them for support when he returned home.

He'd missed his siblings, his mother and his friends. He had so many experiences that he wanted to share with all of them. At least he had that to look forward to when he finally returned home. He smiled and leaned his head on his sister's shoulder. He felt comforted. Everything would be alright.

The next morning Sam was up and off at the crack of dawn. She had meetings in their Boston offices before she had to head up to one of the mills as a favor to their father to meet with some suppliers later in the day. She said her goodbyes to Nathan, hugged him, and reassured him that everything would be okay before getting into her car for the drive back. He opened the garage door and the gate for her.

"Don't be a stranger!" she said, smiling, as she drove away, leaving him standing alone in the secluded driveway.

He closed the gate and walked back into the house to

make a cup of coffee. The bad weather had completely cleared out. The low early morning sun slowly rose into a crystal-clear blue sky. Apart from the damp ground and puddles, you would never have realized there had been such terrible weather the previous day. He felt a bit better now that he'd had a good night's sleep and a chance to talk things through with his sister. He decided to shower and head into town for that haircut and to have a wander around. He felt a bit more like being around people now, and less like hiding in the house, licking his wounds. He still wasn't quite ready to return home, but he was getting there.

The roads were quiet and after a short drive, he parked just off Commercial Street. He locked up and a few minutes later found a place to get a haircut. He sat down in the chair, explained what he wanted, and the barber, named Amelia, began to cut his hair. She was friendly, in an eccentric kind of way. She'd moved to town the previous summer from a small Western Massachusetts town. She thought the people were very nice. She loved the beach. She didn't have any kids and no current prospect of a girlfriend. She had two cats and a parrot named Bob.

He smiled and, on the odd occasion she asked, gave brief answers to her questions. He was usually quiet when he got his hair cut. He preferred to just sit down, get it over with, and go. The guy who usually cut his hair back home was a surly old man. He wondered if he was still there. Before he'd left, as he was getting one last haircut, the man had mentioned several times that he was considering packing it in and heading south to join his sister in Florida.

Half an hour of banter, washing and cutting, and he looked like a new man. He was pleased that she'd done such a great job. He paid, gave her a nice tip, thanked her, and went back out onto the sunny street feeling refreshed. There was something about a haircut that made you feel a foot taller.

He walked back towards where he'd eaten a couple of nights before, meandering in and out of shops on his way. He wasn't in any particular hurry, enjoying the nice weather and the chance to just wander about without any particular agenda. He'd done a lot of this when he was away. It was a habit that he would have to temper slightly if he was going to try to reintegrate into home life.

By late morning he found himself in the West End of town, an area populated by many art galleries. When he was younger, his mother, who knew many of the gallery owners around the Cape, inevitably dragged him round these places; his father usually stayed in the beach house and worked from his study there, oblivious to anything culturally significant. He was the consummate businessman. When it came to the textiles they manufactured, he was emotionally detached—he might as well have been selling toy robots.

Nathan remembered not liking being dragged into galleries when he was younger. But as he'd grown a bit older, he began appreciating the idea of art and history a bit more. He'd visited many museums on his travels, and he knew that he'd end up spending many hours at some point telling his mother about all of his cultural experiences. She would appreciate those stories, as a traveler herself.

Before wandering into the galleries, he decided to take care of his rumbling stomach and ducked into a cafe to grab something to eat. In short order he paid and walked out with an egg and bacon sandwich and a Coke. He walked down past a museum to the pier and found a set of benches where he could sit in the quiet and enjoy his breakfast in the morning sun. He watched as boats bobbed up and down in the water. Seagulls sat on the top of posts along the pier or flew in low swoops over the water. The season was still a bit early for there to be many boats, but in another month or so, he knew, this place would be heaving with activity.

He sat back and watched a couple of guys rigging a sailboat in preparation for heading out into the bay. There would probably be some pretty good sailing, as the storm had left behind clear skies and a stiff breeze. He and Ben used to take small sailboats out when they were younger. It was still a bit too early in the season for him, and as much as he loved it, he wasn't sure he'd want to be out on the water today. Sitting in the sun was fine but the breeze coming in from over the water was cold. Still, he admired their dedication.

Before long the men set their sails, and slowly moved west out of the harbor. He watched them recede into the distance as he finished the last bites of his sandwich. The sailboat grew smaller and smaller as it sailed out into the bay. He got up, threw away the wrapper and his empty can, and decided it was time to wander round the galleries to walk off his breakfast and see what the winter's inspiration had left behind. There was little else to do on the Cape during the bleak winter, and Nathan was sure that there would be an abundance of art to view.

Unsurprisingly, there were many watercolors and oils of boats and beaches, beach huts, dunes, the piers and town scenes. There was a mix of all seasons on display. Some of the galleries carried art from artists who didn't paint seascapes and he found some interesting contemporary abstract paintings in those. There was also blown glass, sculpture and ceramics. Much of it was the kind of art you'd expect to find in seaside art galleries.

He took it all in as he walked around the town, making mental notes of things that he liked and drawing comparisons between the arts and craft style of the works he was seeing and the older, more mature works he'd seen in museums during his time away. Though he'd been exposed to art growing up, he had never appreciated it in the same way that he did now, having visited countries where the old masters had originated and having seen some of the locations made famous by their paintings. He still couldn't fully understand the intricacies of it as his mother did, but his appreciation had deepened to a level of admiration and awe he'd never before experienced.

After a couple of hours, he came across a larger grocery store and decided to pick up a few more things for the house. They had fresh catch of the day and after his experience the previous night, he decided on a couple of fresh fillets to cook later for dinner. He picked up as much as he could carry and set out to find the motorcycle for the drive home.

When he returned, the house was quiet and chilled. He gathered some more wood and kindling from the garage and quickly built a fire. He was practiced at this and in no time it was crackling away, throwing comforting heat into the room. He put away the shopping and grabbed his laptop and camera from upstairs before settling on the sofa. It was as good a time as any to start sorting out the photos that he'd taken on his trip, and he looked forward to sharing them with everyone, having only shared a small portion of them on his social media.

The whole exercise ended up taking him a lot longer than he'd thought, and he was only halfway through sorting them when he noticed it was starting to grow dark outside. Other than periodically getting up to stoke the fire, or at one point to make himself a salad for lunch, he'd hardly moved from the sofa all afternoon. He decided it was time to stop for the day, closed his laptop, and stoked the fire again before heading into the kitchen. It was time for dinner. He prepared the fish fillets and set them in the refrigerator until he was ready to cook them. They would make a nice dinner.

※

He was just about to step out for a walk when the house phone rang. He debated whether to pick it up and then thought Sam and his mother were the only ones who knew where he was.

"Hello?"

"Ha! There you are!"

It was Ben. He smiled. He hadn't been expecting a call from his best friend.

"How did you know?"

At the same time, they both said, "Sam!"

"You know she adores me," Ben said. "She thought that just maybe you could use some company. And as I'm on break for a couple weeks, I thought, hey, I could pop down and see you. So? You up for it?"

He considered it for a moment and thought, why not? He hadn't seen Ben since returning and catching up with him was long overdue.

"Sure! When were you thinking?"

"Well…"

"You're already here, aren't you?"

Ben laughed from the other end of the line.

"I'm in town. I thought you might want to come for a drink and some dinner. Then we could hop back to the house after. You don't mind if I stay a couple of days, do you?"

Nathan laughed and slowly shook his head. He could never say no to his best friend. And it was a chance for them to have some time together and some privacy to catch each other up on everything that was going on in their lives. And besides, Nathan thought, a bit of company might be nice after all.

"Of course you can stay. You're family. But in a good way."

Growing up, Ben had spent a lot of time at the beach house with Nathan and his siblings and some of their other friends.

"Just let me get ready and I'll pop into town and join you."

"Great. I can't wait."

Ben suggested a bar in the middle of town and said that he'd head over and get them a table.

"Alright. I'll see you soon."

He hung up, walked back into the kitchen and cleaned up the counters. The fish would have to wait until tomorrow. He quickly showered, threw on some warm clothes and grabbed the bike. He wasn't sure if it was such a good idea if they ended up drinking, but they always had the option to leave it overnight and take a taxi back when they were ready.

Chapter 7

Unlike much of the rest of the sleeping town at this time of year, the bar Ben had selected was generally busy. However, on a Tuesday night this early in the year it was only inhabited by a smattering of locals, and tourists who came early to beat the seasonal crowds. He scanned the bar as he entered and found his friend sitting alone at a table in a corner.

What a difference a year could make. When he'd left, Ben was a lanky kid with tightly curled black hair and dark brown eyes covered by large thick-lensed glasses. He'd obviously hit the gym and muscled up and now wore tight bleach-blond curls against dark skin and naked big brown eyes. His best friend, waving at him as he approached the table, had never looked better.

"Ha! The runaway returns."

He laughed as he took a seat.

Ben nicknamed Nathan "the runaway" before he left. He knew how much the name irritated him, but over the course of his time away he'd realized that his friend was partially right—it was a running away of sorts.

"You look great Ben! Skinny as ever I see."

Ben flexed a bicep and they both laughed. A few people around the bar looked their way and smiled.

"You look great too! Looks like running away did you some good. You look all grown up."

They smiled at one another; best friends reunited.

"And hey, I'm really sorry about your grandfather. I wanted to come over and see you but didn't know what to say—I knew you'd all have a lot to deal with."

Nathan shrugged his shoulders. He tried hard not to think about why he had to come home so abruptly. Not out of disrespect or love for his grandfather, but because the pain of thinking about it was just too overwhelming.

"Don't worry. I get it."

Ben knew him well enough to know that if he wanted to talk about it or whatever had happened at home, he would, when he was ready. There was no sense pushing it, so instead he changed tack.

"I suppose you've heard the news by now."

There was nothing quite like jumping into the deep end.

"If you mean this," Nathan said as he gestured around at the gay bar his friend had chosen.

Ben nodded. Nathan could see he was nervous.

"Listen Ben, it was about time you came out. I was beginning to think we'd be in a retirement home before you said anything."

His friend rolled his eyes, looking visibly more relaxed. Nathan laughed at his expression.

"You know, you could have put me out of my misery ages ago!"

"It wasn't my place. It was your life and you needed to say it when you were ready. I'm just glad you've moved on now. You really do look great! And it's so good to see you."

They ordered drinks and over the next couple of hours talked over the top of one another, each filling the other in on how they'd spent their time apart. Ben had all kinds of questions about Nathan's time away, wanting to know every detail of the trip. Nathan in turn questioned him about grad school, and the difficulties he'd had with his mother when he told her. Ben spoke briefly about it but obviously wasn't ready to talk about the whole experience.

It was as if the two of them had never spent any time apart. But then, they'd known each other since they were both in diapers. Falling right back into their friendship was as easy for the two of them as breathing. Ben relaxed more and more as the evening went on and the stories flowed from both of them. Nathan, conscious that he'd ridden the motorcycle into town, tried to stem the flow of drinks but finally gave up, realizing that it was going to be a taxi after all.

※

They were just thinking about leaving when the bartender appeared with two more drinks—two reddish cocktails with little parasols sticking out of them. The two friends looked at one another and then quizzically at the bartender.

"Not from me honeys, though maybe next time! No, it was from that girl over there at the corner of the bar."

As they scanned across the room, Nathan's eyes opened wide in shock. A young woman, in her early twenties, black hair and gray eyes, waved back at them. As she stood, he could see that she was of medium height and slender build. Exactly as he remembered her.

Serena. That same Serena he'd met in Dubrovnik nearly eight months previously. What in the hell was she doing in Provincetown? Ben raised his glass to her, and she raised a full glass back.

"We should go thank her."

He was enthusiastic, while Nathan sat in stunned silence.

"Well?"

Ben, already a bit drunk, was eager to meet the strange girl who'd bought them a drink. Nathan was more subdued. He wasn't sure what to say to her. In part he was angry that she'd left him alone and not gotten back in touch, and part of him wondered what the hell she was doing here, now. But she had started walking over and, by the time he stood up, she was standing at their table.

"Hello Nathan," she said. "Are you going to introduce me to your friend?"

"Uh, Serena yeah, sure. This is Ben."

His friend looked between the two of them in confusion.

"Serena? The girl you messaged me about from Croatia. What the fuck?"

Nathan turned slightly red at his friend's sudden outburst, not that he disagreed with the sentiment. She leapt into the confusion.

"You're much more handsome than Nathan let on, Ben. Nice to meet you."

She reached out and shook his extended hand, while with the other she deftly pulled a chair over from an adjacent empty table.

"Listen Nathan, I'm so sorry about Dubrovnik. I was called away at the last minute by my father. There was a bit of a family emergency. I didn't have time to sort things out with you the way I would have liked. When I finally returned, you'd moved on and I wasn't sure where you were. I knew some of your itinerary, but not enough to figure out where you might be. The only thing I knew was where you were from. And so, here I am."

"How did you find me here?"

"You told me where you live."

"Yeah, where I live. Not our house on the Cape. How did you find me here?"

"I called around your house. The Briggs family aren't exactly inconspicuous in New Comfort. I met a nice woman named Sam. She told me."

Even though he'd asked his sister to keep his whereabouts quiet, it seemed that she was practically sending out engraved invitations to everyone. He made a mental note to deal with her when he finally returned home about her serious lack of discretion.

"I don't really understand though. What are you doing here?"

She looked thoughtfully between the two of them.

"I'm here to see you. I didn't like what happened and I wanted to find some way to make up for it. I had to come to Boston on family business and decided to take a side trip to see if you'd returned home—or at least if someone could tell me how to get in touch with you. You never did give me your number or email address."

"Well, I never expected you'd just up and disappear. I thought I had time."

Serena responded with a tight-lipped smile. Nathan couldn't help but think about what a beautiful smile she'd had when they'd first met. He was clearly pressing her buttons now.

"Well, I'm sorry. In my experience, time is never something you can fully count on. But I'm here now. That must count for something."

As she spoke his head began to hurt. He felt conflicted seeing her after all of that time had passed. In many ways he'd moved on from their week together, losing himself in his next set of destinations. But he had continued to wonder what happened to her. Before he could respond, she changed the subject.

"By the way Ben, technically it's Severina. My name. But I usually just go by Serena. Nathan told me a lot about you."

Ben blushed.

"Severina. That's a different kind of name."

"Yes, it's an old family name. My parents have a funny sense of humor."

She didn't elaborate but continued to speak.

"I'm sorry. You both looked like you were ready to head out, and I've already spent more of the day running about than I'd intended. Can I at least walk you both out?"

Nathan looked over at his friend, feeling confused.

"Are you staying over this evening?" he asked.

"No, I'm driving back to Boston tonight. I need to be back in town in for an early morning meeting."

"Aren't you tired?" Ben asked.

"No not really. I slept in quite late this morning, and I like driving at night. Less traffic and it's more peaceful."

He exchanged looks with Nathan and shrugged.

"Why don't you walk Serena out and I'll order us a taxi."

Nathan nodded and turned awkwardly towards the door, ready to walk with her outside. They stood in awkward silence in the cold night air for a moment before either spoke.

"Look Nathan, I understand if you're angry and don't want to see me again. But I'm around New York and Boston quite a lot. It would be nice to see you sometime. If, that is, you want to see me."

She was just as confident and forward as he remembered her. She'd also made the first move when they met in Dubrovnik. He considered her offer for a moment.

"I think that would be okay," he said.

"Why don't we exchange numbers this time. If you can't get me just text or leave a message. I promise I will get back to you."

He nodded and they quickly swapped numbers. As the cold air swirled around them, she leaned in and kissed Nathan gently on the cheek. Her lips were cold, but soft, just as he remembered them.

"I'll speak with you soon, okay?"

He nodded and, in her usual fashion, she walked off into the darkness, quickly disappearing around a corner as though she'd never been there. As he turned back towards the entrance to the bar, he found his best friend standing there, smirking.

"Is she gone?"

"Yeah, but at least we swapped numbers this time."

He shook his head as they stamped their feet in the cold night air to warm up.

"What an odd night," he continued.

They looked at one another and laughed. Ben could see that his friend was clearly rattled by the visit. After a few more minutes their taxi arrived, and they piled in for the short ride back to the warm house.

⁂

"So that was crazy last night, right?"

The next morning all that Ben could talk about was Serena. For Nathan, the whole episode felt unreal. His friend thought it was really romantic that she'd gone out of her way to track him down. Neither one could believe she'd travelled all the way up to his parents' house and then all the way back down to the Cape. Nathan wasn't sure he agreed with the romantic bit, but she definitely seemed determined.

As his friend spoke, he looked over and silenced him with a look.

"Okay, okay. I'll talk about something else."

After a minute he continued.

"You have to admit, it was romantic in a stalkerish kind of way."

Nathan remained silent. His friend had talked incessantly since they woke up. Ben shrugged and changed the subject.

"What should we do today?"

The sun was still low in the early morning sky. Nathan was ready to do anything to get his friend to stop talking about the previous evening. Ben was raring to go and seemed to be suffering no ill effects from their previous night's drinking. Nathan, on the other hand, felt more than a bit hungover and reckoned that he could have used a bit more sleep. He thought it might be nice to spend some time outside and get some fresh air.

It was still too cold to do anything on the water. They could take the bikes out though and head to one of the beaches to catch a bit of sun. And if he felt better, they could even consider heading into town for some lunch afterwards. They would have to double up on the remaining bike until they picked up the one that he'd left in town the night before. He proposed the idea to Ben, who quickly agreed.

Once they arrived in town, they retrieved the other motorbike. Ben took over the one they'd ridden together and tore off, leaving his friend to follow him out of town. After a short ride in the sunshine, they pulled up in a parking lot that led to one of the popular beaches. It was one of their favorite places to go.

They left the bikes and wandered off through a cut in the dunes down a worn wooden walkway leading towards the beach and the glistening water. The sun continued to make its slow ascent from the east. It felt warm in the direct sunlight. They trudged through the loose sand and picked a place to sit down. Over the next half an hour Nathan's mood began to lift and he began to feel better, although he was still hungover and a bit unsettled about the previous night.

༄

As they sat down on the blanket they'd brought along, Nathan began considering the events of the day before. It was a long day, that had begun with getting up early in the morning so he could see off his sister to Boston; and then his best friend had shown up in the evening, before the day culminated with Serena making a surprise entrance at the end of the night. So much for his peaceful retreat to the Cape. It was beginning to feel like he was trying to hide out on the main concourse of Grand Central Station. It didn't help that his friend was clearly thinking about the previous evening as well.

"Severina. That's such an unusual name, don't you think?"

He scowled at Ben, partly irritable from the hangover and partly because he wasn't sure if he wanted to discuss it. Still, he had to admit that his friend was right; it was an unusual name. But then her family was from Croatia, so what was unusual to an American wasn't necessarily strange at all for her. He had encountered many different things while he was away, and his views of unusual or different had been considerably widened over time. With her flawless American English, you wouldn't even know that she wasn't born and raised in the States.

In the time they'd spent together she'd mentioned that her family had global business interests and, as he recalled, she had mentioned New York and Boston. So really, he supposed it wasn't all that odd that she might be in the neighborhood—though tracking him here was a bit over the top. He was surprised to find that after all this time, it still stung that she'd disappeared so suddenly. He rationalized it by admitting to himself that she didn't have the means to contact him, and he had moved on shortly after she'd left. Despite all of that, he still thought that she looked good. Just as he remembered her. He glanced away, hiding a small smile from his friend.

As the waves lapped against the beach, he found himself thinking about her black hair and gray eyes. He'd always thought that her complexion was pale for someone from the Adriatic. Most of the people he'd met in that region had deeply tanned skin. He remembered asking about it and Serena telling him that she spent a lot of time indoors, in meetings and travelling, so she didn't really get back to Croatia, or outdoors, often enough to enjoy the sun and warmth.

As much as he wanted to, she still held a strange attraction that he found he couldn't deny. She was forward, alluring and strangely mysterious at the same time. For all of the hours that they'd spent together, walking and talking, he realized that he knew only as much about her and her family as you might read in the society pages.

He jumped as Ben elbowed him in the side.

"Hey! Do you suppose the water's too cold for a dip?"

He shook his head to clear his thoughts, and looked at his friend like he was insane.

"It's freezing at the best of times. You have to be kidding me."

Ben laughed.

"I know it's going to be cold. But I just feel like taking a dip. It's been too long."

Nathan shrugged. The cold had never stopped them when they were younger. Water was water. They'd practically grown up together in it; cold, warm or otherwise, it didn't matter. Before he could say anything else, his friend was on his feet and peeling off his shirt. Chocolate abs rippled down his stomach. He really had transformed himself. Perhaps coming out had been the start of a new journey and image for his friend. He watched as Ben threw his shirt onto the blanket, kicked off his sneakers and pulled off his socks. He slid his trousers down and pulled them off at the feet and then slid his thumbs under the band of his underpants.

Nathan laughed as his friend glanced at him and began to turn a bit red. It was funny because they'd been naked in front of one another so many times over the years that it shouldn't make a difference to him. But some things were subtly different now, even if they weren't things that affected their friendship. Now that Ben had come out, it opened up a whole new facet of their friendship.

"Oh, fuck it!" Ben finally shouted.

He yanked the underpants down, flicked them off, and turned and ran into the water. The blood-curdling scream as he hit the ice-cold surf could be heard up and down the length of the beach. It was a good thing that the few other people present were a long way off in the distance. Nathan laughed and shook his head. There was no way he was going into that ice-cold water. He'd done it many times in the past, and he knew the initial shock of hitting it felt like running into a slab of ice.

He watched as Ben splashed around for a bit taking some time to acclimate to the cold water, and then turned and looked up and down the beach in both directions.

He really did love the Cape this time of the year, a quiet period just before it became too touristy. Though he'd never considered himself or his family tourists, as they owned a home here, he knew they would never fully be part of the culture that existed there either. Home would always be back in New Comfort.

The sun rose higher into the morning sky and was beginning to warm the sand under their feet. A light cold breeze from the water carried the smell of seaweed and occasionally raised goosebumps on his arms. Ben continued to jump about in the water, trying to taunt Nathan into joining him. He was slightly tempted by the sheer adventure of it. It had been ages since he'd been here, and though during his time away he'd been able to swim in waters from England to Scandinavia to the Mediterranean and Australia, he would always love the familiar blue-gray waters along the New England coast.

"Come on!" Ben shouted. "Don't be boring."

Finally, his resolve broke and he decided to join his friend in an arctic baptism. He quickly shed his clothes, left them in a hasty pile on the blanket and ran directly into the water. When you grew up in New England you learned the best way to get used to the cold was to just suck it up and run straight in. Dipping in a toe at a time did nothing other than to ensure it would take twenty minutes to get used to the water instead of twenty seconds. Even so, the water was ice cold as he slammed into it.

Ben laughed hysterically as Nathan broke through the surface and gasped. He jumped after him and soon the two were play-fighting as they had done since they were children. The cold water cured Nathan of his hangover. For the first time in days, he let go of his angst and smiled and laughed. His sister had done the right thing telling his best friend where he was. He needed a good friend he could talk to, who could provide a distraction from everything that had happened. Her visit had helped him as well. He came to the realization, as he stood in the ice-cold water and sunshine, laughing with his best friend, that when the time came and he finally returned home, he would find a way to smooth things over with his father.

They continued to play for another twenty minutes before they both started to lose feeling in their hands and feet. They knew it was probably long past time to get out of the water. With blue lips and shriveled skin, they made their way back up the beach, shared the towel and dried off in the warming sun. They shook the loose sand out of their clothes and quickly dressed. As they made their way to the walkway, they passed an old couple sitting on the beach together at the edge of the dunes, who shook their heads disapprovingly as they walked past. It appeared they hadn't gone completely unseen after all. They looked at one another and broke out in laughter.

The ride into town was uneventful. Apart from a few missed grains of sand in Nathan's pants, he was glad he'd let Ben talk him into going swimming. He felt wide awake and refreshed and looked forward to wandering around town and getting some lunch. He felt relaxed and stress-free. They parked and locked the bikes and were soon wandering in and out of the small shops, talking and laughing. Even Ben appeared to have let go of the demons that had plagued him in his best friend's absence. They were good medicine for one another.

Though Ben had yet to talk about his worst experiences when they were apart, Nathan knew that he would bring things up when he was ready. He knew that he'd missed his friend while he was away seeing the world, but until this moment he hadn't realized just how much the absence of his friend had meant to him.

After a bit of shopping, where they each purchased shirts, trousers and various bits and pieces, they found a restaurant where they could eat and relax. The morning's activities had made them both incredibly hungry and before too long they were both steadily digging into their seafood pastas. There was near silence while they ate, both having ravenous appetites. Swimming in icy cold water had a tendency to do that. After a long silence, Ben was the first to speak.

"When are you planning to come home, Nate? Sam told me some of what happened. I know you probably don't want to talk about it, but please don't let it stop you from coming back. You've got Chris and Sam. And me."

Nathan shrugged. It seemed to be the big question on everyone's minds, including his own. As he mulled it over, he realized that it didn't bother him that his sister had told his best friend some of what had happened between him and his father. If anything, it saved him the time of having to do it himself.

"Well, if I'm going to be honest, I'm thinking that I might head back with you. Maybe it's time to go home Ben. What do you think?"

His friend nodded as he shoveled pasta into his mouth.

"I think it's a great idea. I've missed you."

His friend's voice quieted as he said the last bit.

"I've missed you too, buddy."

It was all that needed to be said on the matter between the two friends. Ben stopped eating and looked at Nathan.

"I'm sure you've heard. Things got a bit difficult for me after you left."

Nathan had received updates from his mother. And his sister had talked to him about it. He hoped Ben was well on the mend. He seemed alright, if just a little bit sad.

"I'd heard. I'm really sorry I wasn't there for you, Ben."

"You wouldn't have wanted to be there. And to be honest, it was something I had to go through on my own. I've grown up a lot in the last year."

"You've certainly done that."

Nathan reached out and squeezed one of his friend's biceps.

"You look great."

Ben laughed.

"Thanks. Taking care of myself helped, but you know what I mean."

Nathan nodded.

"I do. Well, I mean, I can't really understand everything that happened to you because I wasn't there. But I'm glad that you're okay. I thought about coming back at the time, but my mother said you couldn't really have any visitors for a bit, and afterwards I thought that if you needed me, you'd let me know."

He slid the pasta around on his plate with his fork. He still felt a pang of guilt at not being there when his friend needed him most.

"I thought about you a lot though. I'm really sorry for everything you had to go through."

Ben smiled and put a hand on Nathan's arm.

"It's alright Nate. I know you'd have come straight away if I'd asked it—which was why I didn't."

They finished eating in silence. After lunch they spent a couple more hours wandering around town. On the way back, they picked up a few more things to go with dinner. They strapped everything onboard and rode back to the house, where they spent the rest of the afternoon watching television, making small talk, and enjoying one another's company.

Chapter 8

Back in Boston, Serena was just leaving the office. It was evening as she walked back to her black Maserati parked in the lower level of the garage. She was in one of the many commercial buildings he owned around the world, all held by a series of offshore shell companies. She didn't know exactly how wealthy her family was, but she knew it tipped the scales of extreme wealth. She also knew that her family wouldn't appear on any global wealth lists, as their assets were all private and held in secret, discreet accounts.

Her father, Davorin, had asked her to come to Boston so that he could bring her in on a private matter, something that for the moment only she and her brother, Vilim—or William as he was commonly called—were allowed to know. Incredibly, her father had insisted she return to the Cape and keep a distant eye on Nathan. He wouldn't elaborate on why, and she couldn't fathom the reason—she'd learned over a long period of time that when her father asked her to do something, often without full explanation, it was in her best interest to follow his instructions. He was a kind man in many respects, but he also had an intensity about him that commanded her—and her brother's—full respect.

She couldn't tell in this case if he really wanted her to keep an eye on Nathan—which seemed like an entirely odd request—or if he was trying to remove her from harm's way for a time by distracting her from some other circumstance. She wasn't naïve. She knew that her father's business interests weren't always fully on the level—not that she would have expected that, given the secretive circumstances of their family history. Still, she preferred to know what was going on.

She retrieved her car and prepared for the drive back to Truro. Her father had specifically asked her to keep her distance from Nathan for the time being, to try to blend into the background, keep an eye on him and ensure he came to no harm. For the moment, she would do as he asked without question. There would come a moment when he would bring her closer into the fold—when he was ready, and when he could ensure her safety. She pulled out of the garage into a cool, dry Boston evening and drove south.

※

While Serena was on her way to the Cape, Nathan and Ben were sunk into the sofa with the television flickering away. Ben had fallen asleep halfway through a movie and quietly slid to the side until he was lying on the arm of the sofa, snoring lightly away. Nathan could hear the crash of the surf on the beach. The sun had gone down, and the full moon illuminated the evening sky. He got up, stoked the fire in the fireplace and decided to take a walk on the beach to get some fresh air.

He loved seeing Ben, was grateful that he had come down, but the intensity of the visits from his sister, and now his best friend, was exhausting. He'd had to talk about his experiences and discuss the issues he had with his father more than he'd intended when he escaped to the beach house. He was happy that he was so cared for, but now he welcomed a bit of quiet time, smiling to himself as he snuck out through the back door.

※

As he walked across the back garden and out through the dunes, he could feel a light breeze blowing in from the water. Stepping out onto the silvery sand, he scanned up and down the length of the moonlit beach. There was no one as far as he could see in either direction. It looked like he had it all to himself. He pulled his sneakers and socks off and carried them as he walked across the cool, slippery sand to the water's edge.

Just above the waterline, the sand still held pockets of warmth from the daytime sun. He dug his toes deep into the surface as he walked, and smiled at the feeling of the small slippery grains sliding between them. He turned and walked north along the hard-packed wet sand, strewn with pebbles, broken shells, seaweed and bits of driftwood. The tide rolled gently in and out, covering his feet with icy cold saltwater and froth one moment and leaving them bare and exposed the next.

To the northwest, across the bay, he could see the evening lights of Provincetown twinkling like the stars that filled the sky in every direction. After a while he sat down on the sand. Apart from the crashing waves, the evening was still. It was nice to just sit alone with his thoughts. His shoulders relaxed and he lay down, staring up into the dark, star-studded sky. The moonlight shimmered silvery and luminescent on the water.

After a while, he began to get cold. He'd come out in only jeans and a t-shirt and the temperature had really dropped off. He stood, brushed the sand from his back and legs, turned and began walking back towards the house. The sand had turned cold, and as he reached the path that led back to the house, he stopped and sat at the edge of the dunes, taking a moment to brush off his feet.

Retying his laces, he glanced down the beach in the opposite direction he'd walked. He could see something in the distance, perhaps a cluster of seaweed or a large piece of driftwood on the beach at the edge of the water. Each time the surf crashed onto the beach it edged the dark mass a little higher up onto the sand. He felt a brief itch tickling the back of his neck and reached absentmindedly to scratch it.

As he stood to return to the house, the shape, now

lit by the fully risen light of the moon, became more defined. Everything slowed down. The sound of the surf grew muffled. He could see the body of a man gently bobbing at the water's edge, tangled in seaweed and bits of shells.

He looked up and down the beach. As before, there was no one other than him as far as he could see in either direction. The water began to lap against his sneakers. The tide was coming in and he knew that he'd have to do something fast. He quickly dug his cell phone from his pocket and dialed the emergency services. When they answered, he quickly described what he'd found and his location. The dispatcher asked him a few questions and then said they'd send someone out straight away. They asked that he remain at a distance from the body so as not to disturb anything in its immediate surroundings.

He hung up, stuffed his phone back into his pocket and made his way back up to the edge of the dunes, where he sat down, waiting, and hoping they would arrive quickly. He didn't want to be near the body in any case. He began to shake from the cold—or maybe shock. He sat and quietly waited for someone to come. He really hoped that they wouldn't take too long. He was shivering and he wanted to be back in the warmth of the house, away from the cold, the darkness, and away from that poor man's body.

He could hear the faint sound of a siren in the distance. It grew more and more distinct as it approached, and then suddenly went silent. A few moments later he could see the dancing light of flashlights approaching and hear the crunch of footsteps running swiftly towards him. Two police officers suddenly broke through the dunes and nearly ran him over as they hurried onto the beach. The nearest one spoke first, sounding out of breath.

"Are you the one who called?"

"Yes sir, I am. He's over there."

He pointed towards the edge of the water, where the body was now submerged up to its knees in seawater and surrounded by more strands of seaweed and foam.

"Did you touch or move the body at all?"

"Are you kidding me?"

He didn't want to have anything to do with it, wished that he hadn't come out for a walk in the first place and found it. In the distance he could hear more sirens approaching, and soon the familiar crunching sound of running feet as more people began to arrive. In short order, there were police and paramedics on site. By this time, they had pulled the body further up the beach to secure it from the encroaching tide. A senior officer barked commands at people, while everyone else was busy taking photographs and notes, checking the body or talking to one another. At one point the senior officer turned around and caught Nathan's eye. He walked towards him, followed by another officer, who carried a small notepad.

"Excuse me son. Can I have your name?"

"Nathan. Nathan Briggs."

"And how did you come to find the body?"

"I'm staying at our family beach house—you would have passed it on the way in. I came out for a walk and some fresh air. I noticed it on the way back when I stopped to tie my sneakers."

"Do you recognize the man?"

"No sir. I haven't been here very long. I live north of Boston."

"Where's home, son?"

"New Comfort."

"Nice town. I've been through there a few times."

"Thank you, sir. Do you have any idea what happened to him?"

"The coroner will take charge of the body. It's difficult to tell at the moment how long he's been here."

"It can't be too long though."

"Why's that, son?"

"Because I walked out here the other day and he wasn't here then."

"Just when was that?"

"I walked on the beach on Monday, and my sister walked down this way on Tuesday evening."

"Is your sister around?"

"No sir. She had to drive back to Boston early yesterday morning for work."

The man continued asking questions while the other officer recorded everything Nathan said. He heard more crunching sand from behind and turned just as Ben broke through the dunes.

"Oh, thank God! I woke up and you were gone. I heard sirens and saw all the flashing lights and thought something had happened to you!"

Nathan shook his head.

"I'm fine, Ben."

"What happened? What's with all the police?"

Nathan nodded towards the others standing near the water.

"I found a man on the beach."

He paused for a moment and then spoke in a whisper. "He's dead."

He began to shake with cold and shock. The police officer patted him on the shoulder and turned to Ben.

"Why don't you take your friend back over to the house and get him warmed up. If we have more questions, we'll stop by on the way out."

Ben placed an arm around his friend's shoulders and walked him back to the house. Once inside, he settled Nathan onto the sofa and set about stoking the fire to heat the room up. When it was crackling away and he could feel the heat emanating from it, he found a quilt and covered his friend to warm him. He went into the kitchen to make them both hot chocolate.

He couldn't believe it. A body on the beach. In all the years they had been coming here, they'd never experienced or heard of such a thing. As he stirred the mugs he looked over at Nathan, who was now sitting up and staring into the fire.

Nathan watched as the flames licked up the sides of the dry logs. He could feel the heat and smell the warm comforting scent of the wood smoke. In his mind he could see the body lying on the beach, seawater lapping at its feet, gray lifeless skin, a tangle of seaweed, shells and foam. There was one additional thing that he could remember. The most important thing. The man's neck was cut—not cleanly, but torn on one side. There wasn't any marine life out in the bay this time of year that could do that. Maybe he'd already been in the water for a while and the injury had been inflicted more recently. He shuddered and decided to try to think about something else.

As his thoughts shifted, Ben walked back into the room, placed the hot mugs on the coffee table and put a hand on his friend's shoulder, a gesture of comfort and support. They sat like that for a while, neither one sure what to say to the other. After an eerie silence, the doorbell chimed. Ben leapt from the sofa to answer it, leaving Nathan to sit quietly by himself. He could hear the murmur of voices coming from the hallway and assumed the police had decided to stop by as they said they might. Ben re-entered the room with them in tow.

"Nate, they have a few more questions. Are you okay to talk?"

He shrugged and nodded before responding, "Sure. I'm feeling better now."

"Thanks for your time Mr. Briggs. We do appreciate it. By the way, this is Sergeant Stafford and I'm Detective Hawkins. I realized after you'd left that I've met your father before. He's a supporter of the local police department in Truro."

Nathan smiled. His father always knew how to keep peace in the neighborhood.

"You said you've been around here for a few days. Is that correct?"

"Yes. I came down on Monday. My grandfather passed away recently, and things have been a bit emotional around the house. I just wanted some space and a place to clear my head."

"I'm very sorry to hear that."

The detective seemed sincere.

"Have you seen any strangers since arriving here? Anyone or anything you'd consider suspicious?"

Nathan paused to think. He thought briefly about the guy he kept seeing in town. But it was a small town and off season, so there was no reason to think of that as being odd.

"No, not really. I mean I've spent time up in town, wandering the galleries, the seafront, eating. Apart from my sister and Ben visiting, I've been on my own."

His friend looked at him quizzically for a moment.

"Serena?" he asked.

Nathan shot him a confused look.

"Oh yeah, and Serena. This Croatian girl I met while I was traveling through Europe stopped by to visit. That was a bit odd I suppose. I haven't really seen or heard from her for ages, and she just randomly showed up here looking for me."

The officer was scribbling notes down in his notepad. The detective smiled at his colleague before turning his attention back to Nathan.

"Do you have this Serena's last name?"

His memory leapt back to the time he'd spent with her and he picked through his memories. He realized he had no recollection of her giving him her last name. The detective gave him a moment and then prompted him.

"Well, the thing is, I don't actually know her last name. I know she's Croatian, that she comes from a wealthy family who have business interests in Europe and America. I know they have holdings and offices in Boston. But she never mentioned her last name., and I guess I just never thought to ask."

The sergeant chuckled to himself, not looking up, as he continued taking notes.

"Right, so you said she came here to visit. When was that?" the detective asked.

"She was here yesterday," Ben replied.

"And where is she now?"

"She said she had to go to Boston. Her father contacted her and asked her to return."

"She just came in for the day?"

"Well, the evening really. We ran into her late in the evening."

"Is there anything else?"

Nathan thought about it for a moment. He remembered that he had Serena's number as well now, but for some reason he resisted the idea of giving that out. He felt they'd already said too much, and in any case it was ridiculous to think that Serena had anything to do with it. She hadn't even come to the house.

"No, sir. There isn't anything else."

"Thanks for that, Mr. Briggs. We'll look into this Serena."

"It's Severina," Ben said. "She said her name was Severina, but that she went by Serena."

The Sergeant wrote that down and closed his notebook.

"Is there anything else, Mr. Briggs?"

Nathan shook his head.

"Alright. You're sure you didn't notice anyone else around over the last couple of days?"

"No sir, I'm sure of it."

The detective looked thoughtful for a moment.

"What about the man on the beach? Did you recognize him at all?"

"No, I don't think I've ever seen him before. Though to be honest, sir, I really didn't look that closely at his face. I didn't want to get that close."

The detective nodded.

"Can I ask you a question, sir?" Nathan said.

"Yes, of course."

"Do you have any idea what killed him or how long he's been dead?"

The thought of a body on the beach just a few hundred feet from the house kept playing through his head.

"We're not sure really. The medical examiner thinks he might have been dead a couple of days. But because he's been in the water, it's difficult to tell until we examine him. As to what killed him, until the coroner has a chance to do his work we won't know for sure. For all we know he may have fallen from a boat offshore. There's no way of knowing at this stage."

The detective trailed off and didn't offer anything further.

"Alright, Mr. Briggs. I think we're done here for the time being. The sergeant will get your number and home address in case we have any more questions. Are you staying here for much longer?"

"To be honest, I'd already been thinking about returning home tomorrow."

The detective nodded.

"Alright, well I think we have everything we need from you for now. Give your father my best when you see him."

Nathan winced inwardly at that. The thought of seeing his father and having to explain all of this made him feel slightly ill.

"It's Detective Hawkins, right?"

"Yes, it is."

"I'll be sure to do that sir," he said politely.

※

"So, what do you think? Maybe that's enough excitement for one night?"

Ben flopped down onto the sofa. Nathan nodded and they sat quietly for a few moments before speaking.

"Listen, I've decided I definitely want to head home tomorrow. I came out here for some peace and quiet and I've had anything but—not that I mind the company. I just don't think hiding here is the answer. I need to square things with my father face to face."

His friend nodded. He'd already expected as much. He didn't blame him for wanting to go home. After what had just happened, this was hardly an escape from his problems.

"We can always take the bus or get a taxi to town and get the ferry."

Nathan thought it over.

"I could call Sam and see if she can arrange something."

His sister would have a heart attack when he told her what had happened. He thought about the walk she'd taken on the beach just a couple of nights ago. The man couldn't have been there or she would have said something.

"That's a great idea," Ben said. "She might even drive down herself and pick us up."

"I wouldn't count on it," said Nathan. "She's pretty busy with work these days."

He decided to call her straight away, while his friend got a jump on tidying up the house. The last thing he wanted to do was to leave the place a mess. His mother wouldn't be too pleased, when she came down, if the first thing she had to do was to clean up. He got through to Sam on the first attempt and quickly explained what had happened. As predicted, she freaked out and told him that she'd come to get the two of them first thing in the morning. She told him to be careful and make sure they locked the doors before going to bed.

Satisfied that things were sorted out, his thoughts turned to his growling stomach and the realization that they hadn't eaten any dinner. He mentioned it to Ben, and they decided that they'd go into town and grab pizza as it was quick and easy, and they could be back to clean, pack up their things and get a good night's sleep. Tomorrow would be interesting.

***

When their pizza arrived it was massive, and the slices dripped with cheese, oil and oregano. Ben's focus switched between the pizza and Serena.

"Don't you think her showing up out of the blue like that was a bit strange?"

"Yeah, it was. And by the way, what was that all

about? I hadn't planned to throw Serena under a bus with the police."

Ben blushed.

"Sorry Nate. It just kind of came out. I was nervous."

Nathan nodded as he pulled a long string of cheese from his slice and stuck it into his mouth. It wasn't his friend's fault. It was a stressful situation for both of them.

"I mean, going all the way up to my parents' house, and then down here, just to drop in on me and say hello? It's not like I'd heard from her after Croatia or anything. How did she even know I was home?"

"Maybe she saw in the news about your grandfather and figured you'd have come home to be with your family. After all, unlike you, she knew your last name."

Nathan gave his friend a scathing look, which caused him to laugh. He glared even harder, but his friend had a sudden fit of giggles.

"Not funny. It made me feel like an idiot. I wonder if I should text her and give her a heads-up."

"And maybe ask her for her last name."

This time they both laughed.

"Maybe you should wait and see if the police speak with her."

Nathan nodded. It made an odd kind of sense. It might be best if he just let it go for the moment. He had enough to deal with.

Dragan hovered at the edge of the property, not wanting to be seen. He was well hidden but in a spot where he could observe everything, including the activity in the house, and even the man who appeared each night and waited, believing that he was the only observer. That same car was parked further down the road with its occupant nestled warmly inside waiting. It was the same pattern every night; wait until the lights went dark, sit for a bit longer and then drive back to his hotel.

He'd watched as the police and emergency services arrived earlier in the evening, scouring the area near the body—that same body he'd left to drift in the current further up the beach only a couple of nights before. You win some, you lose some. The seawater would have done its work over the intervening couple of days, and the cause of death would be indeterminate—apart from the large gash in his neck, which could easily have occurred had he fallen out of a boat or been savaged by some creature. He grinned to himself, knowing the confusion and fear such an act would create. Perversely, he thrived on the scent of fear.

He continued to watch the house until the lights went dark, and then nestled into the shadows for a long night. In the distance, like clockwork, an engine throbbed to life, and after a few moments, headlights shattered the darkness and the car slowly pulled away. The mysterious man hiding in the car each night wasn't his concern. Yet. And that was a good thing. He listened to the sounds of wild animals scurrying about and crickets chirping.

In the distance he could hear the water lapping on the beach. But apart from the sounds of slowed breathing, an indication that the boys were asleep, there were no other sounds coming from the house.

※

When they'd returned to the house, they cleaned and packed before making their way up to their respective bedrooms. The stress of finding the body had taken its toll on Nathan and, giving in to complete exhaustion, he fell asleep within seconds of his head touching the pillow. In the other room, his friend contemplated the events of the evening. Between the recent death of his grandfather, and now this, Ben thought his friend must be finding things very difficult to understand at the moment.

Ben had lost his father when he was young. He and his mother had had to learn how to exist together without having a husband and father around. His mother hadn't coped very well, and had retreated from him, immersing herself in church and the friends she made there. He, on the other hand, had learned to keep things to himself. One of the reasons he valued his friendship with Nathan was that his family provided a respite from Ben's own home, and they always treated him as if he were a part of the family.

After sitting quietly for a while in the darkness gazing out of the bedroom window deep in thought, his eyes began to droop, and he reluctantly settled back onto the pillow and fell asleep. Across the way, Nathan woke several times throughout the night from terrible dreams. In one of them he found the body on the beach tangled in seaweed and surrounded by the froth of the surf, and as he looked down at him, the man's eyes opened suddenly, terrifying him. In another dream a dark figure followed him in the shadows. No matter how much he tried to evade his follower, he couldn't shake him off. The figure kept its distance, but he could feel cold eyes glaring at him from the shadows.

※

In the morning he woke to sunlight pouring in through the bedroom window and the slamming of a door somewhere in the house.

"Nathan. Where are you?"

It was Sam! Shit!

He jumped out of bed and quickly threw some clothes on. She'd asked them to get their things together and be ready first thing in the morning. He hoped she wasn't going to be pissed off. Apart from not being showered, it wouldn't take too long for them to get on the road. He was sure he would have to drag his friend out of bed as well. But when he looked into Ben's bedroom, there was no one there, the bed was made, and the room tidied as though no one had ever stayed there. Running downstairs, he found Ben already up, drinking coffee, showered, dressed and ready to go.

"Why didn't you wake me, you idiot?"

Ben laughed and handed him a cup of coffee.

"You needed the sleep. Drink this and shower."

Nathan nodded.

"Yeah, I suppose you're right. I didn't sleep very well last night."

"Are you surprised? We'll load stuff into the car while you get ready."

Sam leaned over and gave her little brother a hug.

"Sorry Nate. You've really had a bit of a time of it since coming home."

"Thanks Sam. Sorry I overslept. I won't be long."

Twenty minutes later, clean, dressed, coffee drunk and cup washed, they locked up the house and piled into Sam's car for the drive home. Nathan sat quietly in the back while his sister and friend sat in the front chatting away. He mulled over the fact that he was going home. He couldn't help but think that he was going from the frying pan into the fire. But he'd keep an open mind and see what his father had in store for him. It was time to face the music.

Chapter 9

Dragan continued watching from the shadow of the woods at the far edge of the property, ever-present steel-gray eyes scanning the Range Rover as it pulled away into the distance. He recognized the vehicle and the woman driving it from a few days before and knew that they were likely heading back home. He walked through the woods until he arrived at an old country lane, where he retrieved his car. He would check in with Jelena and then make his way to New Comfort to continue his duties, stopping only for a quick meal along the way.

As he pulled onto the main road, he noticed the car from the evening before pass by the house, slow, and then continue on down the road after the Range Rover. No doubt Dragan would need to continue to avoid this other mysterious observer. At some point he would identify this mystery man, and perhaps deal with him as he had so many others over the years. For all he knew, it could be Nathan's father keeping tabs on his son—the man in the car looked capable, like he'd come from a military background, or perhaps law enforcement. But it could be something else, and his mother Jelena would want to know about it and decide on a course of action. He was here at her request after all.

※

On the drive home, Sam quizzed her brother about what had happened the night before. His silence implied that he wasn't in the mood to talk about it. Ben filled in all of the details, sensing his friend's thoughts were elsewhere. After a while, Sam dropped it and she and Ben made small talk most of the way back. Nathan wasn't really thinking about the body on the beach. He was thinking about his father and what lay ahead. He wondered where things had gone wrong between the two of them. It wasn't just because he had gone away the previous year. He realized now that he had left in part because the relationship with him had been growing worse for some time. He couldn't think of any precipitating act on his part, which was why he found it so difficult to understand. If he could think of something, anything, he'd at least have a starting point.

He hoped that his father—who was never very open about his feelings—had simply experienced a bad moment with everything going on, and that when he returned he would be in a better place. At least he hoped they could find a way to be civil to one another. Nearly a year of traveling had made him more independent. And while he was convinced that wasn't going to go in his favor, he at least hoped his father would give him an opportunity to prove himself before pouncing again.

"By the way Nathan, you've lucked out. Mom and Dad are giving you the old house down the lane. Apparently, they had it all renovated while you were away. They've even had all of your things moved out there so that it's ready for you when you get home."

He'd only half been paying attention, but now he suddenly perked up.

"What?" he asked.

"Mom plans to tell you when we get home. I think they wanted to give you some space and a place to call your own so that you didn't feel like the odd one out when you finally returned."

He sat quietly thinking for a few moments. This whole time he'd thought he'd end up living back in the main house with his parents. But this was better—a chance for him to start over, to get his feet on the ground, and to have the kind of space that he and his father needed from one another if they were going to work on their relationship. Still, he couldn't help but feel a bit skeptical.

"I really don't understand. That doesn't sound like Dad. And after we fell out… are you sure this is what he wants?"

"Well, I think Mom had a lot to do with it. She thought it would be good for you to have your own place after being away so long. It wasn't being used at all, so she talked Dad into having it fixed up. She told me about the whole thing yesterday. She said she'd spoken with him and apparently he felt that maybe it would help things between the two of you."

His mood began to brighten. Maybe heading back home wouldn't be so bad after all. He wouldn't feel underfoot like he did in his parents' house. And he could have his own space. Maybe this was the best possible outcome for everyone.

"When did all this happen? And why didn't anyone say anything before?"

"Well, to be honest, I didn't know it was happening until yesterday. I don't have any reason to go out to the old place. And you know how Mom and Dad are—always so many different things going on. Apparently, they've been having it renovated for months. I wasn't supposed to tell you, but I could see how stressed you are about going home. And as for them not telling you, I suspect it was because of everything that was going on, you know, with Grandfather. They were probably waiting until the right moment."

He looked out of the window at the passing cars. He remembered when he was little how they used to play "I spy" in the car when they were traveling. Things were so much simpler then. His thoughts turned to the idea of living in his own home. The house was secluded and sat in the middle of a beautiful old garden that he and his siblings had loved to play hide and seek in when they were children. The house had rarely been used but had been maintained in the event it was ever needed. He couldn't really remember much about the house itself as they'd never really spent any time inside it.

"Nate, that's fantastic. Now I have a cool place to stay when I need to get away!"

Ben winked at him from the front seat and laughed. Nathan scowled at his friend.

"I'm kidding. But seriously, it sounds great. You'll have your own space. That should help a bit with things, eh?"

He nodded. His friend was right. Despite everything that had happened, he now had something to look forward to. That was a lot more hope than he'd woken up with that morning.

"Are you saying it's ready now?"

"Yeah, it's been completely refurbished apparently. Mom had all of your things moved over from the main house yesterday. I haven't seen it, so I have no idea what it looks like. But you know Mom. It'll be tasteful and nice. And it'll be perfectly finished, of course."

He smiled and nodded. That bit was true. Their mother was not only meticulous about that sort of thing and would have made sure everything was done to a high standard, but she ran an interior design business for a living. She had higher standards than most. His father would have had nothing to do with it, but would have been burying himself in his work. And in any case, when it came to home and the family estate, his mother had the final say. His father would have kept quiet just to avoid risking her wrath.

The drive seemed to progress more quickly as his mood lightened. They soon passed through, or rather under, Boston. On the approach to the city, he started to feel like he was only just now returning home for the first time. He'd spent a lot of time in Boston, going down for shows, movies, dinners, concerts and shopping. It was such a great city. Most of his friends now worked there or in New York, and he was sure that it would play a significant part in his life going forward.

His family kept the main headquarters for their company there. If he was going to work in the family business, he imagined that eventually he would end up spending a lot of time in the city, as well as traveling to their other business locations from time to time. As the textile trade died off across the country and Asia became dominant manufacturers and exporters, his family had consolidated their manufacturing and traded on making and selling American-made goods. In the early days it had been difficult as prices from China were so cheap, but in recent years it had become a badge of honor to have your products produced in America. And with rising wages in China, the health of the planet, fuel costs and other economic factors, it wasn't always the right decision to import anymore.

His family had purchased several disused mills, modernized them and expanded their business operations. They had gone from strength to strength and exporting goods to other countries was now a major part of it. Even with the economic problems of Europe, they still had a healthy trade overseas. It also helped that their grandfather had an uncanny knack for business and had diversified into properties, investments and other things. The family business had grown exponentially over the years, beyond his own understanding. He wondered how his father would handle things now that his own father was gone.

Soon they were on the final leg of their journey home. He supposed his father would be at work and they wouldn't see each other, at the earliest, until that evening. He hoped that his mother and grandmother would be home though, as he looked forward to seeing them again. The city eventually gave way to suburbs and then countryside, with town after town passing by, and as they left the main interstate, they arrived at a more coastal setting.

On approaching the outskirts of New Comfort, Nathan settled back into his seat and watched the familiar scenery pass by. Having grown up in this town, he knew every inch of it by heart. Sam maneuvered through the streets until they drove past the main part and up into the hills beyond, into more secluded countryside. They eventually reached the turn onto their driveway, and the pillars guarding the entrance passed by as Sam drove up to the main entrance of the house and parked. They all sat quietly for a moment, looking expectantly at the front door. His father's car wasn't in the driveway, so it was a safe bet that he was still at work.

Sam turned and looked at her little brother.

"Well Nate. Welcome home! Again."

※

She laughed as she got out of the car and walked around to open up the rear so the two friends could grab their belongings. Nathan and Ben stepped out of the car and stretched their legs from the long ride. It had taken them a little over two and a half hours to get home—with no stops. His sister was one of those people who just wanted to get on with it when she was driving someplace, and rarely stopped unless there was an absolute emergency.

His bag was considerably more battered than it had been before he'd left on his travels. He rested the stained, worn and patched bag over one shoulder as he made his way with the others towards the house. As they walked up the stone steps, the large, shiny black door opened, and Nathan's mother stepped through onto the porch. Her smile said everything that needed saying. Her son had returned.

"Mom."

"Nathan."

He carried his bag up to where his mother stood, set it down on the cold stone surface, reached out and gave her a long embrace. He hoped that she wasn't too cross with him for walking out like that but knew that if anyone would understand it would be her.

"It's so good to have you back home."

She smiled warmly as she stood back, a hand on each of his shoulders as though assessing him for the first time.

"You know something? I hadn't noticed it before, but you look… different. More grown up somehow."

He blushed. He felt different. He was happy that someone had noticed.

"I see you've cut your hair. Thank goodness! It looks much better now. Come on. Let's get your things inside."

He grabbed his bag, and they all followed his mother into the house. There were two large rooms off either side of the entryway and a large staircase winding up the middle. To the left of the staircase was a hallway that led to the rear of the house. As he walked inside, he could almost feel the weight of all the generations of the Briggs family that would have stepped through that entrance when they returned home from work, some of them from war. He wondered if they'd all felt that same warm feeling of coming home.

For over three hundred years the Briggs family had led a quiet but successful life here. They were never one of the main families that came to mind when people thought about New England history, having lived quietly at the edges, as though they had purposely chosen to remain out of the mainstream. None of them had ever entered politics, they hadn't decided to name the town after the family, and, apart from the large brick edifice of their home, there were no monuments or statues of Briggs family members to remind people who had established the town.

He had attended a private school and then Harvard, but on his own merits, not because his family were patrons. His parents and siblings were also well educated, and like him had all attended good universities on their own merits. In many respects, apart from the large home and successful family business, they all seemed rather unremarkable in comparison to other families of similar stature. His grandfather had instilled a sense of humility in the family. Nathan vaguely wondered what legacy his own father would leave behind.

"I'll ask Camilla to put some tea on for us. Why don't you go into the sitting room and wait for me?"

His mother disappeared into the rear of the house while Nathan, Ben and Sam made themselves comfortable. It was a good-sized room by any standard, with a large fireplace along the end wall. There were comfortable sofas arranged in a u-shape in front of the fire and several other large traditional armchairs with side tables. On the walls hung paintings by old New England artists, some portraits of ancestors and others coastal or seascapes.

He had only just realized that his mother must have changed the wallpaper while he'd been away, having missed it when he'd returned at the beginning of April. It was now a mustard-yellow striped paper with a very expensive-looking finish. He assumed she'd had it custom-made from a pattern she'd seen while visiting some other stately old home. His mother was an absolute perfectionist when it came to decoration—the fact she had advanced degrees in art and design and ran a successful interior design company didn't hurt either.

The house was, of course, immaculate. The Briggs family often entertained, and his mother had a cook, housekeeper, two cleaners and a gardener to oversee things. With ten bedrooms it required a lot of effort to maintain. Fortunately, his grandmother also shared in running the house, which took some of the pressure off of his mother. She soon emerged from the kitchen, trailed by the housekeeper. The welcoming scent of fresh baking preceded them, and he realized that apart from the coffee that Ben had made him in the morning, he hadn't yet consumed anything. And his sister certainly hadn't made any accommodation along the journey to reconcile that.

The housekeeper served up freshly baked muffins and cookies with their tea and he reached for a muffin as soon as they were placed on the table. Ben and Sam also tucked in and soon they were all sitting, sipping tea, sampling the baking and busily chatting away. The subject of the body he'd found hadn't come up, and for good reason; Nathan and Sam didn't want to upset their mother with the news. Nor did they speak about his father or the argument that precipitated his leaving for the beach house in the first place. It wasn't the time really, and until he could speak with his father directly, it really wasn't appropriate to discuss the matter in front of everyone.

His mother's smile was radiant; she was obviously pleased that he had returned home safe and sound. Soon their conversation turned to his travels and he recounted some of the stories he hadn't had time to tell when he'd first arrived home from London. His mother nodded and smiled, very proud of her son for staking out his independence and having the strength and courage to go in the first place. He was both his parents' child. He had developed the strong independence of his father, and his mother's innate curiosity for life. Once they'd had their fill of tea, muffins and stories, his mother stood up with a glint in her eyes and rubbed her hands together.

"Right! Honey, I have a bit of a surprise for you."

He looked up from the crumbs he'd been picking off of his plate.

"Well. Probably not a surprise as such, as I'm sure Sam has already told you."

Elizabeth Briggs glanced between her two children as they exchanged guilty looks.

"Ah, so she did. Well, I'm sure it was a surprise when she told you."

Their mother gave Sam a stern look.

"Sorry Mom. You know me. It just slipped out."

"Of course, Samantha," she said as she winked at Nathan out of his sister's sight.

He nearly laughed, knowing that his mother wasn't really that upset. She wasn't the kind of person that would take offense at something like that. And of course, she also liked to tease her only daughter, calling her Samantha only when she wanted to appear as though she were being stern. He knew that she was probably more interested in showing him the house than in telling him about it.

"Come on everyone. Let's drive him over so he can see it."

They left the sitting room excited. Sam drove down the long driveway, turned left onto the tree-lined country lane and continued on until they arrived at a paved driveway between a row of manicured hedges. She slowed, turning into the long driveway, which curved around in front of an old stone house.

As far as he could tell from the outside, the property had been fully transformed. The garden was brimming with freshly planted flowers and the lush green grass of the front yard was neatly manicured. The stone had been completely repointed and all of the wood trim was painted a beautiful willow green. The wooden window shutters were all painted to match. The house looked beautiful, and he couldn't believe his parents had gone to all of this trouble just for him. With three bedrooms, the house was big for one person and would easily accommodate him and anyone who might come to visit. There was also a brand-new matching two-car, two-story garage in the same stone.

He shook his head as he looked over at Ben. He couldn't believe his luck. He wasn't even working yet, and he had his own house. He'd thought it might take years for him to actually get to this point. And yet here it was, in front of him. His own home. He'd anticipated having to live under the same roof as his parents for some time until he could settle elsewhere, but his parents had devised a solution that provided the best of both worlds for all of them. He was near enough to his family that he could see them, but would still have his own space. There was no doubt that this worked for everyone. His mother reached into her purse and pulled out a set of keys, handing them over to her son.

"Take good care of it. Believe it or not, the whole thing was actually your father's idea. You know I'd rather have you at home. He felt that since your brother and sister have their own places, and with this old house sitting empty all the time, it might make a nice place for you to make a fresh start."

He couldn't believe that it was his father who had been behind this.

"Tell him thank you when you see him Mom. And thank you for everything too."

He hugged her tightly. He felt so appreciative that he didn't know what else to say or do.

"Please try not to judge him so harshly, Nathan. Your father loves you. You know how he is—all business, not so great on emotion. But he does care about you. Even though things have been difficult I am sure the two of you will sort things out. And as for thanking him, you can do that yourself. We're expecting you over for dinner this evening, seven, sharp."

It wasn't a request. He knew better than to question his mother's motivations. She was caught in the middle and worked hard to play peacemaker between Nathan and Jonathan. He would do everything possible to make peace with his father. And after what he'd done for him with the house, he could hardly play the role of the ungrateful son. Even so, there was still the issue of his grandfather's will. He would have to find a way to work through that as well.

"I'll do my best, Mom. Don't worry. I know that things have been difficult for everyone. And I'm sure Dad didn't expect things to turn out the way they did with Grandfather's will. But I'll try harder when I see him."

"Thank you, Nathan. That would help out with things. Let's just have a nice family dinner tonight."

"That sounds good Mom. I'll be there."

He wondered what his mother had been about to say. But it was clear from her change of direction that she didn't want to discuss it any further. She placed a hand on his arm.

"Now let me show you around the place."

For the next half-hour, everyone toured around the house and the grounds. As expected, everything was beautifully done.

"There's one last thing."

She walked up the outside stairs that led to a landing, borrowed Nathan's keys and unlocked the door. As she stepped aside to let her son through into the large open room, she continued.

"This was also your father's idea."

She sounded less enthusiastic about it this time. The space inside was one large open-plan room. In the middle of the room stood a pool table, and around the edges there were sofas and leather side chairs. At one end there was a bar with well-stocked shelves. There was a large flat-screen television mounted on the wall and an Xbox on a stand below it.

"He said you might appreciate this. I expect it's a male thing. I also expect this is the room I never let him put in our house. So, enjoy it."

His mother raised an eyebrow as she said it. No doubt, if they sorted things out between them, his father might come over to visit from time to time. As if to reinforce that idea, he noticed the presence of some of his father's favorite whiskey behind the bar.

"Mom, I don't know what to say. It's amazing. I really can't believe you guys went to all of this trouble."

His eyes scanned the room and he felt moved by the gesture his parents had made. On the other hand, there was probably a payback waiting in the wings somewhere—like when he finally started to work for his father. He would expect something back for the effort.

"Sorry, there is actually one other thing," his mother said as she led them out, locked up, and walked back down the stairs.

She reached into her bag, removed a small black box and pushed a button on it. As the garage doors slowly lifted, they revealed a brand-new black Range Rover

Velar with tinted windows. Nathan looked on with continued shock. His parents had really spared no expense.

"Holy shit! It's like you're on a game show. What's behind door number three?" Ben exclaimed.

His mother laughed and rolled her eyes.

"Your father and I thought you might need something a bit more reliable than that old... truck to get back and forth in, and that rusted-out old piece of scrap metal wasn't reliable enough to get you around."

He thought about his previous car—an old, beat-up eighties brown Dodge SUV that he'd loved to drive around in with his friends, much to his parents' irritation. His father had always expected it to blow up at any moment.

"What did you do with the Dodge?"

His mother shrugged.

"It's gone to a better place. That's all you really need to know, dear."

Ben laughed as he ran his fingers over the hood of the car. Nathan's mother handed the keys over.

"They're all yours now. Don't lose them!"

He couldn't believe his good fortune. He briefly wondered if, given recent events, his father now regretted such generosity—and how much pressure his mother had put him. She was observing his expressions closely during this visit to his new house.

"Don't worry. If you're wondering about your father, I'm sure you'll make up for it with the plans he has for you."

They all laughed at once. His mother knew how to cut the tension. He hoped she'd be as on the ball when he saw his father during dinner later that night.

"And speaking of your father, I'd better get going. I have work to finish before he comes home later. Remember—seven, sharp! You don't want to keep your father waiting."

Well, that was at least something, he thought. If his father knew he was coming to dinner, he would surely try to be civil—especially in front of Nathan's mother.

"Okay then. I'll leave you to get settled in. We'll see you later. Are you okay to take Ben home?"

He nodded. His mother kissed leaned in and kissed both her son and his friend on the cheek, whispering *thank you* in Ben's ear before following her daughter back to the car. They drove off, leaving the two friends standing in front of the house.

"Holy crap, Nate. I can't believe it. This is amazing. I had no idea any of this was going to happen."

He couldn't believe it either. But he had a pretty good idea of what would be expected from him in return. He'd been back a month now and it wouldn't be long before things started in earnest. He shrugged it off for the moment. He'd deal with that when the time came. He slapped his friend on the shoulder.

"Come on buddy, let's get settled."

Dreams and revelations

Chapter 10

Nathan took his bag upstairs to the room his mother had chosen for his new bedroom—and where all of his other things from their house had been deposited. He wasn't sure how he felt about her going through all of his personal things, packing them, having them moved over and then putting them away for him. But he appreciated the sentiment and what she was trying to do. And in any case, it wasn't like there was anything there that could embarrass him.

As he looked around the room—hardwood floors, modern furnishings, wooden blinds at the windows, and a walk-in closet that would do anyone proud—he still couldn't believe that this was his house. He wanted to sort his things out and settle in before anyone could wake him up and tell him that it was a dream, or take it away. While traveling he hadn't been in any one place long enough to really unpack. He was so used to living out of a bag that having all of this space to himself suddenly felt like a luxury.

After putting away the few clothes that he'd retained—and some of his purchases from the Cape—he and Ben embarked on a slower tour around the house and garage just to take it all in. His parents had clearly spared no expense in refurbishing the property. He knew that he would have to show his gratitude at dinner, even if his relationship with his father remained strained. He couldn't deny that his parents had done him a great favor.

It didn't take Ben too long to pick out the bedroom he'd stay in when he visited—which Nathan suspected might be often. He smiled at the thought. Considering the circumstances, he couldn't help but feel a bit more relaxed and happier to be home.

"Hey, we have the whole rest of the day. What should we do?" Ben asked.

"Clothes. I need to buy some proper clothes for tonight. Do you want to come with?"

He looked over at his friend and smiled. Ben didn't need any encouragement to go clothes shopping. As it turned out, it was one of his favorite hobbies.

"Boston?" he asked.

"Yeah, I think we've got enough time to pop in and grab some lunch and clothes before I have to be back for dinner at my parents' later."

His friend laughed and rolled his eyes.

"Yeah, dinner. Good luck with that."

They both laughed.

"Yeah, to be fair I could really do without it tonight. But after everything they've done for me, I could hardly turn them down, right? I don't want to give my father more ammunition by looking ungrateful."

Ben nodded.

"Yeah, I suppose not. Still, I get it. What a place! We're going to have a lot of fun here."

Nathan raised an eyebrow, quizzically.

"We?"

His friend laughed.

"It's not like you're going to shoot pool by yourself. That room above the garage is going to be great for chilling out. I can study there while you play Xbox. And besides, this house is huge. You'll want company! You'll need me to keep you from getting bored."

Nathan shook his head in a mixture of disbelief and amusement. There was no question he was finally home—and Ben was fast-tracking the settling-in process. They locked the house and walked out to the garage. He pressed the button on the remote and his shiny new car slid into view as the doors opened. They'd make a bit of an afternoon of it and still be back in time for him to drop off his friend and get ready for dinner. And it helped to think that the quick trip might settle his nerves a bit and take his mind off the inevitable confrontation with his father.

He slid into the driver's seat and immediately felt the strangeness of sitting behind the wheel of a car again. He breathed in that brand-new car smell as he adjusted his seat and mirrors. He hadn't driven once during his time away, choosing instead to walk or take public transportation everywhere. Of course, the transport links were pretty good in many of the places he'd visited, and he could often get anywhere he wanted just by hopping onto a few trains or buses, which was funny as his family drove everywhere.

Traveling kindled a tremendous sense of curiosity and discovery that, now it was lit, he knew wouldn't disappear. It was a feeling that had built up inside of him a long while before he went away—a feeling that was very much behind his desire to travel in the first place. He didn't want to be told about the world. He wanted to experience it first-hand. He had no regrets, even if it did cause his father personal difficulty. He would have to learn to get over it. And he was sure that his experiences wouldn't go amiss in getting him wherever it was he needed to go with his life. That feeling only intensified the longer he traveled. He felt like he'd gone away and discovered a new part of himself to bring home—to help him grow into being a new person.

Still, he thought, there was something about seeing his best friend and family that made him really happy to be home. If only he could prove himself to his father now, maybe they could finally move on from whatever it was that caused him to be so critical with him. He had come home different, changed, more mature now. His father would have to find a way to adapt and change too.

※

It took a little while for him to get the hang of driving again—he was so used to having been someone else's passenger. As they drew closer to Boston, he realized just how much he missed driving and having the ability to pick up and go anyplace he wanted to at a moment's notice—no schedules to negotiate. And even though he didn't want to admit it, this Range Rover was much better to drive than his old beat-up SUV—even if his memories were filled with nostalgic moments with his friends.

He wound his way through the usual mid-afternoon Friday Boston traffic and when they reached the area he'd intended to shop, he found an underground parking garage and parked. He figured that he would find everything he needed between the shops in the Prudential Center and, across the way, over on Newbury Street. It was where he usually did most of his shopping. They took a long escalator into the main shopping center. As he was about to step off, he stopped dead in his tracks. Ben, caught off guard, slammed hard into his back.

"What the… oh hello," he said.

Standing in front of them, as thought she'd been patiently waiting for them to appear, was Serena. They stepped off to one side, allowing others to exit the escalator. Nathan stood rigid with a baffled expression on his face. His friend took the lead.

"Hello Serena. What are you doing here?"

She laughed, nervously.

"I went back to the Cape to find you, but you'd both left. It seems I've made a habit of late returns. So, I drove up to Boston to see my father. We have offices in a building just off the shopping center. I was just heading there to see him when I saw you both coming up the escalator."

Ben laughed. His friend looked a bit dubious.

"We've come down to do some shopping. Nate's sister picked us up this morning and brought us back. He has dinner with the family later."

They stood awkwardly looking at one another. Ben elbowed his friend.

"Uh, yeah, came down to get some things. So, how are you? Things okay with your dad?"

"Yeah, all good. He's in town for a bit and then heading back to Europe again. I think. I can't keep track of his schedule."

"What are the odds of running into you here? Pretty random, eh?" Ben said.

"Yeah." Serena smirked. "I wonder."

Nathan shook his head. It was the oddest of coincidences. A part of him felt really happy to see her, but it also felt uncomfortable, and he wasn't entirely sure why. And though Boston wasn't the biggest city he'd been in, it was big enough not to run into people as easily as this.

"So, you said you're here for a bit of shopping then?" Serena asked.

He felt slightly on the back foot. It was just as well that Ben was with him.

"Nathan needs some new clothes—he needs to upgrade those rags from his time away. But I'm hungry. I could really do with some food first."

He looked over at his friend. Nathan shrugged.

"I guess we could grab some food first. Didn't you eat enough muffins back at the house?"

"I'm a growing boy."

Nathan laughed. His friend wasn't kidding. He must consume a lot of calories to keep that muscle on.

"What about you Serena? Do you have time to come with us? We'll just grab something in the food court."

She considered his invitation for a moment before responding.

"I've actually already eaten. But I can tag along with you while you eat if that's alright. But after I really do have to go and meet up with my father. He's not fond of being kept waiting. Busy guy, you know."

"Hey, that's fine," Ben responded. "Nathan has to get home anyways, so I don't think we'll be all that long."

"Yeah, we'll be quick," Nathan agreed.

He clearly liked Serena. Ben could tell by the awkwardness.

"Great, it's settled then," she said.

Nathan shrugged off his slightly dazed look and glanced over at his friend. Ben motioned them to follow and they walked through the mall until they came to the food court. They made small talk while waiting in line, ordered and collected their food and found an empty table.

"Your family has offices just off the mall?" Ben asked as they took a seat.

"Yeah, and apartments too. Makes it easier for all of us to get back and forth between where we stay and work. And we can park underground, so there's always easy access."

"You never have to go outside when you're here?"

"Yeah," Serena replied. "Something like that."

Nathan and his friend both nodded as they started eating.

"Where you planning to go shopping?" she asked.

Nathan looked up from his plate between mouthfuls of food.

"Might have a wander around the mall. Probably head over to Newbury Street as well."

Ben watched the two of them. His friend's face flushed when he looked at Serena. It was obvious sitting there with the two of them that he liked her. She was more difficult to read. Her face was quite pale, and her gray eyes were cold, the color of steel. She didn't show any emotion at all, though when she looked at Nathan her eyes burned with a strange intensity.

"That sounds like a good plan. I'm sure you'll find what you need between the mall and Newbury Street," she said.

Nathan nodded and returned to eating.

"How long are you in town?" Ben asked.

"Not sure really. It's up to my father. He wanted to go over a few things with me before he leaves. He might end up flying back to Europe later today, so I'm not sure."

"Back to Croatia?" Nathan asked.

She looked away for a moment, as though the

mention of Croatia raised some other specter. Ben detected a slight change in her demeanor for just a fraction of a second.

"No, possibly London, or Paris. We're in the middle of some delicate negotiations and may have to return for those."

"What kind of business are you in?" Ben asked.

"A bit of this and that. Property, antiquities, investments, some biotech and technology, import and export. It's not one business. It's a group. I'm not even sure I fully understand everything my father is into, to be honest. I usually just go where I'm needed."

Nathan knew that she was part of her family business—like he was about to be—but only now realized that he hadn't fully understood the extent of their holdings. In some ways, the way they were diversified felt a bit similar to his own family's business. Right down to the kids being pawns in it. Clearly, she was very involved in her family's businesses and was much further down the path than he was. It made him feel a bit selfish for thinking so badly of her when she'd left him in Dubrovnik. He was also beginning to see a template for his own life beginning to emerge. He wasn't sure how he felt about that.

After a bit more chat, they finished their meals and discarded the rubbish in the nearest bin. Serena stood, clearly ready to take her leave. Unexpectedly, Ben hugged her, kissing her on the cheek. Her skin against his lips was alabaster-smooth and cold. She pulled back, smiled and turned to Nathan, who stood rigid next to his friend.

She quickly leaned in and kissed his cheek. Nathan stood fast, feeling awkward. He was clearly conflicted where she was concerned, but he took a breath and relaxed his shoulders. They said their awkward goodbyes to one another and then walked out of the food court in different directions.

༺✺༻

As Serena walked away, she smiled inwardly. He was a tough nut to crack. He made her feel warm inside—something she hadn't felt in a very long time. She turned and watched them as they disappeared through the main entrance together. She couldn't read him. He was so quiet—and guarded. His friend Ben though was clearly an open book. She liked him and could see that he was a good friend to Nathan. She brushed her cheek absentmindedly. She wasn't used to being touched and feeling such warmth. She wondered if he'd noticed the coldness of her skin.

She had enjoyed spending time with him in Dubrovnik. She would have spent more had it not been for her father's request to return. She'd left a note but realized now how impersonal that must have felt to him. And now she'd suddenly shown up in his life, on his home turf. It must all feel quite strange. Coupled with the situation with his grandfather, his confusion probably ran deep at the moment.

On top of everything else, there was the request from her father to check in and keep an eye on him. Why had he asked her to keep an eye on some boy she'd randomly met back home? In some ways she felt as confused as Nathan must feel. Why would her father take an interest in him? He wasn't the kind of man who undertook frivolous actions. Everything he did was considered, calculated. What was his plan? The incongruity bothered her. How she felt about Nathan confused her. Nothing about what was going on at the moment made sense.

As the two friends disappeared out to the street, she considered asking her father for more information when she saw him. She was used to doing what he asked of her, but usually his requests made some kind of sense. She understood the context behind them. This time nothing connected. She looked at her watch, shrugged, and started walking back to their offices.

※

"You okay?" Ben asked as they cut through a side street over to their destination.

"Yeah, I'm fine. Why?"

"You seem quiet and weird around Serena. Are you pissed off with her for taking off like she did?"

Nathan shrugged.

"Yeah. No. I don't think so. I get it. I'll be her in a few years. Obsessed with the family business, always at the beck and call of my father. She reminds me of what's coming. That's all."

Ben nodded and, smiling, punched him playfully in the arm.

"But you do like her, don't you?"

"Yeah, alright. I like her. She's different, you know. She's smart, pretty, works hard. She'd make my father perfectly happy if she were his daughter. And that kind of stresses me a bit. But only because she makes me think about things that I'd rather avoid thinking about. She does have a lot of redeeming qualities though."

Ben laughed. He understood how conflicted Nathan felt at the similarities. He hoped that Nathan and his father could find a way to sort things out between them. They hadn't always had such a complicated relationship and he hated seeing Nathan so unsure of himself.

He dropped the subject for the remainder of their shopping trip and focused on helping pick out new clothes. Time was running out, and if Nathan was going to get what he needed and get back home in time to get ready for dinner they'd have to step things up a bit. They spent the next couple of hours wandering in and out of shops, with Ben making faces at his friend's choices. Nathan laughed and managed to smile as they shopped, but his friend could see that the closer they got to returning home, the more tense he got. In the end they walked back to the mall, laden with bags, and took the escalator down to where they had parked. Nathan paid the ticket, and they exited the parking garage into the late afternoon sun.

The drive home was mostly quiet, each of them lost in their own thoughts. Traffic was heavy, which slowed things down a bit, but eventually they made their way back with some time to spare, enough time for him to drop his friend off at home.

"Listen. Your mom has had plenty of time to work on your father. I'm sure things will be fine, Nate. But if you need to talk later, you know how to find me."

Nathan nodded, turned around and made the drive back to his house. His house. He smiled. It would take a while for him to get his head around that idea.

Chapter 11

He spent the next couple of hours fretting, putting his new clothes away, familiarizing himself with the house and wondering if there was any way he could get out of dinner. He knew there wasn't a choice really—he would have to speak with his father sooner or later. And given his parents' generosity, he could hardly give the impression that he was ungrateful. Well, he could, but then he wouldn't be there for very long. Still, it was his father who'd done the hurting, and they would both have to find a way past that or things would continue to be difficult between them.

Eventually the time came to get ready and head over. He showered and changed into some of his new clothes. On the short drive, his mind wandered to the earlier encounter with Serena. When he was around her, he felt nervous and anxious. He couldn't deny that he was attracted to her, and he had been upset with her when she just up and disappeared. But as he understood more about the situation, he realized that he couldn't continue to stay angry—the same thing could easily happen to him in the future.

Recalling their conversations, it occurred to him that while she often spoke about her father—obviously a dominant force in their family—she'd never once mentioned her mother. He wondered if that was a touchy subject—or indeed if her mother was even still about, or alive. She had mentioned brothers, though he couldn't recall their names. If he was going to spend any time with her, he still had a lot to learn about her life. She seemed to know an awful lot about his.

As he turned into his parents' long curving driveway, he snapped back to the moment ahead of him. The real test of his future was about to begin. He hoped that he was ready. He'd made himself neat and presentable as an effort to please his father. There was no sense antagonizing him. He parked in front of the house, locked up and walked slowly up the front steps, composing himself with each labored footstep. He paused in front of the door, just long enough to breathe, before pressing the worn black button of the doorbell. From inside he could hear the muted sound of chimes. His mother promptly opened the door and smiled warmly at him.

Though he'd seen many beautiful buildings and incredible architecture on his travels, in his heart there was nothing that could ever compare to the warmth and familiarity of this house. No matter where he lived, it would always be home. His mother hugged him warmly and ushered him inside. She could feel the tense muscles of his shoulders and back as they hugged.

"Your father has promised to be on his best behavior tonight. Go easy on him, Nathan. He's had a lot to deal with, and he really hasn't been himself lately. But he has had time to think about things."

His mother winked at him. He was sure that she had encouraged much of that thinking. He nodded and managed to smile as he stepped into the foyer.

"Don't worry Mom. I'll do my best," he said.

"That's all I wanted to hear. You look very smart this evening. Dinner will be in about half an hour. We're having a drink in the sitting room first."

He straightened his shirt sleeves and followed his mother. His father stood at the far end of the room holding a glass of what he could only imagine was whiskey. It was his favorite drink and he would have looked lost standing next to the large crackling fireplace in the room without it. He looked up, set the glass on the mantel, and managed a tight smile as he nodded at his son. Nathan smiled and nodded back.

"Dad. I hope you're well."

He crossed the room to where his father stood. They shook hands, and then his father, still gripping Nathan's hand, in a slightly awkward and uncharacteristic gesture pulled Nathan in for a tight embrace. He held him for a moment, patting him on the back, and then just as quickly pulled away.

"You look good."

"Thanks Dad. I've had some time to clean up a bit and get some new clothes."

His father retrieved his glass from the mantel and motioned for him to sit down.

"Can I get you something to drink dear?" his mother asked.

She was clearly relieved that things had started off well.

"Just a sparkling water Mom. Thanks."

She'd barely left when his father spoke.

"So, what do you think about the house?"

"I think it's amazing, Dad! I want to thank you and Mom so much for that—and the new car. You really didn't have to go to all that trouble."

A slightly pained look crossed his father's face and then just as quickly disappeared.

"But I'm appreciative that you did. It's going to be a great place for me to live. Thank you."

His father smiled again, relaxed back into the plush sofa and took a small sip from his whiskey.

"Your mother oversaw the decorating, of course. I think she's done a fine job on it. The games room was my idea."

Nathan smiled as his mother walked back into the room and handed him a glass of sparkling water with ice and a slice of lemon.

"Thanks Mom."

She smiled and settled into the sofa next to her husband.

"So how was the beach house? Everything in good order?"

Nathan gave them a general account of his stay there, skipping over the dead body on the beach. He reckoned if they hadn't mentioned it, then either his sister hadn't said anything or his parents didn't want to bring it up. In either case, he really didn't want to talk about it and ruin what had started out as a good evening.

"That sounds good. We should probably open up the house for the season soon in any case. I'm sure everyone is going to want to start going down."

His father was about to say something further when an older woman entered the room. She was short in stature, with white hair and sparkling blue eyes. She wore a black dress with sapphire earrings and a rose gold and sapphire necklace around her neck.

"Mother. Is everything alright?"

"Everything's fine dear. I'm allowed to see my grandson, am I not?"

She smiled warmly, hugging her son as he walked over to lend her an arm. Nathan could have sworn that she winked at him over his father's stooped shoulder. Alexandra Briggs was strong for her seventy-two years. She had run the business together with her husband for many decades until their son—an only child—had stepped in to take on more of the responsibility. Nathan's grandfather had continued to have some involvement in the business until the accident. And now, of course, he was gone.

Nathan walked over and gave his grandmother a hug, kissing her on both cheeks. He adored his grandparents and had taken care to send them postcards from all the places along his journey. Unbeknownst to him, his grandmother had saved every one of them upstairs in an album.

"It's good to see you, Nathan," she said.

"It's good to see you too Grandma," he replied.

"Let me have a good look at you," she said, stepping back.

She held him at arm's length and peered intently at his face, as though searching for something. Perhaps she was looking to see signs of maturing from his time away, or perhaps she was searching for some detail that would remind her of her husband.

"You look good. Strong. I'm glad you cut that awful long hair you came back with. I'm sorry we haven't had as much time together since you returned. But I'm sure you understand."

"Thanks Grandma. And I do. How are you doing?"

A dark cloud momentarily passed across her face before she smiled at him.

"I'm doing okay. I'm better now that you're around. You can come and see me after you get settled in and tell me all about your trip—or maybe I'll come over to that house of yours, and you can make us one of those wonderful lunches."

"I'd better practice a bit first. It's been a while."

"I'm sure you'd be fine. Listen, I just wanted to come down and see you before I head up for the evening. Don't be a stranger. I expect to see more of you. Soon."

"Won't you be joining us this evening, Alexandra?" Nathan's mother asked warmly.

"No dear, not tonight. I've had my dinner brought up. I just wanted to see my grandson before I head upstairs."

"We'll plan something for another time then."

"Thank you, Elizabeth. And Nathan, I hope you rest well in your new home. Try to have sweet dreams, dear."

This time he was sure of it. She gave a barely perceptible wink and smiled as she turned to leave the room.

"Good night everyone."

"Good night," they said in unison.

He thought about his grandmother's parting comment to him, about having sweet dreams. Between the comment and the wink, it was as though she knew he'd been having increasingly strange dreams of late. He shrugged it off. It was probably just one of those comments older people randomly use in conversations.

༺✧༻

Serena stood on a train platform in downtown Boston waiting to board a fast train. It turned out that her father wasn't in Boston at all. He'd left that afternoon for New York and left a message for Serena to join him. One of his assistants had given her the message and train tickets, with the command to leave at once. Normally she would have driven there, but her father was on a tight schedule and she would have to get the high-speed train if she was going to catch him before he left. She'd left her car in one of their parking spaces under the office building and taken a taxi to the station.

The train pulled slowly into its platform and Serena waited as the other passengers began to disembark before stepping up into a first-class car. She quickly found her seat. As she watched people walking along the platform, she abruptly sat up in her seat. She thought she saw someone she knew, someone she hadn't seen for a very long time—her cousin Dragan. She peered out the window at the passing crowd and saw him making his way towards the turnstiles at the end of the platform. She was quite sure that it was him.

What was he doing in Boston? Her family had a very distant and estranged relationship with her Aunt Jelena and her cousins—so much so, she hadn't seen him or the others for many years. What were the chances of seeing him here on a train platform in Boston? She craned her neck to see better, but he was already gone. The crowd continued to filter past her window and the train filled up for their imminent journey. She wondered what he was up to. That side of the family were never up to any good.

If she hadn't been in such a hurry to see her father, she would have left the train and followed him. Whatever he was doing here, it wouldn't be good. She would have to mention this to her father. They were under orders to deliver news of any sightings of Jelena or her children. Davorin wouldn't be pleased when she told him. As the doors closed and the train began to slowly pull away, she felt a sense of unease, something that she hadn't felt in a long time. It would occupy her thoughts for the remainder of the trip.

※

During dinner, Nathan's mother quizzed him about some of the places that he'd visited. He mentioned museums and galleries and, for his father's sake, managed to work in some of the experiences he'd had in learning about textile production in other countries. He'd had plenty of time to develop some of his own thoughts about things they should consider. His father looked both surprised and pleased with him. Nathan had realized early on in his journey that if he didn't come back with something his father could relate to the whole trip would continue to be seen as an extravagant waste of time. Of course, it hadn't hurt that both his mother and sister had suggested before he left that he consider such things. Now, his mother smiled warmly, expressing pleasure that he'd taken her advice. Inevitably the conversation turned to his future plans.

"Any thoughts on what's next now that you're back?"

It wasn't like his father to ask an open-ended question. The answer was both obvious and expected, and he didn't disappoint. The air between them was heavily laden with expectation.

"Well, I was hoping there was a place for me at the company. I realize I have a lot to learn, but I'd like to give it a go and see how things work out. I won't make any promises that I might not keep, but I'm ready to try."

His father smiled tightly and nodded. Nathan's response wasn't fully what he wanted, but it was a step in the right direction, and more than he'd expected. That would have to be good enough for the moment. Nathan could tell that his father would have preferred a more enthusiastic response. There was still no apology about their fallout on Monday, and there was a part of him that felt rebellious where that was concerned. He had made the right decision for the moment and given as honest a response as he was able to give. He could always change his mind later if he decided that the family business wasn't quite right for him, but he owed it to them to give it a good try first. Especially as they had made such a significant effort on his behalf.

Once they'd finished dinner and after dessert and a cup of tea, Nathan realized how tired he was and decided this might be a good time to take his leave—before things had the chance to turn sour. Before he could go, his father asked him to come to the study for a few moments. Nathan quickly glanced at his mother, who nodded and smiled.

"Yes, of course," he answered.

Closing the door behind them, they sat down.

"Listen, about the other day. I reacted badly. That's not to say that I am happy about the situation, but you are my son and you deserved better. You and your grandfather were close, and whether I like it or not, I will not disrespect him by not honoring his last wishes."

He paused for a moment. Nathan anticipated a "but" coming.

"Even so, I expect you to take his bequest seriously, and also to honor him by working hard. I don't want there to be bad blood between us. But I also won't have anyone disrespect what those who came before us built. We owe everything we have to your grandfather and our ancestors. Do you understand?"

Nathan hadn't expected what, from his father, amounted to an apology. As he'd already made up his mind that he did owe his grandfather and his parents for everything they had done for him, his response was easy.

"I do, sir. And I promise you that I will do my best to make a go of it."

His father nodded, seemingly satisfied, and stood.

"Alright. In that case, why don't you head home and get some sleep. You've had a long day, and I'm sure you're tired. Take the weekend to relax and come over to the mill on Monday. I'll be there for the day, and we'll see about getting you started."

He ushered him back to the front hall, where Nathan said his good nights to both of his parents. His mother hugged him tightly and kissed him on the cheek. He and his father nodded to one another, having come to an understanding, and he turned and walked out into the cold, dark night.

As he started the engine, he thought about their brief conversation. He couldn't believe that his father had come that far in such a short period of time without having been heavily influenced by his mother. On the other hand, his behavior on Monday had been quite poor, even for him. Something—or someone—must have caused him to step back and reconsider what he'd said. Whatever the reason, Nathan was relieved. He could relax now, look forward to his first weekend in his new home, and deal with what came next when he met with his father on the following Monday.

Driving back, his thoughts turned to Serena. He wondered what she was doing at that moment. She was probably relaxing in her family's apartment in Boston. Or maybe she was out partying. Did she party? He wondered if she was thinking about him.

He thought about calling her the next morning to see if she would like to meet for lunch or dinner. He couldn't deny he was glad they'd reconnected, even if the circumstances seemed a bit strange. It seemed to be a week for reconciliations. As he pulled into his new driveway, the headlights swept past the hedges at the side of the yard and in the flickering light he thought he saw something—or someone.

He felt a familiar itch at the back of his neck. He sat in the car with the lights on and the engine running for a few moments as he peered into the shadows. He stared intently but saw nothing. Perhaps it was a wild animal, or just a shadow. Or it might have been the hedges swaying in the light breeze. Nathan decided it was more likely that he was extremely tired and that there wasn't anything there at all. He shook his head, deftly scratched his neck and got out. He stopped for a moment on the front steps, taking one last look, but saw nothing.

As he entered, he switched on the lights and locked the door behind him. Even though he was tired, he wandered around the house, visiting every room. He was so used to sharing spaces with other people when he was traveling that he'd forgotten what it was like to have so much space to himself. His mother had clearly done a great job renovating the old house and Nathan couldn't believe how much he loved it. He changed into sweatpants and a t-shirt and sat on the sofa in front of the television for a bit. It had been a really long day, and he'd covered a lot of ground. It felt like he'd actually left the beach house the day before, not that morning. He reflected on how well the evening had gone. New house and car, and a new job.

One silver lining of working in the family business was that he would occasionally get to spend some time with his siblings when they were around. He missed them and knew that he could learn a lot from them. After a while, still excited about his good fortune, he got up and dragged himself up the stairs to his new bedroom. His head had barely hit the pillow before he was sound asleep.

༺༻

Outside, a familiar pair of gray eyes watched as Nathan wandered around the house and eventually settled on the sofa. That was a close call. Dragan was reflecting on his earlier near miss with Serena when the lights of the SUV picked him out of the darkness. He quickly scrambled into the shadows and held still until Nathan disappeared into the house. Moonlight reflected off his pale skin and black hair as he peered through the windows.

Who are you? Why is my mother so interested in you?!

When the time was right, Dragan would find out everything he could about this boy. It was only luck that he'd been in Boston to encounter his cousin, Serena, sitting with him. He'd followed her to the train station, knowing that he would pick up the boy's trail when he returned to New Comfort. She was on the high-speed train to New York, probably to see her father, his Uncle Davorin, who he knew was there at the moment. He reckoned she'd be back after not too long. He'd have to be extra careful.

His mother, Jelena, had contacted him earlier to say that she thought Serena's trip to New York might be the perfect chance for him to study the object of her attention. He tried to ask her why she wanted him to follow this boy. He looked like a complete and utter boring waste of time—compared to the activities that Jelena usually had Dragan perform for her. But she was playing her cards close to her chest on this one and ordered him to do as he was told.

He stayed until Nathan finally made his way up the stairs to bed and turned out the lights, and stood a few moments more before realizing he felt a deep hunger. He had intended to stop off to feed on his way up here, but his mother had kept him busy. The last time he'd fed was outside the beach house. He glanced one last time at the dark house and then swiftly departed to get his car. He didn't want to feed too close to Nathan's home—doing so in the area near the beach house had been a mistake. He decided to go further afield—perhaps even down to Boston, where another lost soul would hardly be noticed.

※

The train journey to New York was uneventful. Serena had walked the length of the train and back to ensure that there was no sign of Dragan. She was beginning to wonder if she'd really even seen him at all, or if it was just someone who looked like him. It was so long since she'd seen her cousin that she didn't think it possible that she would suddenly, randomly see him standing on a train platform in Boston. It made no sense to her. Still, she'd have to tell her father about it when they met.

On arrival at Penn Station, she disappeared into the chaos of the crowds leaving the train. If Dragan was there—and if he had somehow managed to evade her on the train—she wanted to get away from the station as quickly and quietly as possible. Stealth was one thing that she was expert at—although, of course, so was her cousin. She preferred to avoid a confrontation. He was strong, and although she felt she could handle herself, she didn't want to put it to the test. Even if there was bad blood, they were family, and that still counted for something in her mind. Besides, her father would be angry if anything happened without him there to protect her. It wasn't worth the risk.

She made her way to the building that contained their offices and apartments, a similar arrangement to the one in Boston. She was resolved that—despite his previous protestations—she was going to ask her father why it was so important to shadow Nathan. Not that she minded. But if she was going to be near him, she wanted it to be out of her own desire and not his. As she entered the private elevator, she thought about Nathan and his friend. They were very close. That much was clear. Next time they met, she would make a point of getting to know Ben better.

The elevator stopped and the doors slid open. Davorin stood, still as a statue, in the entrance.

"Serena..."

"Father."

He ushered her into his private study, where she began to tell of her possible encounter with her cousin. They discussed many things long into the night, but one thing was made clear. Her father wasn't ready to divulge anything about his interest in Nathan and now, given her story of her cousin's possible appearance, he was doubly convinced of the necessity to keep watch over him. Serena anticipated some long days ahead.

Chapter 12

He stood on a grass-covered plateau up the hill from the ocean overlooking the settlement of New Comfort. Behind him stood a forest of trees and nearby the beginnings of a foundation for his family's new home. America appeared to be a land of abundant riches and moving there cemented their foothold in both the old world and the new. He watched as the ship that had brought them departed with a load of lumber to be sold back in London. This would pay the expenses of their trip.

His family stayed in the settlement below in a hastily built house until he and the men he'd hired were able to complete construction of their home. He kept a drawing of his large tract of land, to which he occasionally added more scribbles that would act as a plan, not only for the house, but for how to landscape the property in a way that would suit his interests. He needed to be discreet about certain things—after all, this was a strange new world, and severe religious views often drove the minds of men in dark directions. There were things about his family, his ancestry that needed to remain hidden from others.

He could feel this was going to be a good place for them. A place of new beginnings. His brother remained behind in London to run their interests over there, and he would establish new industries right here in America. The Briggs family had taken a risk in coming here, but one that he felt would deliver dividends not only to his immediate family, but also to future generations. He surveyed the settlement below and watched as the ship disappeared into the eastern morning sun. He was pleased. This would be a good day.

⁂

Early Monday morning, he woke with a start. What a strange dream to have. He shook his head to clear away the cobwebs and focused for a moment on the intensity and the sensation of it. He recognized the bay and the view from the hill. He'd grown up knowing both intimately. His dreams were evolving from vague recollections of some distant ancient island to something a bit more recent—the founding of New Comfort. He knew the stories about the town's origin. He'd heard many of them from his grandfather and had read about them in local accounts. It was strange how bits of information locked deep in your brain sometimes had the habit of surfacing when you were asleep.

He looked at his clock and saw that it was still quite early. He decided to get up and get ready for his first day of work. He'd spent the weekend relaxing, food shopping and doing everything he could to prepare himself for the start of the next chapter of his life. He was wide awake now. And while a part of him was excited, there was clearly a part of him that was picking away at the deep anxieties he was holding. Hence the dream—an ancestor starting out on a new adventure. He could definitely relate to that.

The days of his first week at work were a blur, and in the evenings when he came home, he would change into his running gear and go for a run around the countryside. It had been a long time since he'd done any formal exercise, and the first few days nearly killed him. After his runs he usually took a quick shower, made dinner, watched a bit of television and went to bed. Each successive day became more of a routine.

His father had drawn up a list of responsibilities that would keep him busy for a while. Once he had mastered the mills, his father intended to introduce him to their other business interests in order to give him a full view of the breadth and depth of the responsibilities of being a member of the family. It felt like an endless parade of meeting people whose names he could barely remember.

On the upside, he saw Sam and Christopher quite a lot. Though not usually at the mills, they were part of his induction and they answered his endless questions with patience and the understanding of siblings who'd already gone through the process themselves. Having kept out of the business throughout school and university, he had never fully understood the complexity of what they did. As he learned about mills, design teams, distribution, shipping and operations, he began to get a sense of the scale of the textile side of it. They used production facilities in China and Europe for some of their products, though they were predominantly considered an American company.

Over the last couple of years, Jonathan Briggs had slowly begun to hand some responsibilities over to Sam and Christopher, as they continually proved themselves capable of taking on more and more responsibility. Nathan could see the possibility of a similar path being shaped for him. Not one to waste an opportunity, his father made it clear that he intended for Nathan to examine their European operations. He was particularly interested in identifying countries with slow growth, places where labor was more affordable and where people might welcome products produced inside the European Union. He wanted to make use of many of the same nationalistic "made in America" style storylines that he used in America. He conveniently looked past the bits that were made in China.

"I imagine this would interest you," he'd said on their first day together.

It was less a question than a statement. Nathan reckoned that things could be worse. He could be stuck on a production line somewhere learning the difference between a top- and a whip-stitch. He'd overheard those terms while touring the floor of the mill during the week but he still didn't understand the difference. At least it felt like his father was trying to meet him halfway by giving him things that he thought might interest and challenge him. That was a relief.

Between introductions, meetings and a couple of hastily arranged visits to nearby mills that they owned, Nathan began his research of the European business and textile industry, trying to understand where and how they already engaged in the market. He knew that they were considering growing their operations through expansion of their London headquarters. His father had mentioned that his grandfather had been engaged in the planning for that. Trying to get hold of the information that he needed was complicated. Teams didn't talk to one another they way he'd expected. The operations in England were run by different people. He introduced himself via email and phone calls numerous times. As for researching the market opportunities across Europe, it turned out the company had access to external agencies that helped with this sort of thing, as well as its own research libraries and subscriptions to some of the top online research databases.

It felt a lot like preparing to write a research paper at university, the difference being that someone—his father—might be making real-life decisions based on his recommendations. He proceeded slowly and more carefully as a result, looking to avoid disappointing or letting down his father and the company. His schedule remained relentless. He was sure that it was his father's way of ensuring that he didn't become distracted or have spare time to develop second thoughts. Nathan had never realized how much effort went into running this operation—and this was just one of many. Curiously though, as each day passed he found he enjoyed the work a bit more. His father was starting to make more sense. And he wasn't sure if that was a good or a bad thing.

※

When Saturday finally came, he decided it was time to catch up on all of the things that hadn't gotten done during the week—laundry, food shopping, cleaning the house. He realized that he needed to figure out a better way to fit some of these things in during weekday evenings, or he'd never have any time off at the weekends. On top of that, the following day was Mother's Day. His father had organized lunch at the house and invited everyone to join them.

He met Ben briefly for breakfast first thing in the morning and brought him up to speed on his first week of work. His friend couldn't believe that he and his father hadn't fallen out even once.

"Maybe your mother put the fear of God into him," he said.

"Yeah, it wouldn't surprise me. Sam said our mother wasn't very happy about his behavior."

After they finished breakfast, he dropped Ben back at his house before heading to the local shops to find a card and Mother's Day gift and to do some food shopping. He spent the rest of the day catching up on chores, and found time to hop across to the games room to play some Xbox. In the afternoon he decided to text Serena to see how she was doing, but by the time he went up to bed he still hadn't heard back from her. She was probably still busy doing things for her father.

The next morning, he woke and there was still no response. He thought about sending another text but decided it might come across as creepy. She'd respond when she had time. He took his time getting ready before heading over to his parents'. He wrapped the gifts he'd purchased for his mother—photo frames containing pictures of him standing atop the Eiffel Tower and in front of a tall ship in the harbor in Stockholm. He knew that his mother would appreciate something personal and sentimental. His father, on the other hand, would opt for something practical or sparkly.

It was a beautiful bright, sunny day and he felt like he could see for miles. He parked behind Sam's car. It looked like his brother and his wife hadn't arrived yet. As he rang the doorbell, he heard the crunch of gravel as Christopher pulled up and parked. He jumped out, opened the door for his wife Emma, and walked up join Nathan.

"Glad to see you could make it. Your first week didn't kill you?"

Nathan scowled at him. His brother always delighted in picking on him.

"Nope, everything's okay. I don't see what's so difficult about it. I think if I'd been doing it as long as you, I'd be running the whole company by now."

Emma laughed as Nathan leaned in and kissed her on the cheek.

"Next year you'll be on the receiving end of these lunches."

He was commenting on Emma's pregnancy. His sister had brought him up to speed on things that had happened while he was away. Emma ran a hand over her belly.

"I suppose you're right."

She smiled warmly at Nathan. Her husband was clearly still chafed by his little brother's sarcastic comment.

"You wait until the real work starts, little brother. Then we'll see who's ready to run the company."

The front door opened, and their sister stood smiling in the foyer.

"It's about time you three—sorry, four—got here."

She hugged Emma and playfully punched her brothers in the shoulder.

"Everyone is in the dining room. It's a bit of an early lunch. Dad has to head out of town for a few days and has a flight later. Last-minute thing."

They entered the dining room together. Nathan and Christopher placed their gifts on a sideboard with the others. Their mother sat smiling at the table and their father waved them to sit down.

"Come in boys. Sorry it's a bit rushed today. Last-minute business trip."

He grimaced as his wife frowned at him.

"I have to deal with a bit of a supply issue at the mills."

"Anything I can help with, Dad?" Christopher asked.

"No, it's fine. I just need to negotiate a few final details and we're good to go."

"Happy Mother's Day Mom," Nathan said.

"Yeah Mom! Happy Mother's Day," Christopher echoed.

"Thank you, boys. I trust you don't have to run off after as well."

They shook their heads in unison as she smiled back at them.

"Is Grandmother going to join us?" Christopher asked.

"She's gone off to visit Aunt Genevieve in Boston for a couple of days."

A look passed between their parents and they knew better than to ask. Nathan assumed that things were still too recent, and that their grandmother simply wasn't ready for large gatherings. He hoped that she would come around as he enjoyed spending time with her. As they ate lunch, they managed to avoid discussing work—it was an unwritten rule that on holidays and birthdays, work topics were best discussed away from the table. Lunch was loud and festive, everyone talking over everyone else. Not long after they finished, his father excused himself, kissed their mother on the forehead, gave her an apologetic look and grabbed a bag from the foyer before heading off to catch his flight.

Their mother opened her gifts just after dinner that evening and was really pleased with Nathan's framed photographs. As expected, their father had indeed bought their mother a new necklace. It was a shame that he wasn't there to put it on her. When it finally came time to leave, Nathan felt as though things were starting to settle for him at home. He said his goodbyes with the others and drove the short distance home. Before going to bed that night, he checked his phone again. Still no message from Serena.

During his third week, he finally managed to catch up with his sister for lunch. Apart from Mother's Day he'd only managed to see her in occasional induction meetings she held with him.

"So little brother, how are you handling things?"

He shrugged.

"I have no idea. I follow the schedule that Nancy emails me every week and in between things I work on the European research that Dad asked me to do."

Nancy was their father's assistant. She was the fortress that most people needed to get past in order to gain access to their father. She also translated his orders and roughly scribbled notes into intelligible schedules that Nathan followed like clockwork.

"She's good like that. Make sure she's on your side. Sometimes I think it's really Nancy that runs the company and not Dad."

They both laughed.

"So how are you feeling about everything now?"

He sipped his water and thought about the best way to answer his sister's question.

"Well, it's a bit strange. I mean, after spending all that time with no schedules, no responsibilities, no expectations other than my own, it's strange to be a part of something so structured. When I was away, apart from knowing the next general destination, I kind of planned everything as I went along. It's not like that here. Everything is planned out. Scripted. I go where I'm told, listen to what I'm being told, respond when I'm asked a question. It's exhausting. I pretty much go home, go for a run, grab something to eat and collapse on the sofa every night."

Sam laughed.

"Don't worry. You're doing fine. It'll get much worse."

He rolled his eyes and sighed.

"No, I'm kidding. Just give it some time. It gets better. The first few weeks are a complete whirlwind of activity—names being thrown at you, introductions to teams you won't remember. It'll calm down soon and then you'll start setting your own schedules. I remember when I started. I didn't think I'd ever see daylight again. It was the same for Christopher. But now it's pretty much up to us how we do things. And over time, as he develops more trust and confidence, Dad gives us more responsibility in the company. You reach a point where you start to feel more in control of things."

Nathan thought about everything that Sam was telling him and hoped that it was true. If he kept this schedule up for much longer, he might run back home one night, pack a bag and disappear back to Europe. It wasn't that he was averse to hard work; it was the complete lack of balance. He was too tired to see friends, go to the beach, or have any kind of life.

As he sat there, thoughts swirling through his head, he felt a sudden pang of guilt for thinking about it that way given the actual reason that he'd returned home. He briefly wondered how his grandmother was doing. He knew that she was back from her trip. He would have to try to make some time to visit. He looked around the small cafe where he and his sister had come to have their lunch. He realized that it was the first time he'd managed to get out of the mill for lunch since starting.

"Get out this weekend," Sam was saying. "Do something for yourself. Get to the beach. Why don't you grab Ben and take him out? You know how he is. Make him sit on the beach for a bit and get some sun with you."

His sister was right. Getting out might do them both some good. And it would give him a good reason to see his friend—not that he needed one. The waitress brought them their lunch, and as they ate, Sam changed the subject.

"So, have you ever heard anything more from the police on the Cape?"

He shook his head. He'd done his best to put that terrible incident out of his mind.

"I haven't heard a thing. I wonder if they figured out what happened to that poor guy."

He shuddered at the thought of the man's body lying on the beach. Their explanation of an accident seemed likely, though there weren't that many boats in the water that time of year. And what was he doing out on the water anyways? If it wasn't a boat, then the alternative was something much darker—something that he preferred not to think about. Especially as both he and Sam had walked that beach all alone.

"Do you think I should call them?" he asked.

"I'd be inclined to leave it alone. If they need you, I'm sure they'll call. Best to just leave it be unless you hear from them."

He nodded—of course his sister was right. He wished that he hadn't been involved to begin with. While he felt sorry for the man—and his family—there wasn't anything else he could offer other than what he'd already explained to the police. It was probably best to let it go and leave them to handle it. He had enough things on his hands at the moment. Still, he couldn't help but feel bad about it. He shook his head.

"You're right of course. I'll leave it be. They have my number if they need me."

They finished eating and agreed to meet up again the

following week. His initial induction period ended on Friday and he planned to take his sister's advice to catch up with Ben and get some beach time. He'd start to reclaim his evenings and weekends for his own use. And of course, there was Serena. She'd finally texted him back and, as suspected, she was away on business for her father. She agreed to let him know when she would be back in Boston again and they would find some time to meet up. In the end he thought it was just as well that she was away as he'd been so busy the last few weeks, he wouldn't have had time to see her in any case.

※

As he walked from the mill to his car that evening, a pair of gray eyes tracked him from behind the tinted windows of a black car parked across the road from the main entrance. Dragan watched as Nathan climbed into his Range Rover for another inevitably boring journey from the mill to his home. He hadn't known his cousin to take a special interest in anyone for a very long time, and he still couldn't figure out what she saw in this boy. Yet there must be something that was causing both his mother and Serena to take an active interest.

As Nathan drove out through the main gate, he waved to the security guard. Like clockwork, he drove off down the road that led back to his home. For Dragan it would be another long, boring night of observing... nothing. Nothing at all.

He decided to take a break from the monotony of watching, and give in to the familiar pang of hunger. Once satiated, he wouldn't have to feed anytime soon. His side of the family were not nearly as civilized and modern as his cousin's side. His food still walked on two feet. He'd choose his meal carefully, to try to shake things up a little. He wanted to see if another body close to home, so to speak, caused a reaction in Nathan. He was a patient man. He'd find out soon enough.

Chapter 13

He stood on the same grass-covered plateau as before, only this time the foundations had turned into a complete home. The wooden clapboard house had a grand view over the ocean and a significantly larger and more developed town below. It was nighttime. He could hear the sound of crickets chirping, their song carrying out over the hillside drowning out any sound from below. He smelled it before he saw it. The smell of wood burning. Not from the smoke curling up into the night sky from the fireplace, but from the house itself.

Flames began to creep out of the downstairs windows. Within seconds, screams split the air and a husband and wife carrying two children burst through the front door of the two-story home. The fire licked up the side of the house and out of the first-floor windows. The family stood in the front yard and watched the incandescent flames destroy what moments before was their hundred-year-old family home. It was gone before anyone could blink. In the distance the sound of horses could be heard clopping up the dirt lane. The house was burnt beyond salvation.

But its inhabitants had been lucky enough to escape the fire.

He missed the shadow in the trees along the side of the property that watched as the house collapsed in on itself. It watched as residents of the town below arrived to assist the poor family whose home had been destroyed. For a moment the fire lit the shadow's cold white face and gray eyes as they peered out of the tree line at the family. It was a woman glaring at them from underneath a dark hood. Her face was shrouded in anger. She turned and disappeared into the woods before anyone spotted her. A missed opportunity.

Nathan woke the next morning feeling slightly groggy. His dreams were starting to take a strange kind of shape, half dream and half memory, more recalled stories from when he was a child. He assumed that the house in his dream was the one that used to stand where his parents' current house stood, the one that had in fact burned to the ground in the eighteenth century and on whose space their present house, with a much larger footprint, now stood.

He showered and dressed, ate a quick bowl of cereal and drove to work. As he pulled up to the main gates, the security guard motioned for him to stop.

"Hey Sal. Everything alright?"

"Not really, Mr. Briggs. Not sure you've heard yet, but Jess Evans was found dead at his home last night."

Jess worked at the mill and was one of their lead fabric designers. He'd personally taken Nathan through the design process a couple of days previously. He was well-liked, a good man with a wife and two kids. He'd seemed perfectly fine when Nathan last saw him. It didn't seem possible that he was dead.

"What do you mean he's dead?"

"He was off work yesterday. His wife found him out behind their house when she got home last night. My sister Mary, she works for the police, said it was a freak accident. He must have tripped and fallen with a pair of those long trimming shears. Cut his neck wide open and bled to death. That man really did love his gardening. Always got up to it when he had the time."

Nathan couldn't think of what to say. Jess was a gentle man who seemed to really love his work at the company. He was passionate about design and had been with them since graduating university nearly twenty years before. He was considered an expert on fabrics and textiles. His father had commented on how lucky they were to have him, and Nathan had found his time with Jess far more interesting than he'd imagined it would be. There was no avoiding it; his death would be a major loss to the company.

As he drove through the gates and over to his parking space, he couldn't help but make the comparison between Jess' untimely death and that of that poor man on the beach. Both involved serious neck injuries and major blood loss. Nathan was relieved that he hadn't found the body this time, though he felt sorry for Jess' wife. It must have come as a terrible shock. And two children as well. As he parked, he could see that his father and sister's cars were both parked in spaces near the entrance. As he entered the building, the receptionist told him that they were waiting for him up in his father's office. He took a deep breath and made his way swiftly upstairs. His father greeted him as he walked through the door to the office.

"Thanks for joining us. Come in and have a seat."

His sister was already there.

"I suppose you've already heard?"

He nodded.

"Sal told me when I arrived."

"It's a tragedy. A terrible tragedy."

His father wasn't one for too much sentiment and that was about the most emotion they would get.

"In the short term we have to make a decision as to who takes his place. I know there were a couple of people on his team he'd been cultivating over time. We can either choose from one of them or bring someone in from outside."

Nathan noticed at this point that his brother was conspicuously absent.

"Shouldn't Christopher be here? I mean, doesn't he usually deal with situations related to the mills?"

"Well, yes and no. He's more Boston-based these days, working on other things. We've had a bit of a gap with respect to family engagement in the mills. And in any case, the police had some questions, so we sent him along to represent the company. He knew Jess quite well."

That made a certain kind of sense to Nathan. And his father didn't have the right kind of sensibility for dealing with them, in any case.

"Well, if it's any help, I know that he was keen on promoting Madeleine. He dropped a number of hints, saying she had a great eye for fabrics and the technical skills and education necessary to excel in a more senior role," Nathan said.

Their father nodded.

"You don't think she's too inexperienced?"

"Well, Jess seemed to think she had the right skills and experience. In light of being unable to ask him, I'd probably go with his judgment on this. But then, I am new to all of this."

"What do you think, Sam?"

Nathan held his breath, hoping he hadn't overstepped his role. After all, it was only his third week in the business.

"Well, Jess was extremely competent and patient. He spent a lot of time with his team. From what I recall he thought quite highly of her, even back then."

Their father smiled and nodded.

"It's settled then. I'll check with Christopher when he returns just to be sure, but if he concurs, we'll move Madeleine into the position and keep an eye on how she performs. Nathan, can you organize a collection for the family, which we'll match of course? He was a valued member of the team, and we should do something for them."

Their father stood, signaling the end of the meeting. Uncharacteristically, he thanked them both, then returned to his large oak desk. Nathan and Sam left the room. When they got to the area of the office where Nathan worked, his sister spoke.

"Isn't it odd? We were just talking about what happened to that poor guy on the Cape and then this happens to Jess? What a strange coincidence."

He nodded. He couldn't help but think the same thing.

"Yeah, it's very strange. Both unusual accidents. I guess these things happen, but seriously, what are the odds?"

They parted and went about their work until later in the day when their brother returned.

"Hey guys, thanks for helping Dad out with things. I think Madeleine is a great choice. Jess would certainly have approved," Christopher said.

"How did things go with the police?" Sam asked.

"It was fine. They wanted to know if he'd shown any strange behavior at work lately, if he was on any medication, or if there was anything that might have pointed to this being more than an accident."

"And was there?" Nathan asked.

"No; as far as I've heard, he was really happy and healthy. Of course, I haven't been up here much since moving down to the Boston offices. His wife said there wasn't anything unusual either. She said he seemed quite happy. I feel so sorry for her and the kids. She's the one who found him. The whole family are traumatized. Dad said you were doing something about a collection?"

"Yeah," Nathan responded. "I'm going to send an email out to the company explaining what we're doing. Dad agreed to match all donations. I spoke with his assistant this morning, and she's sorting out the actual collection of funds, which is helpful."

"That's great. Well, once it's sorted, let me know and I'll put something in. I really feel for his family. I know he had good insurance, which should help, but a bit of extra money and support from all of us won't hurt. It would be good for her to know how many people around here cared about him."

Nathan nodded. He would make sure they did the right thing. He hadn't known Jess well, but everyone at the mill was like family. And family was important to a Briggs.

※

Over the next couple of days, he finished his initial training and had also managed to sort out a successful collection for Jess' family. He also organized flowers for the church for his funeral. People across the company had been very generous and with their father's contribution, they managed to raise a respectable amount of money. Their father even praised Nathan's initiative in sorting things out so quickly, and, despite the tragedy, he ended the week feeling stronger about family and company. On Friday he received a surprise call from his grandmother.

"Hello dear. I'm not disturbing you, am I?"

"No, of course not. How are you?"

"I'm very well. Sorry I missed you at dinner on Sunday."

"No worries. It would be nice to see you though."

"That's why I'm calling. I was thinking of maybe coming over on Sunday. If you don't have other plans that is. I thought you could give me a tour of your house and we could have tea."

"That sounds great. But why don't you make it lunchtime, and I'll make lunch for the both of us."

"That sounds splendid. Let's say around one then?"

"Perfect. It'll be great to see you."

"I'm looking forward to seeing you too."

They said their goodbyes and he returned to his work with a smile. It was great to hear from his grandmother and he was looking forward to seeing her. They would finally be able to have a proper catch-up.

The rest of his day was taking up with meetings, introductions and checking to see that the final collection for Jess was going well. As he drove out through the gates later that Friday evening towards home, he felt exhausted, emotionally and mentally, but also content with things. Despite the events of the week, he felt that things were settling down for him personally. Maybe life back home wasn't going to be so bad after all.

Chapter 14

The charred debris at the top of the hill had been cleared away and now workmen were busy scurrying about. There was a constant stream of deliveries to the construction site that overlooked the growing town of New Comfort and the harbor below. The old house had sufficed for the first hundred years of their time in the colonies. But it was time to make a statement, as their old home back in England had done. The new house would be unusual for the area, a large four-story red brick edifice with a gleaming white portico and large rectangular windows facing east. Gardens would be designed and landscaped, and follies, small representations of ancient structures, would be built on the grounds, nestled in gardens and bordered by ponds—much as they'd had before their hasty move across the Atlantic.

He watched from the edge of the hill as the masons worked to build this monument to the Briggs family. His family. He had designed the house himself and followed far older designs for the follies and the gardens. The estate would be unlike anything the townspeople had seen before, a private space for his family to feel safe and secure. The workmen had raised eyebrows at some of his designs, but he depended on their skill—and paid them handsomely for their discretion.

As the sun rose higher into the afternoon sky, he admired both the view below and the progress on the new house and the property that surrounded it. It would take a year to complete everything that he'd specified. But when it was finished it would be his new home. His family's home. And the home of future generations. He would protect this house, as he should have done with the previous one. There would be no fire this time. No sabotage. No interference. And he would find the ones responsible and make them pay.

⁂

Nathan woke on Saturday morning to sun streaming through the windows, blinding him, as he realized he'd fallen asleep on the sofa again. It was starting to become an irritating habit. He'd completed three weeks of work and still wasn't used to the idea of a five-day work week. This was the most routine he'd experienced in almost a year, since university really. In the background the television was still playing—last night's movie had morphed into a morning cooking show.

Strange dreams plagued him still, each one feeling as real as the one that came before. Dreams, memories, childhood stories surfacing in his sleep. He wondered why he was having them. He shrugged it off, smiling as he thought about the plans he'd made with Ben. They had seen each other briefly for breakfast a couple of weeks before and that was it. A catch-up between the two friends was overdue. As he grabbed his phone, he noticed the time.

"Shit!"

He was going to be late. They planned to grab breakfast in town and then drive out to the beach for the day. Memorial Day weekend was the following weekend and they wanted to hit the beach before the season descended into complete chaos. He also very badly wanted to spend time outside after having attended endless meetings and training sessions in the mill over the last few weeks. There was so much more to learn about his family's business than he'd ever imagined. And while he'd always thought it would be incredibly boring, he was surprised to learn how challenging his days were. He suffered more from exhaustion than boredom.

He had gained a much better understanding of why his father had often worked so late and come home so tired and irritable. When his father was around, he was pulled in a thousand different directions daily. And with spending most of his time in Boston and traveling, he was always on the go. There were so many things to read and understand. Luckily for Nathan he had as close as possible to a photographic memory and could recall pretty much anything he had read or was shown. It had been invaluable at university and he reckoned that it would serve him well at work.

As he stepped outside, he realized he and Ben couldn't have picked a better day to meet up. The sky was a brilliant blue and the blazing sun steadily climbed from the east. Though it was cool in the shade, once you stepped into the sunshine it was comfortably warm. He looked skyward and smiled as he welcomed the warm rays of the sun on his face. After a minute of quiet indulgence, he left to pick up his friend from the housing development at the edge of town where he and his mother lived.

Ben was sitting on the front steps. Nathan glanced at the time on the dashboard and winced as he realized that it was a little bit later than he'd intended.

"Hey! It's about time," Ben shouted as he jumped up from the steps. "I was beginning to wonder if you were coming."

Nathan grimaced.

"I fell asleep on the sofa again. Been doing a lot of that lately."

His friend smiled.

"The old man working you too hard?"

Nathan laughed.

"Yeah, something like that. Spent the last year waking up to no alarms and going to bed when I felt like it. Not used to all of this routine."

He held off mentioning the strange dreams troubling

his sleep at the moment. They drove into town and he found a place to park near a cafe they both liked. They were quickly seated, and ordered their coffee and breakfast.

"Have you heard from Serena at all?"

"Just a text."

They sat quietly for a moment as the waitress brought them their coffee.

"How about you?" Nathan asked, winking at his friend.

"Yeah, we talk every night. She's my new bestie."

They both laughed.

Recently, Nathan found himself thinking more and more about Serena. She'd become this strange and mysterious girl who dipped in and out of his life, who he still knew very little about. His life was full of mysterious and upsetting events since he got home. His grandfather passing, issues with his father, dead bodies, and these strange dreams he was having. Nothing seemed normal to him at the moment. But he knew one thing. The next time he saw her he was going to try to find out more about her and her family. He could at least try to solve that mystery.

"How's work going at the mill? I've only seen you once since you started. I was beginning to wonder if you'd run off again."

Nathan scowled at his friend's attempt at humor.

"Sorry. Too recent?"

"It's going well. It's exhausting, but it's mostly good,

to be honest. I don't think I ever really appreciated just how much hard work it was."

The waitress brought their food and for the remainder of breakfast they made small talk. When they finished, Nathan took care of the bill and they made their way back out onto the sidewalk, looking forward to the day ahead. They stopped in a small convenience store to pick up drinks to take with them to the beach. Driving out of town, they drove past his sister heading in the direction of town. She zipped right past without a nod, probably not yet used to seeing Nathan's car.

"Was that your sister?" Ben said.

He nodded as he looked into the rear-view mirror and watched her disappear into the distance. He knew that she'd been away the last couple of days. He hadn't seen her since they'd found out about Jess' death on Wednesday. He resisted the impulse to turn around and say hello, instead continuing to drive north out of town and out into the countryside. In short order, they turned down a dirt lane that led to a parking area running parallel to the dunes lining the beach.

He drove straight up to the wooden railing nearest the path and parked. They used to come here all the time when they were kids. Before he could drive, they would ride their bicycles out and lock them to the wooden rails before chasing one another across the beach and into the water. It was a long, popular stretch of sand running along the coastal waters of the bay. It was good to have something like this so close to home.

"I wonder if she's back in Boston."

"Who?" asked Ben.

"Serena, you idiot."

"Oh, yeah. We still on that?"

He gave his grinning friend a dirty look. He was irritated with himself for not being more proactive in staying in touch with her. He rationalized it by reminding himself how busy they both were.

"You know. There are these things called phones. You could always use one."

Ben was on one today. Nathan thought about smacking him on the shoulder, but, glancing over at his friend's newly buff body, decided it might not be such a great idea. Once they were far away from the few people who were out walking, they settled down onto the sand. As they gazed out over the water, he turned to his friend.

"How are things with you, anyways?"

"Well, grad school is great. Mom has been really good. And I'm looking forward to summer. It's been a long year and the break will be nice."

"Any plans for the summer?"

"Just to chill and spend time at the beach. A bit of work on my grad thesis. How about you?"

"No summers off for me anymore. Work. Work. More work. Hopefully we'll have weekends though. We can always hit the beach house and do a bit of sailing. Like old times."

Ben smiled and settled back onto the warming sand. He was glad to have his friend back, even if the circumstances of his return weren't the happiest. He'd gone through a lot of changes over the last year and missed having his best friend around to talk things through.

"Listen Nate. About your grandfather..." His voice trailed off.

"You don't have to say it, Ben. I know."

They sat quietly for a few moments watching the gulls glide over the water.

"I just wish I'd had the chance to see him one last time. I really miss him," Nathan said.

Their trip to the beach was meant to distract him from work and life. But at the moment he wasn't feeling all that distracted. It was as though a dark cloud had briefly passed over the sun. So many things going on in his life. And so much strangeness. And yet here he was, on the beach, on a sunny day, his childhood friend by his side. The dark clouds in his mind slowly passed, and he began to relax into the sand.

Gulls continued to screech overhead and dive low over the water. In the distance a woman and her dog walked briskly along the undulating edge of the frothy surf. Waves came and went and came again, each one washing away a fragment of the past and depositing something new. He took a deep breath, closed his eyes for a moment and exhaled slowly. The air smelled of salt and seaweed, of home and better times. He turned towards his friend, who was also staring off into the distance, lost in his own thoughts.

"So, any boyfriends?" he asked.

Ben's brown eyes widened, and he pursed his lips. "I... I... No."

Nathan smiled at his friend's sudden awkwardness.

"It's alright. You don't have to tell me if you don't want to."

Before Ben could respond, Nathan's phone beeped in his pocket. He pulled it out and checked it, covering the screen in the bright sun.

"It's Serena. She's in London and is heading back to Boston in a couple of days."

"Did she say anything about me?" Ben asked.

Nathan laughed.

"Yeah, she wants to know if that tall, dark hunk of a friend of mine is available."

Ben rolled his eyes. "You just wait and see. She won't be able to resist my charms."

"Yeah, your lucky-charms."

They both laughed.

"At least she's coming back. Maybe you'll get to see her again soon, Nate. She seems nice. You should maybe take her out for dinner or something."

"I was planning to."

Nathan smiled and noted how they'd once again managed to avoid talking about his friend's life. They'd get around to that sooner or later, when he was ready. He nestled his feet into the warm sand, eyes closed, and began to relax. After a time, he realized there was one thing he wanted to talk about.

"Can I talk to you about something?"

Ben nodded and slowly pushed himself upright and brushed the sand from the palms of his hands.

"I've been having these really strange dreams for a while now. Only they feel like more than just dreams. They feel like memories. They are so vivid, like I'm remembering them from when I was young—only I'm not young in the dreams. I'm different ages—and different people. And they aren't from my lifetime. Some of them are from my family's past, and some of them I don't understand at all."

He paused for a moment.

"None of this is making any sense."

His friend looked at him thoughtfully.

"Are you sure it's not that crazy mind of yours? Maybe they are stories that you heard or read a long time ago. And they're just circulating in your head someplace waiting to come out. You've had a hectic time since returning. It might just be a bit of anxiety or stress."

"Yeah maybe. You might be right. But the detail really stays with me. Usually, my dreams fade really quickly once I wake up. Not these though."

He described the dreams to Ben to see if he could make any sense of them.

"I don't know about the first couple, but the more recent ones are like pages out of your family history," Ben said. "I mean, I'm sure your grandfather told you stories about your ancestors, probably even those very stories. They're just in there somewhere playing out in your sleep."

Nathan nodded. He was probably right about that.

"The earlier dreams though—I've no idea. Sounds like something you might have studied or read in school. Something mythic. Sorry Nate. That's all I've got."

Nathan lay on the sand, feeling tired and confused.

"I feel like the dreams are trying to show me something. And I'm just not getting it. Maybe you're right. Maybe they are just old stories from when I was a kid or a student. It's probably nothing at all."

They sat quietly, both mulling over thoughts in their heads.

"I'm thirsty."

Nathan looked over at his friend, watching beads of sweat drip down the dark skin of his forehead.

"Me too actually. It's pretty warm right out in the sun." They'd forgotten their drinks in the car.

"Yeah, agreed. Should we head back to the car?"

"Sure. Let's make a move."

They stood up and walked slowly back along the beach until they reached the trail that led to the parking lot.

"You know, Nate, I'm sure the dreams are nothing. You've been under a lot of pressure since coming back. Enough to stress anyone out. I'm sure you'll be fine. And you can stop worrying about me too. I can see it in your eyes every time you look at me. I'm good now. Really. Okay?"

Nathan nodded.

"Okay. Let's drop it. Summer's coming and we can look forward to having some fun."

"That's the spirit."

He drove Ben back to his house and dropped him off with a promise to find more time to see him. He said that he would also start looking for ways to get out and try not to let work take up all of his time. He was beginning to feel a stronger sense of peace. Seeing his friend and being able to talk about things really helped. He had missed him so much while he was away.

※

After dropping Ben off he drove straight home, and spent a bit of time cleaning and getting laundry going. As the house was so new, and hardly lived in, it didn't take him all that long. He hopped outside and grabbed the lawn mower his parents had provided from the garage and cut the grass—anything to keep him outside for a bit. In short order, the yard was tidied, the house was back to looking presentable and he still had plenty of time left in the day.

He briefly thought about playing some video games but instead, having gotten a bit of sun while outside, decided to lie down on the sofa for a while and channel-surf. His parents had thoughtfully provided cable as well. He wasn't sure who the bill was coming to. After a while his eyes began to close, and he fell asleep.

He woke, disoriented and confused. He pushed himself upright, rubbed the sleep out of his eyes and looked around the room, which was now in shadow. It must be late afternoon now as the sun had clearly moved around to the back of the house. He reached for his phone and saw that it was a little after five. That was a good nap. He must have been really exhausted to have slept that long; he usually wasn't one for naps at all.

He thought about making something for dinner and then decided instead to head into town to grab something to eat. But first, he opted for a shower to wash away the remaining grains of sand. Afterwards he texted Ben to see if he was about.

Sorry. In Boston tonight. Some other time?

It appeared that he had a life outside of grad school and their friendship after all. Nathan smiled to himself, grabbed his wallet and keys, locked up the house and left for town. When he arrived, he parked down by the harbor and sought out a small seafood restaurant—more of a shack with some tables inside and on the dock—that did lobster rolls and lobster bisque. It had been a long time since he'd been there. He ordered a roll, a bowl of bisque and a soda and settled in. The shack was open to the harbor and he had a good view of the boats, moored to their docks, gently bobbing in the water.

Dusk was a peaceful time of day to be down by the docks and he could feel his shoulders and neck relax as he leaned forward and watched the scene in front of him. Most of the other tables were occupied and he enjoyed listening to the buzz of conversation around him. Usually in the past he would have come there with friends or sometimes his sister. It wasn't like him to go out for dinner all by himself. But since he'd come back from traveling, he noticed that he was less bothered by things like that and enjoyed having time to himself more. Sometimes he wondered if he enjoyed spending time alone a little bit too much.

The waiter brought his drink over and said his food would be along shortly. Nathan took a sip of his soda and relaxed back into the chair. He really wasn't in a hurry. His friend had been right; he needed to make sure he didn't just go right from a period of complete freedom to becoming some kind of workaholic. Balance was good, but if you didn't establish it from the start, you'd never have it. Now that his induction was over, he would try harder to enjoy some of that balance and some of the things he'd been fortunate enough to come home to.

After a few minutes his meal arrived, and he started with the bisque. It was outstanding. This was one of those things that when you were away reminded you of home—like pizza for New Yorkers, or wings for people from Buffalo. It wasn't that you couldn't get those things in other places, but they were never the same. The lobster roll was packed full of fresh lobster and crab, in a brioche bun dripping with butter. He couldn't wait to take the first bite. Being a seasoned expert in lobster rolls, he had his napkin ready for the inevitable drip of butter down his chin. He wasn't disappointed.

After finishing and paying he decided to take a walk along the docks. The local fishing boats were in for the night. Pleasure craft were tied off and bobbing next to one another. He wasn't quite ready to go home just yet. He wanted to take in this experience for a little while longer. As he turned to walk back up towards Main Street, he caught a glimpse of his family's house way up on the hill above the town. His ancestors really had chosen an ideal spot to build that house. It overlooked everything and could be seen from miles away. It was almost an embarrassment to him, and he quickly looked away, not wanting to be caught gazing at his own family home like some tourist. He wandered along until he found the ice cream parlor and went inside and ordered a soft chocolate cone. This was another thing he'd missed. He could find soft vanilla ice cream in many of the places he'd visited, but never soft chocolate for some reason.

When he arrived back at the house, he settled in for the night, reflecting on what a great day he'd had. He'd got to spend time with his best friend. He'd shied away from bringing home any work. And he'd had unscheduled, unplanned time out for dinner. He spent a couple of hours in the games room playing music, shooting pool and playing Xbox. He even made himself a couple of drinks—why not? He didn't have to work tomorrow, and he had a ten-second walk home. He made his way to bed late that evening, tired, clear-headed and satisfied.

⚜

The lights of the nightclub flashed to the deep thrum of music as Ben walked across the dance floor to the bar. When he got there, it was three rows deep with people waiting to order. He was considering giving up and trying one of the other bars when a hand grasped his shoulder. He spun around to see that he was facing a dark-haired, gray-eyed man in his early twenties.

"It's crazy, isn't it? All this for a drink."

Ben shrugged. Even through the din of the music he detected a slight accent.

"I'm Ben. You're not from around here, are you? It's always like this." He shrugged and smiled, and the young man laughed.

"No, I'm not. I'm Dragan. Do you come here a lot?"

Ben saw the smirk in his eyes and laughed.

"No. Not really. I'm busy with grad school, so not much time to come out."

"That's a shame. But you're here now."

The line moved and they edged closer to the bar. Ben ordered a whiskey and Coke and Dragan ordered a bottle of water.

"All that for a water?" Ben laughed.

"Yeah, I don't drink much to be honest. Not alcohol anyways."

His eyes narrowed and he looked around the room.

"I like being around people. And the music."

They made their way out through the throngs of people demanding to be served and found one of the quieter areas of the club to hang out.

"You are here with friends?" Dragan asked.

"No. On my own tonight. Felt like going out for a

bit. Can't stay out for long as I'll have a long taxi ride home at some point. How about you?"

Dragan shook his head.

"I too am here on my own. Visiting Boston on some family business."

"Where'd you say you're from?" Ben pressed.

Dragan smiled.

"All over really. Born in Europe. Traveled all over the world. Not sure I'm from anywhere specific anymore to be honest."

Ben nodded. His new friend was mysterious, and it intrigued him. He liked a bit of mystery.

"So, you're staying in town then?"

"Yes. We have a suite of rooms in a hotel that we own. I stay there when I'm visiting."

"Nice, it must be fun traveling a lot. A friend of mine just got back recently from traveling—Europe, Australia. I was supposed to go with him but wasn't able to in the end."

"Yeah, traveling can be fun. But a lot of what I do is for business. It's not as much pleasure as you'd think."

Dragan's eyes narrowed and he looked over towards the main entrance.

"Hey. You want to get out of here? Maybe come back to the hotel with me? I'd enjoy the company."

Ben took one last look around the room. He wasn't enjoying the club on his own in any case. He wasn't even sure why he'd decided to come down to Boston. He should have gone to dinner with Nathan.

"Yeah, sure. Sounds great."

As they left together, he wasn't sure if this was a good idea either. But he figured that he could always make an excuse and leave if he felt uncomfortable.

"Great, follow me."

They walked down the street, around the corner and into a private parking lot, where Dragan clicked a button on his key fob and the lights on a black Mercedes flashed. He opened the door for Ben.

"After you sir."

Ben grinned ear to ear and settled into the sporty red leather seat. Dragan smiled, closed the door and walked around to the driver's side. For someone so young, he was a real gentleman.

"It's not far, but I drove here from an out-of-town meeting, otherwise I would have walked."

They drove literally a couple of blocks down the street, then pulled into the underground parking entrance of a luxury hotel. Dragan held a plastic keycard up to the device at the gate and then drove through as the white metal arm swung upwards. He moved to repeat his earlier chivalry when they parked, but Ben opened the door first and stepped out. He smiled as Dragan gently closed the door behind him.

"Thanks for the offer."

Dragan laughed.

"You're welcome."

He walked over to a private elevator, swiped the same card, and pressed the button. They waited until the doors opened, then stepped inside. Ben was beginning to consider whether he'd made the right decision in coming along. After all, he'd only just met the man, and knew nothing about him—apart from the nice car, good manners and the fact his family owned the hotel. He hoped that he didn't turn out to be one of those rich psychopaths.

They took the elevator all the way up to the penthouse. The doors opened into the foyer of the large apartment. It was a vast structure of steel, glass and marble, and yet as modern as the fabric of the apartment was, it was decorated with antique furniture, oriental rugs, tapestries on the walls, and art—paintings, sculptures and ceramics. Ben looked around in amazement. The juxtaposition of modern and antique was beautiful and somehow really suited the space. Clearly, they came from money. Dragan led him into the living room, where he offered him a drink. The apartment had a full bar at one end of the large room and a fireplace at the opposite end.

"What would you like?"

"I have no idea. What would you recommend?"

"Leave it with me."

They chatted while Dragan retrieved a bottle from the bar and poured a glass. He took a small box from a cabinet, opened it and put a bunch of small biscuits onto a plate. He returned to where Ben was standing and offered him the drink and the plate.

"There you go. Try this."

Ben took the glass and the plate of biscuits and then sat down on a large, overstuffed sofa.

"This is really good. What is it?"

"It's called rakija. Try it with the biscuits. I think you'll like it."

He was right. They made a good combination.

"It's delicious. Thank you."

"It's made in the place where I was born. There is an old man who makes it the traditional way. He learned it from his father, and it goes back many generations in their family. We import it from him. It's a reminder of home."

He paused for a moment as he watched Ben take another sip from the glass and smile.

"I'm glad you like it."

They settled into the sofa. Dragan asked Ben to tell him all about himself, and before Ben knew it, it was well past midnight. Ben learned a bit more about Dragan and his family, most of whom still lived in Europe. For his part, Dragan learned practically everything about Ben, including things about his best friend, Nathan. He seemed fascinated by their friendship. He admitted that given the amount of traveling he did for his family business, he didn't have much time to make close friends.

When it got late, he offered to let Ben stay over at the apartment, but instead of showing him to a guest room, Dragan led him to his own room and closed the door. He dimmed the lights, turned and kissed Ben on the lips. Surprised at first, Ben stiffened, and then slowly leaned into the kiss. This wasn't the evening he'd expected. Usually, his nights out consisted of a few drinks, a bit of dancing and a late taxi home.

The next morning, he woke to an empty bed and sunlight streaming in through the windows. On the pillow next to him was a note.

> Apologies. Had to catch an early flight. Will be in touch with you when I'm back. Enjoyed last night. Leave your number. Stay as long as you want and pull the door closed on the way out. Dragan.

He smiled and got dressed. For no reason other than he found it a sweet gesture, he folded the note and placed it in his pocket. He found a piece of paper and a pen and scratched out a quick note, leaving his number as Dragan had requested. He pulled the door closed, took the elevator downstairs to the lobby and stepped out with a broad smile into the morning sun. He made his way to the train station and took the first train home.

Chapter 15

The carefully designed ornamental gardens were all laid out, the paths installed, and the ponds built. Dotted around the landscape were teams of builders constructing small buildings, follies representing scaled-down versions of an ancient pantheon, a castle tower, and other buildings. One of the construction teams was significantly larger than the others, and the ground they had excavated was much deeper and broader. Below ground level they had constructed a large foundation, laid out like rooms with stone walls and stone floors. It was more complex than any of the other outbuildings on the property.

The family brought the idea of follies over from their former family estate in England where their recent ancestors had constructed very similar, though not so complex, structures. They were a nod to the past, purely ornamental, and were meant to provide aesthetic value to their owners. That was the intent for most of them, in any case. But this structure was very different to the others. It had a more utilitarian purpose. As the workmen went about their duties, he stood and watched for a time, pleased with their progress. This was his own modification and as he watched it come to life, he knew that it would do nicely.

He walked through the edge of the gardens into the back yard of the impressive house that was taking shape on the hill overlooking the town below. He would use all of his abilities to ensure that this house was more secure than the previous one—the one that his enemies had burned down. They would still need to pay for that. But for the time being, he was focused on securing his family's future and safeguarding his wife and children. Keeping them safe was the most important thing he could imagine. Future generations of the Briggs family depended on it.

⁂

He lay in bed staring up at the ceiling. At least this time he'd managed to make it to his bed. He'd slept all the better for it, apart from being plagued by yet another dream from his family's past. He didn't recognize this one as a story he'd been told at any point in his life. Sure, he knew about the fire and the construction of their present home. And he'd walked those very gardens and played in those follies as a child. They'd been a source of great fun for him and his siblings. He even knew the folly in question quite well—an old stone temple with an altar in the center of a square room. But there was no basement, and no doors that led anywhere, apart from the outside door that led into the square temple room itself.

Again, like his other dreams, this felt more like a memory, as though he had experienced it and his subconscious had simply plucked it from his memories while he slept. He pondered why he was having such vivid dreams, and why—apart from some of the earlier ones—they all seemed to revolve around his family history. Not even his own personal or recent family history, but that of his ancestors. It was as if somehow, while asleep, he leapt into their heads and experienced things as they had experienced them. It made no sense.

He pushed himself up and out of bed, showered, dressed and drove to the large grocery store at the edge of town to buy ingredients for lunch with his grandmother. They would have everything that he needed. While he was there, he also took care of his weekly shopping. After half an hour he had filled the cart with everything he needed—and a few things he didn't—and drove back to the house to begin preparing lunch. He boiled water for the crab and turned on the oven. He was planning to do a lunch of summer greens with zucchini, and feta cheese and crab linguine.

When he was younger, he'd spent a great deal of time with his grandmother and mother and their cook. He'd learned his way around the kitchen at a young age, and because he was always in the company of incredible cooks, he'd managed to pick up many skills. He learned about the importance of fresh ingredients and often followed his mother or grandmother, or the cook, into the gardens to pick fresh herbs, vegetables or fruit that would later be turned into a delicious meal or dessert.

He spent the next half-hour in the kitchen preparing food and cleaning as he cooked, leaving the linguine until his grandmother arrived. In between, he managed to set the dining table. He'd grown used to less formal eating during his time away, so it was a treat to set the table for more than one person. While he worked, he listened for the sound of his grandmother's Land Rover Defender, which he assumed she would drive the short distance to his house. Still sprightly, and somewhat eccentric, she drove that car everywhere, much to his father's displeasure.

"If it's good enough for the Queen of England, it's good enough for me," she'd say.

※

A few minutes later he heard the sound of a car pull up. He got up and walked out to the front porch. Sure enough, his grandmother pulled in and parked her old weathered green Defender next to his shiny new Range Rover. He walked over to greet her and to help her get out. She was dressed in gray slacks vaguely resembling riding pants, a white top and a tweed jacket. She looked every bit the country lady.

"It's good to see you, Grandmother. You know I could have come over to the house."

He gave her a gentle hug.

"Yes, yes, I suppose you could have. But then I wouldn't have been able to get away to see your nice house and taste your excellent cooking. It is still excellent, is it not?"

She winked at him, causing him to smile. She had been a willing victim of his many cooking experiments over the years, inevitably suffering through every bad one with a great deal of patience and understanding. She'd always given him advice and tips so that he could learn and improve for the next time. She never wanted to be seen as discouraging him.

"It's alright I suppose. It's not like I've had a lot of practice in the last year, so we'll see."

He took her arm and they walked up the front steps together. She appeared frailer than he remembered, but still seemed to have that fiery spirit that defined her personality. Given all the things that she'd gone through recently, he wasn't surprised at her fragility.

"How are you doing?" he asked.

"I have good days and bad days. It's strangely quiet without him around. It's such a shame it happened when it did. He'd really have loved to see you one last time."

He winced. It wasn't the first time that he'd considered how much time he'd missed out on spending with his grandfather. He knew that she said it as a measure of his grandfather's love for him, but it struck a raw nerve just the same. He led her into the living room, where she sat down on the sofa, and asked her if she'd like a drink.

"Gin and tonic for me. They don't like me drinking

over at the house—your father thinks it's bad for me. I hope you're not going to be so cruel to your old grandmother. And in any case, one won't hurt me."

He smiled and fetched a glass from the cupboard and ice cubes from the freezer. He poured in a single shot of gin and then filled the remainder of the glass with tonic. He placed a slice of cucumber in the glass—just the way she liked it—gave it a good swirl with a spoon, grabbed himself a diet Coke, and, before returning to the living room, he turned on the stove to heat the water for the linguine. He'd already added salt and a bit of olive oil to keep it from sticking.

"Thank you dear. Now please, sit down for a moment. You look tired."

Nathan sat beside her on the sofa. His mother had commented similarly when he visited for Mother's Day. His strange dreams certainly weren't helping—they always seemed to make him feel restless and disoriented the next day. He wondered briefly if there was something wrong with him. There'd been a lot of strangeness since his grandfather's death—and a lot of death. Perhaps everything that was going on was affecting him more deeply than he'd realized. He shrugged it off for the moment though. Now wasn't the time to think about it. It was time to catch up with his grandmother.

"Really, I'm fine."

She looked at him as though she could see into his soul, in the way that a knowing grandparent can. Her look said everything—she wasn't buying it.

"How are you sleeping, dear?" she asked.

"I'm sleeping generally well."

"Really? Because it doesn't look like you're sleeping well at all."

She paused for a moment, then continued, "Are those strange dreams giving you trouble?"

He stiffened and looked intently at his grandmother. What a completely strange and random thing for her to say. And yet so to the point.

"What do you mean by strange dreams?" he asked slowly.

His grandmother let out a long breath and settled back into the sofa, clapping her hands on her thighs as though hearing his response had made up her mind about something. After a moment's pause, she spoke.

"If your grandfather were here, he'd be the one talking to you right now, as it's really his place to do so. But as he's not…"

Her voice trailed off into silence for a moment as she composed herself for what followed.

"Your grandfather started experiencing his dreams about the same age you are now. Strange dreams, about people and places, things that felt more like memories to him than dreams. He didn't know what to make of them until one day his father sat him down and told him what I'm about to tell you."

It was at this point that he remembered the linguine pan was on. He'd either have to turn it off or attend to it while she spoke. He didn't want to slow her down.

"Do you mind if I attend to lunch while you're speaking, Grandmother?"

She laughed and nodded.

"Of course, dear. It wouldn't do to have burnt lunch."

He walked over to the kitchen and stirred the linguine in the pan. He pulled a strand out, blew on it to cool it and popped it into his mouth. Still a bit tough. His grandmother got up and walked over to the dining table, sitting down with her drink so that she could continue.

"Have you ever thought about the origins of the family business?"

As far as he knew, his family had been in textiles going back centuries. First in Europe and then in America, when they moved to the colonies.

"I know we started in Europe before our ancestors moved here."

"Yes. Well. It goes back a bit further than that, you see. Your family comes from a long line of what are called weavers. Now, with respect to the textile business, that's an appropriate name and calling. But the term weaver didn't always refer to textiles. The origin is something more esoteric than that. Weaving, as it's meant in your ancestry, refers to the ability to practice, or weave, magic."

He stopped what he was doing and looked over at her as though she'd lost her mind. Magic? Was she serious? Maybe he shouldn't have given her the gin and tonic after all.

"I know what you're thinking. But you can forget it, young man. My mind's as sharp as a tack. Now, what were we talking about?"

She looked at him with a mischievous glint in her eye before they both started to laugh. He turned back to his preparations while continuing to listen. He drained the pasta in a strainer, and then poured it back into a large bowl and mixed in all the ingredients he'd prepared earlier. Once it was all ready, he placed the bowl on the table with the salad. He made up two plates for them as they both settled back into their seats at the table.

"Grandmother," he started.

"Please, let me finish."

She tried the pasta before saying anything further.

"This really is good. You haven't lost your touch at all. You got the spice just right."

He nodded and tucked into the linguine himself. She was right. It wasn't half bad.

"Now. Weavers. Your grandfather could give you all the fine detail, but for the moment a summary will have to suffice. They originated in ancient times, thousands of years ago. Your grandfather had his theories about their origins, but that would be a little too much for today. They practiced magic but not everyone in their society had the ability to do so. And not every weaver gave direct birth to a new generation of weavers. Sometimes the ability skipped a generation. As was the case with your father. The poor soul had none of the ability that your grandfather had."

He watched her closely as she paused to eat her lunch, seeming to forget she'd left him sitting there with a confused look on his face. A few moments passed while they ate in an awkward silence. Finally, she looked up again and cleared her throat to speak.

"I know that all of this all sounds implausible, like the ravings of an old woman. But what I'm telling you is the truth about your heritage and the legacy that I believe you've inherited. Surely those dreams have given you some clue—an ancient city destroyed by a great flood? That feeling of not just observing everything through the fog of a dream, but of actually being the person sitting on the hillside, present as their beloved home is destroyed?"

He put his fork down and looked at his grandmother. Their simple lunch had taken an incredibly strange twist. He looked into her eyes and they were crystal clear and as intense as he remembered them as a child. There was nothing wrong with her mind. She was telling a truth, as she knew it.

"How could you know that? I haven't spoken about my dreams with anyone."

Of course, that wasn't completely true. He'd spoken with Ben about them. But there was no way Ben could have told his grandmother. She reached across the table and placed a hand over his. He could feel the warmth and strength that surged through her hand.

"They're not dreams per se—they are memories of a sort. Your grandfather called it an epigenetic memory.

It seems that weavers are able to pass actual memories from one generation to the next—even though your father didn't demonstrate the legacy of a weaver, his genetics carried those memories, and passed them on to you. Your brain surfaces those memories through your dreams, guiding you and teaching you about your past."

He listened intently to his grandmother, trying to figure out which one of them had gone insane. Did she really believe what she was saying? He shook his head as if to make it all go away. None of it made sense. Maybe the loss of his grandfather had driven her over the edge. Or maybe he was still asleep and dreaming and none of this was real. And yet, here they both were. She knew specific things about his dreams. If they were a guess, they were a crazy, scary, accurate guess.

"I know what you're thinking—all of this sounds completely unreal. But I assure you that it is the truth. I just wish that he were here to explain all of this to you."

They sat quietly for a few moments.

"What does it all mean? What am I supposed to do with what you've told me?"

She took her bag from the other side of the table, reached inside and retrieved an envelope. She placed it on the table and slid it across to him. He glanced down at it. It was brown, paper-sized, and it had his name written on it in his grandfather's handwriting.

"Take this. It's from your grandfather. He said if anything were to happen to him to pass this along to you. I think this situation qualifies. Don't open it now. Open it later when you're alone."

He took the envelope from her and turned it over in his hands a few times. He could feel something solid in it. He placed it on the table next to his plate, deciding to heed her words and not open it right now.

"Do you know what it says? What's in it?"

"I was there when he wrote it. Of course I know. Your grandfather and I had no secrets."

No secrets. Not from one another at any rate; but they certainly seemed to have secrets they kept from the rest of the family.

"Come on dear. Let's finish this wonderful lunch. We can talk about all of this another time—after you've had time to view the contents of the envelope and to think about things."

Clearly from her perspective that portion of the conversation was over. The remainder of lunch was spent talking about his travel experiences, his grandmother's life at the house, and how much she missed his grandfather. After lunch, he asked if she'd like tea or coffee.

"No thanks dear. It's too late in the day for caffeine for me. I want to sleep tonight. I think it's time I get back to the house before they send out a search party."

He cleared the table before walking his grandmother out to her car.

"It did skip your father, you know. He never knew whether to believe your grandfather's stories or not about the Briggs family legacy. And when your grandfather suspected you might inherit those abilities; well, your father was incandescent. The tension between you and your father is not of your own making, Nathan. And it wasn't your monetary inheritance from your grandfather that caused his irritation. It's the fact that you inherited your grandfather's abilities, and your father did not. It was nobody's fault. It was simply fate."

He nodded as a piece of his life's puzzle fell into place.

"One last thing. You need to know that there are more than just weavers in this world. There are others with different abilities. Your grandfather knew some, and some were allies of a sort. Not everyone sees weavers as allies, nor the other way around. Some of them might do anything to bring the other down. You are about to enter a complicated world, Nathan, with a complex set of rules. You will need to be very careful, and very vigilant."

She put her arms out to hug him, and he bent down and returned her embrace before helping her into the car. She started the engine, rolled the window down and reached out, placing her hand on his cheek.

"You are so like your grandfather. If you need to talk, or anything, you know where to find me. Apart from your father and me, no one else in the family knows of this. Try to keep this knowledge to yourself Nathan. For your own safety, no one else must know."

Her hand slid away from his cheek and she slowly reversed and then drove away, waving as she disappeared down the lane. He stood in the stillness of the afternoon sun. It was warm and large white clouds drifted across the deep-blue sky. As he looked around, he glanced into the shadows of the woods at the edge of the property, wondering what might lie beyond his vision. His grandmother's revelations had only left him with more questions. Unless of course none of it was true. In which case they had other problems. He turned and walked back into the house, unconsciously locking the door behind him.

※

As his grandmother drove away down the lane towards home, she shook her head gently. All she could think about was that poor boy trying to make his way alone in this world, with no one to show him how to claim his potential. Life was cruel sometimes. Even so, there were some people she could reach out to for assistance. But that was a last resort. She wasn't completely sure who she could trust at the moment. A part of her worried what they might do to her grandson. He was alone and vulnerable. If he had a chance at all, it was in the inheritance that his grandfather had left him. He would have to use his own resourcefulness and learn how to use his abilities on his own. She just hoped that there was time.

※

Back inside, Nathan sat at the dining table with the envelope she had left him. He flicked at the closed flap with a finger until he'd plucked up the courage to open it. Inside was a letter and what looked like one of those access cards that you used to gain entrance to a building. He set the card aside and opened the letter, to find that it was addressed to him in his grandfather's handwriting.

Nathan,

If you're reading this letter, then I'm afraid something terrible has happened to me and I am unable to speak with you in person. Hopefully your grandmother has explained some basic things to you about our family and our heritage. I was meant to do this in person, and I'm so sorry that I'm unable to do so.

Being a weaver comes with great responsibility—and great power. Power that must never be used for ill purposes or to harm anyone, unless you are defending yourself. As weavers we have a responsibility to protect others from harm that can come in many forms. There are many more types of living beings in this world than humans. I'm afraid you'll find that fairytales have a strange grounding in fact.

I can't go into detail here. I have provided you with access to a special place—one that now belongs to you. It's not a part of our family business—it doesn't show up on any of the company books. Please see my lawyer. He will provide you with further details. You will need to use those details and the enclosed item to gain access to this place.

Be good to your father. He's a very pragmatic man. He never understood anything I told him about our heritage and always thought me slightly potty to be honest. Perhaps I am a bit. Or was. But he is a good man and takes his role in the family and the business seriously. I know you and he struggle with one another—he suspected that you would inherit the abilities of a weaver, and even if he struggled to believe in them, he was jealous of the bond that you and I had because of what I knew about you.

Go to the address the lawyer will provide to you. I'm sorry to be so mysterious about it. But it's necessary. It is imperative that you take ownership of what you find there—and I assure you that the answers that you need will be found there.

Take care of yourself Nathan and be strong. There is darkness ahead. I'm sorry I'm not there for you.

Always,
Grandfather

He retrieved the access card and turned it over in his hands. It was made of matte black brushed metal. There were no markings on it, no clues as to what it opened— or hid. He would have to save his curiosity until he could see his grandfather's lawyer. For the moment, he placed everything back in the envelope, closed it, and hid it behind some books on his bookshelf. Not very original, but he had no reason to suspect that anyone knew about it and would come looking.

He spent the remainder of the afternoon and evening going through work emails, doing some research and preparing for work the next day. The lawyer would have to wait until he had time. His grandmother's story continued to play in his head, making it difficult for him to concentrate. On the surface the whole thing seemed crazy. His grandparents were sensible people—or so he'd thought. The last thing he wanted to do was to doubt their sanity—to consider that they might have lost their minds together, creating some fantasy. But he knew them both to be exceptionally sound people with sharp minds. They were anything but fantasists. Nothing made sense to him. He continued to work while turning things over and over in his head, until tiredness finally got the better of him and he made his way up to bed and slowly drifted off to sleep.

Chapter 16

He dreamt of a dark place. The flicker of candlelight cast shadows on blackened stone walls. He was cold and surrounded by complete silence, yet somehow sensed that he was not alone. Ahead, in the blackness, red-rimmed eyes peered from the shadows. He felt danger, something deep, dark and primal. And yet through his own fear he also sensed something familiar reaching out to him, as though there were something trying to calm him in the midst of his fear. He closed his eyes and reached out to it with his senses, as though he might be able to grasp on to it and pull it close to him.

A face took shape from the shadows. It was a soft, familiar face, a face completely at odds with those eyes. As it came closer it became more defined—it was a face he knew completely, one that enthralled him, that sought to capture his heart. The young woman peered at him briefly, smiled, almost sadly, receded into the darkness and was gone. He knew this face. Serena. A deep snarl broke from the darkness, shattering the silence and dissolving the dream.

He woke with a start, struggling to catch his breath. This dream was different to the rest, darker, more of a nightmare. It wasn't a memory; it wasn't something he'd ever experienced. And yet there was something familiar about it. He could still smell the residue of the smoke from the candles in his nostrils. If his grandmother was right, this could be an ancestral dream. But how could Serena be in it? They were the same age. It didn't make any sense. He shook it off, got up, showered, dressed and went in to work.

For most of Monday his time was taken up working on research for the European project. He wanted to make a good impression on his father, so he poured himself into the work, adding some thoughts from his own travels and observations to his notes. Throughout the day, his mind kept turning to the weekend, the surreal lunch with his grandmother and the note from his grandfather. And of course, there was the dream. His head was filled with confusion about everything and, in some moments, he wondered if maybe he was the one who was starting to lose his mind. His dreams were persistent. And it wasn't as though he'd led the most normal life since returning from his travels.

At lunchtime he remembered to call his grandfather's lawyer and make an appointment to see him the next day. That was the soonest that he was available. The lawyer said he would drive up to New Comfort and meet Nathan at a local restaurant for lunch. With that task accomplished, he buried himself in his work until it was time to head home.

When he got home, he realized that he was feeling tense and anxious about the next day. He decided to change into his running gear and head out for a quick run around the neighborhood. He jogged until his legs began to cramp, forcing him to walk the full distance back to his house. As he walked, his head began to clear, and he could feel tension start to drain from his shoulders and neck.

※

The next day, he was both nervous and excited about meeting the lawyer for lunch, and even though it felt like the morning was going on and on, every time he looked at his watch only five or ten minutes had passed. He wasn't sure if he'd be able to make it to lunchtime. Eventually, he buried himself in the work he was doing and when he next checked it was half past eleven. He cleaned up his desk, closed his laptop, and walked out to his car. He waved at the security guard as he drove out through the gates and made his way towards town.

Although it was only midweek, New Comfort was busy. After finding a place to park, he made his way to the restaurant they'd chosen. He checked his watch and realized he could slow down, as he was running a bit early. When he arrived, he went inside and asked for the table reservation in the name of the lawyer. He was seated straight away, ordered a glass of water and watched as people passed by the large restaurant windows. Eventually his grandfather's lawyer appeared at the door. Nathan stood as he walked over and extended his hand.

"Mr. Eddington," he said as they shook hands.

"Hello Nathan. And please, call me Carl."

They both sat down, and the lawyer ordered a glass of water. They took a moment to review the menu and place their orders before getting down to business.

"So, how are you settling in?"

"It's fine at the moment. I'm in the middle of reviewing our European strategy for Dad."

"Ah, that's good. I know he's hatching some big plans at the moment. He's away this week, traveling, isn't he?"

"Yeah, he's always really busy. It's all good though. He loves what he does. And I'm well looked after by the management team at the mill headquarters."

Carl took a sip of water and looked around the restaurant, then opened up his briefcase and took a manila envelope from it. He set it on the table between them.

"I think this is what you are looking for. Your grandfather left it with me some time ago to give to you at the right moment. I'm guessing this is that moment."

Nathan put his hand on the envelope and slid it across to his side of the table. He started to peel back the sealed flap.

"No, don't open it here. Wait until you are alone. Your grandfather was very specific that this information was for you and you alone."

Nathan pressed the flap back down and slid the envelope to one side.

"Mr. Eddington. Carl. How well did you know my grandfather?"

The lawyer sat back in his chair, contemplating his response before speaking.

"Well, I think I knew him quite well. We did a lot of business together over the years."

"Was there anything about my grandfather that you think that I should know about?"

Carl sat quiet for a moment.

"In what way?"

"In any way. I mean, are there things about his life that you are aware of that you think I should know?"

"Your grandfather was a hugely successful businessman. He was also very lucky. He had a knack for investing, playing the markets. He understood the real estate market implicitly and he had a deep understanding of the textile business. There's no question that he was a weaver through and through."

Nathan froze at the word "weaver". He started to question it, but their food arrived. They ate, and chatted between bites. Carl was keen to understand how he intended to proceed once he inherited his shareholding. As a partner in the same firm as Arthur Johnstone, he was clearly knowledgeable about Nathan's inheritance. Nathan explained that he hadn't given it any thought since they'd initially discussed it and was trying to focus on learning about the business first. And in any case, from his perspective his father was running the company, and by all accounts was doing a great job. Carl nodded as he spoke. When they finished their meals, he tried to question Carl's use of the word weaver, but before he could do so the lawyer summoned the waiter over, paid the bill and pushed himself up from his chair.

"I hate to eat and run, but I'm afraid I need to get back to Boston for a meeting with another client. I'm sure we'll find time to catch up again soon. Come to Boston sometime and we'll go out for dinner."

Nathan stood and shook his proffered hand before the lawyer turned and hurriedly left the restaurant, leaving him standing at the table wondering about his cryptic comment. Carl clearly hadn't wanted to discuss it any further, and had looked as though he thought he might have already said too much.

On the drive back to the office, all Nathan could think about was the envelope sitting on the passenger seat. As he parked, he thought about opening it before he went inside, but thought better of it, locked it in the glove compartment and went into the office to finish work.

If he'd thought the morning dragged on, the afternoon seemed to last ten times longer. Several times he considered going out to the parking lot and retrieving the envelope, but each time thought better of it and returned to the task at hand. When it finally struck five Nathan grabbed his things and made a hasty retreat. On the drive home all he could think about was what the envelope might contain. He already had the strange metal entry card—a card that unlocked something unknown and mysterious. What else could there be to come, apart from the location of the place that he was meant to use the card?

When he got home, he quickly parked, removed the envelope from the glove compartment, and went into the house. He set the envelope on the dining table and sat down nervously in front of it. He flicked a fingernail against the loose corner of the flap and, with a great amount of reserve slowly peeled it back. When it was open, he slid the contents out onto the table. A long, dark, etched metal object, a standard white envelope, and a small leather notebook lay on the table in front of him. He picked up the metal object first and turned it around in his hand. It was about four inches long. It had a base like a standard key, but the shaft was triangular in shape. There were fine dots etched in the length of the metal shaft, as though something—perhaps a laser—had etched the metal. It looked like an unusual kind of door key—or a key to a safety deposit box, perhaps? He couldn't figure out what it opened from looking at it.

He picked up the notebook. Inside there were sketches and notes in his grandfather's handwriting. There were symbols he didn't recognize and drawings that looked somehow familiar to him, but which he couldn't quite place. He put the notebook on the table next to the key and picked up the envelope. It wasn't sealed and as he opened it, he could see there were two sheets of paper inside. The first sheet contained the address of a building on the outskirts of town. The second held a small hand-drawn map.

As he looked more closely at the map, he recognized it as a drawing of his parents' property. There were several locations marked, including the main house. There was an "x" with a circle around it over a location in the rear of the house at the edge of the forest in the main gardens. He was puzzled for a moment, but then he grabbed the small notebook and opened it to a page containing a familiar-looking drawing. Suddenly it occurred to him why some of the sketches in the notebook seemed familiar. This was a sketch of one of the old follies built by one of his ancestors on the property. The notebook had a sketch of the folly itself, with annotations that drew his attention to the altar in the center of the folly's single room.

He placed everything back in the envelope and hid it on the bookshelf behind some dull-looking old encyclopedias, where he'd also placed the envelope his grandmother had given him at the weekend. He needed time to think. As he paced the room, he recalled the dream about the construction of the gardens, and the larger works concerning that very same folly. All he had were questions—and there was no one he could turn to for the answers. Everyone and everything around him, his grandmother, the lawyer, his dreams, held fragments of a story, but only his grandfather could have explained it all. He missed him more than ever at that moment.

※

The next morning on his drive to work, a light rain began to fall. He figured that it was a good thing he'd decided to go for his run earlier, even if it was supposed to clear up in the afternoon. He passed through the main gates in short order, pulled into his space and parked. He ran the short distance to the entrance to avoid getting too wet.

He'd start to assemble the research that he'd been doing for his father into a presentation. He wanted it to be ready for when he returned from his business trip. It was slowly coming together, and he found that he was enjoying it. There were so many things still to learn, but he was happy that he could contribute something to their efforts in his own small way.

Late morning, deep into his work, his phone buzzed. He picked it up and was surprised to see a text from Serena. She wanted to know how he was doing. He texted back that he was fine and was working. She asked if he wanted to meet her in Boston after he finished for the day. He thought about it for a moment. He hadn't seen or heard from her in a while but the idea of seeing her felt nice and he thought maybe he could use a break from everything, if only for one evening. He would have to put off his exploration of his grandfather's notebook and a visit to the mysterious address, but he figured he'd have plenty of time to get back to it. He told Serena that he was free, and they quickly settled on a location and a time.

He returned to his work with a smile and a renewed enthusiasm. He spent the rest of the day in meetings and working on the research, and before he knew it the day was over. He packed up his things and joined the queue of people exiting the building for the day.

On the drive to Boston, he thought about his strange on-again off-again friendship with Serena. He liked her, but she was so elusive and difficult to pin down. He supposed it was because of her responsibilities with her family's business—something he was becoming all too aware of with his own situation. The traffic going into the city was heavy but moved steadily for a Wednesday evening—northbound traffic was far worse. Fortunately, he would avoid that later on the drive home.

When he arrived, he drove to a parking garage near their meeting place and parked. The rain had stopped in the afternoon as predicted and the sun had now been out for most of the day. He walked a couple of streets over until he reached the cafe they'd chosen. He checked his phone to be sure that he wasn't too early and was relieved to see that he was nearly right on time. As he arrived, he looked through the cafe window and saw

Serena sitting alone at a corner table. He took a deep breath to compose himself and walked inside.

"Hello," she said without looking up.

She must have seen him approaching. He smiled and took the seat opposite.

"How have you been? Where have you been?"

She smiled at him.

"Always with the questions."

They both laughed.

"I ended up having to take care of a few more things than I'd expected. Sorry. My father's like that. A very intense man. But then I don't have to explain fathers to you."

He winced.

"No, I guess you don't. It's good to see you."

"That's better."

The waitress appeared, ready to take their order.

"Serena?"

"I'm okay actually. I had a late lunch. But please, you go ahead."

"I'll have a white americano and a toasted ham and cheese sandwich."

The waitress smiled and disappeared as quickly as she'd arrived.

"How's the family business?"

"It's good. It's intense and fun and challenging all in one go. I have a better sense now of what my family does on a daily basis. As much as I hate to admit it, it puts my father into perspective."

"That's good. Your whole life hasn't ended then?"

He laughed.

"No, I still seem to be alive."

The waitress arrived with his americano and a small pot of steamed milk. He poured the milk into the coffee and stirred it.

"How about you? Things going well with you and your family?"

She nodded.

"Yeah, the usual stuff. Always some deal being made or problem to solve. My father tends to hold the fort with my brothers, so I usually have a bit more freedom than they do."

Nathan sipped his coffee and looked around the cafe. It seemed unusually quiet for the middle of the week. He supposed everyone must have other things to do with their time. Not that he'd know, since he'd become a bit of a hermit, shuttling between home and work on a daily basis.

"How are you and the family coping with things?"

He winced.

"My grandfather, you mean?"

"Yes, is everyone okay?"

"We all seem to be getting by. No one really talks about it. They still haven't found any wreckage from the plane. I guess he must have gone down in the ocean. We'll probably never know."

He glanced away briefly.

"I'm really sorry to hear that. He was a good man."

He looked up.

"What?"

"I'm sorry I didn't mention it before. My father knew him. I think they had some common business interests from time to time. I met him a few times. He seemed like a really nice guy."

Nathan was shaken. How had this never come up before? How was it that this random girl he'd met in Croatia, who kept turning up at the strangest moments, turned out to know his grandfather?

"I don't understand. Why didn't you ever mention this before?"

"Well, I hadn't put it all together before a few days ago that he was your grandfather. While I was away my father mentioned that he'd lost a friend in a plane accident. I eventually put two and two together and realized the man he was talking about was your grandfather."

Nathan settled back into his chair. Both their families had business interests in Boston, and both were wealthy. It probably wasn't that surprising that they might have met, or even done business together. Still, the admission had put him on the back foot. And given the conversation he'd had with his grandmother, the letter, keys, journal and everything, he couldn't help wondering what else Serena knew. More fragments. More pieces of the puzzle. He wasn't willing to risk opening up that can of worms. If she didn't know anything related to what his grandmother had divulged to him, he'd have to open up about something that he still knew very little about—or avoid the subject altogether. And of course, there was his grandmother's warning not to speak about it with anyone.

"Fair enough. Sorry, I didn't mean to appear rude."

"No Nathan, I understand. It was awkward for me too. Just such an odd coincidence really."

The waitress brought his sandwich over and he ate while Serena sat for a few moments in silence, seemingly lost in thoughts of her own. After a time, they moved the conversation to safer ground, talking about what they'd each been up to. He omitted details about dead co-workers and focused on what he was learning at the company and things that he was working on, and she talked a bit about what she'd been doing the last few weeks. After an hour or so had passed, she checked her watch and reached down for her bag.

"It's been really good seeing you. Unfortunately, I have to see my family to prep for a meeting that we have tomorrow. I really wish I could stay longer."

"Me too," said Nathan. "Don't worry. I have the drive home and I have work in the morning too. It was really good to see you, Serena. It'd be nice to see you again soon—if you can find some time."

He paid for his meal and walked her outside into the gas-lamp-lit street.

"I'd like to see you again soon too," she said.

They stood awkwardly for a moment, then Serena leaned in and kissed him on the cheek.

"I'm sorry, I really do have to run. But I'll be in touch. Have a safe drive home."

She turned and walked in the opposite direction from where he'd parked his car. He watched her until she disappeared into the distance.

On the drive home two confusing thoughts ran through his head. The first was that Serena and her father knew his grandfather. At the very least they'd done business together. There was no telling what else Serena's family might know. What if her father knew something about the strange things that his grandmother had told him? That was too much to comprehend. The second thought was about the ice-cold feeling of Serena's lips on his cheek. It wasn't that cold outside, but her lips had felt like ice against his skin. He vaguely remembered having those same thoughts when they'd met in Croatia, even though it had been warm weather there too. It was odd. Still, he smiled to himself at the thought that she'd given him a kiss.

His drive home went by quickly. The traffic had eased and in no time, he found himself making the turn into his driveway. He parked in front of the garage and locked the car. The sky was clear and filled with stars. The vast ocean of them made him feel very small as he stood alone in the darkness. The temperature had dropped since he'd left Boston. He shuddered, rubbed his goosebump-covered arms, and went into the house. He was exhausted from the long day. Two more days until the weekend. He looked forward to it, and to what he might find.

※

Outside, a car slowly pulled up on the lane near the end of his driveway. The driver sat in the car with the lights out and watched as Nathan walked through the front door. He wasn't sure what he hoped to get out of his surveillance, but he was on a mission, and anything might give him another piece of the puzzle he was trying to solve. He sat until the downstairs lights went out and an upstairs light came on. After about ten minutes that light was extinguished, and the house sat in complete darkness. After a bit, he started the engine and slowly drove off into the distance.

Chapter 17

He was surrounded by complete and utter darkness. Cold, damp air clutched at his skin and clothes. His body ached and he fought the beginnings of a terrible dread. And yet someplace deep inside he felt something else, something hopeful. He reached out towards that feeling with his mind, an invisible tendril reaching out from deep inside himself. He could almost feel it, something he would never be able to grasp with an outstretched hand, something that only his mind could touch.

Out of the darkness, a light spluttered and then sprang to attention. Dark shapes took on definition as his eyes adjusted to the sudden flickering light. Candles in twisted iron holders lit the slick hewn-stone walls of a room. Able to see more clearly now, he saw that he stood in the middle of a circular room with corridors going off in different directions. In the center of the room stood a solitary round stone table with books on it, encircled by chairs.

As his vision slowly cleared, he felt warmth and strength flow into his body. Something tugged at the corners of his consciousness. There was something he needed to remember but he couldn't quite grasp onto it—a thought? A memory? Something that was going to happen—or something that had happened? He shook his head gently to try to clear away the cobwebs, but whatever it was—thought, memory—it remained elusive. And then suddenly it was gone

※

He had never felt privileged, even though he knew the reality of his situation growing up. He never thought differently of anyone based on their background. People were people, and he had been friends with all kinds over the years. It was his experience that it was often others who kept him at a distance or treated him differently because of his family. That was one of the things he loved most about traveling. No one knew who he was, and he could be a normal young guy seeing the world on his own and being who he wanted to be. The anonymity had provided him with a great experience.

Work was different. Everything about it reminded him about who he was and what family he belonged to. There was no escaping it. He managed to get through a full day of meetings, doing very little of his own work. He guessed this was the way of it sometimes—and the reason so many people, including his father, worked such long hours. When he'd finished, he drove home, and spent some time thumbing through his grandfather's journal trying to decipher the scrawled handwriting and sketches. He'd figured out that the key belonged to a hidden lock on an altar inside the folly at his parents' house. The keycard must be for the other building at the edge of town. He needed to make time to visit them as soon as possible.

He wasn't sure why he felt so reticent—why not just hop in the car and check out the building and the folly? Part of him wanted his grandmother to be wrong, the letter not to be real and all of this just to go away. Stepping onto that path felt like it might lead to a level of craziness that he wasn't ready to accept. If it wasn't real, then what the hell was it all about? He watched television until ten that evening and then decided it was time to turn in.

He woke to dark gray skies, rain and the distant rumble of thunder. Occasional flashes of lightning lit up his bedroom like the flash from a camera. He looked at his alarm clock and realized that the weather outside must have woken him earlier than usual. He switched it off and lay in bed for a few minutes listening, before eventually crawling out of bed to shower. Downstairs he had a couple of chocolate pop-tarts and a banana. Not the healthiest option, but it was Friday and the weather outside was crappy, so he thought, why not?

He stood on the porch for a few moments, inhaling deeply—the air always smelled so fresh when it rained.

Overhead, the sky was a jumble of light and dark gray punctuated by flashes and streaks of lightning. *It was going to be a great day,* he thought with a hint of sarcasm. He wrestled his car keys out of his pocket and pressed the unlock button from the porch. As the lights flashed and the side mirrors swiveled into position, he decided to make a run for it, knowing that he wasn't going to avoid getting wet. It hadn't occurred to him to grab an umbrella.

By the time he drove through the front gate at the mill the wind had picked up and the rain was lashing down sideways. As he opened the car door there was resistance from the wind, and he had to push back against it. He made a mad dash to the door. With his bag flung over a shoulder, he burst through the front entrance. He walked into reception, nodded to the receptionist, who looked at him quizzically, and headed straight for the guest bathroom in the lobby. He quickly toweled himself dry and fixed his hair. He made his way upstairs to his corner table in the open-plan space next to a large window, where he quickly sat down and placed his bag on the table in front of him.

The offices still had the patina of an old mill—they had converted the front third of the building to create the mill headquarters, and the rest was still an active manufacturing space, filled with modern equipment. There were wide wooden floorboards, brick walls, and large windows that let floods of sunlight into the space—though not today. Today they kept everyone sheltered from the rain and wind lashing the other side. He sat briefly at his desk, took out his laptop and checked his emails. Afterwards, he went to a small kitchen area to make a cup of coffee. He really felt the need for it this morning. He was chilled from the commute in and his clothes were damp.

Around mid-morning, he received a text from Serena.

It was great to see you the other night. Sorry I had to run. You know how it is. Look forward to seeing you again soon. Sx

He smiled and texted back that it was alright, and that he was looking forward to seeing her again too. He touched his cheek briefly, remembering the kiss—that ice-cold kiss.

At lunchtime, he decided to get lunch in the cafeteria where most of the mill employees ate. He had no desire to go back outside into the rain and wind. He was still slightly damp from his experience in the morning. While standing in line, he overheard a conversation between several of the mill workers.

"You heard about that too?"

"Yeah, happened last night according to the news."

"Can't believe it. I mean, this area is pretty safe and quiet. Who would kill that kid?"

"I don't know. But my cousin is with the state police. He said they didn't think the kid was killed where they found him. There was a lot of blood missing around the body, and they reckon that he must have been killed someplace else."

"That's not right. Just a kid! I hope they catch whoever did it."

When Nathan's turn came, he ordered a salad and some fries. He wasn't sure that he could stomach anything else. He somberly took his lunch back to his desk and ate while he worked. He could hear occasional snippets of conversations as people passed, commenting on that kid's brutal death. Apparently, his body had been found quite close to the mill boundary. There was a housing development that ran along the east side of the property and kids often played along the border between the development and the mill. He shook his head. Another body. More blood. Apart from proximity to the mill, he couldn't claim any association with what had happened. He was relieved about that, at least.

He continued working until mid-afternoon, when he received a phone call from reception that there was somebody waiting for him. He wasn't expecting anyone. He hadn't really done anything work-wise to expect visitors this early in his time here. He locked his laptop, got up and walked down to reception. The only person there—other than the receptionist—was a middle-aged man in a beige raincoat. His balding head was damp from the rain. He carried a leather bag with him. Nathan didn't recognize him and had no clue as to why this gentleman—if it was him—wanted to see him. As he approached the bottom of the stairs, the man looked over as though he recognized him.

"Mister Briggs," he said before the receptionist could introduce them.

"I'm Nathan Briggs. Are you sure you're not looking for my father?"

"No, I'm definitely looking for you."

The man produced a hand from his pocket, but not to shake Nathan's hand. It held a leather cardholder, which he opened to show federal identification.

"My name is Mark Ellison. I work with a government crime task force. Is there someplace we can talk?"

Nathan took a step back. What would a federal agent want with him?

"Mister Briggs. You can use conference room one."

The receptionist had very kindly put them in a conference room on the ground floor around the corner. It was out of the way from the rest of the office, so they would have some privacy.

"Right, thanks. Well, Mister Ellison, please come this way."

Nathan nodded his thanks to the receptionist and motioned for the man to follow him. He shut the door behind them, and they both sat down at the long conference table. They wouldn't be interrupted. He was sure that the receptionist would see to that.

"What can I do for you, Mister Ellison?"

The man hung his coat over the back of the chair beside him and placed his leather bag on the seat.

"I'd like to ask you about the gentleman you found on the beach on the Cape. And also discuss the death of your lead designer, Jess Evans."

Nathan suddenly felt sick in the pit of his stomach. He'd hoped all of that business was over. It had been a little over four weeks. He hadn't heard anything further from the police, and it wasn't something that he wanted to discuss or think about again.

"Mister Ellison, there isn't much more I can tell you. I've already given a report to the police. And as for Jess, I didn't really know him all that well. Whatever happened did so at his home, outside of work time. My only involvement was to organize a collection for his family from the company."

His statement hung heavy in the air for a moment before Ellison spoke again.

"Were you aware that there was another death close by the mill last night? Did you know that, Mister Briggs?"

Nathan sat still, perplexed by the direction this conversation was going.

"Mister Ellison, I heard about that for the first time today at lunchtime. I'm afraid that I don't really know anything about that either, other than what other people were saying. Just what is it you are trying to get at here?"

"I'm sorry. Let's start over, Mister Briggs. I'm not trying to upset you and I do apologize if I have."

Ellison switched gears, taking a different tack now.

Whether he'd unintentionally upset Nathan or done so on purpose wasn't clear.

"The reason I'm here is that there are some similarities between these cases, and some previous cases I've investigated. I would be remiss not to speak with the person who found the victim on the Cape. And as your lead designer was affiliated with your family's company—and you work here too—it seemed like the prudent thing to speak with you."

Nathan settled back into his chair and waited for the conversation to continue.

"So, with that in mind, can you describe the circumstances of finding the victim on the beach? Please take your time and provide as much detail for me as you can."

Nathan took a deep breath, closed his eyes for a moment to recall the evening, and then began to tell his story. Ellison interrupted a few times with questions and to get him to focus on specific details. He scribbled notes in a notebook as Nathan spoke. When he finally finished, he waited for Ellison to stop writing his notes.

"Now, with respect to Mister Evans. Can you tell me everything you can—from your perspective—about what happened?"

Nathan briefly recounted what he'd heard and what the local police had said. That was all he knew. Again, Ellison interrupted a few times with questions, before finally finishing.

"Is that all, Mister Ellison? You mentioned the person killed near the mill. I'm afraid I can't help you with that one. I left work and went straight home last night. I stayed in for the night, watched some television, made some dinner, read a bit. It was a quiet night."

"Yes of course. I'm quite sure you did."

Ellison put his pen and notebook back into his bag and pulled out a business card. It was plain apart from his name and a phone number. He slid it across the table.

"Should you remember anything else, Mister Briggs, please call that number."

Ellison stood, put his coat back on and hefted his bag. The interview was clearly over. As Nathan walked him out to reception a final question occurred to him.

"Mister Ellison. You mentioned that these deaths all had something in common with one another—and with previous deaths you've investigated. Could you tell me what that is?"

"I'm afraid not. There are certain details we prefer to keep out of the public eye."

Nathan supposed that made a kind of sense.

"I have one last question for you Mister Briggs, if I may."

Nathan nodded.

"Have you met anyone new since your time on the Cape? Anyone strange or unusual who might have a connection?"

Serena. Nathan hesitated for a second and then shook his head.

"No, not that I can think of. The Cape was pretty

empty and since I've been back home, I've been too busy with work to meet anyone."

Ellison squinted his eyes briefly and nodded.

"Okay, Mister Briggs. Thank you for your time. And remember to call me if you can think of anything else. Especially should you recall meeting any new people."

Ellison left that comment hanging in the air as he turned and walked out. Feeling shaky, Nathan thanked the receptionist for calling him down and for her discretion, and went back upstairs to his desk.

He sat down at his desk and collected his thoughts. After he calmed down from the conversation, he texted Ben to see if he was free later. His friend quickly got back to say that he didn't have any plans. They agreed to meet for dinner, deciding on a small Italian restaurant in town. Nathan didn't feel like sitting alone in the house that evening, and after Ellison's visit he needed someone to speak to.

As the day dragged to a close, he decided to leave a bit early. The stormy weather had passed and overhead the sky was now a mix of departing clouds and blue patches. He drove back to the house for a quick shower, wanting to change out of the morning's rain-soaked clothes. He had some time to kill before he needed to meet Ben, so he reflected on the afternoon's encounter. Having to relive the beach house experience was difficult. He'd encountered so much death since his return—his grandfather, the man on the beach, Jess. And now another body found near the mill. Death seemed as though it was following him around like a shadow. It was unsettling.

As he thought about the meeting, he couldn't shake Ellison's last question. The only person who had entered his life of any substance was Serena. She'd been both on the Cape and in New Comfort. Why hadn't he mentioned her to Ellison? He didn't need to think about it too deeply. He knew why. It was because she couldn't possibly have anything to do with any of it. That would be ridiculous.

There was something more to all of these deaths than he understood. Ellison saw a connection between them—he had mentioned that there was something they all had in common. Why would he mention this if he wasn't willing to elaborate any further? Was he baiting him? Did Ellison somehow think that he was involved? Nathan clearly had more questions than answers. As the time for meeting Ben grew closer, he hopped into his car and drove into town. The restaurant had a small parking lot in the rear, and he drove around back and pulled into an empty spot.

He locked up and ran around to the front of the restaurant, where he ran into Ben, who was waiting near the front door.

"Hey!"

"Hey Nate. How are you?"

He shrugged and nodded towards the restaurant.

They entered together and were seated at a table near the window.

"How's work going?"

"It's fine. I've been busy working on a report for Dad. He's been away this week, so other than meetings and the report, work has been quiet."

His friend nodded as he looked at him over the top of the menu.

"What's bugging you?"

"Is it that obvious?"

"Yeah, you seem really agitated."

Nathan composed himself before starting. He hadn't seen Ben since last Saturday—before he'd had lunch with his grandmother, had lunch with his grandfather's lawyer, before seeing Serena and before the unsettling visit from Ellison. How had so many things happened in only a week?

"Well..." he began.

For the next twenty minutes he filled Ben in on a week's worth of events, only stopping long enough for them to order food.

"Nate, I hate to say this, but are you sure your grandmother is all there?"

Nathan shrugged.

"Look, she had the letter and the metal keycard, and the lawyer had the other details. If anyone is crazy it was my grandfather, sending me on some wild goose chase. And all this crap about our family history. I mean. It's insane, right?"

Ben looked at his friend and shook his head.

"I don't know what to believe. Your family is an old family here. They've always been wealthy and successful. Who knows where all of that came from originally? You know the only way to figure all of this out is to go to the folly on your parents' estate and that building at the address the lawyer gave you and see if there is anything there that would help. Maybe you'll find nothing—empty buildings. Maybe it's just some strange game your grandfather concocted to test you or something. I really don't know. But what I will say is that your grandparents always seemed quite solid—not the kind of people who would play those kinds of games."

The waiter interrupted with their food and they quietly set about eating.

"Did you say that you met Serena?"

Nathan looked up to find his friend smirking at him.

"Yeah. It was good to see her. It's frustrating. I'd like to spend more time with her, but she's always so busy that it's impossible. I feel like she's always slotting me in between other things. I really hope that's not how my own life is going to be. I can't imagine living that way for the rest of my life."

His friend nodded and gave him a warm smile. Nathan was a good guy and had always struggled with the idea that one day he might be locked away in the business and never be able to get out. Being trapped by his family's legacy had always been one of his greatest fears.

"I'm sure it won't be. It'll be whatever you decide you want it to be."

That was the most he could offer for the moment. He knew that his friend had deep-seated doubts and there wasn't anything he could say to convince him otherwise.

"And this other business?"

Nathan just shook his head.

"Yeah, and then there's that."

"It's crazy stuff Nate. I know it must all feel related somehow, but you can't really think about it that way. Look, shit just happens. That's it. This guy is obviously on some mission, and you're on his list of people to check out. We both know that there's nothing more to it than that."

"I hope so. I mean, it does seem odd though, right? How can I go my entire life without anything like this happening, and then suddenly I come back to be with my family and all hell breaks loose?"

He kept Ellison's final question to himself. He didn't want his friend's mind to wander down that path.

"Anyways, that's my week. How's yours?"

They both looked up from their food and laughed.

"Well, the week was fine," Ben said. "But after we hung out last Saturday I caught up on some things in the afternoon and then went out to a club in Boston in the evening. I just felt the need to get out for a bit."

Nathan understood that feeling. He could probably do with a night out himself.

"And?"

"Well, I did meet this guy. He was kind of cool. We had a really great time out and then I... well... I kind of stayed over at his place. I ended up getting the train back Sunday morning."

He blushed and looked away. He still wasn't used to having this conversation with Nathan. Things had really changed after he had left. But they were close friends, and he was sure the awkwardness would soon pass. For his part, Nathan still wasn't used to seeing this side of Ben. Before going away, his friend had been kind of introverted and geeky. He was nothing like that now. Now he was more outgoing, happier. He'd bulked up. He wasn't the quiet, lanky kid who stayed behind. On the whole he was really happy for his friend.

"So, what's next? Have you spoken with him or seen him again?"

"We texted a couple of times over the week but he's really busy with work. Sound familiar?"

They both laughed. Nathan could relate.

"Good luck with that."

Ben rolled his eyes.

"Yeah, I know, right?"

The waiter came over to collect their plates. They decided not to get any dessert and asked for the bill.

"When are you going to go check things out? At the folly and that building, I mean?"

Now that the weekend had arrived Nathan figured it was probably time to do some digging.

"I'll have to make an excuse to visit the parents to

check out the folly. I can hit the other building anytime over the weekend."

"You are going to do it though, right?"

"Yeah, I don't think I have a choice really. I've got to know one way or the other what's going on. Maybe I'll find some answers. Or maybe there won't be anything, in which case I've got nothing more to think about. But I can't shake the feeling there is a lot more to this. These dreams I've been having are more vivid and feel so real. And my grandmother knew exactly what I was experiencing even though I'd never once mentioned it to her."

They paid the bill and walked outside.

"Do you need a ride home?" Nathan asked.

"No, I'm going to stay in town for a bit. I have a few things I need to do."

"Alright. I think I'm going to head home then. It's been a long week and I just want to collapse for a bit. Thanks for listening."

"No worries Nate. Listen, if you need anything. If you want me to come with you to check things out, just let me know. You know I'm here for you, right?"

Nathan smiled at his old friend.

"I know buddy. I'll let you know. I just need to sort things out in my head. But you'll be the first person I talk to about it—whether I find anything or not."

Ben nodded and they said their goodbyes. Nathan retrieved his car and drove home for the night, happy that he'd seen his friend and that he'd taken the opportunity to talk things through with someone. The rest was now up to him.

✧

As he walked into the house his phone buzzed. It was a text from his father asking him to come around the house the next morning. As he wasn't that into texting, Nathan wondered what was going on. At least it gave him an excuse to visit the house. He texted his father back to say that he would be there. He switched off the downstairs lights and for a brief moment thought he saw a flicker of light outside on the lane. But as he looked into the darkness, he couldn't see anything. Before going upstairs, he checked the envelopes on the bookcase behind the books and was satisfied that they were still there. He figured that tomorrow he might want to find a more secure place to hide them. He climbed into bed, pulled the covers up, and within a few moments was sound asleep, the stress of the day—and week—slowly drifting from his mind.

✧

Sat in his car, parked on the dark lane, Mark Ellison watched the lights switch off. For a brief moment he was sure that he could see a face outlined in one of the downstairs windows. A few moments later the upstairs lit up, then after a few moments also went dark. Everything was quiet and still. Another dull night. Still, he sat for another half an hour to reassure himself that there was nothing more to see, and then started his engine and slowly drove away down the dark lane. He would continue to watch Nathan until he found the answers he was looking for—he was sure this kid was the key.

Chapter 18

Nathan woke early on Saturday to a beautiful late May morning. It was early, so he decided to go for a quick run to start the day. He locked the house, stretched for a few minutes on the front lawn, and then set out at a slow and steady pace. Spending time with Ben the previous evening had been fun and had given him a chance to talk about everything that was going on. He could feel the stress draining away from his body and continued his run with looser shoulders and a clearer head. When he returned home, he made a cup of coffee before putting on some laundry, showering and getting dressed. He felt a little anxious about why his father wanted to see him; he wasn't the most sociable person at the best of times.

He retrieved one of the envelopes from behind the books and took out the strangely shaped key from inside, putting it into his pocket for later. He left the notebook, letter and keycard. If he had time, he would stop back at the house later and retrieve them for a drive over to this mysterious building that it seemed he now owned. He wondered how his father's business trip had gone. Hopefully well. He was usually in a better mood when things went well.

Here's hoping, thought Nathan as he got behind the wheel of his car. While the early morning air was still cool, he could feel signs of it starting to warm up. As he drove, he opened his window to feel the fresh air. He turned the radio on, finding a station that he liked, and listened to music for the short drive to his parents' house. He could feel a small knot forming in the pit of his stomach as he drew closer.

∽⋏∾

When he pulled up to the house, his mother and grandmother were outside tending the rose bushes that grew alongside the driveway, chatting away as they worked. Even though they had a gardener they liked to spend time outside tending to the plants. They found it relaxing and something that they could do together. For his mother it was a break from the weekly routine of working with her clients and running her own business. He walked over and gave them each a hug and a kiss.

"How are you both this morning?"

"We're good. We decided to get up early and enjoy a bit of morning sun and fresh air in the garden," his mother answered.

He laughed as he watched the two of them with their small pile of clippings gathering on the yard. They made quite a pair. There was none of the stereotypical bad blood between this mother and daughter-in-law. They'd liked one another from the beginning and had become hard fast friends over the years.

"Your father is inside. We thought we'd give you two a bit of privacy," said his grandmother.

"Ah. Yes. How is he?"

"He's good. He had a successful business trip and seems to be in good spirits."

His mother was ever optimistic.

"Fair enough. Well, I guess I'd better not keep him waiting."

"He's just finishing up a call. Wait in the sitting room and he'll come and get you when he's ready."

His mother returned to tending roses as he walked into the house. He took a seat on one of the large sofas. On the table in front of him was a fresh pot of tea and a plate of biscuits. The housekeeper must have seen him pull up. He poured himself a cup of tea and added some milk from a small jug. He held his cup between both hands and gently blew across the steaming surface to cool it before daring to take a sip.

There was a fire in the fireplace, taking the edge off the remaining chill from the cool late spring morning. He leaned back and gazed at the walls covered in paintings of his ancestors. He could name each and every one of them, having learned all of their names as a child. Paintings of his father and grandfather hung on the wall at the end of the room nearest the door to the hallway. He'd been assured as a child that if he was good, one day there might be a painting of him on the wall. He doubted it as his brother was the oldest. And in any case, it had always felt like an antiquated ritual to him—and more so since his travels. He felt less like he was sitting in his own family home and more like he was visiting a European portrait museum or the home of an old aristocratic European family. After finishing his tea, he warmed his hands by the fire and was just about to sit back down when his father strode into the room.

"Nathan," his voice boomed across the room. "Come along. Let's go sit in my study."

He followed his father into the study, where they once again faced one another across the large desk. He'd had mixed experiences sitting in that study and he momentarily experienced that fight or flight feeling you get when trapped in a place that you can't easily escape.

"How are things going for you at the office?"

Nathan shifted uneasily in his chair, wondering if this were a trap.

"I think they're good. I feel like I'm learning a lot. Everyone on the team has been really helpful. There's still a great deal to learn, of course."

His father smiled broadly.

"I must admit, I didn't think you'd take to it. But by all accounts you seem to be engaged and picking things up quickly. I've read the draft of your report, and apart from a few things I might have put differently, the work is solid."

He sank a little deeper in the chair, waiting for the slap.

"Look, to get to the point, about that business regarding your inheritance. I just wanted to apologize and put things on an even footing. There's no need to have any bad will between us."

He was surprised by his father's approach. This wasn't like him at all. He wondered if this was some new game that he was playing, or if he'd really just had some time to think about things, calm down and decide to bury the hatchet.

"Look Dad. I didn't want there to be anything bad between us. I know we haven't always seen eye to eye on things, but I'd like to think my decisions haven't resulted in complete disaster either. I just wanted the chance to be my own person and not feel or look entitled just because of my family. It's been important to me."

His father nodded while he spoke and at long last smiled.

"I can understand that, Nathan. And I appreciate you being candid with me about it. I'd like to get some of the team working with you on the ideas from your report and see if there is something further that we might do with it. We have some plans for our European operations and I'm keen to get you involved. In the meantime, let's just get on with things and make the most of it. There is enough work for everyone in the family to stay busy. Your brother and sister are pretty deeply engaged, so it would be good if you could spend a bit of time at the mills and give it some focus. And with Chris and Emma about to have a baby, Sam will have her hands full when she steps in to cover your brother's duties."

Nathan nodded. He knew that there was quite a lot to manage. It would take time for him to get his head around all the things that they were involved in. For now, getting to know how the mills operated would be enough of a challenge for him.

"That sounds fine to me, Dad. I think there's enough for me to learn where I am for the moment."

"Good, it's settled then. I'll speak with some of the management team and get them to start spending more time with you."

He nodded and his father pushed himself up from his chair.

"If there's anything you need, just let me know. I'll do what I can to help you find your way through things there. I'll mostly be in our Boston offices but will continue to come up from time to time to check on things."

He stood up and smiled at his father.

"Thanks Dad. I appreciate your support."

"Do you have any plans for the day?"

"Well, I was thinking, if you don't mind, I might take a walk around the gardens. It's been a long week and I could do with stretching my legs."

"Of course. You may not live in the house anymore but it's still your home too. You don't have to ask."

They walked out of the study together. His father turned and walked towards the front of the house, while he left through the back. A gate at the bottom of the yard led to formal gardens, ponds and the follies. He knew that he would find the one he was looking for out at the edge of the woods.

※

He stepped through the gate onto a single gravel path that split into several paths, each of which snaked its way out into the gardens. Just as in his dreams, he knew the gardens had been constructed at the same time as the current house and managed and maintained by generations of Briggses ever since. They reached out as far as the base of the hills beyond and the edge of the forest. There were ponds with ducks and frogs and fish, formal manicured spaces and wildflower meadows.

As a child he'd spent a lot of time playing with his siblings and friends in this space. It was a magical garden that created a place to play games and dream in the summer sun. He selected the path that led to the spot marked in his grandfather's notebook and, as he walked, he reflected on the conversation he'd just had. He wanted to believe everything that his father had told him, but it wasn't like him to be so effusive with his praise. Still, it was good to hear acknowledgement of his good work. It was a start and that's what mattered.

He continued towards the edge of the woods where the folly was located, thinking about the generations of Briggs family members who had wandered and played in these gardens. There were six follies in all, each one a kind of caricature of a building from ancient history. His family were big on ancient history, generations past having donated to excavations, museums and the preservation of ancient artifacts.

The one that he was walking towards was a smallish replica of an Ancient Greek temple, complete with columns and a small enclosed room where ancient priests would have held ceremonies to the gods. The map indicated that there was a hidden stairway leading to a series of rooms beneath a stone altar in the middle of the room. Somewhere on its side was a keyhole that he would have to find hidden amongst the ornate carvings. He recalled his dream of the construction of this very folly. Of the rooms laid out beneath the ground. A dream he'd experienced before inheriting his grandfather's sketches and notes.

He specifically recalled playing in this folly as a boy, pretending that he was an ancient general, conquering the lands. It was almost funny to him that this turned out to also be a secret hiding space that his grandfather had used—he wondered how many times he'd been playing above ground while his grandfather secretly hid below. As he neared the western edge of the garden and the start of the forest, the gray weathered-stone folly loomed ahead. It didn't look as big as he'd remembered it. His fingers briefly brushed the key in his pocket as he drew closer and he felt anxious as he finally found himself standing at the foot of the old worn steps.

As he ascended to the stone landing, the large wooden temple door loomed ahead. A cloud briefly crossed the sun and he stood for a moment in shadow, the sound of birds chirping in the woods beyond, before it silently slid past once again, leaving him standing in the full morning sun. He felt reticent about entering the building but knew that he'd come too far to stop now. He had to see whether his grandfather's musings were lunacy or, perhaps even worse, some kind of crazy reality. He wasn't sure which he hoped for.

He walked up to the imposing door, grasped the ringed handle and pulled it open. Antique-style lanterns instantly lit the inner chamber of the faux temple, and ahead he could see a large stone altar in the center of the room. At some point, one of his ancestors had run electricity to the folly—likely his grandfather. The soft yellow glow of the lanterns gave the impression of flames flickering on the stone walls. Overhead there were long narrow windows that ran just below the ceiling that allowed natural overhead light into the space. The effect created a somber tone. He remembered thinking of this building as a more happy place.

He stepped into the room and approached the altar. If he recalled his grandfather's sketches correctly, the key slot would be on the right-hand side. He walked around the imposing stone box and was struck by the beauty of the ornate carvings on the weathered surface. He could remember running around inside the folly when he was young, playing hide and seek. But it wasn't until now, when he was much older, that he'd come to appreciate the craftsmanship that had gone into creating them.

He ran his fingers across the carved stone surface. There were several indentations that looked large enough to house a secret lock. Eventually he found one that seemed to go deeper than all the others. He removed the key from his pocket, and slowly inserted it into the hole, noting that it slid firmly in place until it clicked. He gave it a slow turn and stepped back as he heard a sudden grinding sound as the top of the altar lifted up, driven by a set of gears, and the side facing the door slowly slid downwards into the floor, revealing a set of stairs. As it opened into the secret space below, the stairs were suddenly alight with a similarly yellowish glow to that of the lights in the temple. They must be triggered by the key opening the entrance. He quickly looked outside to ensure that he was alone, retrieved the key from the lock, and began to carefully make his way down.

Chapter 19

As he walked down the old, pitted and worn stone steps, he realized that even though this building was meant to be purely ornamental, it was clearly constructed for some other purpose. His dreams, his grandmother's stories, and his grandfather's letter and notebooks took a step closer to reality. He wondered briefly if any of the other buildings on the property hid similar secrets to this one. When he reached the bottom, he found himself standing on a medium-sized circular landing. Set in the wall was a handle that presumably closed the entrance, and a keyhole, which he assumed reopened the exit at the top of the steps.

Deciding against closing himself in the space without better understanding what was down there, he left the hidden entrance open to the outside. Though that wasn't as secure, it would sure be easier to get out in the event he needed to leave quickly. As it was the weekend, there shouldn't be any gardeners on the property. His mother and grandmother were out in front of the house, and his father never ventured into the garden. The house staff mostly kept to the immediate environs of the house. From his point of view, he was out there on his own.

There were two doors set in the opposite wall. He grasped the handle of the door to his left and slowly pulled it towards him. It revealed a corridor that—like the temple and the stairway—flooded with light as soon as the door opened. It appeared to run for around twenty feet before coming to a dead end. He could see doors set into the wall on either side. Not knowing how large this underground space was, he made a mental note, closed the door and decided to see what was behind the other door before proceeding.

Instead of a corridor, this one led directly into a similarly lit furnished room with wide oak floorboards, sofas and recliners, bookcases filled with books on most of the walls, and what looked like a wooden library desk with a computer screen and keyboard on it. The room had many of the same traits as the library room in the main house. Only in this space, the books looked much older than the ones in the house.

He stepped into the space, sensing a calm peacefulness as he entered. It was as though his grandfather was there in the room with him. He could imagine him sitting in this space, thinking, working, reading and having his own little escape from life. He could even smell the faint scent of the pipe tobacco that his grandfather smoked—a habit his grandmother had tried to disabuse him of. No wonder he used to take such long walks in the garden!

He was curious about what else there was to see, and decided to inspect the rest of the space. At the far end of the library there was a door set into the back-left wall that presumably led back out. He walked across the room and opened the door just to be sure—and, just as expected, stepped into the yellowish glow of the corridor. He crossed over and grasped the handle of the opposite door. This one was locked. He tried inserting the key, but it didn't fit the type of lock. He wasn't sure what else to do, so for the moment decided to leave it alone and return to the library. There must be a missing key.

He began looking at books on the shelves. Some of them were very old, from what he could see. He was hesitant to handle them for fear of causing them damage. Some of the older ones were in languages that he didn't recognize. There was a section of one bookshelf labeled *Briggs family*. They appeared to be journals of some sort and were arranged in chronological order. He picked up the oldest one first, but again, like many of the other books, he didn't recognize the language. He placed it back on the shelf and took one marked *1682*. It appeared to have been written by one of his ancestors in the early years of the Briggs family settling in New Comfort. Written in script with large swooping strokes, this one was in English and he could read most of it.

He placed that book on the library table and then moved to the section that appeared to hold more recent entries—journals from his grandfather's era. He removed the earliest of those and the most recent and placed them on the library table with the older journal. After a time, he sat down in front of the computer and tapped a key on the keyboard. It quickly hummed to life and the screen flashed on. Of course, it asked for a password—which he also didn't have. Another mystery left to be solved.

As he stood to investigate the room a bit more, he noticed the air in the space appeared to be much cooler than outside, and dry. He wondered if his grandfather had installed some kind of air conditioning unit to help maintain the condition of the library. Maybe that was what was in the other room. He rubbed his arms to warm them up as he continued to look around the room. He noticed that the books seemed to be themed by section, but for the life of him, he couldn't make out the language of any of the early works on the shelves. Many of them contained sketches with handwritten notes. This wasn't a typical library or collection. These were people's personal notebooks, journals, thoughts, all transcribed. What an odd collection for his grandfather to own. He briefly wondered where they had all come from. Were they written by his own ancestors? If so, these books likely went back many generations beyond the Briggs family's time here—and perhaps before their time in England. He wondered just how old these handwritten documents were.

He spent the next half-hour randomly pulling books off shelves and carefully thumbing through them. It turned out that they weren't all in languages he didn't understand; there were many in English that looked like they may have been transcriptions of earlier books. There were handwritten notes on the pages and highlighted sections. He read snippets but, unless he was willing to lock himself away for a very long time, they didn't really add up to much. He found references here and there to an ancient island-based civilization and stories of the lives of people who had lived there. Was his grandfather some kind of secret crackpot collector of other people's fantasies? Was that the purpose of these books? Was it possible that his grandfather had created some fantastical story about himself and his family from spending too much of his time lost in his collection? Nathan didn't feel any closer to the truth than before; if anything, he was even more confused now.

Eventually, he ended up back at the computer. On the floor next to the table was a folded canvas bag—the kind of bag a librarian or schoolteacher might carry their books or papers in. He collected together the journals he'd removed and put them in the bag. He'd have to sneak them past his parents on the way out, as he obviously hadn't arrived with a bag filled with books. Taking one last walk around the room to see if he'd missed anything of substance, he grabbed the bag, pulled the door closed behind him and examined the door seal, finding that when it closed it appeared to remain airtight. He hoped that he hadn't caused any issues by opening and closing all the doors. He shrugged and walked back up the stairs.

Assuming the altar closed the same way that it had opened, he inserted the key and turned it in the opposite direction, quickly stepping back so he could watch the mechanism in full play. The end slab rose up from the floor and the top of the altar rotated down until it was in place again. He removed the key and walked around the altar to see if there were any signs that the secret stairway existed, but as it didn't open across the floor there were no drag marks or scratches to be seen. The mechanism was ingenious really. The room looked completely untouched, with no evidence that he—or anyone else—had ever been there.

He hefted the bag and made his way outside, standing for a moment with his ear to the sky. He could hear the faint hum of a generator—or perhaps an air conditioning unit. It must be cleverly concealed on the roof of the old building, fully out of sight. He smiled to himself as he turned and walked back down the paths, around the ponds, through the gardens and into the back yard. This time, instead of walking through the house, he walked around one end of it to avoid its occupants. His mother and grandmother must have finished their tasks and gone back into the house. He quickly placed the bag inside the car and then went into the house to say his goodbyes.

His father was already back at work in the study, so Nathan left him alone. He again hugged and kissed his mother and grandmother, the latter smiling and asking if he'd had a nice walk in the garden. She obviously knew more than she'd let on about things. He'd have to pick this up with her again at some point, but now wasn't the time with his mother standing there. They walked him out to the car, where they said their goodbyes. He waved as he drove off. On the drive home he called Ben to briefly explain what he'd found. They agreed to meet later in the afternoon and look through the books together.

Before heading over to the other building, he finished a few house chores. His stomach rumbled and he realized it was just turning midday. Only a few hours had passed, but he already felt like he'd been on some grand adventure. And yet there was more to come. He quickly made a sandwich, not wanting to waste any more time. He double-checked the address in his grandfather's notebook. It shouldn't take him too long to get there, and he could still be back in time to get Ben and bring him over to the house. He removed the books from the bag and slid them into his bookshelves amongst the other books. He figured that hiding them in plain sight might be the best way to keep them safe. He hoped they wouldn't get damaged being outside of the library.

He took the cloth bag, believing it might be useful again, and retrieved the black keycard and the journal from the envelope. He kept the other key in his pocket just in case it came in useful where he was going. He punched the building's address into the car's navigation system and quickly found the location that he was looking for. His drive led him away from town to the north, first on a main road and then down a busy two-lane road. After about fifteen minutes he pulled up to the main entrance of an industrial park.

He followed the navigation, with the map indicating he should follow the road around to the left and all the way to the back. The park itself looked active, with automotive repair shops, welding companies, a storage unit company, and a bunch of other industrial-style buildings housing companies of different types. There was a fair amount of traffic in and out of the park and as the old building was located all the way at the back down its own cul-de-sac, he reckoned that no one must really pay it much attention as it was out of the way of all the other businesses.

There was a large abandoned parking lot off to the side, fenced off, with weeds growing up through cracks in the tarmac. He noticed a padlock on the gate and drove on until he arrived at a circular drive located at the front of the building. As he scanned for any signs of life, he spotted security cameras dotted around the approach and on the building itself. Signs on the fences and building indicated that it was private property and under managed security. He wondered if this was going to cause him difficulty getting into the building. He parked near the front door, and climbed a set of crumbling concrete steps to the front entrance. The building looked old and unused. Still, through the look of abandonment, all the windows appeared intact. The security cameras looked active. And the front doors looked new. As did the card reader at the side of the doors.

He took the card from his pocket and tapped it against the reader. He heard a click and reached out to pull one of the glass and metal doors open. He quietly entered the building and as the door swung shut behind him, he heard the metallic click of the lock. He took a moment to get his bearings. He was clearly in what would have once been the lobby of the old warehouse. There were several doors off the lobby. The building itself was three stories tall, in the usual style of old New England warehouses. There hadn't been any indication when he drove up of what the building had been used for in its day. In general, it still looked quite solid. Had it been closer to town and not located in an industrial park it would probably have been converted to loft-style apartments by now. As it was, its location was against it and from its look, it was much older than the rest of the buildings in the park.

He tried each of the doors off the lobby. One led to a corridor with disused bathrooms. Another looked like a storage cupboard. The third door he opened led into the main part of the ground floor of the warehouse itself. It was a long rectangular room with high ceilings, old wide wooden floorboards, and several rows of periodically spaced metal columns that held up the cross beams of the ceiling. Large metal-framed windows punctuated the walls at regular intervals down each wall. They all appeared to be intact and well maintained. The warehouse might be old and abandoned, and the grounds outside dilapidated, but someone, likely his grandfather, had done their best to ensure the fabric of the building was well maintained and didn't fall into disrepair.

As he stood considering his options, he wasn't entirely sure where to go first. He noticed about a third of the way down there were stairs on either side of the room going up to the next floor. Just past it on the left side there were four garage-style doors. This must have been where any loading or unloading took place. There must be a dock running along that side of the building on the outside. In the center of the room, there was a large square mesh-metal cage that ran from floor to ceiling and disappeared up into the next floor. This must be an old freight elevator for moving goods easily between the three floors. On the furthest side there were three wooden doors set into the wall. Nathan decided to check those out first.

He walked the length of the room to the other side, noting the solid hardwood floors and generally good condition of the inside of the building. None of the windows running the length of the room were broken. The fabric of the building appeared solid. Light flooded in through the windows—there was no need to turn any lights on. The ceiling looked to be about thirty feet high.

The walls were made of exposed brick. Light switches and metal industrial-looking electricity conduits ran along the walls. The electrical work looked new. He wondered if his grandfather had maintained and updated the building with the intent to do something with it. Sell it perhaps?

He approached the far end of the room, stepped up to the middle door and tried that one first. It led to what looked like an old abandoned kitchen. There wasn't really anything to be seen there. The next door led to another set of bathrooms. And the third one led to a corridor with another door at the end. He walked down and opened the door into what looked like a large utility room. It was filled with different kinds of equipment, pipes, and electrical boxes. The pipes went up to the upper floors and also seemed to go down through the floor. There must be a basement in the building. Everything in this room looked new and well maintained.

He looked around to see if there was a way to get downstairs—not that he really wanted to go down into the basement of some old abandoned building by himself. He walked around the equipment, careful to avoid touching anything. He checked the back area first, noting that the back wall of the room appeared to also be the back wall of the warehouse. All of the equipment looked new and completely out of place in this building. He was beginning to wonder what his grandfather was doing here.

As he walked along the wall, he arrived at a metal rail and set of stairs that looked like they led down to the basement of the building. He took a deep breath and carefully made his way down the stairs, wondering if the basement ran the entire length of the building. When he got to the bottom, he flicked a light switch on the wall and a long row of lights came on, disappearing off into the distance. The floor was concrete, and the walls were made of stone. There were metal columns spaced periodically, running far into the distance.

He figured that there may have been machinery down here at one point, perhaps old steam engines for powering the lift. He looked around and could see sections of the floor where things had been bolted down at one point. But all of that was gone. Perhaps the gear in the room above had replaced all of it? He wondered if the lift in the middle of the floor still worked or if that was just ornamental. He could see that the cage for the lift extended down into the basement, and assumed it had run from the basement to the top floor. He took one last look around the area, but there didn't seem to be anything further to see—and he didn't want to walk the length of the room on his own. What if something happened? No one would ever find him here. He walked back up.

It made no sense. He walked over to the stairway nearest the garage doors. Before ascending the stairs, he looked out through one of the large windows and confirmed that there was indeed a dock that ran a portion of the length of the building, as well as a side lot for large vehicles to load and unload. It was obviously unused as it was covered in weeds. He walked up the stairs to the next floor. It was very much like the first, except there were no rooms at the front of the building, and there were only doors to bathrooms at the far end. Again, not much to see here. He continued up until he arrived at the top floor. And this was where the building got interesting. As he reached the top of the stairs, he was met with a steel security door. There was a camera mounted in the ceiling that could capture the entire stairway. Next to the door there was a black pad—just like the one for the front entrance to the building. He removed the black metal keycard from his pocket and tapped it. Once again, he heard the familiar click of a lock. He turned the door handle and pushed.

It opened into a large space that spanned the width of the building. There were bookshelves and wooden tables scattered about, interspersed with sofas and armchairs. This was a space made for relaxing, reading. Researching? He immediately noticed a difference in the air in this room. It was cooler than the air in the rest of the building. And the air felt dry, not humid as other parts of the building had felt. Just like the room under the folly, this floor was climate-controlled. That explained all of the equipment in the utility room and the pipes disappearing up into the ceiling. Though here it was on a much grander scale than in the folly.

As he stepped into the room he could see row after row of bookcases, their shelves filled with old books. It looked as though it took up just a little over a third of the length of the upper floor and extended to the front of the building. Another much larger library. The windows were covered with some kind of translucent sheets—maybe to protect the contents of the room from the sun? At the other end of the room there were again three doors leading into a space beyond. He walked towards the front of the building.

He found a large desk with a keyboard and six screens, mounted three by three on a central pedestal. There were sofas, armchairs, more bookcases lining the end wall, and an Eames walnut and black leather lounge chair with a matching footstool. This last had his grandfather written all over it. He sat at the desk and tapped a key on the keyboard. Like the computer back at the folly, this one required a password. He wondered why his grandfather had gone to such a great extent to ensure that he was able to find these computers but didn't provide him with a password to access them. Maybe he'd intended to, but the accident happened before he was able. He searched around the space but didn't find anything else. It looked like a comfortable space to work.

He crossed to the opposite side of the room. He tried the two normal doors first and discovered a nice new kitchen, stocked with drinks and food to snack on. Obviously, no one had been inside this space in over a month and the milk was certainly off. He'd have to deal with the mess in the refrigerator. The second door led to a large executive-style bathroom, wood-paneled walls and a large walk-in shower. His grandfather obviously spent long hours in this space.

He turned his attention to the third door. He swiped the card, heard the familiar click and opened the door. He found himself in a square room that ran the depth of the bathroom and kitchen. On the opposite wall was another door, all glass. He walked across the room and once again had to swipe to enter. As soon as the card passed over the black plate, soft lighting came on. The windows to this room had been completely covered over with black steel plates. No outside light came into the room at all.

He stepped into the space and immediately saw dozens of glass cases holding artifacts. Along both walls running the length of the room were low cabinets, of the type that architects used to store blueprints. Above those were glass cases containing scrolls and parchment. He walked over, carefully slid one of the drawers open and saw more sheets of what looked like papyrus. They looked ancient. He closed the drawer and carefully walked around the room looking at the objects in the glass cases.

It was as though he'd entered a private museum. There were beautiful artifacts made of various metals—gold, silver, other metals he couldn't identify. There were enameled artifacts, ones that had precious stones set into them, and even some made of stone and wood. Wherever they were from, he thought they must be worth an absolute fortune. He wondered why they were here and not in a museum or someplace far more secure than an old abandoned warehouse.

He pulled his phone out to check the time. If he was going to pick Ben up in time, he'd have to make a move. He took one last look around and then quietly left his grandfather's—now his—space. He shook his head as he pulled the door to the stairway closed behind him. He had no idea what he was meant to do with all of this. As he crossed through the middle floor, he noted that although the freight elevator cage extended from the basement to the middle floor, it did not extend up into the top floor. He could understand why.

He made his way outside to the car, ensuring that he locked everything behind him. He still had no answers, but whatever it was his grandfather was into, he had been serious about it. He rolled the window down, put some music on, and did his best to calm his mind.

<hr />

He was a little bit early, so he sat for a moment, composing himself, before locking up and walking up to the front door. He knocked a few times and then stood waiting. After a minute, Ben's mother answered the door.

"Hello Ms. Evers."

"Nathan. Come in. Ben will be down shortly. Honestly, that boy changes his clothes fifty times a day."

She offered him a seat in the living room.

"Can I get you anything to drink?"

"Actually, some water would be great."

She poured him a glass of water from a bottle in the refrigerator.

"Here you go," she said as she placed it on the coffee table in front of him.

"Thank you."

"He'll only be a minute."

She walked back into the kitchen, leaving him to wait. The house was clean and well organized. Ben's mother was a bit of a neat freak. Though his mother went on the odd date from time to time, she'd never gotten close enough to anyone again to remarry after Ben's father left. They had made the space their own and seemed content enough to share it. Nathan watched as she tidied the kitchen, and wondered how she was really handling his friend coming out. She seemed alright. With Ben in grad school during the day and sometimes early evenings, and his mother often working overnights and sleeping during the day, they had an arrangement that worked for them. After a few moments, Ben came downstairs.

"Ready to go?" he asked.

His mother walked back into the room.

"You have a nice time honey. I probably won't see you back here this evening before I leave?"

"Not sure Mom. We may only be a few hours over at Nate's, so I might see you before you head out later. But if not, have a good night."

"You too, dear. Nathan, it's good to see you again.

Try to get him back at a reasonable time. I think he has studying to do."

"Of course, Ms. Evers."

"Bye Mom. See you."

He closed the door behind him and followed Nathan out to the car. On the drive, Ben tried to get him to talk about how his day went, but Nathan just responded that they'd talk about it once they got back to the house. They drove the rest of the way in silence. When they got there, Nathan made sure to lock the front door behind them before walking around the downstairs closing the blinds on all the windows. He was concerned that they might be observed, and wanted as much privacy as possible. He got them drinks, retrieved the books, envelopes, journal and keys and set everything out on the table.

Ben took a few moments to pick each item up in turn and look closely at it.

"Is this all?"

Nathan laughed.

"Seriously? No. There are hundreds, probably thousands of books split between a room hidden under the folly and out in the old abandoned warehouse—which isn't so abandoned."

Despite his grandmother's admonition against telling anyone else, he spent the next half-hour explaining everything he had found to his close friend. He knew that he probably shouldn't be telling anyone anything, but then it wasn't exactly as though he'd been given a set of written instructions—more like a mystery to solve—and he needed someone to talk to about things. His friend interrupted from time to time to ask questions or clarify his understanding of what Nathan was telling him. It all seemed so completely unbelievable, and yet the rooms beneath the folly and the old warehouse suggested there was substance to what his friend had been told. Neither of them was sure exactly what it might be.

Over the next few hours, they sifted through the books to try to gain an understanding of what was going on. Whether it were true or just all some sort of fantasy, hour by hour it was becoming clearer that it stretched back into Nathan's family history. The old journal told stories of one of his ancestors and the family's move from Europe to the new world. It spoke of a grand home in England. It talked about the transport of artifacts, scrolls and books that had been collected or passed down through generations and it referred vaguely to the Briggs family heritage.

There were also descriptions of weavers and their ability to weave magic. In order to hide from their heritage, or legacy, they became literal weavers of textiles. There were rumors about them but they managed to escape the horrific culling of witches in England and Salem, leveraging wealth and status to avoid scrutiny. As early evening approached, they decided that it was time to stop for the day. Nathan carefully re-hid everything and drove Ben into town, where they stopped for food.

"What do you make of it all?"

Nathan sat quiet and thoughtful, considering his friend's question.

"Well, either my entire family, going back generations, are fantasy-obsessed nuts, or there is something more to all of it. Not that any of it makes sense. I feel like I'm even more confused than when my grandmother came over."

"You said there are a lot more of these family journals?"

"Yeah, there was a whole section on the Briggs family in the folly. I didn't spend enough time looking through all the shelves in the warehouse to see if there were more there."

"So presumably there is going to be a complete record of everything."

"Yeah, I suppose so. The thing is, if it all reads similarly to the journals we've just looked at, it doesn't really get me any nearer the truth. Right now, it's all stories. I have no idea what to make of it."

"I guess you're going to have to spend more time and see if anything more tangible turns up."

Nathan stared moodily at the menu. His friend wasn't quite ready to let go of the conversation.

"Let's assume for a moment that it's true. There are so many fairytales and myths and legends. What if they aren't all stories or fantasy? What if they have a basis in truth?"

"What if they're the hallucinations of my crazy family," Nathan responded.

"Yeah, or that."

They ordered and sat quietly contemplating the day while they waited for their food to arrive.

"The thing is Nate, if the stories about weavers are true, and there is some kind of magic that runs in your family, doesn't this mean that you might have some kind of ability too?"

Nathan scowled at his friend. What a ridiculous thought. Still, the idea had briefly run through his head in one of his crazier moments.

"Yeah, that's what my grandmother implied. But I can assure you that apart from some crazy dreams in the last few months, I haven't noticed any weird powers."

His friend laughed.

"Okay, but just because you haven't experienced them doesn't mean you don't have them. I mean, wouldn't it be cool if you did?"

Nathan thought about it for a moment and then shook his head. His friend read a lot of fantasy novels and would like nothing more than to discover that everything he read was about somehow true. But for Nathan, following in his family's footsteps with the business seemed daunting enough. It was going to take an unimaginable amount of hard work to be successful. He didn't need another thing to distract him—even if his own grandfather must have taken the same path and was successful in business. Maybe that was because of the magic—not despite it.

"I don't know about cool. It feels like a lot of responsibility if it's true."

Their food arrived. After a bit, Ben looked up at his friend as though he'd made a decision of sorts.

"Nate, if you need any help, let me know. I'd be happy to come and see what's in either of the libraries and help you try and sort through it. Like a research assistant of sorts."

"Thanks Ben. I appreciate it. And I'll probably take you up on that at some point. There's just too much to go through on my own and too many things I don't understand yet."

His friend smiled. He really did want to help Nathan figure it all out.

He dropped Ben back at the house just in time for him to see his mother heading off to work. She waved and smiled as she got into her car. When he got home, he settled in for the evening with his grandfather's journals. He paid close attention to the journal he'd received from the lawyer. There was a specific reason that he'd been given this one and he wanted to find out why. He also had to figure out how to access his grandfather's computers and where the key was to the other room hidden under the folly.

※

That evening as Ben sat home, studying and running through the events of the afternoon, the doorbell rang. He wasn't expecting anyone. As he peered through the window, he saw a familiar and completely unexpected figure standing outside. *Dragan*. He hesitated for a moment. How did he know where Ben lived? What was he doing in New Comfort? Why hadn't he called or texted first? Awkwardly, he reached for the handle and opened the door slowly.

"Hey."

"Hey Ben. How are you? Sorry to just stop by like this but I was driving past the area and thought I'd detour and say hello."

Ben raised an eyebrow, feeling skeptical about the unannounced visit. After all, he hadn't heard from Dragan since they'd met up that night.

"Are you going to invite me in?"

"Yeah, sure. Sorry. Come in."

Ben stepped back from the threshold and Dragan smiled and crossed into the house. He followed Ben into the living room.

"I'm afraid that I can't stay long but I didn't want to miss the chance to say hello."

They both sat down on the sofa.

"How did you find out where I lived?"

"I checked you out after we'd met and found that you were from here. Sorry, I hope that doesn't freak you out. And New Comfort isn't that big a town. I stopped and asked. The lady at the diner seems to know you really well."

Ben laughed. He'd spent enough time there over the years. He started to relax a bit.

"Fair enough. How have you been?"

"I'm good. Was busy with work all week. Usual stuff. Weeks are really hectic. How about you?"

"Yeah, I'm good. Been busy with school. Studying. Spent some time today with my friend Nate."

Dragan looked sideways for a split second, then nodded.

"That's cool. Is he a close friend?"

Ben laughed.

"Not like that. We've known each other since we were kids. He was always there for me when we were growing up."

"Sounds like a good friend. What does he do for a living? Is he a student too?"

Dragan already knew the answer, of course. He was a boring kid who worked and jogged, visited his family and spent time in his house. A lot of time in his house.

"No, he got his undergrad degree and took a year off to travel. He works for the family business now. A bit like you."

"Ah, I know that feeling. What do they do?"

"Oh, all sorts. They have textile mills, make clothing of all sorts in the US and Europe. Own lots of real estate. Lots of investments. I think they're into other things too. We don't really talk a lot about work or family business stuff. He keeps it all low-profile. And of course, his father runs the whole thing now that his grandfather has died. Nate and his dad have a complicated relationship."

Dragan nodded, noting Nathan's issues with his father. That was probably why he didn't live in the family home—and why he'd left to travel instead of joining the family business. Nathan sounded a bit like an outsider to his family—or at least to his father. He was starting to see a little bit why Serena might be interested in him. She was always a bit of an outsider too.

"What did you guys get up to today? Anything fun?"

Ben shifted uncomfortably in his chair.

"No. Just got a bite to eat."

Ben didn't elaborate, but Dragan sensed that there was more to this story. It was a shame he'd been away doing things for his mother, but he was back now, and would start keeping a close eye on Nathan again. He decided not to push his luck and moved the subject on.

"At the diner?"

Ben laughed.

"No, a restaurant we like to go to."

They sat quietly for a moment. Dragan looked briefly at his watch.

"Oh sorry, you said you couldn't stay long."

"No, I have to get back on the road I'm afraid, but I really wanted to see you."

"That's cool. It's nice to see you again. Maybe we can hang out again sometime?"

Dragan smiled.

"I'd like that. I'll drop you a text and let you know when I'm free again."

"Sounds great. Don't be a stranger."

Dragan laughed.

"Well, you've invited me in now. How could I possibly be a stranger?"

He grinned mischievously and stood as if to go. Ben got up and followed him to the front door. As they reached it, Dragan turned, leaned in slowly, and kissed Ben softly on the lips.

"I'll call you."

Ben held the door open as Dragan stepped out into the darkness.

"Now if I can just figure my way back out of this town."

They both laughed. Dragan walked out to his car, waved at Ben one last time, got in and started the engine. As he drove off, Ben stood in the doorway and watched the car drive into the distance. He hoped that he would call him soon. He was too lost in thought about the visit to consider Dragan's unusual interest in his best friend.

Legacy

Chapter 20

He stood just inside the main doors of an airport hangar looking outward. It was nighttime and the sky was overcast, a light rain falling on the tarmac. A private jet sat idle outside—it looked like the one his grandfather used when he traveled, the one that went down in the Pacific. There were people standing around the base of the extended steps that led inside. Through the darkness and falling rain, a man who looked like his grandfather stopped at the base of the ramp and turned; he looked directly at Nathan, smiled and nodded.

As he entered the jet, the ramp closed and the engines fired up. It began to make its way out to the taxiway. Near the edge of the hanger, he saw a dark shadow detach from the building, its gaze following the plane as it disappeared into the distance. It was too dark for him to make out any of the shadow's details. After a moment, it turned and disappeared around the side of the hanger. The jet was also now out of sight. The rain continued to fall, and he stood there for a moment more, unsure of what to do next. And then everything dissolved.

Nathan woke in a sweat. He lay there trying to hold on to the substance of the dream. It was so vivid and frightening—were these his grandfather's last moments on dry land? After a time, he crawled out of bed and went downstairs. He fixed a coffee, sat down and picked up his phone. There were two messages. The first was from Serena. She wanted to know if he was around that evening and if she could stop by and see him. He texted her the address and they agreed she would be there around eight. The second was from his mother, reminding him of the Memorial Day family BBQ at the house the next day. He was expected around noon. It wasn't an invite. It was a friendly reminder. He knew better than to skip a family gathering.

Instead of showering, he went out for a run. His mind played through the events of the week. He had so much to consider—the space under the folly, the warehouse, Mark Ellison, Serena. So many things happening at once. And still, so many questions. He could feel the tension begin to ease as he ran. The sound of his sneakers slapping the pavement provided a steady cadence in his head. He made a mental note to get some headphones so that he could listen to music.

By the time he returned to the house, he had formed the skeleton of a plan. He would start with the journals and the notebook that his grandfather had left him. There had to be answers in there somewhere. He opened the blinds, letting sunshine flood into the downstairs, before heading up to shower. He stood under the showerhead for several minutes, feeling the muscles of his neck, back and legs begin to loosen. As he reached to turn off the water, his head felt clear, and he felt ready to face the day.

As he made his way downstairs his cell phone rang. He skipped down the last few steps and grabbed it off the dining table. It was Ben.

"Hey."

"Hey! How are you today?"

"I'm good. Went for a run this morning, all showered and ready to start my day. You?"

"I'm great! I had a surprise visitor last night."

"Oh really? Who?"

"The guy I met last weekend at the club. He stopped by out of the blue. He didn't stay long. He was passing through and wanted to say hello."

"Get you! Are you going to see him again?"

"I think so. I hope so. He seems like a nice guy. Reminds me of you and Serena. He's always busy with family business. I don't really know much about it, but I know it keeps him busy. His mother runs things."

Nathan laughed and rolled his eyes.

"Good luck with that. Though I guess you're getting used to it with my schedule."

Ben laughed.

"Yeah, I guess so."

As they spoke, the conversation from the previous night ran through Ben's head. Dragan seemed unusually interested in Nathan—or maybe he was just trying to show interest in Ben's friends. Only time would tell, but he would have to be more careful next time they spoke.

"Ben? Everything okay?"

"Yeah, no I'm good. Sorry my mother's calling. I'll get back to you later, okay?"

"Sure, no problem. And I'm happy for you. I'll talk to you later."

"Thanks Nate. Bye."

They phone went silent. He was happy for his friend. He deserved to have someone special in his life. He smiled to himself as he set his phone back on the table, and then retrieved everything he'd brought home from the folly, warehouse and the lawyer. He emptied the envelopes and spread it all out like the pieces of a puzzle. He reached first for the notebook from the lawyer. That seemed the most obvious place for him to start.

It was a curious mix of notes and sketches. After an hour of flicking back and forth through the notebook, he noticed some pages had a character scribbled in the bottom outside corner—a jumble of upper- and lowercase letters, numbers and symbols. He couldn't see anything they might correlate to in the book, and eventually decided to write them down reading from front to back to see if they made any sense. He flipped through each page until he was sure that he'd captured every single character.

At1aN982bCx)!7/\t15.

At first glance, he thought it might represent some kind of formula. But it didn't look like anything he'd seen before. The more he looked at it the more the jumble began to look familiar. It wasn't a formula. It was a password. Had he found the password to his grandfather's computers? If so, it would give him access and he would be able to see more clearly what it was his grandfather had been working on. And maybe there were further clues to be found there. He was sure this was why the notebook had been passed to him. His grandfather hadn't forgotten or been unable to relay the information he needed—it was there in plain sight all along.

He was just about to pick up one of the other books, his grandfather's most recent journal, when there was a loud knock at the door. Startled, he scooped everything up from the table and put it into the cloth bag. He hid the bag inside a cupboard in the kitchen before going over to the front door. As he looked through the peep hole, he was surprised to see Mark Ellison standing outside. What was he doing here? Why was he bothering him at home on a Sunday? Nathan unlocked the door and opened it a few inches.

"Yes?"

"Mister Briggs. Good afternoon. I'm sorry to bother you on the weekend, but I have a few more questions and I thought it might be better to speak with you at home, away from the office and the people you work with. May I come in?"

Nathan stood at the entrance contemplating the man standing in front of him. He was around six feet tall. He looked like he was in good shape. Nathan would have expected that for a federal agent. He was middle-aged, perhaps in his early to mid-forties. He was casually dressed, in jeans and a polo shirt under a dark blue jacket. He looked like he wasn't going to take no for an answer. He stood back, opened the door and gestured for Ellison to come in. He led them to the living room.

"Before you start, Mister Ellison, can I ask you a question?"

Ellison shifted in his chair. He was clearly used to being the one asking the questions.

"Sure. Go ahead."

"Why are you so interested in me? I get that I was staying nearby, but I had nothing to do with what happened to the poor man on the Cape."

He shuddered at the memory of what he'd found on the beach. Ellison sat quietly listening before answering.

"Look Mister Briggs, I'm going to level with you. The man on the beach, Jess Evans from your work, and the boy we found near the mill were all murdered. In each case they'd bled out. But there wasn't enough blood at any of the scenes for them to have been murdered there.

Someone killed these people and then moved their bodies to where we found them. It's a murder investigation. Do I think you were involved? Honestly? No. I don't believe you are a suspect. But you may know something without realizing it, and that's why I'm here. Does that satisfy you?"

Nathan considered what he'd just been told. It felt like Ellison, though exasperated, was being upfront with him. Though he also knew that his job was putting people at ease and getting them to tell him more than they'd intended. He wasn't yet entirely sure what to think, but decided he'd give Ellison the benefit of the doubt.

"Fair enough. Thanks for telling me. But can I ask why you're here today?"

"Ah that. Well, do you know a woman by the name of Serena?"

Nathan stiffened. Where was this headed? He hadn't mentioned her to Ellison when they'd met. How could he know about her existence? Maybe he got her name from the police. Damn Ben for blurting that out. How should he play this? Clearly the man knew more than he'd been letting on. He decided to go with the truth. He had nothing to hide—other than the fact that he hadn't mentioned her previously. And that ship had sailed.

"Yes, I know a Serena."

He decided to make Ellison ask the questions—make him work for the answers.

"What can you tell me about her?"

"What would you like to know?"

A look of irritation crossed Ellison's face.

"Look kid, don't fuck with me. I'm asking the questions here."

Nathan sat back into the sofa, instantly regretting having let this man into his house. For the first time he felt under threat, and he didn't like the feeling.

"I'm sorry sir. Can I ask on whose authority you're here?"

Now it was Ellison's turn to shrink back into his chair. He looked around the room for a moment and took a deep breath. The look of irritation was gone, replaced by a somewhat paler, worried look.

"I'm here as part of a government investigation into a possible serial murderer. Look, I'm sorry, but I've already said more than I should have done. Let's start again."

He paused for a moment before continuing.

"In the course of our investigation we've previously come across a Serena and her brother William. We're not sure if they are directly involved in the murders, but they are persons of interest to the organization and we would like to know more about them. Unfortunately, we haven't been able to track them down, as much as we've tried."

So, one of Serena's brothers was called William. Maybe Nathan could turn this to his advantage and learn something more about Serena and her family in exchange for speaking to Ellison.

"All I'm asking is could you tell me a bit more about

the Serena you know? Anything might help us with this, and I'd be very appreciative."

Nathan could tell that Ellison wasn't used to playing nice. There was something inherently dark about this man—he would have to be careful. He didn't know enough about Serena to implicate her in anything, so he decided to tell Ellison what he knew, starting with meeting her in Croatia. From time to time Ellison interrupted to ask questions. Nathan stuck to facts and kept his answers brief. He left out his plans with Serena for that evening. He wasn't about to complicate this further. He wanted this man out of his house as soon as possible. By the time they finished, Nathan had learned Serena's brothers were called Thomas and William. Her father was called Davorin.

"Where are they from?"

"As well as we can tell—and this is from their names—they are Croatian. However, they have homes all over the world and are extremely difficult to get close to."

Ellison looked closely at him.

"Is there nothing else you have for me? Met in Croatia. Saw her a couple of times since you got back. Nothing more specific? How about her cell number? Can you give that to me please?"

Nathan retrieved his phone and read out the number.

"Thank you for cooperating. Could I trouble you for a glass of water before I go?"

Nathan got a glass and poured water from the dispenser in the refrigerator. As he stood there, he began to feel that odd itch on the back of his neck. He rubbed it until it went away. He brought the glass of water to Ellison, who was now standing, jacket on, ready to go. He thanked him for the water, took a few sips and handed it back. They walked to the door and Nathan wondered how much Ellison had learned—apart from the cell number. That was probably going to get him into trouble with Serena. Right now, he was beginning to wonder just who he could trust.

"Thank you for your time, Mister Briggs. Again, I'm sorry for disturbing you at home on a Sunday, but as you can imagine, it was a conversation better had in private."

Nathan nodded.

"Is that all, Mister Ellison? Can I assume I won't be seeing you again?"

"You never know, Mister Briggs. I'm good for the moment. Have a nice day."

As Ellison drove off, Nathan felt that he'd missed something. The agent clearly couldn't be trusted. He was done with journals, federal agents, and death for the day. He felt numb. He was tired. He was afraid. But there was something else happening. Something deep inside was trying to tell him something. Like that itch. He shrugged it off for the moment. He would think about it later.

He had fallen asleep on the sofa. He woke to the sound of his cell phone beeping. He got up and checked the message—it was Serena saying she was on the way and would be there soon. He looked out the window and saw that it was already dusk. How long had he slept? He checked the time—it was almost eight o'clock. He couldn't believe that he'd fallen asleep. He quickly tidied the living room and kitchen and made a cup of coffee to wake up. The week had taken its toll. After a short time, the doorbell rang. He looked out the window to see Serena standing on the front porch. He opened the door and stepped out to see her.

"Hello there!"

"Hey Nathan. It's so nice to see you again. So soon."

She stepped up and kissed him on each cheek. He needed to get used to her being so forward if they were to continue whatever it was that they were doing. Her lips weren't as icy cold, though still nothing close to warm. He hugged her back. They stood looking at one another for a brief moment.

"Shall we stay out here? It's a nice evening."

"Oh, uh, no. Would you like to come in?"

"I'd love to."

She smiled and followed him into the house.

"It's a nice place you have here. I love the area. And so close to the ocean."

He nodded.

"Yeah, it's on my parents' estate. They renovated the house for me while I was away. It was a bit of a surprise. It's more than I need really but after all that travel it's nice having a place that's my own to come back to."

"I can imagine. It's pretty rural here too."

"Yeah, my family settled here in colonial times and pretty much own all the land around here, so no neighbors."

"We have a similar ancestral home in Croatia. There are little villages nearby, but our family have lived in seclusion for many centuries. We only have apartments in London, Boston and New York, so no outside land there."

Nathan nodded. It was good to hear her talking about her family.

"By the way. Since we're talking about it—and this is kind of embarrassing—what is your last name?"

Serena gave him a serious look for a moment and then started laughing.

"Have I never told you?"

"Nope."

"I'm so sorry. It's Vidaković."

He got his cell phone out.

"Can you spell that for me?"

"Here, let me type it in for you."

He handed her his phone.

"Thanks. I've been meaning to ask you but just never found the right moment."

Serena smiled at him.

"Don't worry. I would have cleared that up a long time ago if I'd realized."

"What does it mean? I mean, where's the name come from?"

"Well, it's son of Vidak or Vid—Vidak means to see,

and Vid goes back to Vitus, a Roman name derived from the word *vita*, or life. Also, back to Saint Vitus in the fourth century. I guess if you put it all together, it means to see life."

He nodded. He liked that she was so forthcoming. Maybe she hadn't been evasive in the past. Maybe it was just that he'd never asked. He'd try to remember that going forward.

"So does your family still mainly live in Croatia?"

"No, our ancestral home is still there, and we own a lot of real estate, but my father and brothers mainly live in London. They say it suits them and it's kind of central to everywhere they need to go. We own real estate all over Europe and America. And there are many other businesses in my father's holdings. That's what keeps all of us so busy all the time. There is always something that needs to be dealt with somewhere."

"Don't you ever get tired of it all?"

"Not really. We all support one another. It's not all work. We get time away too, which makes it all worthwhile."

He took it all in. It sounded a lot like his own family.

"I'm familiar with that."

They both laughed.

"You're on the start of a long journey. Enjoy it. Don't take it too fast. You have time. That's part of the pleasure of it. Learn everything you can along the way."

"You sound like my grandfather. He always spoke that way."

"Your grandfather was very wise."

"How well did you know him?"

"Me personally? Not well. I mean, he and my father knew each other from their work. But I only met him a few times when I happened to be around when they were meeting. He seemed like a very kind man. I know my father had a lot of respect for him. And that's saying a lot. He's not always the easiest man to get along with."

"You and I have that in common at least."

Serena smiled. As she was about to respond her phone rang.

"Hello? Yes. Yes Father. Of course. Straight away. I'll be around an hour. Okay. I will see you soon."

Nathan looked at her phone and then up at her face.

"Duty calls?"

"Yes, I'm afraid so. I don't want to disappoint you, but my father is really insistent I get back down to Boston as soon as possible. I hope you're not cross with me."

Nathan shook his head.

"No, no of course not. I understand. I'm not upset."

She smiled.

"Listen, I feel I really owe you. I promise I will make some proper time for us to get together. I really would like to spend time with you."

She paused for a moment.

"If you'd like to spend time with me of course."

He smiled in response.

"Of course I would, Serena. I hope you know that

I do. I get that our lives are both a bit crazy at the moment. But it can't always be that way."

Can it, he thought to himself.

"Alright then. It's a deal. I'll look to sort something out as soon as I'm able. And you really do have a nice house, Nathan. It suits you."

"You should see the games room over the garage," Nathan said.

"Well, maybe next time you can give me the grand tour of the Briggs family estate."

They both laughed. He reckoned that her family estate would be far more impressive.

"Seriously. Thank you for understanding."

He nodded and walked her out to her car, which was parked next to Nathan's SUV. A matte black Maserati with dark-tinted windows. Mysterious car for a mysterious girl.

"I like your wheels."

"Thanks. It's one of my father's cars, but it's my favorite one to take out when I need to drive somewhere."

They stood quietly next to the car for a moment while she reached into her pocket for her keys. She pushed a button and the car unlocked, lights flashing.

"Have a safe drive back to Boston, Serena."

"Thanks Nathan. I'm sorry I have to run. But you'll hear from me soon."

This time he leaned in and kissed her on the cheek. She smiled and climbed into the car, started the throaty engine, and waved to him before putting it in gear and driving off down the lane. The sun had now set, and Nathan stood listening to the sound of crickets and the rumble of Serena's car disappearing off into the distance. A few seconds later another car drove past, heading down the lane in the direction Serena had gone. It was quiet where he lived and with no houses nearby and very little traffic on the road, it was unusual to see another car, especially at that time of night. He watched as the taillights disappeared down the lane.

He stood outside for a while longer, listening to the sounds of the night, and considered that he really didn't mind the solitude of living here. Maybe it wasn't right for someone his age to live in such a quiet place, but he had never been the typical kid. As the temperature continued to cool, he turned and walked back into the house, locking up behind him.

❦

Mark Ellison sat in his car listening to a small transceiver. He could hear conversation inside the house as clear as day. The small bug he'd placed in the living room picked up everything he needed to know to understand that Serena was visiting Nathan. He would have planted more if he'd had a chance, but Nathan hadn't left him much time. A built-in recorder had captured the full conversation, which he would play back later when he retired for the night. Right now, it was more important to follow Serena back to Boston to see if he could identify where she and her family lived. He'd come to spend a few hours of surveillance on Nathan, but had hit the jackpot when she'd arrived.

He wasn't close enough to see the license plate—he should have captured that while they were in the house. She would be difficult to keep up with, but he was determined. He would figure out what to do with Nathan later. Clearly, he hadn't been completely forthcoming about Serena coming to visit. And they were closer than he'd realized. Even so, they hadn't discussed his visit earlier in the day. Maybe this kid wasn't so stupid after all. He felt confident that he was getting closer to getting them now. He would be relentless.

He wasn't the only observer that night. Steel-gray eyes watched everything from the edge of the woods across the road. They saw Ellison's car parked up the lane. And they saw Serena visit Nathan. So many things to observe and report on. This other interloper had been around for a while now and Dragan reckoned it was time that he did some digging and identified him.

Unlike Ellison, Dragan had memorized Ellison's car license plate, and would pull in some favors to find out more about him. Who would sit outside the house and listen remotely to conversations? This was getting more and more interesting. He thought for someone so young, Nathan had strange taste in hobbies—visiting an old monument at the back of his family property, and an old abandoned warehouse in an industrial park. He had watched quietly, on more than a few occasions. All he'd been able to ascertain was that Nathan was a strange kid with strange habits. And Serena seemed to have more than a passing interest in him.

His mother's orders had been to observe but under no circumstances interfere. Apart from occasional meals and other business she'd sent him on, he'd managed to accomplish that so far. He wondered if her orders would soon change. He'd sensed during their last conversation that something was coming, and hoped that he'd be a part of it. He stayed a while longer before disappearing off down the lane for the evening. He was bored. And in any case, there were more interesting games to play now.

Chapter 21

Nathan woke early, feeling briefly disoriented before remembering that it wasn't a workday. He could feel the warmth of the early morning sun streaming through the windows on his bare arms. It was Memorial Day and the weather looked as though it was going to cooperate—a good day to be outside. He looked forward to a day where he could spend time with family, relax and just let the stress and confusion of recent days pass.

Since he wasn't expected until late morning, and as he'd woken up so early, he decided to go for a run. He got ready, went downstairs and brewed a shot of espresso to wake up. He shook his head to clear it as he walked down the front steps, did a few stretches on the warm grass, and then started off. As he jogged down the driveway and turned left to head up the lane, he noticed that the weeds on the side of the road nearest his house had been knocked over. There were tire treads running through them and then back onto the lane again. That seemed odd to him. He hadn't noticed them the day before. He shrugged it off and continued his run. It was likely that someone had swerved to avoid an animal. There were plenty of deer, squirrels and other creatures about.

He enjoyed the sun on his face. It was still and peaceful out. The more he ran the better he started to feel. He thought about his visit from Serena the previous evening. It had been really nice to see her. And unlike the previous times, he'd managed to ask her questions and learn a bit more about her and her family. Probably better he'd done so after Ellison's visit than before. He wondered about not having told the federal agent about the impending visit. He was still trying to figure out things for himself. He wasn't ready to tell Serena that there was someone enquiring about her and her family—he wasn't looking forward to the moment when it eventually came up. He probably should have said something sooner.

He ran for around twenty minutes before deciding to turn around and head back. As he returned to the house, he was sweaty, over-heated and breathing heavily. He used to run nearly daily before he'd gone away. Now that he was trying to get back into it, he could see just how out of shape he'd gotten over the last year. He'd thought all the walking would help, but it obviously wasn't a great substitute for a good run. He'd just have to keep working at it. He showered and took his time getting ready. He put the keycard and key into his pocket. If he was able to get away from the family for a bit, he wanted to see if the characters he'd deciphered from his grandfather's notebook might be the password for the computer. He felt that he should at least try, having saved a picture of the jumbled letters, numbers and symbols on his phone.

After a while he grew restless, and decided to head over to the house early. His mother would be happy to see him no matter when he arrived. And he figured that he might be able to make himself useful. When he arrived his brother and sister's cars were already there. He guessed that everyone had had the same idea. He could hear voices coming from the kitchen. They would be busy getting ready for the day and socializing while they worked. He wandered down the hallway to join them.

He stepped through the kitchen doorway into the noise and bustle of activity. His mother and grandmother were preparing food. His father was chatting with his brother Christopher and Christopher's wife Emma, and Sam was busy stacking plates and cutlery on the table. There were no staff to be seen. Memorial Day was usually just a Briggs family affair and an excuse for the family to be in one place for a day, leaving all of their work behind. Noticeably absent from the commotion was his grandfather, who usually tended the grill during the cookout. He felt a momentary pang of sadness thinking about that. He guessed this year that duty would fall to his father.

"Nathan," his mother said, looking up.

A chorus of *hellos* came from the room.

"Hey everyone. If I'd known everyone was coming so early, I would have come sooner."

"No, you're fine. Your brother and sister decided to come early."

Their father seemed unusually jovial this morning.

"Give me hand with these plates and things."

Sam leaned over and gave him a hug.

"You look good Nate. It's good to see you. Sorry I haven't been by, but I've been back and forth between Boston and New York. It's been busy."

He knew that his siblings were on the go a lot recently as he hadn't seen or heard from either of them. That was the way of things. He scooped up an armload of plates and napkins and followed his sister out of the house. Partway down the garden there was a brick and slate patio with a shed that had been converted into a bar, a BBQ and an outdoor pizza oven. There were tables and chairs scattered around. He and his sister placed their load on one of the tables and went back inside to repeat the trip until everything was fully set up. The food would come later.

"I hear Dad had you working on thoughts and recommendations around our European plans. He said you'd done a good job on the report."

Christopher smiled at his little brother.

"Welcome to the treadmill."

They both laughed. Their father had disappeared into the house, probably into his study to take care of something.

"Thanks Chris. It's a lot to get my head around. It's very different working there as opposed to being around it as a kid. There's so much to learn."

"You'll get the hang of it. It took both Sam and me a couple of years to really sink our teeth into things. You have plenty of time. Don't rush it. You have a lot of good people around you. Make sure you ask loads of questions—don't be afraid to look stupid. They've already had Sam and me to deal with, so they're used to it by now."

Nathan hadn't thought about it that way before, but he would be sure to take his brother's advice. And he was right—they were used to Briggs siblings by now, so his questions, and his mistakes, should be taken in stride.

"How's the new digs? Mom put a lot of effort into it. Dad too. They really wanted you to feel like you could be home but still have your own space. Are you enjoying it?"

Nathan nodded.

"I haven't really gotten time to use the games room as much as I'd like, but I'm planning on it. I feel like I've been on the run since I returned. I need to find some time to chill out."

"Well, like I said, take your time. Enjoy it a bit. You don't have to try and do everything all at once."

Nathan wasn't completely referring to work, although of course his brother didn't realize that. There were so many other things going on that filled the rest of his time. Things that he preferred not to talk about.

"Come on Chris, don't monopolize him."

Sam put her arm around her younger brother's shoulders and dragged him outside.

"So little brother. What have you been doing? Is it all as scary as you'd thought?"

He laughed. He'd only flown back a little over eight weeks ago but it felt a lot longer than that somehow.

"I've been pretty busy with work. I see Ben from time to time, which is good."

He neglected to mention Serena. He wasn't really sure how to bring her up with his family, and as their friendship was still so casual, he didn't want anyone to read any more into it than there was. And of course, there was the fact that a federal agent was interested in her and her brother. As he thought about that, he considered that maybe he should get to the bottom of whatever that issue was before anything more serious happened between them.

"Have you heard any more about that mess on the Cape?"

She almost whispered the last bit. That was another can of worms that he wasn't ready to discuss. Today was a day for family. He would try to leave work and death off the agenda for the day.

"No, nothing more. I don't see any reason why they would get in touch."

He left it at that. She was about to say something further when their mother called, asking Sam to give her a hand. Standing outside on his own, he decided it might be the perfect time to sneak off into the gardens and try that password. When he arrived, he did a quick check to see if it looked disturbed since his recent visit.

Everything was just as he'd left it. He removed the key from his pocket and inserted it into the lock, turning it until it clicked in place. The mechanism ground into gear and slowly revealed the entrance. He quickly retrieved the key and made his way carefully down the stairs.

He walked through the door into the library and sat at the computer desk. He didn't want to be absent from the house for very long as he wanted to avoid uncomfortable questions. He laid his cell phone on the desk and brought up the picture of the password that he'd written down to photograph before tearing the paper up into small pieces. He tapped a key on the keyboard and the computer hummed to life. After a few seconds the screen lit up and the log-in box appeared. His grandfather's name was in the username field. He slowly keyed in the letters, numbers and special characters exactly as he'd copied them. When he'd finished, his finger hovered over the return key for a moment before he pressed it.

The screen quickly dissolved, and he was in. He had the right password. He scanned the screen, noting folders and files on the desktop. One folder instantly stood out.

Nathan read me.

His grandfather had been more prepared for something to happen to him than Nathan had thought. He clicked on the folder and opened it. There was a text file, a Word document and what looked like a bunch of video files. He opened the text file first.

COPY THIS FOLDER ONTO A USB FLASH DRIVE.

His grandfather had left a trail of clues like breadcrumbs for his grandson to follow. He looked around the desk but didn't see anything he could use to copy the files. He felt under the top edge of the desk and found a small drawer. He opened it and found several cable adapters and a couple of USB flash drives. He found the adapter that worked for that computer, which had a USB port on it, and plugged it in. Instantly a drive icon appeared on the desktop. He clicked on it and an empty folder appeared. He checked that the items in the folder would fit onto the flash drive and then dragged the folder onto it.

It took about half a minute for everything to copy over, then he unplugged the flash drive and put it deep into his pocket. He logged out of the computer. He would come back another time to look through its contents in more detail. He briefly wondered if the computer in the warehouse used the same password. It would be lucky for him if it did. He made his way back through the gardens to the back yard. Thankfully, his family were still inside preparing for the BBQ.

He went back into the house and easily slid back into conversations with his family. After a while his father came back into the kitchen and rejoined the festivities. Before too long they were all enlisted to carry bowls of salads and trays with various marinated meats out to a long table near the grill. They spent the rest of the afternoon eating, laughing and enjoying the good weather. There were a few somber moments as they recalled past family gatherings with his grandfather, but they all worked hard to keep their spirits up and enjoy the day.

That evening, when he finally returned home, he was stuffed from eating, sunburnt and tired. Instead of his usual routine of television and something to eat, he decided to just head up to bed. As curious as he was, he was too tired to look at the contents of the flash drive. Just before going upstairs he hid it on the bookshelves with the other items.

The next day, he took his brother's advice and reached out to people in the business to set up opportunities to shadow them. He wanted to gain a better understanding of their roles and how they worked to make the business so successful. Everyone he spoke with was accommodating and in nearly every case—unless they hadn't been with the company at the time—they talked about how they'd also helped his siblings to settle in.

He spoke with one of their IT team about ordering him a personal MacBook that he could keep at home for his own use. He wanted to have a computer that was not associated with the company. The IT guy was helpful and put him in touch with their supplier. After Nathan made arrangements to pay, they agreed to have one couriered over to the company that afternoon for him. He split the rest of the day between making updates to the final version of his strategy document and beginning the process of shadowing people to meetings. As promised, the courier arrived that afternoon with his new computer. He retrieved it from reception and left it on his desk to take home with him at the end of the day.

On the drive home he reflected on how the day had gone and made the decision to take more direct control of his onboarding into the company. He wanted to find a way to add more value. Shadowing was the first step, but he also wanted to learn how all of the companies fit together. As he drove towards his house, the sky began to darken, and clouds rolled in thick and fast. As he pulled into the driveway the wind started to pick up and rain began to fall. He grabbed his backpack and the bag containing his new computer and ran from the car onto the front porch. The rain was crashing down now and there were flashes of lightning and thunder. It was going to be a stormy night—a good night to set up his new computer and view the files he'd copied over from his grandfather's computer.

While he was waiting for updates to download and install, he made dinner. He needed to go shopping at some point to buy food. He was getting low on everything. He ate while the computer restarted over and over, typing in his password periodically and moving onto the next set of updates. He purchased and downloaded several software packages that he knew he'd use, which added to the time it took to update.

Eventually, it was set up the way he wanted. He got out the USB drive and plugged it in. Once everything was working, he opened the drive and copied the files onto his desktop. His grandfather had helpfully named each file with a number in front of it. The sequence ran from one to ten. He clicked on the first video. The screen was instantly filled with the image of his grandfather.

"Nathan, as you're viewing this I knew that you would figure it out. I want to apologize for not being there in person. Clearly something has happened and you're on your own... I never intended for that to happen."

He paused the video for a moment. It was one thing to receive the notebook, keys and access to all of the spaces his grandfather's clues had led him. It was another thing altogether to watch the older man speaking to him as though they were actually sitting together in the same room. He choked back unexpected emotion and wiped a tear from the corner of his eye.

After a few minutes, he hit play and settled back in to watch the rest of the video. It turned out that his grandfather had recorded a series of tutorials for him. Each clip was a different lesson, and it was important, he said, to note that there were more on the computer system in the warehouse. These first ten were the lessons that his grandfather felt formed the foundations for what followed. They were meant to teach him about being a weaver—how to access and use his abilities, warnings and what was expected of a weaver. The notes and thoughts had been compiled by his grandfather over the years and were meant to go along with his training.

He wasn't sure what to make of it all. None of it made sense to him in practical terms. His family ran businesses, were respected, worked hard. They were sane, normal people. And yet, his grandfather exposed him to a side of their life that he couldn't reconcile with his own view of his family. Was the businesses a mask for their real purpose? Or was his grandfather a crazy closet fantasist? The folly, the warehouse, all of the books, scrolls, artifacts, the secrecy—it was all a lot to take in. It presented him with a conundrum if none of it were real.

He continued to watch as his grandfather explained the first lesson—how to get into the right mental state in order to perform what came after. It was a type of meditation that he was meant to learn in order to clear his mind. He shook his head in disbelief. His grandfather was teaching him mindfulness. He could get an app for that.

Still, there was only one way to debunk this madness. To go forward. He would go along with it for the moment and see where it led. With a high degree of skepticism and a belief that his grandfather was mad, he would learn to meditate if that's what it took to put an end to all of this. For the rest of the evening, he practiced until he felt like he was beginning to get the hang of it. It was only meditation—nothing strange about it yet. Nothing to change his mind. But he had to admit, by the end of the evening his head felt still and clear and when he went to bed, he fell asleep almost immediately.

After rushing through the next day at work, he was ready to move onto the second lesson. Maybe he was trying to move too fast, but it wasn't like he had anyone there to advise him properly. Lesson two required a candle. He retrieved one from a shelf in the living room that his mother had kindly provided when decorating. He set it in the center of the table and sat down in front of it. The video showed his grandfather concentrating on it. He uttered a single word; *ignis*, Latin for fire. Nathan recognized it, having learned Latin in school. The candle flared to life. A trick? Maybe the great secret was that the Briggs family came from a long line of stage magicians. Illusionists. He rolled his eyes and prepared himself.

First, he let thoughts come freely. He wasn't sure if there was relevance to the use of a Latin word for the exercise or if use of a word just helped to focus the mind on the task. He looked at the document that accompanied the videos, a brief set of notes for each exercise. If this was all fantasy, then his grandfather had gone to great lengths to create it. His grandfather wrote that the word was not that important as long as it helped you visualize the thing that you were trying to do—it provided a focal point to channel power.

He found a comfortable position on the chair and closed his eyes. He practiced taking deep breaths in, holding them for a second before letting them out slowly.

He continued for several minutes, allowing his breathing to slow and his mind to quiet down. When he was ready, he opened his eyes, looked intently at the candle, and whispered the word.

"*Ignis.*"

Nothing. Not a spark or a sputter. He looked at the candle for any sign that something had happened. There was nothing. He got up and walked around the room to shake off the failed attempt. Outside, the evening was still apart from the steady thrum of cricket song—it was the complete opposite of the previous night's storm. He dimmed the lights, as if creating an air of mystery would make a difference to his efforts, and returned to the table. It was just him and the candle. He closed his eyes and ran through the same exercises again, only for longer this time, until his mind felt perfectly quiet and still. When he was ready, he opened his eyes, and spoke more forcefully this time.

"*Ignis.*"

The wick sputtered, making a crackling sound for a split second, and then small sparks and smoke leapt from the wick until it suddenly burst into flame.

"Holy shit," Nathan shouted as he pushed himself up from the chair, knocking it backwards onto the floor.

The candle flickered and cast a gentle yellow glow across the dimly lit room. He stared at it, then looked around the room as if trying to detect some trick being played. Nothing. He placed the chair upright, sat back down, gently blew out the flame, and then repeated the entire exercise. The next time it felt perceptibly easier and the candle sputtered quickly to life. He continued practicing into the evening, each time feeling more effortless than the last. He could feel something changing inside of his body and his mind. Something slowly unlocked, allowing him access to a part of himself that he had never before realized existed. Before the night was over, he'd managed to scrounge up four other candles and found that he could not only light each one individually, but with a bit of concentration he could light them all at once.

As he crawled into bed late that evening, he was both exhausted and elated. He lay in bed thinking about what he'd accomplished. He'd made an incremental leap away from being a skeptic. It looked as though his grandparents weren't crazy after all. How was this possible? It was a long while before he could sleep. He was curious and excited and couldn't wait for the next evening to come around.

The next day he and Serena texted one another. He still didn't mention anything about Ellison or his investigation. Nor did he mention anything about his other discoveries. This newfound world scared him and made him feel more cautious than usual. He had a nagging feeling that his new abilities somehow put him in more danger than before. His grandmother's warning came to mind and he realized that it was already too late. He'd already involved his best friend without understanding there might be implications to doing so. He promised himself that he would be more careful going forward. There was no telling who or what was out there waiting.

On the way home from work he stopped in town and bought groceries. He needed to eat, and the refrigerator and pantry weren't going to fill themselves—unless he could use magic to do that too. When he got home, he quickly put everything away, sat at the dining table, and picked up where he'd left off the previous evening. During the day he wondered if the spell was strictly about lighting candles or if more generally it was about conjuring fire. He understood the use of the candle as it was literal and provided a specific focus for him. He thought he'd try something else first, before proceeding.

He placed a crumpled-up paper towel in a metal mixing bowl on the table before sitting down. He practiced clearing his mind and when he was ready, he spoke.

"*Ignis.*"

The paper towel flared up and burned inside the metal bowl. It was so instantaneous and intense that he pushed back and nearly fell out of his chair again. So that settled that. He took the bowl to the sink and doused the paper towel with water and left it there. He continued practicing that evening, wanting to ensure that he was proficient enough at that lesson before proceeding to something new. He wasn't sure if he was meant to leave time between learning new magic, or if he was meant to progress once he proved to himself that he'd mastered the lesson at hand.

He decided that he would try something new the next night, Friday, when he didn't have to go to bed so early. His head reeled at this new world that he'd entered. He wondered where all of it would lead him—he was learning, sure, but why? Why was he learning these things? Was he meant to do or be something once he'd mastered them? He missed his grandfather more than ever and wished that he had someone who he could ask about all of this.

Dragan was also on a mission to discover new things. His mother Jelena had tasked him with finding out more about the mysterious man who kept turning up near Nathan's home. She decided that it was time to do something about that. He drove back to Boston, where he used one of his contacts to run the license plate of the car. It turned out to be registered to a federal agency carpool. This was going to be more difficult than he'd thought.

He spent the next few days running down every lead and contact he had to see if there was an easy way to identify this stranger. He even traveled back up to Nathan's house a couple of times to see if the man turned up again—but no such luck. On Wednesday night it rained, and he decided to give it a miss. He also began to take precautions—being watched by two people was bound to be noticed sooner or later. Even though there was no possible way that Dragan could have been spotted lurking in the shadows of the woods, he took no chances. Each time he kept watch he made sure that he was well hidden. You could say he had a knack for this, having performed these kinds of services for his mother Jelena for a very long time.

By Thursday night, after striking out on his search, he decided to return to New Comfort. Having expended a lot of energy, he was hungry and needed to replenish. He made a quick side trip before driving up and parking in his usual place to camp out in the woods outside of Nathan's house. Perhaps this time he'd get lucky. As he waited outside the house, the air was clear and calm, just the sound of crickets making their usual racket. Not like the previous night's storm, which he'd been happy to avoid. He watched as Nathan carried bags of food into the house.

As darkness settled the lights inside the house suddenly dimmed. Dragan felt a sudden crackling in the air, like static electricity across his skin. Inside the house a light flared. This wasn't good. He recognized that sensation. He'd felt it many times before over the years—the unmistakable feeling of magic being practiced nearby. Nathan was clearly more interesting than he'd realized, and his mother's mission suddenly began to make more sense. He'd have to report this back to Jelena. She would decide what to do next. It was out of his hands now. He left Nathan to his own devices while he set out to get his car and ready himself for reporting back to his mother. She hated weavers. This wasn't going to go well.

※

Nathan woke early on Friday morning, feeling clearheaded and energized. He stopped in town to grab breakfast from a local diner on his way into the office. While sitting at the counter waiting for his food, he overheard two people talking about another murder.

"Yeah, they found her on the walking paths near the park this morning. Not sure what happened but they said there was foul play."

"Such a shame. Who could have done such a thing?"

"I know. What's this town coming to?"

Nathan's food eventually arrived, and he hopped into the car and drove into the office. He half expected Mark Ellison to be waiting for him. He spent the morning in meetings and responding to emails while waiting for the inevitable call from reception. Around lunchtime his mother texted to ask if he could stop by the house on his way home. He texted back that he would see her after work. He hoped it wouldn't take too long as he was looking forward to moving on to the next lesson that evening.

The rest of the day felt like a distraction—both from fear that he might receive another visit from an agitated federal agent and from the excitement of what might happen that evening. He was grateful that his grandfather had been so prepared for this eventuality. And yet, he'd rather have him around to help him now. Each time he played the videos he felt his grandfather's absence all over again. His world was rapidly changing, and he had no choice but to find his way on this journey alone.

Chapter 22

The end of the day finally came, and he made his way out to the car. Like everyone else, he had that Friday feeling. On top of that it was now June and he could feel the alluring tug of summer. As strange as the idea seemed, most of his excitement came from the thought of going home and learning the next lesson. Before he could do that though he had a stop to make. As he climbed into the car, he took one last look around the parking lot. He couldn't shrug off the nagging feeling that Ellison would show up with more pointed questions. As he scanned it, all he could see were company staff heading out for the day. As he drove out, the guard waved to him. He smiled and waved back.

"Have a good weekend Sal."

"You too Mister Briggs."

It was still nice and warm outside, and he drove with the window down, music playing on the radio. As he got close to his own house, instead of turning down the lane he continued on towards his parents'. His brother was just leaving as Nathan turned in to their driveway.

"Hey Nathan."

"Hey Chris, how are you?"

"I'm good. Did Mom text you too?"

"Yeah, any idea what she wants?"

Chris reached across and picked something up from the passenger seat.

"It's blueberry season. Obviously, Grandmother and the cook have been busy in the gardens and the kitchen."

Nathan laughed. He'd have to get used to this new arrangement. Before leaving the previous year, living in the main house he had been used to coming downstairs at various times of the year to fresh-baked pies, cakes, breads and whatever else came out of the kitchen.

"Fair enough. I'd better head in then. Will I see you around the mill anytime soon?"

"Yeah, I'll actually be around next week. Let's get some time together."

"Great! I'd like that."

"Alright buddy. I have to run. Emma's waiting. I'll catch you soon, okay?"

"Sure Chris. Have a good weekend."

His brother drove off and Nathan pulled up in front of the house.

"Mom! I'm here," he shouted as he walked through the front door.

He still felt awkward about walking into his parents' home since returning, especially given that he no longer lived there. His mother appeared from the kitchen with a big smile.

"Hello honey, it's good to see you. We were so happy you came to the BBQ on Monday."

"Of course, Mom. Why wouldn't I?"

"I don't know. You seem so independent these days. I miss seeing you."

He sensed that this was her not-so-subtle way of dropping a hint that he wasn't visiting enough. In some ways she was right. There were so many things going on—some of which he could do without, and some of which excited him. He reassured her that he would try to do better. She led him to the old antique pie safe, where there were several pies lined up on the long oak shelf.

"Take your pick. We have blueberry, raspberry and Boston Creme. Your grandmother and the cook went all out today. You can have two if you'd like. There's plenty."

He selected a Boston Creme and a blueberry—his favorites growing up. His mother covered each pie with clear film for him to take and put them in a cardboard box so it would be easy for him to carry. He'd have to invite Ben over at the weekend. He loved these pies even more than Nathan did.

"Thanks Mom! And tell Grandmother thanks for me."

He kissed her on the cheek. She opened the door for him and walked him out to the car.

"So how do you like your house?"

"I love it Mom. I really appreciate what you guys have done for me."

"You're not too lonely out there by yourself?"

"No, I seem to be busy all the time. It's nice and quiet there, so when I'm home I can just chill. I've started running again too, and it's such a nice area to run in."

"That's good to hear, dear. And don't be a stranger. You're welcome here anytime. You do know that, right?"

Which reminded him that since he was there, he should pop out to the folly and see if the computer contained any more useful information.

"Actually, since I'm here, would you mind if I walked out into the gardens and picked some flowers for the house?"

"Not at all. You'll find some shears in the shed at the bottom of the lawn."

"Thanks Mom! I'll find my way out when I'm done. Tell Dad I said hello."

His mother nodded and gave him a last hug before disappearing back into the house.

※

He made his way around the side of the house to the bottom of the yard, retrieving a pair of pruning shears from a garden shed on the way—it would look odd if he came back without the flowers that he said he was planning to cut. He made his way out to the folly and downstairs into the library. He scratched his head as he entered the room—he still hadn't found a key to the other mysterious room at the back. He'd have to sort that out at some point.

He sat down at the desk and tapped the keyboard. When the screen came to life, he keyed in the password which he'd now memorized. He spent the next twenty minutes clicking through different folders. There were a lot of notes and documents to read. He couldn't find any more videos though. Perhaps there were more on the warehouse computer. Or maybe the videos he had held all of the information and lessons he needed—perhaps they were the only ones his grandfather had time to make before the accident.

He copied a few of the more interesting files onto the spare flash drive in the drawer, stuck it in his pocket when he was done and logged out of the computer. On the way out he closed up everything and stepped outside, taking a deep breath of fresh air. He took his time walking back to the car, taking cuts of flowers from the garden. He laid them on the passenger seat next to the pies and enjoyed the warm weather, and the scent of flowers and blueberries, on the short drive home.

※

As he pulled into his driveway, he was confronted by a familiar Maserati parked in front of the house. He smiled as he got out of the car.

"Oh nice, flowers. For me? And pies?"

He laughed as Serena stepped up to give him a hand carrying everything into the house.

"You can thank my grandmother. She and the cook can't help themselves sometimes."

Serena laughed.

"My family are never in one place long enough to do those things. I sometimes wish we were."

He unlocked the door and held it open. They walked inside and laid the flowers on the kitchen counter.

"Do you have a vase and some scissors?"

He found a vase in a cupboard and scissors in a drawer in the kitchen. His mother had thought of everything when she stocked the house. He handed both to Serena, who separated all of the flowers, and took her time cleaning each one individually and trimming all the stems until she was satisfied. She filled the vase with water and carefully arranged them.

"There, how's that?"

Nathan looked on with interest. The arrangement was beautiful.

"If you ever decide to quit your career with your family, you could always open a florist shop. They're beautiful."

Serena smiled as she placed the vase in the center of the dining table.

"I'm glad you like it."

He nodded, admiring her handiwork.

"What brings you here? I didn't know you were going to be in the area today."

"I had a bit of free time, so I decided to pop up and surprise you. Surprise!"

They laughed and smiled warmly at one another. He was happy to see her, even more so as it was unexpected.

"So how was your week?"

"The usual. Meetings, work, bit of jogging here and there. We had a family BBQ on Monday, which was nice. It was great to see everyone. A bit of work talk, but most of it was just friendly chat."

"It must be nice to have family time like that. My family are always on the go, and we don't often get that kind of time together. We used to, but not for a very long time now."

A shadow briefly crossed her face before she shrugged it off. He decided not to press the issue. He figured if she wanted to elaborate, she would; and in any case, he didn't feel that he knew her well enough yet to pry. Instead, realizing he wasn't being much of a host, he changed the subject.

"How about a piece of pie?"

Serena smiled.

"I'd love to, but I ate on the way over. I wasn't sure if I'd find you here, so I stopped for a quick bite—just in case."

"No worries. Do you mind if I make something?"

"Not at all. Don't let me stop you!"

He grabbed a few things out of the refrigerator and made a sandwich. He joined Serena in the living room and slowly ate while they talked.

"Any plans for the weekend?"

She shrugged.

"I may have to go out of town. I'm just waiting to hear back to be honest."

She seemed a bit down on family and work tonight. It wasn't like her. She usually appeared to be into the part she played in her family. He admired that about her.

"Is everything alright?"

"Yeah. No, it is. It's just I sometimes envy the things other people do with their families. You seem to be close to yours and aren't always on the go. It must be a nice feeling."

He hadn't really thought about it that way before. He supposed from her perspective he appeared relatively normal.

"I suppose so. I mean my relationship with my father can be like a rollercoaster at times, though at the moment it seems to be in a good place. And my father, brother and sister are often on the go. I guess I'm lucky as I've only really just started working with them. I don't have the same responsibilities that they have. It means I get more time to myself. I'd imagine that will change in time."

"Get the most out of this time, Nathan, because when you lose it, it'll be the time you'll think about the most."

As he sat with her, there was another thing that was weighing on his mind.

"Serena, can I talk to you about something?"

She nodded.

"Sure, go for it."

"Promise me you won't be upset. Hear me out before you judge me?"

She looked at him quizzically and nodded.

"Okay. I promise."

He then proceeded to tell her about Mark Ellison, the interactions they'd had and the reason for those encounters. He mentioned Ellison's interest in Serena and her brother William. She quietly listened throughout. When he finished, he looked at her expectantly, wondering how she was going to react. When she said nothing, he spoke.

"Are you upset with me for not having said anything sooner?"

She looked away before answering.

"Nathan, there are things about my family that you don't understand. Things that I can't really talk about. Not yet anyways. It's not unusual for people to believe that we are—well, that our family is doing things that they shouldn't be doing. Your story does explain something though. There has been a man nosing around our apartment building in Boston asking questions. It must be this man Ellison you are talking about."

She hadn't reacted to his mention of the strange deaths. He could see from her posture that she wasn't going to say much more on the matter. He hoped that she wasn't angry with him.

"Thanks for saying something. I do appreciate it."

"No worries Serena. Look, I'm sorry if I upset you, but I thought it was something you should know. I'm just sorry that I didn't say anything sooner."

After a moment she changed the subject to Nathan's house. He realized that he hadn't even given her a tour yet, so he quickly put away his plate and took her around the house first, and then outside and up to the games room.

"Clearly this isn't your mother's idea. Your father had a hand in this space."

They both laughed. He explained that he hadn't had much of a chance to use it since moving in.

"You should use it more. It's a nice space. A place to unwind and forget about work and life."

"Yeah, I just never seem to get the time. But you're right, I should use it more."

"Remember, no regrets. Enjoy your life while you are living it."

He thought how she sometimes seemed older than her age. She came across as someone who had lived a long lifetime and spoke with the wisdom of hindsight. They sat and talked for a while longer before Serena stood.

"I think it's time to get back. If I do have to head out on business I may have to leave tonight or very early in the morning."

He stood up, nodded and walked her out to her car. He plucked up the courage to lean in and kiss her. She leaned into him, returning the kiss. They stood like this for a moment, an awkward embrace, before she pulled back and smiled.

"I do have to go. It's getting late."

He cleared his throat.

"Yeah, of course. Will I see you again?"

"Of course you will. Soon. Things are complicated but I promise I'll let you know when I'm free again."

He nodded in understanding. Not because he understood what complicated meant for her, but because he was getting used to her being constantly on the go.

"I'll text you and let you know if I have to go out of town."

"Sure, no worries. Thanks for coming up to see me."

She smiled, got into the car and opened the window.

"You take care of yourself, weaver."

Before he could respond, she drove off down the lane and disappeared into the night. He stood frozen on the spot. What did she mean by that? Was she being clever about his work, or was there something more to it than that? He thought about the lawyer's strange comment at lunch. Did everyone know about his family secret? Was everyone in on this all along? And there was Ellison's interest in her and her brother and everything that was happening. And the fact that she had met his grandfather. What did she know that she was not telling him?

He looked briefly up at the stars.

"Grandfather, I really wish you were here right now."

Dragan returned in time to follow Nathan from the mill to his parents'. He parked down the road and walked up to the edge of the property through the woods to the side, watched Nathan go into the house and then watched him disappear out into the back. He decided to follow—at a safe distance, of course. Not that Nathan would be able to detect him. Dragan was very adept at remaining hidden. He watched as he disappeared into one of the outbuildings on the property. Why were the wealthy so fascinated with recreating miniature versions of ancient buildings?

He kept his distance and waited about half an hour before Nathan emerged from the building. On the way back he watched as Nathan clipped flowers before disappearing back toward the house, presumably to make his way home. When he disappeared around the corner of the house, Dragan wound his way back to the small outbuilding and stepped inside. It looked like a miniature version of an old temple.

He opened the door and walked into the room that housed an altar in the center—the only object in the room. He walked around it. He ran his hands over the carved surface. He could feel the faint hum of magic, like static, crackling on the palms of his hands. There was clearly something hidden here, and Nathan had access to it. This boy was growing more interesting day by day. Another thing he would have to convey to his mother. He decided to skip another night of surveillance and drive back to Boston to await his orders.

Chapter 23

The next morning Nathan awoke to the sound of his phone ringing.

"Hello?"

"Nathan, it's your mother."

"Hey Mom. What's up?"

There was a brief pause and he could hear the sound of muffled voices in the background. After a moment his father came on the phone.

"Hey Nathan, it's your dad. It's about your grandfather. We've just received a call from the Washington state police. Part of the fuselage of your grandfather's plane washed up onshore."

Nathan pushed himself upright. He sensed there was more coming.

"And?"

"The body of the pilot also washed up nearby."

So that was it. Confirmation. Even though they had all suspected the truth, it was impossible to rationalize away facts like these.

"I'm really sorry Dad."

His father remained quiet and his mother's voice soon came back on the phone.

"I'm so sorry to wake you up like this, Nathan. But we thought you'd want to know right away."

He shook his head. He didn't quite know what to say.

"Yeah, of course Mom. I understand. And thanks for letting me know."

"We're here if you need anything."

"I know that Mom. I'm going to get up now. I'll call you a bit later."

They said their goodbyes and he made his way downstairs for a cup of coffee. He sat at the dining table for a while staring at the steam rising off the slowly cooling cup. He had always been particularly close to his grandfather. And in light of recent events, he thought maybe he understood that interest a bit more now. Still, he wanted to believe it was about more than their shared abilities. His grandfather was a good man, and he'd looked up to him. He poured the cold coffee into the sink and made another cup. This time he sat on the sofa watching the morning news on the television. He was half listening when a news segment came on that made him sit up straight.

"And in other news, local businessman Hedlund Briggs' plane was found earlier this morning washed up on the coast of Washington state. The body of the pilot was found nearby but no sign of Briggs. It is too early to speculate as to the cause of the accident that brought his jet down a little over two months ago. The small town of New Comfort, where he's from, has also recently been rocked by a series of gruesome murders. Police and federal authorities are investigating possible links between those murders and other unsolved murders around the country in recent years."

As he listened to the news, he wondered briefly just how unrelated those two things were. The murders had started just after his grandfather's disappearance. Maybe there was more to it than anyone realized. And here he sat, square in the middle of both sets of events, connected in ways that he had yet to understand. Ellison knew something though. He clearly hadn't divulged everything that he knew—or suspected—when they spoke, Nathan was sure of it; but for the moment he felt the need to shower and head over to his parents' house. It was the right place for him to be.

On the way to the house, he carried the heavy burden of his grandfather's loss. In light of everything that had surfaced over the last couple of months, he needed him around now more than ever. How could he just spring all of this on him without being there to provide answers? Of course, it wasn't as though Nathan had been around either. He'd left as soon as he graduated university. What was his grandfather supposed to have done—stopped him from going away? Showed up one day in some random country that he was passing through and dropped it all on him there? His grandfather had respected his wishes, and in the end, they'd both simply run out of time. It wasn't anyone's fault.

This was clearly a part of the responsibility that his father always droned on about. For the first time, instead of feeling defensive about it all he felt remorse. Maybe his father was right. In his desire to carve out his own independence, maybe he had let his family down.

When he got to his parents' house the situation didn't improve. His mother greeted him and took him into the sitting room where his grandmother was sitting on the sofa with a cup of tea.

"Hello dear. We didn't expect you to come over."

He sat down on the sofa next to his grandmother and put a hand on hers.

"I needed to come over, Grandmother. I'm so sorry. I miss him so much."

He choked back tears as he sat with her.

"Now, now, dear. We all knew. At least now we might have some closure. I just wish they had found him too."

His mother sat opposite with her hands folded, looking contemplative.

"Your father isn't in the best of moods, as you can imagine. Up to you if you want to see him."

He considered it for a moment and decided that he was damned either way. The right thing to do was to go and see him, regardless of the outcome.

"I'll go see him. Where is he?"

"He's outside in the back yard."

Nathan nodded and pushed himself up from the sofa.

"Will you be okay, Grandmother?"

She nodded and smiled, brushing a tear away from a wrinkled cheek.

"I've already made my peace dear. I'm alright. You go and see your father."

His father stood on the patio looking out across the yard and the gardens towards the woods in the distance.

"Dad."

His father stood silent for a moment before turning.

"Nathan."

"I'm sorry Dad."

His father nodded.

"Nothing to be done about it son. He's gone."

"Yes, I know—"

"Not now Nathan."

His father stood looking reflective before continuing.

"I understand from people at the mill that you've been distracted and seem to be in a rush to get out of work. Is there a problem?"

Nathan stood fixed to the spot, trying to figure out a response. He hadn't realized his behavior was that obvious to people. But of course, it made sense that word of how he was progressing—or not—would get back to his father. He also wasn't prepared to have a discussion with his father about the things he'd learned from his grandfather, or the visits from Ellison. There was a lot going on around him, just not a lot he could easily talk about.

"No sir. No problems. It's just a lot to take in is all. I promise that I'll be more aware of things going forward."

His father considered him for a moment.

"You know Nathan, I was opposed to your grandfather leaving you so much of the company in trust. But he saw something in you. I have to believe that he knew what he was doing and that he did the right thing. He was a brilliant man. Don't dishonor his memory by betraying his trust in you. The best thing you can do is focus on becoming the best grandson to him—and son to me. Learn to love and respect what our family has built. In that way you don't just bring honor to yourself, or me or your grandfather, but to all those who came before us, who worked hard to provide us with a life we could be proud of."

He looked at his father, unsure how best to respond. It was a rebuke from his father, but not like their past interactions. He felt disappointed in himself for appearing not to care about the opportunity his father had given him and decided that no matter what else was going on, he would try to do better.

"I will do my best. I'm sorry if I've disappointed you."

"You've not disappointed me. Not yet."

His father turned back towards the gardens, quietly dismissing him. He walked back into the house and said his goodbyes. His mother walked him out to the car.

"He loves you, Nathan. He just has a difficult time expressing it."

He nodded and hugged his mother before climbing into the car. As he drove off down the driveway his sister was just turning in. She stopped and rolled down her window.

"How are they?"

"Mom and Grandmother are doing alright. Dad's in one of his moods."

"Ah, you got a lecture then?"

He looked properly chastened. She laughed.

"Don't take it so seriously, little brother. You know Dad. You did the right thing stopping by. He'll remember that more."

"Yeah, I suppose so. Anyways, I should let you go in."

"Thanks. I'll message you and maybe we can meet up. It'd be good to see you."

"I'd like that."

As he drove towards home, he thought about his father's words. He was right, even if there were mitigating circumstances. He vowed to work harder to separate his responsibilities to his family and work from his extracurricular activities. He wondered how his grandfather had managed it all those years. Not for the first time he wished that he was able to speak with the older man.

Dark clouds began to form overhead and he could feel that there was a storm brewing. As he walked through the front door the first drops of rain began to fall. The weather mirrored his dark and gloomy mood. He locked the front door out of habit and sat at the dining table for a few minutes to gather his thoughts. He clearly needed to focus more on the family business. If his father had thought it was out of control, he would have received a more severe lecture. Instead, his father had fired a shot across the bow and would leave it up to him to decide if he'd received the message properly, which he clearly felt that he had.

He had the weekend to put his head in order and be ready to return to work on Monday with full concentration. That said, he also had the rest of the day and all of the next to review his grandfather's videos and practice the things he was tasked with learning. As the weather continued to deteriorate, he got up and closed the blinds for privacy. He had a general feeling that he was being watched, a feeling not out of character for someone who had federal agents showing up at his work and home. But it wasn't just that. He couldn't help but feel that there was something else out there, something that he couldn't yet put his finger on, that presented a real danger to him.

He walked around the house to ensure that everything was secure and that he was alone, before retrieving his laptop and a candle, which he placed on the coffee table in the living room. He logged into the computer and opened the next video. He pressed play and settled back on the sofa to watch the next lesson.

"By now either your skepticism and disbelief have been put at ease, or I was wrong, and you are not the one. But let's assume for a moment that I was right, and you've been successful with things this far. In today's lesson you are going to learn how to use your power, and the focus of your mind, to move objects."

Move objects. Like a fork? A rock? A car? He decided to find an object that would give him a higher possibility of success. He got up from the sofa and walked into the kitchen, where he looked through various drawers until he came across the lightest thing that he could find—a paperclip. He pressed play again and continued watching. Now came the hard part. Clearing his mind of thoughts. He sat upright, hands folded in his lap, eyes closed, and relaxed his shoulders. He took a few slow, deep breaths and then settled into a normal pattern of breathing while letting thoughts flow into—and then out of—his mind. After about five minutes his mind began to feel clear. He opened his eyes and spoke the word that his grandfather had used in the video.

"*Demovere.*"

There was a second of stillness, and a feeling as though the air were being sucked out of the room, as the paperclip shifted slightly on the table. Well, that was something at least. It worked better than his first failed attempt at lighting the candle. He'd have to work harder to let go of his thoughts and his emotions; a clear mind was one of the keys that enabled him to access whatever it was that flowed through—or from—him.

He decided to take a break. He got up from the sofa and walked over to the front door, unlocked it and stepped out onto the front porch. The rain was falling steadily now. The wind had died down and somewhere in the distance he could hear the steady rumble of thunder. He let his thoughts wander until they began to settle on the agitation that he felt with himself over his encounter with his father. He'd brought that one on himself. His father was just doing his job of parenting and being a boss. He couldn't be faulted for that. Nathan was irritated with himself for having let his focus go at work. And now it was interfering with his ability to learn the lessons his grandfather was trying to teach him.

He stood on the porch for a while, until his head began to feel clear. When he felt ready, he went back inside the house, locked the door, and once again sat comfortably on the sofa. He closed his eyes, took a few deep breaths and continued to calm his mind. Soon he felt like he was in the right space to try again.

"*Demovere.*"

The paperclip slid forward, across the coffee table and onto the floor. He felt a sense of elation knowing that he was able to advance his abilities. As if to ensure that everything else he'd learned still worked properly, he turned his attention toward the candle.

"*Ignis.*"

The candle wick flared to life. It worked. Clearing

his mind and finding focus helped him to better access his abilities. He spent the next half-hour practicing on the paperclip and found that he was able to successfully move it across the table each time. He decided to be more ambitious and turned his attention to the candle, using a word he'd learned in the previous lesson to extinguish it.

"*Extinguo.*"

The flame flared and disappeared. Before his mind could fill with more fragmented thoughts he spoke again.

"*Demovere.*"

The candle inched forward across the coffee table. It took slightly more exertion for him to make it move than the paperclip, but it worked. He was sure that if his grandfather were here with him, he would be very proud of what his grandson had accomplished. Or at least he hoped that would be the case. The video contained other commands for moving objects, enabling him to bring things towards him, or move them away, and also to regulate the speed at which objects moved or to move them even more forcefully. He decided for safety to stick with the paperclip for the moment, until he learned how to control it. He found that he was able to move the paperclip both away from and towards him, but he struggled trying to move it with greater force.

After a few hours of mixed results, he decided to stop for the day and give it a rest. He had a slight headache from the exertion. Magic clearly took its toll. It was time to switch gears and do something fun—no work, no lessons. Playing a bit of pool, some Xbox, listening to music, and not worrying about work, life, or learning to be a weaver seemed like a perfect distraction. He just wanted to feel normal for a bit.

He spent the rest of the afternoon having fun, relaxing and shutting out the world. He even made a few drinks. As early evening approached, his stomach began to rumble, and he remembered that he hadn't eaten anything all day. He shut everything off and ran through the rain across to the house. He'd just started getting things ready to make pasta when he heard a car pull up out front. Through a window in the dining room he could see the lights of the car switching off, but he couldn't really make out the details of it or its occupant. He walked over to the front door just as a loud knocking broke the silence. He opened the door to a wet, disheveled-looking Mark Ellison.

"You have a lot of nerve," he shouted as he shouldered his way into the house.

Taken aback, Nathan stepped away from the door and the intruding visitor.

"Excuse me? You can't just barge in here."

"I can't believe you're trying to interfere with my investigation. Calling the offices and speaking with my superiors. You have a lot of nerve, kid."

Nathan looked perplexed. He didn't have a clue what the agent was talking about.

"Mister Ellison, I think you've got your wires crossed. I haven't spoken with anyone about you."

Technically that wasn't true but certainly not in the context that the man was implying.

"Someone is trying to get me thrown off this case. You and your family have those kinds of connections and would be able to pull a stunt like that. Don't tell me you haven't."

Nathan shook his head.

"My family might, but I don't. And right now, we have other things taking our attention. If you don't mind Mister Ellison, I'd like you to leave. Or I just might be tempted to see if we *do* have the kind of connections that you're referring to."

The agent stood his ground for a moment, looking angry and slightly menacing, before his shoulders sagged and he looked away.

"Well, if not you, then who?"

"I'm not the federal agent here. That's your job to figure out. I suggest you stop wasting your time on me and figure out who's really behind it. Maybe you're getting too close to the killer. Maybe they're the ones with the connections."

Ellison looked sharply at him as though he was about to say something, but then seemed to decide against it.

"Now please. It's Saturday night. I'm tired of you intruding on my time."

"Fine. But if I find out you're involved in this you can bet that I'll be coming for you."

"You do that, Mister Ellison. But I'm afraid you're going to be very disappointed."

He walked over to the front door, which was still slightly ajar, and motioned for Ellison to leave. Without comment, the angry man stormed out, got into his car, and drove off. Nathan locked up, for good reason this time, and returned to the kitchen to finish making dinner.

Later, as he flipped through the TV channels, he thought to himself that this guy was getting to be too much. There was something really wrong with him. The way he acted, it was as though he was somehow personally involved in whatever was going on—not like the kind of professional that Nathan would have expected. As he settled on a movie it occurred to him that he didn't even know which federal agency the man worked for. The next time they crossed paths, and he was sure that they would, he would ask to see his identification again and get the details of his department. He'd had enough of being pushed around by this guy and it was time for it to stop.

Chapter 24

At Boston Logan Airport a black private jet taxied over to a terminal for private, non-commercial flights. Dragan waited in the terminal, patiently. It was three in the morning on Sunday and he'd been summoned. The terminal was quiet, and it wasn't long before his mother Jelena emerged.

"Dragan. It's good to see you."

She kissed him on both cheeks, hugging him close.

"You spoke with our contacts in government?"

"Yes Mother. They said they would do their best. It seems this Ellison is running rogue from the agency he works for."

"And who does he work for?"

"He's with the CIA."

Jelena stopped in her tracks.

"Why is he involved in these cases then? Surely these deaths are a local police issue. And we never have problems with them. We'll need to tread carefully. Still. I have many friends."

"My understanding is that he isn't on an official case

at the moment. He's taken leave for a few months. No one is quite sure what it is he's working on."

Jelena shook her head as they walked towards the car.

"I don't like it. Something doesn't feel right about this. I want you to stay on top of it."

"Of course."

"Now about this other matter. You're sure about it?"

"Yes, there's no doubt about it. This kid is a weaver."

"Just like his grandfather."

"I'm sorry?"

"I'm afraid I haven't told you everything, my son. But there's not enough time for that now. Let's get to the apartment."

The driver dropped them at the hotel. Jelena and Dragan went upstairs and talked into the early hours of the morning.

In the middle of the night Serena's phone rang.

"Hello?"

"Your aunt has arrived in Boston. This can't be a coincidence."

"No, I suppose not. What should we do?"

"Come into the office. I've summoned your brother."

Davorin wasn't meant to be in Boston. What was he doing there?

"Are you at the office now?"

"Yes, I arrived a few hours ago."

"Alright Father. I'll be right over."

He clicked off and Serena was left sitting in her apartment, wondering what was happening. Davorin and his sister, Jelena, had had a very tenuous relationship through the years, down to bad blood between two of their children that resulted in the deaths of them both. They each blamed the other for those deaths, and though they had generally kept a respectful distance from one another, there was a constant tension between them.

She changed into more suitable clothes. She took the elevator downstairs to the lobby and stepped outside into the cool air. Boston at four in the morning was peaceful and still. It really was a beautiful city, many who'd had the good fortune to experience it in their lifetimes holding it fondly in their hearts. No matter where she traveled, she would always be fond of it.

She walked four blocks to the office building. Davorin and her brother William were already waiting for her. She wasn't entirely sure what was going on, but from the looks on their faces she could tell that it was something serious.

※

On Sunday morning Nathan slept in. The rain had ceased overnight and by morning clouds had given way to crystal-clear blue skies and sun. The chaos of the prior evening felt like a distant memory. He wasn't entirely sure what Ellison was on about. The man had seemed slightly unhinged during the visit—not the kind of behavior Nathan would expect from someone with authority.

He roused himself from bed, changed into his jogging gear and walked downstairs. He made a quick shot of espresso and downed it in one go. He needed it to wake himself up. He wasn't about to let the agent's visit the prior evening stop him from having a good Sunday. He laced up his running sneakers, and stretched before setting off on his morning run. The rain had freshened the air, and everything around him was green and vibrant. He took his time and found a pace that allowed him to look at everything in his surroundings while he jogged. He decided to run towards town this morning and see if he could make it all the way.

As he approached the outskirts, he slowed to a walk and took his time wandering down Main Street, occasionally waving and saying good morning to people. When he caught his breath, he wound his way around the narrow streets and back in the direction of home. He managed to jog at a sedate pace most of the way back and walked the last bit to cool down, before finally ending up at the bottom of his driveway.

With the good weather it was a good day to air the house out, so he walked around opening windows and letting fresh air stream throughout the house. A salty sea breeze blew in from the ocean and he could hear the screech of gulls flying overhead. The weather certainly improved his mood and he felt clear-headed and energized. On his way in from the run he noticed that the garden needed tending, so after breakfast, he went out to the garage and got the lawn mower out. When he was finished cutting the grass, he got out the gardening tools his mother had helpfully supplied with the house and spent the rest of the morning pruning, weeding and tidying plants around the property.

By lunchtime he had finished, and stood back to admire his handiwork. His gardens and yard looked beautiful and he was proud of the hard work he'd put in to get things looking smart once again. As his gaze passed across the front porch, he noticed for the first time a series of six hooks spaced evenly along the underside of the porch roof. His mother must have intended for him to hang flower baskets if he wanted. He decided to drive to the garden center at the edge of town to see if they had anything that he liked.

He parked and wandered inside. It was full of people looking at plants, pushing flat carts stacked up with various things for the garden, or just wandering about, like him, enjoying being outside in the good weather. He made his way to a section that held hundreds of hanging baskets and picked out the ones that he liked. He found a pushcart and, in short order, loaded it with six baskets. When he got home he lined them up on the ground, figuring out which order he wanted to hang them in. As he finished, he stepped back and admired them for a bit before tidying up all of the gardening equipment. It looked great.

Before doing anything else, he took another quick shower, changed into shorts and a t-shirt and walked outside to sit on the front porch for a while. Soon after, he spotted a familiar figure cycling towards him.

"Good morning stranger," he said as Ben walked up the steps.

"It's afternoon. And what's so good about it?"

Nathan raised a questioning eyebrow at his friend.

"Somebody woke up on the wrong side of the bed this morning."

Ben scowled.

"Where have you been? I haven't heard anything from you."

"It's been a bit of a hectic week."

"Too busy for your friends?"

He was clearly in a bad mood. Nathan offered him a seat on the porch, and they sat together in silence for a few minutes.

"What's up Ben?"

His friend stared off into the distance.

"Nothing. Sorry. It's just that with your job and all this other shit you're into now it feels like we never get time together. I'd been hoping once you got back, I'd see you more. But sometimes it feels like you're still away."

Nathan thought about what his friend was saying. Maybe he had kept himself to himself too much. It wasn't the first time someone, including Ben, had suggested he get more of a life.

"I'm sorry Ben. I didn't realize that my going away bothered you so much. And it's not like I haven't seen you or spent time with you since getting back. It's just been, well, complicated."

His friend shrugged.

"You used to tell me everything. Now I feel like you have all these secrets and I'm not a part of your life anymore."

That stung. Especially since Ben was the only person he had confided in. He wasn't sure what to say to his friend.

"And now you have this other thing. And what about that anyways?"

Under other circumstances he might have held back from telling Ben anything further about all of that, but given what his friend had just expressed, he decided that he didn't have any other choice.

"Well. About that. It turns out that there's more truth to it than I'd believed. I'm not sure how to say this. Or maybe I shouldn't say it. Maybe I should just show you."

He got up from his chair and disappeared into the house, reappearing a minute later with the candle. He set it on a small side table between their chairs.

"Give me a moment—and please don't say anything. Let me just see if I can show you."

Ben looked at him with an odd expression. Even

though he obviously wanted to say something, he kept quiet as he'd been asked. Nathan scanned the property quickly just to be sure they weren't being watched, and then closed his eyes and started to clear his mind—which was difficult as his best friend was sitting there staring at him and he was completely unsure if he'd be able to do this in front of someone else. As his mind began to feel still and his thoughts calmed, he took a deep breath and opened his eyes, looking straight at the candle.

"*Ignis.*"

The candle flame burst into life. It was much easier to do than he'd thought. He figured that it must be because of all of his practice during the week. Ben jumped back in his chair.

"Jesus, fuck. What was that?"

Nathan looked up to find his friend staring at him with a look of horror on his face.

"What the hell Nathan. Is this some kind of trick?"

He shook his head as he leaned over and blew the candle out.

"This is what I've discovered about myself, Ben. About my family. My grandfather left a bunch of videos on his computer for me to watch. He created these, I don't know, training videos for me. It's crazy, right?"

Ben picked up the candle and turned it over, looking for a mechanism or something that would explain what he'd just seen.

"I really don't get it."

"There's nothing to get. Everything my grandfather

wrote about is real. At least, this thing about being a weaver is real. I'm also beginning to think my dreams are tied up in it—that they have some kind of significance as well. I don't know. I don't exactly have anyone to talk to about it."

They sat in silence. His friend slowly recovered before he spoke again.

"Is there anything else?"

"Well…"

"Go on then."

"Set the candle back on the table."

He set the candle back in the center of the table while Nathan once more cleared his mind, letting all thoughts fade away until he was ready.

"*Demovere.*"

The candle slid towards Ben, who caught it just before it fell off the edge.

"Holy shit. Nate, this is completely nuts."

Nathan just smiled at his friend.

"Tell me about it. To be fair, that's about as much as I've learned so far. There are more lessons, but I'm trying to get my head around each one before moving onto the next."

Ben shook his head, his eyes darting from the candle to his friend.

"So, it is all real then. What the hell was your grandfather into? Some kind of black magic or something?"

Nathan shrugged.

"I have no idea. But you can count on the fact that

he knew a hell of a lot more about this than the couple of things I've just shown you."

His friend didn't know what to say. He didn't know how to react to this and wondered, selfishly, what it meant for their friendship.

"No wonder I haven't heard from you in a week."

"No, it's not just that. It's work. I've been to the house a few times. And yesterday part of my grandfather's plane washed up on the beach in Washington state—along with the body of his pilot. It's been... stressful."

"Oh Nate, I'm so sorry. I had no idea. Are you okay?"

Nathan thought about it for a moment. He felt like he'd been trying to avoid thinking about how he felt. He felt emotional as he spoke about it with his friend.

"There's just so much going on all at once. I feel like I'm juggling lots of balls, and none of them very well."

"Well, judging by what you just showed me you're not doing too badly. I'm sure things will get better, Nate. It's just a tough time at the moment. You're strong though. You'll be fine. And you've always got me to rely on."

They both laughed. He knew that Ben was there for him. He just didn't want it to feel like he was burdening him with everything that was going on. Instead, he changed the subject. He'd figure out later where his friend fit into things. Maybe there was a role for him to play.

"So enough about me. What about you? What have you been doing?"

Ben talked to him about his classes, homework and how studying seemed to take up so much time. Nathan sensed there was something else bothering him.

"What's stressing you out, Ben?"

His friend looked away for a moment.

"I told you about that guy and how he stopped by. Well. I haven't seen or heard from him since. He hasn't responded to any of my messages or calls. I've no idea what's going on."

Nathan smiled.

"Ah so that's it. Listen Ben, you said he works with his family. Like I do. Like Serena. And you know how crazy things have been for me. Maybe it's the same for him. I'm sure he's just been busy. And let's face it, if he didn't like you, he wouldn't have stopped by to see you, right?"

That brought out a smile from his friend.

"Yeah, I suppose so. I guess I just need to be more patient."

They both laughed. Patience had never been one of Ben's best character traits.

"Thanks Nate. I'm sure you're right. I'll just give it some time. Listen, I hate to chat and run but I need to get back into town and pick some things up for Mom for dinner. I just wanted to swing by and see if you were around."

Nathan nodded as they got up from their chairs. He walked his friend down the front steps to his bicycle.

"Keep practicing. It's weird but it's part of who you are, right?"

"I guess so. I can't pretend it's not real now."

"No, you can't. Take some time to read those journals. History is important, and they might help you to understand more about your family and your abilities. I'm sure your grandfather would have insisted you learn everything, not just how to use this power but why you have it and when to use it."

"I think you're probably right. I just wish he were here for me to talk to. I miss him so much."

"I know you do Nate. But you'll be fine. He's left you an awful lot to learn from. And you're one of the smartest people I know. You'll figure it out."

Ben lifted his bike from the ground and hopped on it.

"Call me later if you need to talk. I'd better run before my mother kills me."

Nathan laughed.

"Say hi to your mom for me. And safe ride home."

Ben smiled and set off down the driveway. As he turned onto the lane he waved at his friend, and then disappeared off into the distance. Nathan gathered up the candle and walked back into the house.

Chapter 25

Over the course of the week Nathan buried himself in his work, and in the evenings, after he was sure he'd completed everything he needed to, he continued to practice his grandfather's lessons. He managed to get through just one more video during the week, as the lessons were becoming progressively more difficult. He learned how to form a ball of energy and then throw it at other objects. It took him a few evenings to learn to properly form the ball between the palms of his hands without it dissipating. It took a couple more evenings to learn how to properly direct the energy at an object without it going off in the wrong direction. He practiced this in the back yard, out of sight from anyone, and away from possible breakables inside the house.

After the news of their grandfather's plane wreckage, his father decided not to travel and spent much of his time at the mill attending to business issues from there. As a consequence, he and Nathan saw a great deal of each other. He was still distant after the news, but he made time to sit with Nathan throughout the week and answer questions that his son had about the mill and their other operations. Despite his variable mood, he showed moments of genuine interest in his son's progress, and at times a bit of pride that he had listened to him and was showing a deeper focus while at work.

"So, the parent company for all of our holdings is run out of our Boston offices?"

"Yes. That's why your sister and brother are away from the mills most of the time. They range across a much wider portfolio than the mills these days and help me out with running those. The mills have good strong management in place, and practically run themselves. We also have a European headquarters in London that answers to our head offices here."

Nathan had seen the strength of the mill operations management team in the meetings he'd attended with them over the past couple of months, and he'd been able to learn a lot from their approach to running the business. Still, it was no substitute for having his father around. For all of his ability to be a massive pain in the ass, his father was incredibly business-savvy and had a strong handle on running things. Nathan realized that he could do far worse than spend time learning from him. As the week progressed, he developed a much clearer understanding of the reach of their businesses and learned that in addition to the Boston and London headquarters there were offices in many different countries for those who wanted to deal with the Briggs family and everything that they were involved with.

※

With Jelena's arrival, Dragan redoubled his efforts to keep an eye on Nathan. The experience was slightly uncomfortable for him as it was clear that Nathan's effort to engage in his abilities was increasing—and clearly he was very adept at it, as he had never seen a young weaver progress as quickly as this one seemed to be doing. Each attempt crackled across his skin like electricity, even at the distance he kept himself from the house. He didn't need to see what was going on. He could feel everything. Jelena was going to have to decide soon if her campaign against weavers, and this family in particular, would continue, or he might find himself unable to stop him. Things had definitely taken a bad turn.

Acting against weavers was a violation, unless she or her family were in imminent danger. Which they clearly weren't. Even so, this hadn't stopped her before, and she had proved herself willing to risk everything to accomplish her own ends. This couldn't go on forever though. Eventually someone would step in and stop her. But so far, she'd been good at creating misdirection. It had been difficult to hang past indiscretions on her. But she was sailing too close to the edge at the moment and even Dragan was worried about his mother and their family. He didn't feel able to confront her, but he was also increasingly concerned about carrying out her inevitable orders. For now, he sat, and waited, and endured.

※

On Wednesday, Nathan received a call from Serena.

"Hey Nathan. Are you okay?"

There was a harder edge to Serena's voice.

"Yeah, I'm good. You? Is everything alright?"

"I'm well. I'm tied up with things with my father. He's in town and it's always chaos when he's around."

He understood even if his own father was currently distracted by other things, creating chaos of a different sort. As they spoke, he recalled her last words to him as she'd pulled away from his house the previous Friday. He wanted to say something about it but then decided against it. And as his father periodically passed by where he sat, he wasn't sure how he would react if he overheard his son speaking with someone about weavers. He didn't know how much his father knew, but he probably knew enough to react if he heard it.

She explained that she wouldn't be able to stop by during the week. She'd been hoping to find some time, but her father had her running around taking care of a few things. She promised to explain more when she saw him next. It was probably just as well, as he wanted to remain focused on work for the week and pursue his lessons in the evening. He could use a week with no other distractions, to get himself back on track.

"Yeah, sure, that's no problem. Maybe we can find some time at the weekend or next week."

"I'd like that, Nathan. It would be great to see you. Listen. I'm sorry, but I do have to run. Do me a favor, okay? Be careful. Keep your eyes open. Not everything going on around you right now is what you may think it is. I'm sorry I can't explain more now. I promise I will when I see you."

He said that he would, even though he had no idea what he was meant to be careful about. Before he could say anything further the phone clicked off. He sat and stared out of the window and considered calling her straight back. What was she on about? This was the second time in the last two conversations they'd had that she'd said something cryptic, catching him off guard. His suspicions about her previous comment were now heightened by her call. She clearly knew more about Nathan than he knew about her. And given her family's relationship with his grandfather, he was beginning to suspect some of the things that she might know.

Reluctantly, he returned to his work. He'd promised to remain focused and he meant it. It was hard, but he found that he was able to use the technique he'd learned from his grandfather to calm his mind. Before too long, the end of the day arrived, and he'd managed to get through everything his father had left for him.

As expected, he didn't hear anything further from Serena for the remainder of the week. He continued practicing in the evenings, taking periodic breaks to rest, go for runs, and eat. He even spent some time in the games room, as he needed distractions to reduce some of the frustration levels he felt when his attempts didn't go quite as expected. If the rest of the lessons were as difficult, it was going to take him a while to get through all of the ones that his grandfather had left for him. He supposed that he had the time. It wasn't like he was going anywhere anytime soon.

On Friday evening, he decided that it was time to take a break. On the whole he felt work had gone really well, his father seemed pleased, and his lessons had progressed. When he got home, he changed clothes and went for a run. His legs burned a little, and he still didn't have quite the endurance that he'd had before going traveling, but he thought he was seeing improvements and was beginning to enjoy running more and more.

Later that evening he was sitting on the sofa flipping through the different movie and series options on Netflix when the doorbell rang. He froze in his seat. His first thought was that it would be Mark Ellison. Why couldn't this man just leave him alone? He pushed himself up from the sofa and much to his relief could see that it was his best friend. He opened the door with a big smile.

"Ben," he said as his friend pushed in past him.

Something wasn't right.

"What's up buddy?"

Ben turned to him with a look of anguish on his face.

"I still haven't heard from him."

"Who?"

"That guy I met in Boston. I've messaged and everything and no response."

Nathan offered his friend a seat at the dining room table.

"Ben, I…"

"No Nathan. You don't know what it's been like for me. You were away the whole time. I had no one to talk to about anything."

"No, I guess I don't. And I'm sorry that I wasn't here for you. I'm sorry I wasn't here for a lot of things. But I'm here now."

Ben looked up and winced. He'd unintentionally struck a nerve with his friend. He knew that he felt guilty for missing out on time with his grandfather. They'd always been really close when Nathan was growing up, and now he'd never see him again. Ben hadn't meant to stir that up.

"I'm sorry Nate. I know. It's not your fault. None of it is your fault."

They sat at the table in silence for a few moments, each one running things through their head, each one soothing their own personal wounds.

"I guess the thing is I was never as good at making friends as you. I take things like that really personally, and I hate the idea that I might be rejected."

Nathan had always known his friend had insecurities about himself and he reasoned that the last year probably hadn't helped any of that. As confident and strong as he looked on the outside, Ben still held onto the same insecurities he'd always had.

"I'm sorry. I really am. Like I told you last time, I'm sure he's just busy. I heard from Serena the other night and it's the same thing. Her dad's in town and she's always tied up with things. All I'm saying is that he's probably really busy and when he's free he'll surface. You just need to give these things a chance to happen naturally."

In his head he was comparing his friend's situation to his own, though in light of recent events he wasn't sure how similar their issues were. Serena was turning out to be something different than what he'd originally thought. It was something he'd have to figure out how to address when they next met. But for now, his friend was the one who was right in front of him, hurting.

"Yeah Nate, I'm sure you're right. I'm just being impatient. But is it so much to ask to find someone who likes me for me?"

Nathan put a hand on his friend's shoulder. There wasn't any simple answer where relationships were concerned.

"I like you for you. But I know what you mean. I think sometimes you have to just let go and not try so hard. You need to give things—and people—space to breathe and come around on their own."

Ben nodded and smiled.

"I guess you're right. Is that what you're doing with Serena?"

Nathan winced.

"I have no idea what I'm doing with Serena. This week it's had to be about work and learning what my grandfather is trying to teach me. Next week, who knows?"

They both laughed as Ben's stomach rumbled.

"You hungry? I was just about to cook some dinner. Would you like to stay and eat?"

"I don't know. What are you making?"

"How about some spaghetti carbonara? It's quick and we can take it across to the games room and chill. You don't have any plans tonight, do you?"

Ben shook his head.

"No, not really. Let me call Mom and let her know."

"Sure. You do that and I'll get started."

While Ben went out to the porch to call his mother, Nathan set about cooking dinner for the two of them. When it was ready they filled their plates and took them across to the games room, where they ate their dinner and played pool. When they were too tired to stay up any longer, they walked back to the house and Nathan convinced his friend to crash in one of the spare bedrooms. They were both pleased to have spent an evening together chilling, chatting and hanging out like they used to.

Chapter 26

On Saturday morning Nathan was the first one to wake up and make his way downstairs. He made two cups of coffee, figuring that Ben would quickly follow. Within a few minutes the smell of coffee did the trick, and he could hear his friend come rumbling down the stairs.

"Morning Ben. Have you seen the weather outside?"

His friend blinked a few times, clearing the sleep out of his eyes, and looked out through the dining room windows.

"Oh yeah, it looks great."

Nathan laughed. His friend was still half asleep as he sat at the dining table and reached for his coffee.

"It's supposed to be in the low eighties today. What do you say we head to the beach? It's been ages, and I'd really like to get out of this house."

Ben nodded as he took another sip of his coffee.

"Alright, it's settled then."

Ben gave him a thumbs up as Nathan downed the last of his coffee and jogged upstairs to get ready. After twenty minutes, showered and wearing shorts and a t-shirt, he appeared at the bottom of the stairs.

"Ready!"

Ben was just finishing his second cup of coffee.

"That's better. I think that I'm awake now."

After they threw some large beach towels and Ben's bicycle in the back, they climbed into the car and Nathan drove towards his friend's house.

"I won't be long," said Ben. "Let's grab some food and drinks on the way."

Nathan nodded and got out of the car to wait. The morning skies were clear, and the air smelled fresh and clean. It was already beginning to heat up. There was a little traffic going in and out of town, but not too much. It wouldn't take them very long to get to the beach once they set out. After around fifteen minutes Ben appeared at the front door.

"Ready."

"All set?"

"Yep. Shower did the trick. Town first?"

They agreed and drove the short distance over to Main Street, where they parked and quickly figured out the stores they wanted to visit. There was a nice deli that made fresh sandwiches. They went there first and ordered egg and bacon sandwiches for breakfast and subs for lunch. Afterwards they went to a small supermarket just down the street, where they purchased a small cooler, a couple of bags of ice, snacks and drinks.

"I think we should grab some sunblock. It's going to be intense out there."

Ben was right. Nathan had caught a bit too much sun the previous weekend when he cleaned up the garden, and didn't want a repeat of that. They walked to a nearby drugstore and made their purchase before heading back to the car and setting off for the beach. They drove with the windows down, enjoying the rush of wind and feeling full. The early June weather was promising, and they looked forward to putting home, work, school and life generally behind them for a few hours. Sand and seawater were good healers.

When they arrived, the parking wasn't too full. They grabbed the cooler and beach towels and walked down the trail. As they broke through the dunes into the broad expanse of beach, they both stopped briefly to admire the view of the ocean stretching away into the distance. Gulls cried out and the air was tinged with a salt and seaweed smell that was both familiar and friendly. These views and scents made them feel relaxed.

They lay in the sun, enjoying the moment, listening to the crash of the surf. The sound washed over them, clearing away difficult thoughts or anxieties. The beach was their therapist, and they were happy to lie on its warm, sandy sofa. They made small talk as they lay there catching up on bits of their lives around family, work and school. They reminisced about growing up and the amount of time they'd spent coming here as kids. As midday came and slowly started to pass, they opened up the cooler and retrieved their drinks and sandwiches. They sat quietly, eating and people-watching and listening to the waves as they rolled in and out. Out over the water there were a few sailboats and motorboats and further out there were a couple of larger ships, likely heading towards the docks.

At one point, Nathan felt a familiar feeling edging up the back of his neck—that feeling of being watched. He propped himself up on his elbows and scanned the beach, but he couldn't see anyone looking their way or acting in any way threatening. He settled back onto the towel and closed his eyes, taking in the warmth of the sun as it rose higher into the sky.

Finally deciding it was getting too warm, they packed up their things and walked back down to the trail to the parking lot. Nathan dropped Ben off at his house with a promise he'd call later to see how they felt about going out for drinks that night. Neither one felt quite like giving up on the day just yet.

✺

When Nathan got home, he parked and walked into the house, taking the cooler with him. He dumped the water out on the way in one of his flower beds, and put the remaining drinks in the refrigerator. He showered to wash away the sand and put fresh clothes on. The sunblock had mostly done its job, though it was clear as he stood in front of the bathroom mirror that he'd caught a bit more sun than he'd intended. Still, it was the start of a summer tan and he wasn't too worried.

Afterwards, he went back downstairs and spent a couple of hours practicing the lessons he'd already learned. The more he did it the more confident he was starting to become. He guessed that the whole thing was like working a muscle—the more you used it the stronger it got. A couple of hours went by quickly, with flames flickering, objects moving and energy balls bouncing off of objects in the back yard. He had just decided to give it a rest when his cell phone rang. It was Ben.

"Up for some food and drinks still?"

"Yeah, I was thinking, what if we grabbed some lobster rolls and then went to that outdoor bar down by the dock?"

"That sounds great. Say in an hour?"

"Perfect. I'll swing by and pick you up."

They hung up and Nathan cleared away his laptop, the candles and other objects he'd been using. He put everything away and then went outside to water his flower baskets. The sun was moving lower in the sky now as evening approached. After a while, he grabbed a light jacket and set off for Ben's house. As he pulled up, Ben jumped up from the steps and walked gingerly to the car.

The lobster shack was near the docks. They each ordered two lobster rolls and sat at a nearby table, slowly savoring each bite as the butter ran down their chins. These were a common treat since they were kids and they rarely spoke while there was still a lobster roll to be eaten. When they finished, they wiped their hands and faces with wet napkins and set out towards the bar.

About halfway down the dock Nathan's phone beeped. He pulled it from his pocket and stared at the message with an odd look on his face. It was from a number he didn't recognize.

Nathan. It's an emergency. I need to see you right away at the warehouse. Serena

She had added the address of the warehouse that his grandfather had left to him. How did she know about that? He tried calling the number back but there was no answer and no way to leave a message. He looked at his friend and then held the phone out, showing him the messages.

"What is that?"

"It's the warehouse I told you about that my grandfather left me. The one with... you know. All the stuff in it."

"Did you tell Serena about it?"

"No, I didn't say a thing to her. I haven't spoken with her about any of this."

"Isn't that a bit odd?"

"Yeah, I don't get it. Why would she be there? And what's going on?"

"I think we'd better get up there, don't you?"

"I don't know. This feels really strange. Are you sure you want to go? I could drop you off at home first."

"Are you kidding? Let's just get moving. The only

way we're going to find out what all of this is about is to go and meet her."

Nathan nodded and they turned and headed back to the car. The hairs on his neck stood out and he felt a sudden chill run through his body. This didn't feel right.

"What do you think this is all about?"

Nathan shrugged.

"I have no idea. Seriously. I've never mentioned the warehouse to her."

They drove most of the way in silence, both lost in their own thoughts and neither sure what to say. Nathan clearly felt uneasy about the whole situation. Ben guessed that they would know soon enough what was going on. His friend's life had grown more complicated since his grandfather's death. He hoped this wasn't going to turn out to be something serious. Nathan could really use a break. No matter what though, Ben was there to support him.

Eventually they pulled into the industrial park and Nathan drove around the darkened buildings to the back where the warehouse sat in silence. It loomed ahead like a dark, abandoned ship in the night. The emptiness and silence of the park gave them both a deep sense of foreboding as they drove down the lane. They didn't see any cars—or people. Not for the first time on the trip up, Nathan wondered what was going on.

"Did she say she was already here, Nate? I don't see anyone."

"You saw the messages. I guess she could have been on her way here as well. I don't know why she'd want to meet here and not just come to the house. I've been running through everything in my head on the way up and I'm sure I never mentioned this place to her."

They parked in front of the dark, imposing building and sat for a few moments before deciding to get out. It felt different at night than during the daytime. The large structure had a haunted quality about it. The lack of moonlight didn't help. It sat shrouded in a cloak of darkness and abandonment. Nathan briefly considered going inside and up to the top floor but then remembered he didn't have the entry card with him. Another oversight; he should have stopped by the house on the way and picked that up. As he stood next to the car with his best friend, he suddenly felt very exposed. It certainly wasn't the day he'd envisioned when he woke that morning.

"This place is pretty creepy."

"Yeah, I know what you mean. Honestly though it's not so bad during the day. There's a lot of activity in the industrial park and it doesn't feel so abandoned."

Ben nodded and pulled his jacket tight. When the sun set the temperature had dropped and it had turned cold. Nathan leaned against the side of the car, closed his eyes for a moment, and listened to the night sounds while he instinctively cleared his mind. He had no idea what to expect and no idea where Serena had gotten to—or why she'd wanted to meet him there. Goosebumps ran down his neck and arms and he felt a strange, intense itch on his neck. He couldn't tell if it was from the cold or something else. Either way, he couldn't shake the feeling that something was very wrong.

They wouldn't have to wait long to find out.

Chapter 27

As they stood still, feeling chilled in the darkness, a figure detached itself from the dark shadow of the building. It was too dark to see their features, but Nathan assumed it was Serena.

"Serena," he said, almost in a whisper.

The figure walked towards them. A deep masculine laugh cut through the darkness. Definitely not Serena. As he stepped closer, Nathan could see that he had dark hair, gray eyes and pale skin. He looked vaguely familiar. The closer he got, the more the hairs on the back of Nathan's head stood up, and he could feel static running up and down his body. This was a new sensation to him. His entire body felt like it was being charged with electricity.

"No, weaver. Not Serena. Your precious Serena can't save you now."

Ben suddenly shot forward from behind Nathan.

"Dragan? What are you doing here?"

Nathan turned and looked at his friend.

"You know this guy?"

"Yeah, he's the guy I've been telling you about. The one I met when I was out in Boston. The one who hasn't been returning my calls or messages."

A look of surprise and then menace crossed Dragan's face.

"Well, well. I didn't think I'd see you here. Stay out of it, Ben. It's the weaver I want."

"I don't understand. I don't even know you. Who are you? What is it you want from me?"

"What do we all want from your kind? To get rid of you and your meddling ways. Things need to change, and my family are willing to sacrifice to bring about that change."

Nathan was taken aback. His kind? Were there more weavers out there? He realized it was a kind of arrogance that had led him to believe that he was one of a kind. He realized in that moment that even though he'd traveled through many parts of it, his view of the world was still incredibly narrow. He hoped his ignorance didn't cost them their lives.

"My kind?"

"Weavers. Surely you know about the history of your kind. Weavers can't help but talk about themselves, and their heritage. And by now you must know something of my kind. The evidence has been all around you for a while now—and of course there's Serena. You can't be that stupid."

Nathan stood feeling helpless. He clearly knew nothing of the things that Dragan spoke about. How had he missed so much of what was going on around him? Dragan stepped back and assessed Nathan carefully before laughing—a cruel, almost inhuman sound.

"You have no idea, do you? You thought you were the only one. You don't even know what I am."

Nathan felt ice running through his veins. He shook his head, bewildered.

"No. I guess that I don't."

"Your grandfather didn't tell you anything. You have no formal training. All that fumbling around in your house evenings. How pathetic. This will be too easy."

Nathan felt the imminent danger of the situation. But what came next caught him completely off guard.

"I guess we took care of the old man too soon. Didn't give him a chance to train you properly."

Dragan's words struck the air like a thunderclap as Nathan stood with his feet strongly rooted to the ground. Every word passed through his head as though in slow motion.

"My grandfather died in a plane crash. You have no idea what you are talking about."

Dragan laughed.

"Yeah, well the jet was sabotaged to make it look like an accident. Killing the old weaver was meant to send a message to his peers. And don't worry. It wasn't me. I've been busy. I only found out myself what happened in the last week. I would have gladly done it though."

Nathan's hands clenched into fists. As he felt a sudden deep anger wash over him, he took a step forward.

"What are you going to do, weaver? Fight me with your fists? Good luck with that."

As he took another step forward Dragan lunged. In a flash, Ben shot forward with his arms outstretched to protect his friend. Dragan turned at the last second and lashed out, biting him in the shoulder. Ben screamed out in pain and fell writhing to the ground. Nathan froze in his tracks, his attention on his friend. Dragan stopped, stepped back and looked at them both with dark menace in his eyes.

"You should never have done that, Ben. I'm going to have to finish it now."

He wiped a spatter of blood from his lips.

Nathan knelt down to check on his friend, who was lying on his side on the pavement curled into a ball, moaning, as a car approached and came to a screeching halt behind them. Two figures emerged from the car. As they crossed in front of the headlights, he immediately recognized one of them.

Serena.

She was accompanied by a young man who Nathan had never seen before. His appearance was similar to hers. As they approached, Dragan stepped back a few paces and snarled.

"Severina and Vilim. Good to see you, cousins."

Cousins? Serena knew the guy who'd attacked his

best friend. His gaze swept back and forth between all of them. He hadn't realized it when he first saw Dragan come out of the shadows but looking at them all together, he could now see that they shared similar features. What was going on? Who were they and why was Serena's family out to get Nathan? Was this her interest in him all along? A cry rang out from Ben. Nathan's attention turned back to his friend, who clutched his bloody shoulder and sobbed.

"What's going on?"

He looked up at Serena.

"Your *cousin* attacked us and bit Ben in the shoulder. I mean what the fuck. Who attacks people and bites them?"

Serena looked at Dragan, who still had a drop of blood on the corner of his mouth. She motioned her brother over.

"You bit him? Why? Why would you do that?"

"He got in the way. What's the big deal? I'll kill the weaver and then finish him and that'll be the end of it."

Serena knelt down with Nathan to look at Ben's wound. Nathan pushed her away.

"Get away from him. You've done enough. I need to get him to a hospital."

She looked from Nathan to her brother.

"A hospital can't help him now. Please, let me."

She gently removed Ben's jacket and laid it under his head as a cushion. She pulled back the collar of his t-shirt and looked at the wound beneath. There was congealed blood around two sharp punctures in his skin. Ben was writhing in obvious pain from the bite.

"Leave him, cousin. He's finished. Take your brother and get out of here. My mother won't be happy you interfered."

Serena ignored Dragan.

"William, we're going to have to help him."

Her brother looked on silently while she tended to Ben.

"Leave him William. Let me finish this. This is my kill."

"Your mother's gone too far this time, Dragan. As we speak, Father is bringing her actions to the conclave."

Dragan appeared to pale at the mention of that.

"What? Why would your father involve the conclave? This will look bad for him as well. His own sister breaking the compact. Davorin's reputation will be in ruins."

"No, Dragan. She's gone too far this time. She's interfered with one of the old families. The council members will stop her and anyone who helps her. She won't get away with it this time. You won't get away with it."

Serena and Nathan were both trying to comfort Ben. William stood behind all of them and Dragan tensed, a look of anger crossing his face. Nathan could feel anger rising inside of him and at the same time that familiar feeling of static electricity running across his skin. Suddenly, a gunshot erupted from the darkness and William pitched forward, nearly falling onto Ben.

He caught himself at the last moment and spun around to face the direction of the shot. Blood flowed from a wound in his arm.

"Stand back, all of you. And put your hands where I can see them."

A figure stepped out of the darkness and into the headlights of Serena's car.

Mark Ellison.

What was he doing here?

This was becoming a party, thought Nathan, who only wanted to find a way to extricate himself and Ben from the situation and get Ben someplace safe. Ellison pointed his gun in the direction of Serena, who now stood next to her brother.

"After all of these years I've finally got you both."

Serena and William looked at one another questioningly. From the expressions on their faces they clearly had no idea who he was.

"I'm afraid I don't understand. We don't know you."

Serena spoke calmly so as not to provoke Ellison further.

Dragan moved further back into the shadows. Nathan felt anger welling up inside him. His best friend was injured. Ellison wouldn't leave him alone. He was being pursued by someone he'd never met—who admitted to being responsible for his grandfather's death. And the girl he liked was related to this same person. Life had become so damned complicated, and he'd felt powerless. But he wasn't powerless. He wasn't powerless at all. As he stood, thoughts swirling around in his head, he could hear his grandfather's voice whispering to him.

Calm your thoughts, Nathan. Let them go. Be still.

"No of course you don't know me," said Ellison. "Why should you. But you knew my mother. You killed her when my father was assigned to the United Nations. I was just a boy. I was only four then."

Serena glanced quickly at William, who shook his head and shrugged his shoulders in confusion. They clearly didn't know what he was talking about. Ellison looked from one to the other, deep-seated hatred on his face. Nathan was thinking about what Ellison had said. If he was four when it happened, and was in his forties now, it had to have happened before any of them were even born. They couldn't possibly have done anything to his mother.

"You can't even acknowledge what you've done? How pathetic. Clearly your kind have no morals or values. You take life, consume it and feel no sense of responsibility for what you've done. But you'll pay tonight. You'll take responsibility for your actions."

He kept the gun pointed at them.

∽🙵∾

Behind all of them, at the edge of the shadows and nearly forgotten, Dragan started clapping his hands together slowly while laughing.

"Nice performance everyone. And good try Agent Ellison. You were close. But you got the wrong siblings.

It wasn't dear cousins Serena and William. They don't have it in them. I'm afraid my brother and I are responsible for what happened to your mother. Not that I put any of this together until recently. You've been following the weaver hoping to get close to my cousin Serena this whole time. That's why I kept seeing you watching him on the Cape and outside of his house. You've been looking for a way to track her and he was the bait. Well done. Unfortunately for you, you've got it all wrong."

Serena and William turned, facing Dragan.

"You did this? You killed his mother?"

"Oh please, Serena. Don't go getting all preachy on me. It's what we do. Do you want me to starve? We can't all live on that crap that you and your family eat."

Serena's fists clenched in rage. She blamed her aunt for all of this. Jelena was a dark element in the family. After her husband was killed by members of the conclave for serious breach of the compact, she had gone underground, and she and her children had gone rogue. And after what happened between Serena's sister Dajana and Dragan's brother Antun resulted in both of their deaths, there had been bad blood between her father Davorin and his sister Jelena. It was a dysfunctional family of epic proportions.

"We made a choice to honor life, to live that way. You could make that choice, but instead you look to defy everyone at every turn. This won't end until our entire family is dead."

"Well Serena, maybe that's the endgame. I guess you'll have to wait and see."

Ellison had been slowly advancing towards the group while the cousins argued with one another. Ben was getting worse and Nathan realized he that had one chance. He took the opportunity with all of them being distracted to clear his mind. His friend was lying on the ground bleeding and writhing in pain and he had to try something. Otherwise, what good was everything that his grandfather had taught him? He didn't understand yet the role of a weaver or their place in the larger order of things, but he knew that he had to do something, or else he and his friend would both die.

Confronted with the knowledge that the family of the girl he liked was trying to kill him, and a crazed federal agent threatening them with a gun, he took a final deep breath and felt everything go still. He turned just in time to see Ellison rushing in from one side and Dragan from the other. In one split second his head cleared and without further hesitation a sound screamed out from the depths of his body.

"*Concito!*"

There was a sharp snap in the air, and suddenly everyone was flung backwards into the darkness. The corners of Nathan's vision blurred, and he slowly sank to his knees. As he went down, falling alongside his friend, the last thing that he saw was Dragan pick himself up, stagger for a second, and then run off into the distance. And then everything swirled around inside his head and went black.

Chapter 28

Nathan woke with a start, feeling disoriented and light-headed. He gasped and reached out a hand as if to protect himself. As his vision cleared, he looked around and realized that he was in his own bed. Sunlight streamed in through the partially open blinds but otherwise he was alone, and the house was silent and still. He pushed himself up with one hand and ran the other gingerly across his forehead. He had a pounding headache. He sat on the edge of his bed for a moment, cradling his head in both hands. The events of the previous night slowly trickled back into his mind and then in a flash he remembered everything.

Ben!

He reached for his cell phone, which sat on the bedside table, and quickly pressed the contact for his friend's number. The phone rang and rang and then went to voicemail. As he reached over to place his phone back on the table, he noticed a small piece of folded paper next to the base of the lamp. The note read:

> So sorry about last night. We're taking care of Ben, but we will need to talk about things. Ellison is in the hospital with a concussion. Watch out for him. My cousin and aunt have fled the country. They shouldn't pose an immediate danger. Please don't be angry with me. We'll be in touch when it's safe.
>
> Serena

He got up and went down to the kitchen, made coffee, got a glass of water and found some aspirin to take. What the hell had happened last night? Who was Dragan? What was the conclave? What were Dragan, Serena and William? Clearly, they weren't what they seemed. And yet the thoughts that went through his head made no sense. They couldn't be what he thought they might be. That was pure fantasy. But then so were his own abilities. And what had happened with those? Luckily, he'd practiced that command when he'd practiced moving objects, but he had never experienced that level of intensity before. Maybe the magic worked on a sliding scale—the more energy he put into it, the stronger the response. He shook his sore head as he slowly sipped his coffee. He was worried about his friend.

༺✲༻

After a while, and after the aspirin had kicked in, he showered and got dressed. He was growing increasingly agitated about not knowing what was going on with Ben. He picked up his phone and sent him a text message to see if he would get a response.

Ben, I'm so sorry about last night—for dragging you into this. I hope you can forgive me. Nx

He then set about cleaning the house and doing work outside in the garden to pass the time. He needed to clear his head. Doing physical work allowed his brain to process everything that had happened the night before. By late morning he had finished all of the things that he needed to do, and he headed back into the house. When he retrieved his phone from the dining table there was a message.

Nate! I'm okay. Serena and William are looking after me. I'm not angry. It wasn't your fault. I have a lot to deal with right now. Please just give me some time and I'll be in touch. Also, I hope it's okay, but I told my mother that I'm staying at yours for a bit. I'll be in touch soon. Bx

At least he was alive. His shoulders relaxed and he felt somewhat relieved knowing that his friend was able to respond to him. They'd have to deal with things once he was ready and able to talk about them. Why did Serena and William have to look after him? Thinking about the possible consequences of his friend being bitten was too much for him to consider at the moment—if what he guessed about them was correct. Another thing that he would have to find a way to deal with when the time was right. He shook his head to try to clear it. The headache had passed. With a clean house, and a lot of questions circling in his mind, he decided to drive over to his parents' house. It was time he had a chat with his grandmother.

On the drive over he replayed everything that he could remember about the previous evening, right up to using his power. What had made him decide to act at that moment? He remembered hearing his grandfather's voice telling him to calm his mind. The same voice from the video lessons that had taught him how to access his abilities. His training must have caused his mind to react like a muscle when feeling threatened. While he was grateful, he also harbored a slight fear that he might not be fully in control of it. As he drove, he thought about Dragan, Serena's strange and dangerous cousin. It was then that he recalled the boy from Provincetown. They were one and the same. He'd been tracked for weeks.

As he pulled into his parents' driveway, he let it go for the moment. He'd have plenty of time on his own to work through things. He didn't want to appear too troubled as he entered the house, and cause his family to ask questions that he wasn't prepared to answer. He composed himself for a moment before twisting the door handle and stepping inside. As he walked in he startled Camilla, the housekeeper, who had just been reaching for the front door handle.

"I'm sorry. I didn't mean to scare you."

"No worries Mister Briggs. My own fault. I should have looked through the window first."

"No really. I should have rung the bell."

He stepped politely out of her way as she exited through the front door. He heard voices coming from the kitchen and stepped inside to see who was around. His mother and father were sitting having a cup of tea. There were two pieces of luggage on the floor next to his father.

"Good morning dear! What brings this unexpected visit?"

His mother stood and gave him a hug and a kiss on the cheek.

"I thought I'd stop by and say hello. I was wondering if Grandmother wanted to go for a walk in the gardens."

"Oh, that's a lovely thought. I'm sure she'd like that. I'll go up and get her."

"Thanks Mom."

His father stood as well. He kissed Nathan's mother on the cheek.

"I should be going. I have a plane to catch."

"Are you off on another trip?"

"I'm heading to our London office for a few days. There are some things that I need to sort out there. Everything alright with you?"

"Yes, I'm well. It was good to get time with you this week at the office."

"I agree."

His father checked his watch.

"I'd really better get moving or I'm going to be late."

"No worries Dad. Have a safe flight."

"Thanks Nathan. You have a good week. I'll be in touch."

His father hefted his bags and carried them out to the car, where he loaded them for his trip to the airport. A few minutes later his mother returned to the kitchen with his grandmother in tow.

"I hear you're planning to escort me through the gardens."

Nathan laughed.

"Just thought a walk would be nice, Grandmother. If you're up for it."

She winked at him and smiled.

"I'm always happy to spend time with my grandson."

His mother smiled as the two walked out through the back yard towards the gardens.

"You two have fun! Don't be too long. I'll have some lunch ready when you return."

They waved goodbye as they walked arm in arm across the yard.

The sky was clear and blue, and the late morning sun warmed the air. Birds sang and bees hopped from flower to flower as they walked. After the cold dark events of the previous evening, he welcomed the warmth of the sunshine.

"Now dear, what is it that you need to talk about?"

He could never get anything past his grandmother. Her mind and powers of intuition were as clear as ever.

"Is it that obvious?"

"It doesn't take the power of a Briggs to figure out you have a lot on your mind. Why don't you start at the beginning?"

For the next hour Nathan brought his grandmother up to speed on everything that had happened over the last couple of months, all the way through the events of the previous evening. She occasionally, and politely, interrupted to ask him questions or to clarify something but in the end, having made a circuit around the gardens, he managed to tell her everything that had happened.

"Your friend Ben will be alright?"

"I assume so. Even if I wanted to know more, I wouldn't know where or how to find him."

"You're going to need to make contact with the conclave at some point. Or more likely, they will reach out to you."

"Grandmother, what is the conclave? And what is this compact they spoke about?"

"Well, that would really have been a question for your grandfather but as I best understand it, the conclave is made up of a mix of old weaver families and ranking members of the other, shall we call them, tribes. They collectively keep an eye on one another to ensure everyone follows the compacts—or rules agreed by the members of the conclave. Your grandfather was a member. As I said, he could have told you much more than I can about the whole thing."

As they continued to walk back towards the house, he and his grandmother spoke about everything that had happened.

"Did you know about the rooms beneath the folly? And the old warehouse?"

"Oh yes, of course I did. Your grandfather didn't keep too many secrets from me. Unless he had to. You see dear, my father sat on the council too."

Nathan stopped and looked at his grandmother.

"You mean, your family are weavers too?"

"No, my family are from one of the tribes. It was a bit of a scandal you see, your grandfather marrying me, but he was very stubborn. He often got his own way."

He was about to ask her more questions—he had so many now—but she held her hand up to stop him.

"That's enough for one day. We have lunch to enjoy and we don't want to keep your mother waiting. I promise you that we will pick this up another day. For now, the best thing you can do is to keep following your grandfather's teachings and start catching up on a bit of history. Your grandfather's libraries will contain everything that you need to know. Perhaps you haven't gotten that far yet, but I am sure you will find a lesson that will enable you to translate and read all of the old texts that he has."

They made their way back through the gate into the back yard and stood for a moment admiring the old house, before walking up to join his mother. Before they entered, his grandmother stopped, placed a hand on his arm and looked up at him.

"Promise me that you will not give up on becoming who you are. It's important, Nathan. It's what your grandfather would have wanted. And it's your legacy."

He nodded and promised her that he would continue what he'd started. She smiled and led him into the kitchen, satisfied for now. They joined his mother for lunch. She was happy that he'd come to visit and when he finally left, she sent him home with leftovers for dinner.

"Don't be a stranger Nathan. It's good to see you and your father getting on better these days. I knew that things would eventually work out for the two of you."

"Thanks Mom. I appreciate it. And I promise I'll come over more often."

They repeated their ritual hug and kisses. Nathan hugged his grandmother and kissed her on the cheek.

"Thanks for the walk, Grandmother. We'll have to do it again soon."

She smiled warmly as she held both of his hands.

"Anytime. And you take care of yourself."

He nodded and left them both standing at the front of the house as he drove away.

When he got home, he put the food into the refrigerator and decided to go for a run. It was warm outside.

After recent events he needed to get out and stretch his body and clear his head. He ran down the lane onto the main road and headed off in the direction of town. When he got there, he wandered down to the docks for a bit, where he stood, breathed in the clean sea air, and watched the gulls glide past and boats coming and going in the harbor.

He was trying to unpack everything that had happened of late. Chatting with his grandmother about it had been helpful, even if that had resulted in him having even more unanswered questions. What were these tribes? And if she wasn't descended from weavers, what was she? He struggled to grasp the breadth of everything that he'd learned, but he was coming to terms with the fact that there was more to his life than he'd ever realized. Returning home, he stretched a bit more in the front yard to unwind from the run and burn off excess energy, before finally going inside. He retrieved his phone from the kitchen counter to check for messages. There was one.

Still okay. Stop worrying. Bx

He laughed. His friend knew him too well.

Later that evening he ate the leftovers his mother had given him and, after locking up the house, went upstairs and was in bed by nine. As soon as his head hit the pillow, he was sound asleep. No dreams. No interruptions. Just a long and very deep sleep.

Chapter 29

Over the next week Nathan buried himself in his work. It was a welcome distraction from everything that had happened. His world had changed, and some things could never go back to the way they were. Several nights he woke covered in sweat and breathing heavily as his brain replayed the events of that evening. Each time, he had to get up and walk around the house checking that all of his doors and windows were secure, even though he knew he was being careful to lock up before bed. On the upside Ellison had checked out of the hospital and appeared to have left town. Dragan was gone too. Serena confirmed through a text that he and Jelena had indeed returned to Europe—and that Nathan should leave them to her father. William was looking after Ben, as she had to go to London and might not be back for a while.

As the week progressed his worry grew about his friend. What did Serena mean that they were looking after him? What kind of looking after did he require? And just what did the bite mean for him? Every time he considered the situation something stepped in and sought to repress what he thought he had figured out. He knew that things wouldn't be the same. He just didn't know the specifics of what this would mean for their friendship—or for Ben's life.

At work, their father had instructed Sam and Chris to spend more time giving him a deeper understanding of what they each did. For some reason, he clearly wanted to accelerate Nathan's understanding of the business. Over the course of the week he learned more detail from them of the planned expansion of their operations in London and the rest of Europe, which was the focus of their father's trip to London. There was a great deal of work to be done there and they'd all be involved in it one way or another. As the week drew to a close, he didn't hear anything further from Serena or Ben. He entered the weekend in a dark mood, detached from everything and everyone and feeling alone.

On Saturday morning he woke with the early morning sun. He rubbed his eyes and felt relief that he had managed to sleep through the entire night with no significant dreams or interruptions. The sun warmed his skin as it streamed in through the windows. He was starting to leave his blinds open again now that he was sure that his pursuers had taken flight. He couldn't live in an enclosed tomb for the rest of his life. He wouldn't live like that.

He got up and decided that he could either sit in the house feeling gloomy about everything or go outside into the sun and enjoy his day. When he was ready, he grabbed his keys and a beach towel, locked up the house and drove into town. He found a parking space and hit the shops, quickly finding everything he needed to spend the day at the beach.

The sea air and familiar cries of gulls relaxed him as he made his way back to the area where he and Ben had hung out the week before. There were few people on the beach at that time of the morning. The wind off the water was cool, but the direct sun warmed him as he settled in. It wasn't anywhere near its zenith but still, he sprayed himself with sunblock, then lay back on the towel and closed his eyes.

After a while he sat up and looked out across the dark waters of the Atlantic. Serena was out there on the other side of this great expanse of water for who knew how long. He was conflicted about his feelings for her. On the one hand she'd held back a great deal from him, putting both him and his best friend in danger. And yet, when it counted, she and her brother had been there to defend them. He liked her but he wasn't sure now that he could ever trust her. Her family was responsible for what happened to Ben. She should have foreseen that. She should have told him. And yet, he'd also kept his own secrets. Life was complicated.

He shrugged. For the moment, none of it mattered. She was gone. His best friend was gone, and he was left on his own to sort through everything for himself. At least he could speak with his grandmother. That was some comfort to him even though, as she hadn't been there, she would never fully understand everything that had happened. And of course, clearly even she had her own secrets that she wasn't ready for him to know. It seemed that everyone around him knew things about him—but he found that as time passed, he knew less and less about them. He was beginning to think that his father was the only one he understood in all of this.

One thing that he was clear about was that he was a weaver. He could no longer deny the existence of the legacy that he had inherited. Whether his grandfather was there to teach him in person or not, he had to find a way to learn about his abilities and what he was capable of—and to learn how to control it and not accidentally hurt those he cared about. He needed to push himself to learn the extent of his power. He didn't want to black out if he were to find himself in another life-and-death situation. He needed to learn to control it better. He lay back on the blanket once again and cleared his mind, listening only to the undulating sound of the surf. He spent the next couple of hours drifting in and out of sleep, until the steadily rising sun grew too hot and he decided it was time to head out.

On the way back he drove into New Comfort. The next day was Father's Day and his mother was having a dinner at the house. They were all expected to be there. He bought a bottle of a whiskey that he knew his father liked and a card. He spent the rest of the afternoon and evening in the games room, out of the sun, away from people, forgetting everything while he soaked his brain cells in video games and pool. He wasn't ready to return to his lessons just yet, even though he knew he should. That night he slept like the dead.

He woke to the abrupt sound of his phone ringing.

"Hey. It's me. I thought I'd give you a quick call."

Serena's voice reached across the vast gulf. He wasn't sure if he felt relieved to hear her voice, or angry. He looked at the time. It was seven in the morning. It would be midday for her if she was still in London.

"Serena."

He paused. There were so many things that he wanted to say. He had so many questions. Before he could say anything, she spoke.

"Look. I'm sure you have a lot of questions but this really isn't the time for it. I wanted you to know that Ben is doing alright. I can't imagine what you must be thinking right now, but you have my word that we'll look after him."

There was awkward silence as he tried to find the right words to express what was in his head. But she spoke first.

"Nathan. It will be alright. I promise."

She could clearly sense that he was conflicted, and wasn't giving him any room to maneuver.

"Fine. But we're going to have to talk about all of this at some point. Soon. It's killing me not being able to see Ben. I get that you're taking care of him—even if I don't fully understand what that means."

"You'll just have to take my word for it. I know that's probably not worth that much right now. But please believe me. It will be alright."

He shook his head. He was still confused about all of it. But she was right about not doing this over the phone; after his recent experiences, he didn't know who might be listening. Over the last week, while cleaning the downstairs, he'd found the listening device. He assumed it had been planted by Ellison when he'd visited. He scoured the rest of the house and couldn't find anything else, so he hoped that was the only one. Ellison hadn't been alone in the house for very long so he wouldn't have had much time to plant any more. Nathan was still shaken by it though.

"What about your aunt and your cousin?"

"Just leave them to us. My father will deal with them."

Her voice lowered as she spoke as though she found the conversation difficult. He sensed there was more to this than Serena had told him. She obviously wasn't prepared to go into it on the phone though.

"At some point I want an explanation for all of this, Serena. Not just your aunt and cousin, but everything that you know. You clearly know more than you've ever let on."

The phone was silent.

"Well? Are you still there?"

"When the time is right, we'll speak about it. But for now, Nathan, you need to continue with your studies. You need to become stronger—you have a great deal of potential, but not enough control. There may come a point when your life—and the lives of others—depends on it. I know that you're not happy with me right now. That you don't trust me. But you have to promise that you won't give up. You've shown great ability but there is so much more that you need to learn."

He thought that they could at least agree on that. He wasn't happy. And he didn't trust her. He needed to get more serious about all of it. He was fairly sure that he should have been able to do what he did without passing out. His power had overwhelmed him. He'd lost control and that scared him. He had been lucky this time, but if that were to happen when he faced an adversary alone, it could kill him—or, worse, someone he loved. His grandfather's lessons might teach him how to access his power, but there were nuances that were missing from his training so far. He would have to find a way to address some of those himself.

Before he could say anything further, she spoke.

"Anyways, I have to run. I will be in touch. And I'll ask Ben to get in touch with you too. You take care of yourself, weaver. I will see you again soon."

The call ended abruptly. Everything to do with her was complicated—just like everything about his life was starting to be.

Since he was awake, he decided to start reading the journals he'd brought home from his grandfather's library. He didn't have to practice any more lessons if he wasn't quite ready, but he could start filling in some of the gaps in his knowledge. It took him most of the day to get through them, but he realized that his ancestors and grandfather had kept fairly precise diaries of everything they did and everything that they were going through. He felt almost embarrassed reading someone else's private thoughts, but realized that much of the nuance that was missing from his grandfather's videos was contained in the journals. He made the decision that before dinner that evening, he would make a quick side trip out to the gardens and borrow more journals to read. They contained a lot of the inner monologue that he was missing out on.

He got ready and drove over to his parents' house. He arrived early so that he could sneak out to the folly first. It took him twenty minutes to grab a stack of journals and return his filled backpack to his car. He grabbed the card and the whiskey and entered the house, where he joined his siblings for a drink and a chat. They seemed to be in a good mood and before long, their father and mother joined them. They'd all placed their gifts on a side table and their father made a point of opening and reading each card in turn and expressing his gratitude for each gift he'd received. Even he was in a great mood. Everyone but Nathan seemed to be quite buoyant that evening.

Their father brought them up to date on his trip to London and hinted that there were interesting opportunities there. He was looking forward to the coming weeks and having conversations with each of them about their roles in the company. He even appeared to include Nathan in his plans, though he didn't elaborate further. They enjoyed dinner and after it was over, everyone excused themselves to head back to their homes. As Nathan was about to step outside, his grandmother reached out for a hug and as she pulled him in close, she whispered in his ear.

"You can't give up, Nathan. You need to work harder than ever to learn what your grandfather has been teaching you. He was strong, and it wasn't enough in the end. You need to become more."

Before he could question her about it, she pulled her cashmere cardigan closed, said her goodbyes, and turned and walked back into the house. He waved to his parents as he drove away, feeling somewhat confused, tired, and full. Whether he fully understood her request or not, he was determined to try harder to do as she'd asked.

When he got home, rather than going straight to bed, he retrieved his grandfather's journals and read late into the night. There was more in these books than he'd realized, and things that, had he read them sooner, might have prepared him better for what had happened to him. His grandmother was right—he would have to redouble his efforts to become more. He had two full-time jobs now, and he would have to find a way to balance both of them without failing.

He was in a circular stone room. In the middle of the room was a large, round stone table. A mix of men and women sat around the table. They appeared to be deep in debate.

"*The compact is our most sacred agreement. It binds us all together. You can't ignore it.*"

"*I'm not asking you to ignore it. Or to set it aside. I'm asking you to let me resolve things.*"

Their voices rose over the top of each another before one man stood. His grandfather.

"*We should give him the opportunity to resolve this within his tribe. If he fails, then we will do what we must.*"

"*And if there are more victims before he succeeds?*"

"*I am sure that he will do everything within his power to ensure this doesn't happen.*"

The man who'd proposed handling whatever the situation was nodded.

"*My family and I will do our best to handle this to the satisfaction of the conclave.*"

His grandfather nodded his assent and sat down. The others debated amongst themselves for a few moments before they too nodded. They would leave whatever matters required resolution in the man's hands. For the moment. They concluded their business and shuffled out of the room, one by one. Though they'd agreed, it was clear that they weren't all happy with the assent they'd given. Some of them went out in pairs whispering to one another, clearly angry at his grandfather's intervention. His grandfather, the last person to leave, had a look of concern on his face. Before walking out, he looked over towards where he stood in the shadows, nodded and quietly left the room.

<hr />

The next morning, he woke with a start. Another strange dream, but one that he was growing used to having. This was the conclave—the council who ruled over his kind and the other tribes. His grandfather was clearly troubled. And though he didn't know the nature of the problem, between the journals and his dreams, the one thing that had been circling around the edges of Nathan's mind was confirmed. The one truth he'd been trying to avoid was laid bare.

Serena and her family were vampires.

Nathan Briggs
will return in
OLD BLOOD

Love this book? Share the love, support independent authors, and make me your best friend forever by posting a quick review on Amazon.
Thanks!

Want to be alerted when the next OLD BLOOD SERIES book is released? Sign up for e-mail updates at https://bscotthoadley.com/subscribe/ and we'll keep you updated. (We'll never share your address or use it for anything else.) And you can follow B. Scott Hoadley on Facebook (https://www.facebook.com/bscotthoadley), Twitter (@bscotthoadley) and Instagram (@bscotthoadley).

Thanks & Acknowledgements

I'd like to thank and acknowledge my partner for all of his support—the long hours waiting for me to come down from the study, and the many hours he spent as a reader and personal editor. I'd also like to thank my friends and family for their ongoing encouragement for the many years it took me to get to this point. I owe a debt of gratitude to the workshops, students and faculty at Emerson College in Boston, where I received my Master of Fine Arts in Creative Writing. I'd also like to make a shout-out to the Red-liners, my writing group at the time. I'd like to thank my friend Michael Stephen Fuchs, author of the Arisen Series, for all of his advice and support, and Christina Clarke for helping me unravel the mystery of using social media to engage with my readers. I'd like to thank my wonderful support team, Ben (cover design), Jacqui (copy-editor), Jason and Vidya (bookmakers) for helping me assemble this book.

And finally, I'd like to thank all of my readers who make it all worth doing!

Printed in Great Britain
by Amazon